OTHER BOOKS OF FICTION BY JOE LYON

The Provenance (Book 1 of Astar's Blade)
Temple of Valor (Book Three of Astar's Blade)

Poetry is Cool (another book from Joe Lyon)

CHECK OUT MORE STUFF AT THE WEBSITE:
www.astarsblade.com

MUSIC BY PURPLE TOAD:
available on iTunes and streaming services.

Music to Swim By (1984)
Legacy (2013)
Self-Inflicted Wounds (2016)
Anything You Want (2017)

ASTAR'S BLADE

KILMER'S GHOST

AN EPIC FANTASY

JOE LYON

First Edition

Printed in the United States of America.

© Copyright 2021 by Astar's Blade, Lyonic LLC

978-1-956189-22-3 (Paperback ISBN)
978-1-956189-05-6 (Hardcover ISBN)
978-1-956189-07-0 (Kindle ISBN)
978-1-956189-06-3 (Audiobook ISBN)

Many thanks to the following contributors:

Copy Edited by Anne-Marie Rutella
Developmental Editing by Deborah Murrell
Developmental Editing by Sophie Lyon
Proofreading by Amanda Rutter
Audiobook Narration by Lisa Negron
Cover Design by Story Wrappers, Artist K.D. Ritchie
Songs by Purple Toad

 AMPERSAND BOOKERY

Typesetting by Colleen Sheehan at Ampersand Bookery

THE WORLD SETTING

ONLINE VIEW OF MAP:
Map of Odessa—Astar's Blade
(astarsblade.com)

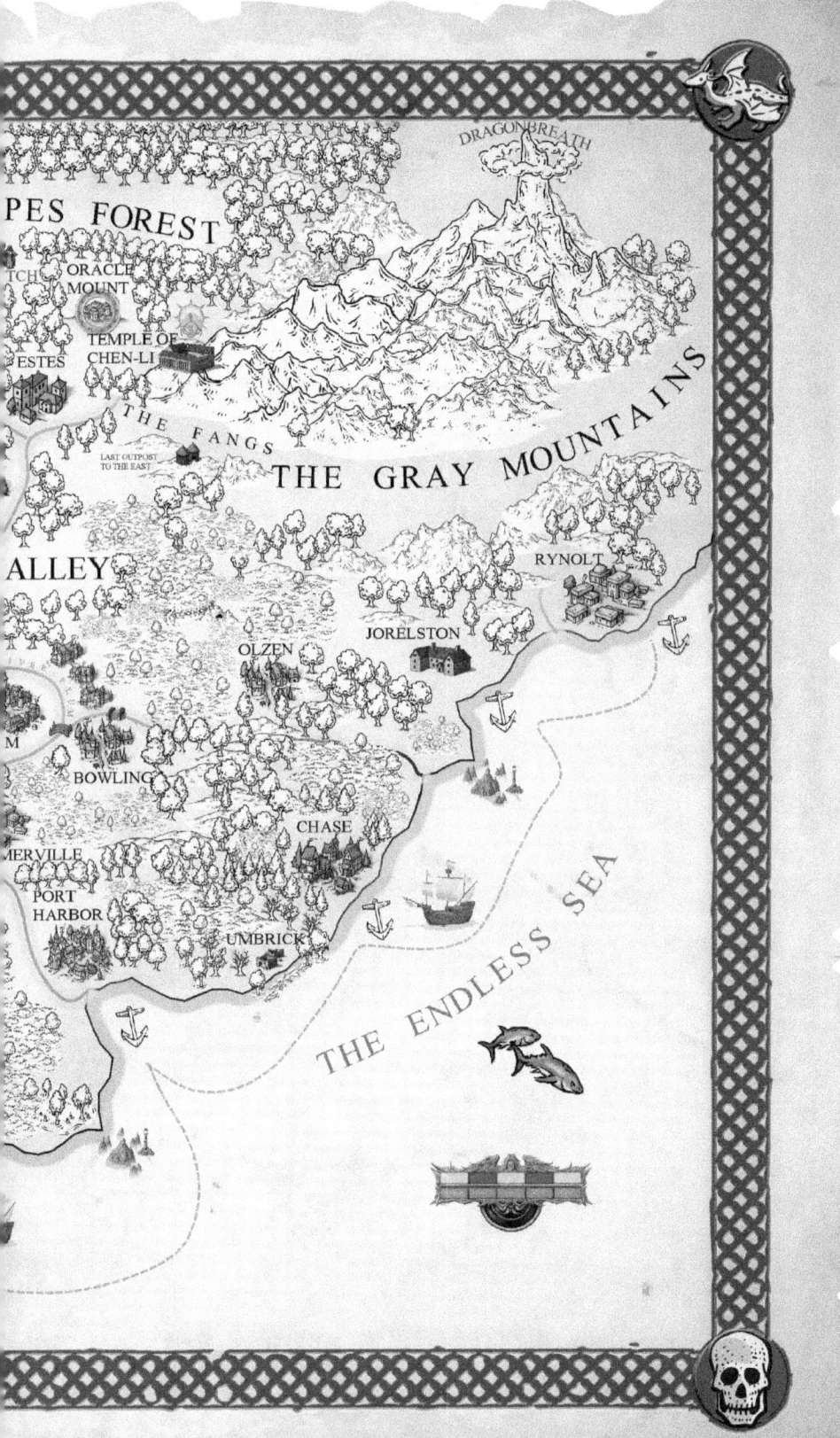

INTRODUCTION

Welcome back, dear reader, to *Kilmer's Ghost*, the second book in the Astar's Blade Epic Fantasy series. If you are just joining us, this book is written to be enjoyed without reading the first book in the series. *The Provenance* told the origins of the world, the places of interest, the events, and the characters set in this book. Although it is unnecessary to read *The Provenance* first, it is certainly recommended for a more enriching experience. At any rate, I want to thank new and returning readers for this second installment of the Astar's Blade Epic Fantasy series.

Kilmer's Ghost is written in four acts, although, once again, there is some creative license in storytelling, and not all the chapters are in chronological order. For those repeat readers, I am sure you are used to this style by now. But for any new readers, I want to point out that as you explore the following pages, I have firmly planted signposts to tell you where/when the chapters take place and any relevant reference to special events. For example:

CASTLE ODESSA IN THE YEAR 830
HUMAN RECORDED TIME (HRT)
(THREE HUNDRED YEARS AFTER THE GREAT COOLING)

Once again, for those just joining us, and as a reminder for those veteran readers, Human Recorded Time, or HRT as it is referred to in later chapters, is the time recorded to mark the planting and harvesting season for humans in the world. The Gods, if you should run into any, do not follow or respect HRT. These timelines are relevant only to humans and will give you a good idea of the timeline referenced in the story, whether it is told from the past, current, or future. So, I invite you to look at the signposts; I would not want to lose any of you, especially in the places where we are going.

— Joe Lyon

FOREWORD

There were no bells that rang out when the era of the Gods ended, but they were gone just the same. Swept up in an endless battle, a conflict called the Great Negation. They returned to the Cosmic Creation. Forever trapped there, in a sun of their own making, high overhead its rusty-colored surface. This was their punishment, for any direct violence between the Gods of Day and Night was strictly forbidden. A third God existed with them, the Goddess Ehlona, to keep their balance, but she failed miserably when she took one of them as her husband. Because of their jealous conflict, the twin Gods triggered a vector that sent them back to the Cosmic Creation to fight each other for all eternity. And the Goddess Ehlona, pregnant with both the twin Gods' offspring, went running into the world, lamenting, and blaming herself for the Gods' disappearance.

Ehlona found solace with a group of women, former Acolytes from her Temple of Valor. These women formed the Sisters of the Orphans and assisted her in her labors of birthing her two children. The first son, named Marus, was the child of Heironomus. She blessed him with the ability to control body and soul. The second, named Hazor, was prophesied a horrible and bloody future.

The Goddess Ehlona bestowed the Sisters of the Orphans with Beautiful Blessings, giving them all of her beauty. But by doing so, she turned herself into a monstrously hideous and ugly figure.

Running far away, she declared herself the Witch of the Great Mapes Forest. The living things of the forest bargained their safety to give her a home among them. However, far from keeping them safe, the witch endangered and harmed the forest with a new form of life she created—the tiny golden orbs of the microscopic society of the Timmutes. Finally, in recompense for harming the forest, the witch deformed herself by sacrificing her left arm.

On his eighteenth birthday, her son Marus visited. Now calling himself Chen-Li, the warrior-priest trained an army to protect the world from his powerful brother, Hazor the scorned.

Hazor, now calling himself the Zorn, summoned a demon to assist him with establishing the Zornastic Order, his own army of dark obedient priests. The demon's name was Langula and agreed to call the Zorn her master. Hazor had recovered the witch's severed arm to create the most powerful weapon in the world—a golden blade named Soothsayer.

The era of the Gods ended when the witch took her own life. The spirit of the Goddess Ehlona was prophesized to rise again someday with a star but that had so far remained unfulfilled.

In the meantime, in the realm of humans, the War of the Mid-Run Valley had been waging for years, with the emergence of a new power, King Leopold. The Amalgamate forces of the Mid-Run Valley had formed to defy him. In the final Battle of Mauveguard Pass, King Leopold succeeded in ending the war and established his new Kingdom of Odessa.

Our story now begins five years after the surrender of the Amalgamates to King Leopold. After the war, the opposing forces were united under the single rule of the one king. Ruthless in war, King Leopold has changed to a benevolent monarch, though still aloof and mysterious.

With Castle Odessa now finished, the king has declared a holiday celebration to remember and honor the Battle of Mauveguard Pass and acknowledge the first five years of his rule over the Kingdom of Odessa.

Everyone loves a holiday, and the anticipation of King Leopold's celebration is no exception. The five-year anniversary of the unified Kingdom of Odessa has everybody charged with excitement, and throughout the kingdom activities are under way to make it a memorable one.

There. I believe you are all caught up, and we can now continue. Oh, I almost forgot, I should warn you. Now that you have come this far, you should not stop, for once you have entered the darkness, the spell has already been invoked. You do not want to expose your back to the unknown here. It is best to keep pressing forward. Keep turning pages—it may be your only hope, for sometimes the best way to get back to where you came from is to plow ahead. As you will soon see as you begin *Book 2 of Astar's Blade*.

We now join *Kilmer's Ghost*, already in progress, as the king's First Archer and his spotter hunt for game to provide venison for the feast, a seemingly harmless event. But before one can lay their claim to the feast at the king's banquet table, one never knows what dangers lurk in the depths of the dark forests, and in the wilds of *Astar's Blade*.

ACT I
Death of
Identity

Can you hear it? It sounds like thunder.

The beast is out there with a savage hunger.

We can't stay at home, and we can't go to sleep.

We're on the bloody trail into the jungle deep.

Excerpt from *The Witch's Songbook*

Today marks the end of your hunt in this world.
Now, you can begin your hunt in the next one.
— Excerpt from *The Provenance* (Chapter One)

THE SANGUINE FOREST

THE SANGUINE FOREST IN THE YEAR 841
HUMAN RECORDED TIME (HRT)
(ONE WEEK AWAY FROM THE KING'S CELEBRATION)

Yori steadied his bow and took aim at the big buck. Isse quietly looked on, hardly breathing. Yori let the arrow release with a *twhip*! Swiftly it found its mark deep in the animal's side with a lethal *thunk*! As the arrow struck right behind its front leg, the deer startled. But rather than drop, as it should, the big buck lurched and turned to run.

"Oh no, no!" Yori yelled at it. The buck darted through the trees, still under its own power.

"You missed him, Yori."

"The hell I did, Isse, I got him all right."

"Not good enough." Isse motioned with an empty hand. "Now there goes dinner. Tell me again how well you got him."

Yori squinted his eyes. "Yes, sir, I got him all right. He won't get too far."

The buck left a trail of blood, and the two followed it. It led away from the tiny brook and through the trees. For a full two hours, they were on the buck's trail. But all the signs were there that the big buck was not through yet. They followed the path deeper into the forest until the shadows grew long.

"There's no quit in this one," Yori said, stopping briefly to wipe his brow with a dirty kerchief. "Must've had a big heart."

"You think he's close?" asked Isse. "I don't want to be out here after dark."

"Just a bit," Yori said. "He can't get much further."

Just then, they heard a guttural scream.

"What was that?" Isse asked. "Was that the deer?"

"Never heard a deer sound like that," Yori remarked. "I think he's down. But look alive! Might be that a bear got involved."

"You go ahead, Yori," Isse said. He took a step back.

"You're not turning back?" Yori turned to look at him.

Isse did not answer. He was trembling.

"Look here, Isse, you mean to leave our little hunt? You know that Leopold paid you seven metros to assist the senior archer, and you know who the senior archer is? Me, Isse, that's who. You can't just turn tail and run."

"It's not safe here. Come on, Yori! I've heard the stories, and so have you."

"You believe the ghost stories?" he laughed.

"You know it's not safe to be in these woods after dark."

"You believe the stories of the haunted Sanguine Forest?"

"Forget the buck, Yori, please. We'll say we didn't see anything this trip."

"But we did see something, Isse. We saw a great big strong buck, at least eighteen points! Fit for His Majesty's celebration table. Why, that stag's got my arrow in him, stuck in his side there. And there is nothing wrong with being in the forest after dark."

"King Leopold's five-year coronation anniversary is not worth losing our lives over, Yori."

"What is this, Isse? You're scared of the stories old women tell around their washing basins? The Sanguine Forest? Why, it is nothing but trees and leaves out here, and look—it is certainly *not* haunted."

Just then, Isse's eyes widened, and he grabbed Yori by the arm. Out in the trees, a figure of a man walked some distance away from them.

"Look there, Yori! Who is that? A ghost?"

"The hell it is a ghost! Probably another hunter about to lay claim to our buck! And without so much as taking a shot. We cannot give up our prize, Isse, now come on! Be a man about you."

They continued tracking the blood trail again, but then, after just a few more steps, Isse stopped again.

"Oh, Yori, I can't explain it, but I am so scared. I don't know why."

"Courage, Isse." Yet Yori was feeling it too. Isse's fear was getting the best of him as well. "Stay close to me."

Isse held Yori by the arm, fighting against his desire to run. Quietly they went through the underbrush, following the mysterious figure. Then, the trail of blood ended. The big stag lay on its side in front of them. But the deer was not right.

"Is that my buck?" Yori said as a whisper. He saw his arrow sticking out of the deer's side. But this could not be his deer.

"It can't be," Isse replied. "Look at it."

The deer was in a state of advanced decomposition, moldy brown hide, torn and rotten, stretched across ivory bones. Its head had no flesh and the dried skin had been drained of blood. Yet sticking up high and prominent was Yori's red-and-blue arrow of Leopold's First Archer.

"This is impossible. That is my arrow, it's a fresh new one, but this deer has been long dead."

"Oh, Yori!" Isse declared. "This forest is haunted. Look!"

Isse reached down and wiped the dirt away from a half-buried human skull, covered only by a dusting of soil. The skull's dark eye sockets and open jawbone seemed to mock the hunters.

Yori looked around the area and found more. There were further skulls and other bones, buried just inches in the ground, or lying fully exposed on top. Skulls and spines, feet, hands, legs, and ribs. Yori and Isse had wandered into a sea of human bones.

They dropped to the ground and crawled on all fours behind a bush. They looked aghast at each other with pale faces, afraid to stand in fear of being seen by the man who walked in the woods.

"Who is it that walks in this forest?"

"And where is he now?"

They both raised their heads up over the bushes to see where the man had gone and what he was doing. Soon, they could see him. He wore all black, and his adornments were fresh, but still odd, like maybe from some other time. Upon his head he wore a jeweled crown as if he were royalty.

He continued to walk away from the two behind the bush. But then, abruptly, maybe sensing their eyes upon him, he stopped in his tracks. He lifted his head, appearing to sniff the air, and he stiffened.

"Oh, Yori, I don't like this. That is not a fellow hunter or a companion," Isse whispered in growing anxiety.

They watched him scan the area, first to the left, then to the right.

"Oh! Damn you, Yori. I'm so scared!"

Yori was scared too. Their hearts beat faster as fear seized them.

The man slowly turned in their direction. Yori and Isse got their first look at him now. The decayed skin of his face stretched taut over his skull and an enormously pronounced chin. Unable to close his mouth, rotten teeth lay bare and exposed. The gristle of his nose, long since deteriorated, left uncovered bare nasal passages as two open, long slots. Darkness filled his hollow eye sockets, except for the fiery lights of two tiny yellow orbs, with which he used to stare directly at Yori and Isse.

They dipped behind the bush, but it was too late. They had been seen.

The Skeletal King raised his hands, lifting them in front of his yellow eyes, and blue-and-silver energy crackled, arcing between his hands. With a sudden flash of blue light, some shadowy movement spilled from the man in a blur, causing a commotion in the bush, like a noise of a hundred sticks clicking against each other. The sound got louder and rustling in the leaves got nearer. Then, like a wave riding through the underbrush, suddenly it hit them: cockroaches! Hundreds, if not thousands, of cockroaches charged them in waves, attacking Yori and Isse ferociously.

The force knocked them backward as the cockroaches smashed into them. They both ran away, trying to swat them off their bodies. Yori dropped his bow and ran as fast as he could. Isse was already far out in front. The cockroach horde jumped on their backs and crawled on their heads. They swarmed in piles and tangled their feet; it was everything Yori and Isse could do to keep from falling.

But then as suddenly as they had appeared, the cockroaches disappeared in the same pale blue mist that had created them, not that Yori and Isse took the time to notice. They continued to run wildly. When the blue fog cleared, and the cockroaches were gone, they soon discovered something even more dreadful; they had lost each other. They had run haphazardly in different directions and were now standing alone in the dark forest.

Yori looked for him, but Isse only wanted to get away. His fear finally overwhelmed him. He ran as fast as he could back in the direction they had come into the Sanguine. Isse had scratches from the thorns of the forest, and he was bleeding from the cockroach attack. For several minutes, he ran until he was almost out of the

Sanguine Forest. But then, much to his horror, he stopped as he realized he had run directly back to the Skeletal King, back to the very place he had just left.

The Skeletal King had been waiting for him to return. Now, he stepped closer to Isse. Crackling blue energy emanated once again from his bony hands. But this time, having been successful at separating the men, there would be no more cockroaches; they would not be needed. Isse suddenly felt weak as the blue energy filled his body, and he fell to the ground. He fell in front of the Skeletal King. His life force was being pulled out of him. Being drained of power, he could only lay there trembling, trying to get up, trying to run but unable to. The skin on his body started to tighten and open with his blood steaming through the ruptures. The golden-clad boots of the Skeletal King approached and stopped in front of him. The lich allowed Isse to look upon his face, and then to let out a loud scream.

"Isse! Isse! Oh, where are you, Isse?" Yori said in a whisper, trying not to yell. He stood behind a tree, shaking in fear. He had dropped his bow while escaping the cockroaches, losing most of his arrows when they spilled from his quiver. Taking the now useless quiver off and throwing it down, he tactically traversed from tree to tree, being cautious not to remain exposed for very long.

Then he heard a loud agonizing scream.

Was that Isse? he wondered. The scream sounded so terrifying there was no way to be sure who it was. Yet, he was sure; he knew it was Isse. This was not a time for false bravery. For now, it was every man for himself, and Yori strategically moved between trees desperately trying to find his way out of the Sanguine Forest.

Peering through the trees, the dark figure was moving again with no discernible connection to the ground, rapidly closing the distance separating them. Yori turned and ducked behind the tree again, breathing heavily, knowing the Skeletal King was getting closer.

Then, the Skeletal King called out, in a calm, raspy voice, "Come out, oh Noble Archer. Come out and see my magnificent Castle Orlo."

Yori did not move, could not breathe—the voice paralyzed him with fear.

He felt a heavy movement on his boot, and gazing down, saw a snake crawling over his feet. But the snake soon became larger and larger, until it grew in size to form the bottom half of the demon Langula. Her lower serpentine body slid around the tree and revealed her womanly upper half, complete with shapely form, sharpened black fingernails, black hair, and two large horns. Looking at him with her sparkling silver eyes, she opened black lips, revealing pointed fangs.

Yori's mouth screamed soundlessly in terror. Impulsively he tried to run away from her, and he pivoted from the cover of the tree. But there, the Skeletal King stood in front of him—they had him trapped.

The hideous figure wore a crooked golden crown and a black uniform buttoned smartly to his chin. There, in the dark woods, he stood in front of an enormous castle with seven tall, spiraled towers and a domed roof over its walled stronghold, a massive castle that was not there mere seconds ago.

"I see you have met Langula," the Skeletal King said to him. "I am the Zorn."

A large dark-haired demon covered in yellow-and-brown spots appeared with them. He approached Yori from behind. Upon seeing the third demon, Yori collapsed in the spotted one's arms. The monster did not let him fall or moved to harm him. Instead, he dragged him off toward Castle Orlo.

"Welcome to your new home," the Zorn said, flashing his teeth in what could only be his way of trying to smile.

Langula sang sweetly to the unconscious Yori.

> *Your days are gone, never to return!*
> *In Zornastic fire your spirit will burn!*

"We are going to get very acquainted with the king's First Archer."

Their laughter filled the forest as they made their way into the castle with Yori. Once the heavy doors closed behind them with a loud clang, the castle was gone, and only the Sanguine Forest remained.

I can't recall it all, but I,

I seemed so different at the time.

Aye! Aye! Aye!

I can't remember, but the ghost cannot lie.

Excerpt from *The Witch's Songbook*

The Plum family will remain forever blessed.
— Excerpt from *The Provenance* (Chapter Two)

THE VILLAGE OF PLUM

THE VILLAGE OF PLUM IN THE YEAR 832 HRT
(NINE YEARS EARLIER, BEFORE YORI'S DISAPPEARANCE)

With a faraway sound of falling chimes, the ghost emerged, materializing in dull light just before the sunrise. A deep hood covered the awful sight of its face, leaving only a darkened void. Having no mouth to speak with, the ghost did not say a word as it loomed over the boy in his bed.

Darius Plum lay on his back, mouth stretched open in a silent scream. In widening terror, his eyes stared toward the ceiling, as he watched the images of violence and death replaying in an endless loop in his mind—the implanted visions the dull specter forced onto him.

He'd had visions before but nothing like these. These were the worst ever—scenes of his father burning in flames, his mother screaming in agony, his sister calling out for mercy, the whole village consumed in sweeping fire. The vision ended in a river of blood; it washed over him, pulling him under its crimson surface. Then, as long as the ghost remained, the vision would start over again.

"Please stop, Hollow Face," Darius said, pleading with the faceless ghost looming over him. "I can't stop it. Please! Help me, Hollow Face."

Hollow Face—Darius Plum gave the ghost that name long ago. If the ghost had once lived and had a real name in life, it had been lost to time.

For as long as he could remember, Hollow Face had been a part of his life. The spirit would appear to him anywhere, anytime, sometimes in the middle of the night, sometimes during the day. But whenever and wherever the ghost would show itself, only Darius could see him. And when the ghost shared its visions, only he could see them.

Over the years, Hollow Face not only materialized, but took solid form, just long enough to knock over a bottle or move a dish, knock on the wall, tap the window, or make heavy footsteps above on the ceiling. But Hollow Face was far more than just an invisible phantom that liked to move things around and make disembodied sounds. Hollow Face shared visions with the boy, causing a sort of paralysis, and had done so for as long as Darius had been alive.

Now the ghost loomed over him and remained. But he heard Darius's pleas and finally released him from the visions. Then, he too faded to dust with the coming sunrise.

Immediately, after regaining control of his mind again, Darius sat up abruptly, sweating profusely. His eyes cleared and the bedchamber returned to his vision. Exhausted, he rested his head in his hand, listening to the only sound, the monotonous ticking of the clock.

He stayed in bed, watching the glow of the morning light continue through the curtains of his window. He was certain the fear would pass. Instead, it lingered and grew.

Why did Hollow Face show me such awful scenes?

Outside, for the villagers of Plum, it was just another ordinary day. Dew covered the fields of mud, hard and frozen. Still warm from their beds, people started to stir, dressed in layers of itchy wool and cold, stiff boots. The aromas of baking bread, browning bacon, and percolating coffee permeated the morning air.

With the first rays of the sun, Kilmer awoke too. He breathed into his good hand to warm it, then rubbed it against his useless one, the one withered and curled against his body. People called him the village beggar, the cripple, or even more cruelly, the town hunchback. He had been born with a spinal deformity that left his back crooked. His hair grew in random patches. He was poor. His clothes were threadbare, and his body mangled and road-dirty from his adventures. He made his way to the town square with considerable effort, taking his place and waiting with his empty cup under the giant bronze statue dedicated to the village founder.

For as long as anybody could remember, Fortis Plum stood watch over the village of Plum. The statue, cast in bronze, preserved the likeness of the man who was best known for his long, distinctive, flowing mustache that extended an entire foot from either side of his cheeks. But after years of youthful mischief, his mustache had long since broken off on both sides, leaving just two tarnished blemishes where it had been. Regardless, the statue was the pride of the village.

Kilmer, with his little tin cup and exposed missing teeth, smiled at all the passersby. He went about begging for his breakfast, talking to the citizens, enjoying telling the news and relaying stories from his constant travels. He always listened for the *clink* of coin into his little dented cup. But whether he received a coin or not, he expressed his gratitude to everyone who passed, giving each one a sincere blessing.

Justus Plum considered it his duty as the Head Council of the village to stroll through the town every morning. He made it a point to stop and speak casually with anyone he encountered along the way, including Kilmer, who was no exception.

Justus wore a velvet hat on top of his curly black hair, a luxurious navy blue coat with yellow stitching and bright yellow lapels and cuffs, and his boots were made from soft leathers. Kilmer saw the colorful Head Council coming and extended a greeting befitting the most important man in all of Plum.

"Good morning, councilor," Kilmer said to Justus Plum. "It is a fine day today. Yes, sir! A fine day today."

Justus knew what Kilmer wanted, and eventually plunked not one, but two, coins into his little tin cup: *clink, clink!*

Kilmer gave him a warm, and mostly toothless, grin. "Oh, thank you, councilor. May the Goddess Ehlona bless you," he said in raspy spits.

He was surprisingly well traveled for having been born with a crooked spine and had a penchant for connecting with people. News traveled faster through Kilmer than in any other way. Kilmer talked to anyone who showed interest, but he especially enjoyed the company of Justus Plum. Justus took a moment to converse with Kilmer.

Kilmer shambled through the Mid-Run Valley collecting stories and local news from all the surrounding villages. Today was no exception, and he told Justus about the big news in the village of Bowling: the case of the sick pig was currently the topic of debate.

While Kilmer spoke, Justus took a moment to admire the statue of Fortis Plum above him. His wife, Rosa Plum, was a direct descendant, and when the two of them were married, they held their lavish wedding right here under the broken, mustache-less statue in the town's square.

Justus had been just a commoner then, only to rise to his current position as executor of the Plum family's sizable fortune. First, he had to not only win over Rosa's heart, but prove his worth to her parents as well. In that regard, he had two qualities going for him. The first was that he had a natural flair for politics, which pleased her father, Eben. The second was that Rosa loved him more than anything, and that pleased her mother, Dalla.

After their elaborate wedding under the statute, Justus—not having a surname to share because of his family's common situation—adopted her family name to ensure their wealth would stay within the Plum family. Their children would be Plums forever, and executors of the family's vast riches.

But with the security of the aristocracy came a curse.

The Plum family curse did not directly affect Justus because he was only a Plum by marriage, nor did it affect Rosa, because the curse only affected males of the family. Their first child, a daughter named Mara Plum, was unaffected too. But their second child, a son named Darius, who was the only living male with the family blood, took the full brunt of the curse from an early age.

The only chance of understanding the curse ended when Rosa's father had died months before Darius was born. Eben Plum was rumored to have been possessed by the spirits of the dead in the final days of his life. He had become highly eccentric in his remaining years. His death left his grandson, Darius, with no one to help him understand the curse. Darius was on his own.

After the loss of her husband, the matron Dalla lived several more years as the genial grandmother. She was ultimately buried beside Eben in the Plum family cemetery, not far from here, along with all the other generations of the family. Nearby lay the mortal remains of the old village founder himself, Fortis Plum, with his fully intact flowing mustache and all.

Marrying into such a powerful family like the Plums, Justus had the honor—or burden, depending on one's perspective—of sitting on the village council. Soon after the senior Plum's death, he eventually became the Head Council.

"I'll be going to the village of Bowling tomorrow." Kilmer suddenly asked him a question that broke into his thoughts, "Do you have any news to pass on, councilor?"

"Oh sorry, Kilmer, yes, I do! Please give my regards to the Honorable Head Council, Jakob Whitney. And let me know how this case of the sick pig resolves itself, won't you?" Justus tipped his velvet hat and continued on his way. "Good day, Kilmer."

"Take care, councilor," Kilmer continued to call to him even after he left. "May the Goddess bless you and Rosa, and your children, Mara and Darius. Tell them that Kilmer said hello."

Justus approached home now. The Plum's lived in an enormous, spacious family house by the Plum River, the largest residence in the village, the House of Justus. Seeing his wife, Rosa, working outside, he walked up to her and gave her a kiss on the forehead.

"You wouldn't believe what Kilmer just told me," he said, laughing. She quickly interrupted him.

"I have no time for foolishness," Rosa said. She turned; her hair was pulled back in a loose bun. Rosa could have hired servants to do the chores, but as a proud Plum, a dedicated mother, and a hardworking woman, she demanded to do things herself. She continued talking loudly while focusing on her laundry.

"Kilmer embellishes stories only to pique your interests. He will say anything he thinks you want to hear. He is hardly a reliable source of information. Not worth the coin that would otherwise put food on our table."

"What's a couple of coins to us? Where is your spirit of community, of charity, of giving to those less fortunate than ourselves?"

"You would give it all away?" At this, Rosa stopped her work and turned to face her husband, wiping the loosened hair from her eyes with a blow upward in a deep breath. Rosa could be abrasive as she was harsh sometimes, but she had a kind soul and a good heart. And she certainly did not appreciate the insinuation where Justus painted her out to be heartless. He received a haughty stare.

"I have never known him to lie," Justus said with a shrug,

Rosa said nothing, and that was about as close as he would ever get to her agreeing with him. She looked around the yard.

"Go get your children," she said, giving him a quick grin. Then she got back to work. They both enjoyed a little verbal sparring between them.

"I will take that matter under advisement, Miss Head Council," Justus said with a smile.

Mara was by the river, picking flowers when her father saw her halfway down the steep riverbank that dropped sharply to the Plum River. His heart nearly stopped as he saw how close she was to the rushing water.

"Mara! Get away from the river!"

Mara looked startled and held tight to the bundle of yellow-and-white flowers she had just picked. Carelessly, she slipped, tripped, and nearly fell, all to the shock of her father. But eventually, she scaled the slope back up to the top of the ridge. Justus watched her all the while, worried she would tumble backward and disappear into the murky water.

"Mara, you are the oldest. You are almost seventeen. You are supposed to set a better example than that. What have we told you?"

"You told me not to play next to the river. But I was not playing, I was gathering flowers. Look!" She extended the bundle of flowers to her father. He looked at them, then back at her.

"Humph," he grunted. "Beautiful, but are they worth the risk of falling in the river?"

"But I didn't fall in the river. I was careful." Mara was sixteen going on seventeen years old. She had big brown eyes and brown hair tied with ribbons. Her blue dress hid grass stains from her adventures. Barefoot, she ran and found her white shoes in the grass. "See? I took off my shoes so I wouldn't slip."

"Do not go down there again, Mara, especially by yourself," he scolded her. "Stay away from that river, understand?"

Mara nodded.

Justus gave her a stern look, but he could never stay angry at her. She was his heart. Youthful and headstrong, but as his child, he would expect nothing less. They walked away from the riverbank and Justus put his arm around her shoulder.

"Are those for your mother?" Justus asked and pointed to her yellow-and-white flowers.

"No, these are for Darius. He hasn't left his room, and it's almost midday."

"Is he having nightmares again?"

Mara nodded.

"Well, you're a good big sister, watching out for your little brother like that."

"I hope Darius likes them," she said.

Darius sat on the edge of his bed, staring with empty eyes out the window, hoping Hollow Face would not appear again to show him any more visions. The door of his room opened, and his father and sister walked in. It startled them to see him sitting in his bed with dark circles around his eyes.

His father sat on the bed and put his arm around the boy. "Rough night?"

Darius nodded and looked out blankly.

"Are you sick?" Justus asked him. Mara came and sat on the bed too, her flowers in her arm, and a worried look on her face.

Darius shook his head. "I feel all right. Just a little tired."

Justus leaned forward and kissed him on the forehead. He did not feel warm. No fever. He ran his fingers through his son's curly red hair.

"It's too late to go back to sleep now. Since you are up, why don't you go outside and see your mother?"

Darius nodded blankly again.

Justus stood up and started to leave. Looking back, he said, "Oh, I almost forgot. Kilmer's in town if you want to go see him. Just don't tell your mother, yeah?"

Darius smiled and nodded.

Once their father was gone, Mara turned and asked, "Was it Hollow Face again?"

"It was horrible. The worst ever." Mara was the only one Darius ever talked to about Hollow Face.

"No wonder you have nightmares. What did he say?" They talked like this. Mara knew Hollow Face never actually spoke.

"Last night, he showed me fire, blood, water, and death." Darius could not tell her all he had seen, especially not about her and the whole family being murdered in the vision.

She paused and looked down at the bouquet in her hand.

"I picked these for you. Do you like them?"

Mara gave Darius the yellow-and-white flowers. He looked at them blankly. Then he stuck his nose into them, giving them a long sniff.

"They're nice. Thank you."

Outside, Justus went back to Rosa, who was now at a washing basin by the well.

"Guess where I found your daughter?"

Rosa looked up, flustered. She knew that could only mean the girl was down by the slippery banks of the river again. She was not pleased at all.

The two children walked to the town square and up to the founder's statue, where they knew Kilmer would be. Both of them held a flower, one white, one yellow.

"What pretty flowers you have there," Kilmer said.

"They are for you, Kilmer." The children handed them to Kilmer at the same time.

"Oh joy! You brighten my day. May Ehlona the Goddess bless you."

"But don't you want coins instead?" Darius asked. "Sorry that we don't have any."

"Oh, flowers are better. I have plenty of coins here in my cup. Do you want some? You can have some—let me pay you for the pretty flowers! Go buy yourself a tasty sweet roll. One for both of you!"

"We won't take your coins, Kilmer," Mara said. "But you are such a kind soul."

Kilmer grinned and blushed, unaccustomed to compliments.

Darius tried to be happy but could not forget the visions. Something was wrong. Something terrible was about to happen. He felt it but could do nothing to stop it. He would not have to wait long—the bad was already on the way.

I remember fields so green in the corners of my mind.

I remember stars so bright every night I walked outside.

———❖———

For as much as he wanted not to believe,
he could only stare at what he knew was really there.
— Excerpt from *The Provenance* (Chapter Three)

DETAIL ON THE HIGH GREEN

CASTLE ODESSA IN THE YEAR 841 HRT
(THREE DAYS AFTER YORI'S DISAPPEARANCE,
JUST DAYS AWAY FROM THE FIVE-YEAR CELEBRATION)

Hard boots pounded down the polished hallways of Castle Odessa, as the messenger pushed his way through the unsuspecting soldiers. He slid around a corner, quickly shuffled down the stairs, rounded the turns of each landing, and continued descending as fast as he could. Eventually reaching the ground floor, he burst through the doors and went back to dodging the armed troops casually going about their duties.

"Excuse me! Excuse me!" the messenger said, bumping into them.

At last, he came to the end of a hallway, and approached the heavy double doors painted deep green. They were the biggest doors in all of Castle Odessa, and he strained to pull one of them open. Bright sunlight burst forth into the hallway. This way led out to the Green.

Made from luxurious green limestone, the Green served multiple functions for Castle Odessa as the parade grounds and a rally point for King Leopold's Red and Blue army. The large overhanging balcony overlooked the peaks of the Blue Mountains and spied down upon the Mauveguard Pass.

The messenger hated coming out this way, onto the Green. Inside the interior confines of Castle Odessa, he could easily forget they were on a mountain peak. But once out here on the Green, the heights were impossible to ignore. And some, like the hurrying messenger, were prone to bouts of paralyzing vertigo. He took a deep breath trying to collect himself. Walking cautiously in a slow, measured, controlled pace, he stayed as close to the middle as possible. Still, he could feel the elements all around him—the wind, the cold, the mountain peaks. Without looking at the stone railing, he knew that over it was the dizzying vertical drop down to the valley below. He got woozy thinking about it.

A work detail of a dozen soldiers with buckets and brushes scrubbed on their hands and knees, polishing the green limestone to a brilliant shine. Overlooking the detail stood a tall, athletically built officer of the Red and Blue, his back to the castle and the messenger. Looking out over the mountains, the captain was deep in thought and did not notice when the messenger approached.

"Captain Kilmer?" the messenger asked with a soldierly salute. "Lord Whitney sends his compliments, sir!"

The captain turned to face him, with the fresh mountain air moving through his red curls. Returning the salute, Kilmer flashed a spark of impatient intensity behind his green eyes after seeing the face of the messenger.

"A message from Lord Whitney, sir," the messenger said, handing Kilmer a slip of paper, daunted by the alertness of his eyes.

Captain Kilmer accepted the note with a nod, unfolded the paper and read it. Afterward, he refolded the message, tucking it away in his pocket. Giving a quick glance to his detail, they turned quickly, once again busying themselves scrubbing the limestone. Kilmer smiled, knowing their curious eyes had been watching him and the messenger all along.

He kept his arms behind his back while considering the messenger. "Please extend my compliments to Lord Whitney; tell him I'll be there immediately."

The messenger bowed his head and turned to go, all too happy to vacate the Green. Kilmer watched him, taking some small amusement as the messenger strained to open and shut the heavy green door behind him.

Once the messenger was out of sight, Kilmer reread the note:

Dear Captain Kilmer,

Please see me immediately. I want to discuss an important mission that comes from His Majesty, King Leopold, himself. I think you are perfect to complete the action.

In the service of the king,
My compliments,

— Lord Whitney.

Captain Kilmer placed the paper back in his pocket, then turned to address his work detail.

"Wrap it up, boys!" he said. He called the work detail to attention. Once gathered, Kilmer dismissed them, after which, the soldiers relaxed among themselves.

"Any news, sir?" a young soldier named Melvin approached him.

"Lord Whitney has a mission for me."

"Can I go with you, Captain Kilmer?"

Kilmer liked Melvin. The boy reminded him of a childhood friend he had lost a few years ago. Kilmer could not help watching over the boy.

"We'll see. It all depends on what the mission entails, Melvin. But I'll take that matter under advisement."

Kilmer nodded at Melvin, then turned to go.

When Kilmer approached Lord Whitney's chamber, a woman waited there outside his office. She wore all black and looked worried, frantic even. She gave Kilmer a most desperate look as he passed her. He politely excused his way through, entering Lord Whitney's hall.

A visit to Lord Whitney was an informal affair. The senior officer had the tall, well-heeled look of a nobleman with short-cropped white hair cut in a proper military cut. His real name was Oskar Whitney, but the title he was known by was simply Lord Whitney because of his education and family wealth.

Almost seven years ago, Leopold commissioned Lord Whitney to be the chief architect to construct Castle Odessa, the very space they now stood within. Not only did he build the castle to Leopold's specifications and aggressive schedule, but in the War of the Mid-Run Valley he helped lead King Leopold's Red and Blue army in a successful defense against the Amalgamate armies at Mauveguard Pass. In addition, and at the king's command, his forces arrested and executed the king's own shock troops, its sadistic and bloodthirsty leader LaNew, and the rest of his murderous Red Guard. The king rewarded Lord Whitney with the second-highest position in the kingdom, subordinate only to himself.

He had first met Captain Kilmer at the Battle of Mauveguard Pass when the boy had saved the life of Leopold's former Minister of War, Amtor, who was severely wounded. For this act of heroism, the king promoted Kilmer to the rank of captain. But Amtor had never fully recovered from his wounds. It ended his fighting days. He married and retired to the relative safety and quiet of a cottage in the village of Homestead.

"How is the detail on the Green?" Lord Whitney asked Kilmer. He put down some papers he had been reviewing. Rounding the front of his desk, he offered his hand to greet Kilmer.

"Perfectly boring," he told Lord Whitney.

"A beautiful view on the Green, and it never looked so good. I am a bit envious. While you are out there, I'm in here reviewing invoices for Leopold's five-year celebration next week. There are times I would gladly trade places with you."

"As uneventful as polishing the Green is, I would rather be outside. Plus, I cannot do what you can anyway. You handle these heady things, like Leopold's finances. I handle the more laborious mindless things."

Lord Whitney returned to his desk and took a seat behind it. He motioned to Kilmer to sit. "You sell yourself too short, Kilmer. Why, I believe you could do anything you set your mind to."

"I am flattered you think so."

"Quit being so humble," Lord Whitney said. "You were there too—Castle Odessa, the defense against the Amalgamates, Mauveguard Pass. Everything."

Kilmer looked at the Badge of Heroism Lord Whitney had hanging on the wall. Just hearing that name, Mauveguard Pass, caused memories to come flooding back, remembering sounds of battle that day. He abruptly drifted off, and it did not go unnoticed.

Lord Whitney knew about Kilmer's melancholy and the tendency he had to get lost in the maze of his own mind. But Lord Whitney had something to discuss which he knew would bring Kilmer out of it quickly.

"I have a mission, something that may interest you," Lord Whitney told him. "Have you ever met Leopold's First Archer? His name is…"

"Yori, yes. I've met him on a couple of occasions, but I don't know him well."

"Couple days ago, Yori and a spotter, a man by the name of Isse, went into the Sanguine Forest on a hunt. They never came out."

"And you want me to find them?"

"This is a rescue mission direct from His Majesty, the king."

"There's more, isn't there?"

Lord Whitney nodded. "I want you to meet someone."

He stood up, opened a door, then motioned with his hand. The lady dressed in black from the hallway walked in, the look of despondency still on her face. Kilmer stood up politely and helped her to a seat.

"This is Lara, the wife of Yori, His Majesty's First Archer. Lara, this is Captain Kilmer."

"Thank you for helping us. I have heard so much about you, Captain Kilmer," Lara said through her tears. "Yori has been gone for days now. He has been away on many trips, but he has never been gone this long before. I fear the worst and am so frightened that he is lost or in some trouble. But I know he is not dead. I can feel it; I still feel his presence. He's still alive, Captain Kilmer, Lord Whitney. Can you help us? Can you help him? Won't you find him and bring him back, Captain Kilmer?"

"We will do our best, Lara. Of that I can assure you," Kilmer said, touching her arm. He looked at Lord Whitney, who gave him a slight nod of his head.

"Please find him, Captain Kilmer. Bring my husband back home."

"We will do whatever we can, Lara," Lord Whitney said, comforting her.

At length, Lord Whitney started to walk her out. But then, she stopped and turned to face Kilmer again. "Oh! Bless you, Captain Kilmer. May the Gods shine down on you and guide you."

She left and the two men stood alone in Lord Whitney's office.

"Well?" Lord Whitney asked him.

"Well? That was a dirty trick, Oskar."

"I know, but highly effective, you must admit."

Kilmer nodded. "Yes, I will search for the archer. Providing I can find him, I will return what is left of him back home to his wife and to our king. But I cannot promise whether he will be alive or dead."

"You'll need security, of course. Take as many men as you deem fit. Yori's last location was in the direction of the Sanguine Forest."

Lord Whitney searched Kilmer's face for any indication of reservations. Kilmer heard the words *the Sanguine Forest* but did not react.

"I will want to travel light," he said. "I think six good men, fully armed and with ample supplies, should be sufficient."

"Since this is coming directly from King Leopold, he told me to spare no expense."

"I'll just need the six with me. But additionally, I will depend on you to set up a string of couriers, to track us and our progress."

"I'll handpick the couriers and have them ride out to your search party daily."

"Have them stay close. I will send messages back once or twice a day, to meet your riders, carrying updates of the search. If you don't hear from us by the end of the day, send out the Red and Blue in force to sweep the Sanguine. Whatever we may encounter, the Red and Blue can handle it. But for now, let's not overreact."

"I agree," Lord Whitney said. "Anything else?"

"We'll need the basic supplies—ropes, bags, linens, shovels, and face coverings."

"Face coverings?"

"The smell of death," Kilmer said.

Lord Whitney nodded grimly and watched as Kilmer opened the door.

"Good hunting, Kilmer," Lord Whitney said, patting him on the back. "Be careful."

Kilmer walked out of the door. But before he left, he stopped and turned. "You sure you don't want to trade places now?"

"Not this time, old boy. This mission is your hour to shine."

"Then we leave immediately for the Sanguine Forest." Kilmer gave Lord Whitney a nod and left his office, knowing he would be spending the next few nights under the stars.

I want you to hear me,
I want you to fear me,
fear me, fear me
Come, and feel my pain.

Excerpt from *The Witch's Songbook*

They created red banners and hung them in the caverns in his honor.
— Excerpt from *The Provenance* (Chapter Four)

THE RED GUARD

A rapping on the window awakened Darius in the middle of the night. At first, he tried to ignore it, thinking Hollow Face was making sounds again. But the rapping continued in intensity and became more frantic. Darius knew that this could not be Hollow Face, the ghost was never this agitated.

He got out of bed and opened the window. The pale light outside revealed a shadowy person moving in the bushes. Kilmer, with his crooked back, stepped into the light. Darius opened the window fully, sticking his head out.

"Kilmer? What are you doing?"

Kilmer frantically tried to tell Darius something, but he was incoherent, talking so fast, his thoughts so scrambled, that Darius could not understand a word of what he was saying. It had to do with something about killing, blood, and fire. Darius had flashbacks of the vision Hollow Face had been showing him, a day ago, and he feared it was coming true. In all his time knowing Kilmer, he had never heard him complain about anything or seen him so desperate. His tone and urgency frightened Darius.

"Kilmer! Slow down. I can't understand you! Take a breath, start from the beginning."

Kilmer did as he was told. He took a deep breath, nodding in agreement. Calming himself the best he could, he began speaking slow enough so that Darius could understand.

"They are killing people, burning them alive," Kilmer whispered to the young boy at the window.

"Burning who alive?" Darius said, more frantic this time. "Where? Who? What people?"

"I don't know. A man, I heard his name. Leopold. He's gone mad! In the village of Bowling last night. I was there, I saw them burning. Oh, it was horrible, Darius. Horrible!" Kilmer cried.

He calmed himself, wiping his face on his sleeve. "They came after the city leaders first, 'Surrender the town or burn,' they said. But they were foolish and resisted. Leopold took them, strapped, and tied them to poles, then they set fire to them, burning them. Women and children..."

"What of the children?" Darius asked.

"They were rounded up, taken away. Children in one cart, women in another. Slaves, no doubt. And now he's coming this way! Leopold is coming!"

Darius saw that Kilmer kept rubbing his face in his sleeve. "Kilmer, you're bleeding."

Kilmer let out a cry that sounded alarmed and scared.

"They only wanted the healthy ones, those that can work." Kilmer held up his shriveled arm. "As for me, they beat me, and beat me, left me for dead. But they didn't kill me, Darius, and I got away from them and came straight here. Darius! We must warn your father, make him understand. Leopold is coming, and he is out for blood."

Darius rushed into his parents' room. One by one, the lights inside the house started to illuminate all the windows in their home. Justus hurried outside to speak with Kilmer. The realization that the village of Plum would soon be under attack became apparent.

At the first rays of the sun, an emergency meeting of the village council of Plum convened, the Honorable Justus Plum presiding. All seven members of the committee rushed to the council hall in the morning, wondering at its meaning.

"Council members," Justus Plum began. "I thank you all for coming so early in the morning to this emergency meeting."

"What is this meeting all about, Plum?" Councilman Delmont Botta asked among the other murmurs.

"Let me explain—last night news came to me that the village of Bowling has been attacked by forces commanded by a man named Leopold, a commoner who is championing an army of rebels and cutthroats. Yesterday they seized the council of Bowling, executing the entire council, every single board member."

A general gasp erupted around the table.

"Now this Leopold is looking at our village," Justus continued. "Which leads us to a dilemma. How do we defend ourselves, and what do we do?"

"Just one moment, Justus—where did you hear this information?" Councilman Delmont Botta asked.

"A survivor of the attack made his way to my home, just a few hours ago. He informed us of the attack, the brutal executions, the cruel beatings, and the suffering and surrender of the village of Bowling to the forces of this man Leopold."

"Why have we not heard this news from anyone else?" Delmont Botta asked. "Can we confirm that it is true? Who is your source?"

Justus reluctantly admitted that it had been Kilmer.

"Kilmer, the hunchback? The homeless beggar? Are we to believe this roaming vagabond on his word alone?"

"I have never known him to lie, Delmont," Justus told him. "I believe we need to secure our village, close our doors, close our businesses, and arm our citizens. We have to defend ourselves."

"On the word of this cripple?" Delmont asked.

"On the word of a survivor of the massacre in Bowling," Justus said.

"Alleged massacre, you mean, Justus," Delmont Botta told him. "At least, let us corroborate this report. Let's not overreact. I propose sending a scout to Bowling—a simple rider could confirm it. Let us take our own exploratory action to define our options before we handicap our businesses and our economy to shut down for a defense that we might not even need."

"Delmont," Justus said in reply, "have you not looked out the window? You can see the black smoke rising from the direction of Bowling. We can smell it here in this very chamber."

"Have we not had forest fires before? A brush fire? A farmer burning manure? But a massacre? We do not know it is that just because we see smoke. I, for one, am not taking the word of the hunchback. Let's stay in control—let's put our own eyes out there before we set panic upon our population. Don't we, as council members, have the responsibility to do so?"

"Maybe you are right, Delmont," a frustrated Justus said. "It should only take a rider an hour to make the round trip and return with a report that would either confirm Kilmer's story or not."

The council agreed. They quickly procured the services of a local stable to send a scout on horseback to the village of Bowling and return with a report. Soon the scout pounded away down the road in a cloud of dust from the village of Plum heading toward the black smoke rising out of Bowling.

The council waited for his return, but they never saw their scout again. Instead, they saw the banners, the red-and-blue flags of Leopold, carried by a double line of mounted cavalry warhorses as they came riding into the village of Plum. These were soldiers, not cutthroats, and they marched with orderly discipline. They soon gathered in force in the heart of the village.

So quick did Leopold's attack force unexpectedly ride into Plum that the village attempted no resistance. Most of the villagers continued eating their breakfast uninterrupted, only looking up from their eggs to remark upon the brightly adorned warhorses they rode in on. The scene looked more like a parade than what it was: an invasion. Children laughed and waved, running beside the column of the heavily armored killers. As the realization set in, a general panic ensued. Soon parents scrambled after their children, removing them from the street.

The cavalry rode in first, in front of Leopold's Red and Blue infantry, and thundered into the village square through the west of Plum. To the east, the Red Guard appeared, Leopold's intelligence and security forces. As Leopold's Red and Blue regulars stayed together in a show of power, the Red Guard quickly dispersed in a designed pincer movement to seal off all the roads coming in and out of Plum. All of Leopold's military units executed their actions with rehearsed military precision. The Red Guard harassed villagers of interest, searched them, and confiscated their possessions. Then they rounded the villagers up and detained them for later interrogation.

Before the village knew what was happening, the Red Guard and the Red and Blue were in control. With no resistance, they rounded up the available able-bodied citizens and corralled them in the middle of town. These prisoners were kept under heavy guard and were not allowed to return to their homes.

The village council members were equally as shocked at the suddenness and precision of the attack. The Red Guard surrounded the village leaders gathered on the steps of the council building.

The commander of the Red Guard approached the council building on his horse. He dismounted and walked through the middle of soldiers. He stood significantly shorter than the rest of the others, with blond hair and sideburns angling sharply across his cheeks. Looking over the scene, he motioned with his hand, and dozens of men leaped to work digging holes. Approaching the huddled leaders, he addressed the entire council with a shout. "Which one of you is Delmont Botta?"

"I am Delmont Botta," Delmont answered, squeezing his way through the council members to the front.

"Well done, Botta! Now, go with the Red Guard to collect your payment."

Justus Plum and the rest of the council looked at Delmont, confused. All were slow to realize what had just occurred.

"Delmont?" Justus asked, realizing he had been working with the Red Guard all along. "You stalled the actions of the council to betray your own village? To save your own skin?"

"I had no choice." Delmont approached Justus and whispered, "They approached me two nights ago. They were going to kill me then. They said they would kill my whole family if I did not cooperate. Forgive me, Justus. May the Gods forgive me... may they forgive us all."

As treacherous as Delmont's betrayal was, Justus had weightier matters to attend to at the moment.

"What is the meaning of this? I am Justus Plum, the Head Council here."

"So, you are Justus Plum, huh?" The commander pulled off his glove. "The Head Council of the village of Plum?"

"Yes, I am, and are you Leopold?"

The commander of the Red Guard slapped Justus backhandedly, knocking his floppy hat off his head. "Show your respect! He is to be addressed as King Leopold!"

Justus absorbed the pain and slowly turned back to face the commander, who got closer to his reddening face.

"I am Captain LaNew, commander of the Red Guard. I am here to accept your surrender of the village of Plum on behalf of the king. Are you prepared to surrender?"

"This is an unprovoked attack," Justus Plum said.

"Your surrender?" LaNew asked again with upraised eyebrows, walking around the council. "You must make a decision. You must surrender to my authority, on behalf of King Leopold, or... Here, let me raise the stakes a little."

By now, the Red Guard had completed digging holes behind LaNew and had begun centering tall wooden poles in them. Just then, a wagon pulled up flying the Red Guard banners. In the wagon were the families of the council members. They threw Rosa and Mara out of the wagon first, and they hit the ground. There in the dust, Justus' wife clung to their daughter.

"Rosa! Mara!" Justus called. He did not see Darius with them, and this immediately frightened him. Why was Darius not with them? Was he already dead? "Do not harm our families."

"Take them!" LaNew ordered. Agents of the Red Guard rushed the village leaders with military precision. All the council members were detained in the arms of two agents each. The Red Guard roughly handled and shoved the council members across the town square. Held against their will they were tied to the poles. They struggled against their constraints, but they held secure, and bound them in place. They could still talk, but not move, and everyone—soldiers and prisoners alike—were talking at once.

LaNew silenced the crowd.

"I tried to give you a chance. But even in the face of overwhelming force, you still cannot overcome your snobbish pride. It is easier for you to die than to part with your wealth and resources." With another motion of his hand, Red Guard agents stacked kindling around the base of the poles. "In this, we can oblige you."

"What are you going to do?" Justus called out.

LaNew approached him and looked at his luxurious navy blue coat with the yellow stitching and lapels. A soldier produced the expensive floppy hat Justus wore and handed it to his captain. LaNew dusted it off then placed it back on Justus's head and adjusted it properly.

"Take your silly hat," LaNew told him. "Now you pigs will know what it is like to suffer. We knew where to find your homes, your families. Thanks to the honorable Delmont Botta. He drew us a map."

Delmont Botta was brought to LaNew and forced to drop to his knees in front of the council. He had been stripped naked and beaten and was bleeding.

"I can give you one piece of solace," LaNew told the council, dousing Delmont in a bluish liquid. Then LaNew took a torch from one of his men. "No one likes a rat like Delmont Botta. Someone who would sell out their own kind is a man who just cannot be trusted."

LaNew touched Delmont Botta with the torch. He struggled and screamed as the fire spread over his body. He jumped up to run, but only survived for a few steps before collapsing on the ground motionless. The townsfolk and the council members gasped and screamed hysterically. The captain and his Red Guard laughed in delight. Justus watched in horror but could not help thinking about the whereabouts of Darius.

What happened to my son?

Shortly before the Red Guard arrived in the village of Plum, and the death of Delmont Botta in the town square, Hollow Face appeared to Darius once again. This time the ghost had a new vision for him. Darius's mind flooded with visions of yellow-and-white flowers. At first, Darius thought it was a pleasant memory of the flowers Mara had picked earlier. But Hollow Face was insistent with this vision, replaying it over and over. The more Darius tried to push the vision from his mind, the closer the ghost approached the boy, pressing the vision on him with growing intensity. Nonstop showing him the flowers, always the flowers, and again with flowers.

Darius wondered why the immediacy. What could be so important about yellow-and-white flowers to his ghost? He eventually thought he should find out. At any rate, he reasoned, they made a nice gift for Kilmer, they would make a nice gift for Mara or his mother.

Casually putting on his shoes, he lazily walked out of the house. He walked through the yard and headed off in the direction of where the wildflowers grew.

Stopping at the top of the riverbank, he knew better than to go down there, as it was strictly forbidden by his parents, and he did not want to get into any trouble. He could see many yellow-and-white flowers matching the vision blooming just down around the middle.

He looked left and right. Despite the warnings of his father, he took off his shoes. He did it just like Mara did earlier, to be doubly careful not to slip down the bank. Leaving his shoes in the grass on top, he dragged on his bottom slowly and carefully down the steep bank, moving closer to the flowers until he reached the top of a large patch of them.

Darius heard horses coming in the distance, many hooves thundering down the road close to their house. He stood to see over the hill. Wagons with red banners were approaching. Then a dark figure appeared next to him. It was the ghost.

"Oh! Hollow Face," Darius said, startled. "What are you doing here?"

This short greeting was all Darius had time for. Hollow Face materialized from his ghostly spirit to solid form and gave Darius a solid push with humanlike hands. The boy fell away backward from Hollow Face, tumbled violently through the flowers and down the riverbank, where he splashed into the freezing water and went underneath the Plum River.

Struggling for air, he came to the top, surfacing just in time to see the rumbling horses of the Red Guard coming to the House of Justus. They pulled their wagons to a halt, kicking up clouds of dust, and men with red headbands dismounted, ran through the yard, and into their house. When they came out, they were roughly handling Rosa and Mara. The men threw them screaming into the wagons.

The hunchback was hiding close by too. He came out of the bushes and bravely tried to protect the women. But they caught him and beat him mercilessly.

Darius watched silently while immersed in the deep river. He was helpless standing on his tiptoes in the cold water, leaving just part of his eyes and nose exposed above the rushing waters that pushed him downstream. He could only watch the scene unfold, mesmerized.

The soldiers surrounded Kilmer beating and kicking him. Darius could hear the poor man scream, as his mother and sister were taken away by force.

He realized Hollow Face had helped him, saved him. First to get him on the riverbank, then materializing to push him into the relative safety of the river. In the river was the safest place for him to be. Darius struggled against the current to get a better idea of the commotion in the town square.

Under the village statue, his father and six other council members were tied to stakes. The Red Guard had spread wood kindling around their feet. LaNew turned to face them, holding a large clay pot. He approached Justus Plum and gave him a splash of bluish liquid from the big jar. Justus reacted to the harsh fluid, the fumes filling his eyes.

"Please! Plum is yours! Take it! I surrender!"

LaNew laughed and kept splashing the remaining bluish liquid on the rest of the council members. He threw the jar aside and it broke. LaNew shouted so all of them could hear.

"Plum has always been mine!" LaNew said. "You have always been mine! You just didn't know it! The time to negotiate is over. The time to surrender is over. Personally, I never wanted to offer you surrender anyway. That's something that King Leopold insisted on. But I like doing things my way."

"Please, my family!" Justus pleaded. "Rosa, Mara!"

"Father!" Mara called to him.

"Worried about them?" LaNew asked. He motioned with his hand, and soldiers pushed Rosa and Mara down to the ground.

"Nice-looking family you got there, Plum," LaNew said, giving Justus a sideways look. "It would be a shame if anything happened to them."

Justus said, "Rosa! Mara!"

"Rosa, Mara!" LaNew mocked him. Then a puzzled look crossed LaNew's face. He asked one of his soldiers, "Aren't we missing one?"

A soldier stepped forward with a list. "The young son, Darius Plum, sir."

"Well, where is he?"

"He wasn't at home when we got there, sir," the soldier told him.

LaNew looked at Justus. But now, soaked in kerosene, his expression was silent and defiant. He knew his boy still lived.

"Well, find him and kill him," LaNew said. "But before you send out the detail, deal with these two."

LaNew stepped back and motioned with his hand. Two soldiers of the Red Guard rushed up with swords drawn.

"No!" Justus shouted along with the others.

From the river, Darius saw the Red Guard surround his mother and sister. An audible gasp erupted from the villagers that Darius heard clearly, even chin-deep in the river. He saw his father scream and struggle against his bindings. When the soldiers parted, Mara was the first to fall. She fell quickly and quietly, succumbing to death as if she was laying down to go to sleep. Rosa had more fight in her, and as the red stain grew wider on her dress, she held her throat. She tried to protect her daughter. Then, seeing it was too late for her, she reached back for her husband tied to the stake with a blood-filled hand. Justus called to her. Then she collapsed at his feet on top of the fueled kindling.

Justus wailed in agony. Likewise, Darius dropped under the surface, rolled himself into a tight position, and screamed in the water, trailing long bubbles of agony. Long moments passed before he could find the courage to come back to the top. By the time he broke the water's surface, the other council members were engulfed in raging flames, leaving only his father remaining.

Justus Plum silently hung his head in capitulation while the others burned. With his murdered family at his feet, and the cries of the others in his ears, he mercifully would not last much longer.

They handed LaNew the lit torch. He switched the torch away from Justus so as not to accidently set him on fire. He would not want that to happen prematurely. He lifted the man's chin and saw he had tears streaming down his face.

"If you cry hard enough, maybe you will be able to douse the flames," LaNew said. Then, he backed safely away and applied the torch. Fire erupted underneath. The rolling blaze enveloped him, and the body of his wife, spreading quickly up his body with thick black smoke. After a brief but painful struggle, Justus Plum became still in the smoke.

Darius realized the terrible vision had become real—the blood, the water, the fire. Now he was forced to witness the final fulfillment of the vision. Darius looked on in horror. Behind them, the homes of the village were on fire, burning out of control. The scene was just as Hollow Face's vision showed him days ago. But Darius had ignored the warnings.

By now, he could see the Red Guard trampling down Mara's yellow-and-white flowers under their heavy boots. They had found his shoes and were looking for the boy, obeying the order of their commander: find him and kill him.

"Darius! Darius!" they called out.

"We will not harm you!" they mocked and laughed.

He wanted to die. Lying back in the water, he lifted his feet from the bottom, allowing the river's current to carry him. Floating along on his back he saw the blue sky, the puffy clouds, it was such a beautiful day; its only flaw was that occasionally the sky was obscured by pillars of thick black smoke. His ears stayed under the surface. He could no longer hear their screams, the guards calling, the mocking of his name.

"Darius! Darius! Where are you? Darius!"

In the currents of the Plum River, the very river that his ancestor aptly named, he put his fate in the Gods to take him wherever the water would have him go.

I had this feeling
That I can't feel anymore
But I... feel
So far from my home.

———— ✦◈◆◈✦ ————

Excerpt from *The Witch's Songbook*

Rest his soul. By thunder, they are dead now.
— Excerpt from *The Provenance* (Chapter Five)

THE SEARCH PARTY BEGINS

Castle Odessa in the Year 841 HRT
(Four Days After Yori's Disappearance)

Kilmer and his six companions followed the winding road down and away from Castle Odessa, which turned east and went through the Mauveguard Pass. They rattled down on horseback through the steep cliffs and rocks that flanked them on either side. The pass narrowed like a giant funnel from its highest point and opened to gently slope down for the next three miles to the Mid-Run Valley below.

This had been where the final conflict in the War of the Mid-Run Valley had been decided. Twenty thousand men died in the pass. Almost five years later, the memories of war stood like ghosts in a multitude of granite statues of the units and heroes who fell here. Along the way, they passed the monuments like tombstones, and pointed out the places where they fought, the sacred ground where their friends had fallen. No matter how many years had passed, the veterans never quit fighting the Battle of Mauveguard Pass.

Rhodes rode upright in the saddle, an experienced combat soldier. The large muscular veteran started talking first.

"I was right here in the front lines, standing in the third rank of the Red and Blue's First Infantry Spears when the command came. 'Spears at the ready,' Amtor directed, screaming at the top of his lungs. 'Stand your ground, boys,' he said."

Rhodes paused. He relived that day with the sun in his eyes, his black hair cropped tightly in a military cut. After taking a breath, he continued.

"Then came the push of the Amalgamates, and we all resisted with everything we had. But they just kept coming, pushing us. Those Amalgamates slammed into us powerfully, in waves of spears, clashing into our own. They pierced our shields, our armor. They ran our boys through, impaled us. Bloody frightening, it was. Terrible! It was chaos! And we impaled them right back. In the end, the fighting broke down to hand-to-hand combat. A bloody murderous affair. At the time we used whatever we could: fists and feet, heads and rocks."

"With you, Rhodes, there is little difference," said Curtz, another veteran of Amtor's First Infantry. The others laughed.

But Rhodes ignored them.

"We picked up their spears, pulled them out of our dead, used them over and over again. We died together along with those brave Amalgamates. It was a bloodbath."

Curtz glanced at Hanson riding next to him. Hanson had been an Amalgamate and fought on the other side during the Battle of Mauveguard Pass. Both sets of combatants had been merged as equals after the war. Once enemies, they had to accept each other, forming a corps of fighting men under the Kingdom of Odessa. By decree of King Leopold any retribution, by either side, had been made strictly forbidden but some still harbored hard feelings for their former enemies. Curtz looked at Hanson for a way to aggravate him.

"At least the Amalgamates were good at marching," Curtz said with a shrug, while continuing to look at Hanson. "Even better at dying."

"You know, Curtz," Hanson told him, plodding alongside him, "the Battle for Mauveguard was only one battle in the long War of the Mid-Run Valley. There were others in that war. Why, I can remember pushing you First Infantry ladies all across the Mid-Run for over a year. And when we reached Mauveguard, we were forty-five thousand strong. Oh! How I remember the looks on the faces of you Red and Blues when you were shitting yourselves behind your fortifications as we came up that hill."

"Well, we are all friends now," Curtz replied and gave him a little smirk. Curtz was an ornery man with a quick wit and sharp attitude. He kept his yellow hair long below his helmet and stubble on his chin, but he could have been mistaken for a much younger and inexperienced man. He was smaller and shorter than the rest. But he had incredible agility; he could run circles around anybody in a fight.

"I lost a lot of good friends here to the spears," Hanson remarked to both Rhodes and Curtz as they silently rode on. "We all lost at Mauveguard Pass."

Melvin, the youngest of the group, was not only too young to shave, but he was also the only one that had not been in the war. He was barely more than a kid, just a little more than a recent recruit, who had not yet shed his baby fat and possessed a round youthful face. His uniform looked new, clean, and crisp in contrast to the veterans' old and worn uniforms. He rode next to Kilmer who insisted he stay close to him.

"Thank you for letting me come with you on this mission, Captain Kilmer," Melvin told him.

"Don't thank me, Melvin, I'm not sure what we are getting into. So, just look alive and stay alert. And don't do anything stupid."

"I don't mean to question you, sir, but why did you select me?"

Kilmer looked at Melvin. "You remind me of someone, a friend of mine. Someone who needed experience too."

Melvin accepted that as the best response he was going to get. He wanted to ask Kilmer what happened to his friend, but he thought it best to leave that unsaid for now.

Kilmer, Rhodes, Curtz, Hanson, and Melvin rode in the front, while two other veterans took up the rear.

The largest man in the search party was a man by the name of Laws. He rode with an enormous double-edged long sword strapped across his back. Laws wore his suffering on his face, quite literally, made by an Amalgamate battle-axe. A scar sliced him diagonally across his face; it ran from the top of his left milky eye and cut a divot across the bridge of his nose, splitting his lips vertically in two, making it difficult for him to speak or eat. Had the axe not been a glancing blow, he would not have survived to be here today. The wound left him self-conscious with little to say so as not to draw more attention to himself. Outwardly Laws appeared to others as morose, but Kilmer handpicked him because when a sword needed swinging, there was none better than Laws, an excellent swordsman. But until that time, he brooded along behind in silence.

Then there was Givens, the party's best cavalry man and horseman. He rode with Amtor's cavalry in the war. Kilmer brought him along to take care of the horses and considered him an expert in horseshoes, saddles, and bridles. He expected Givens to keep the mobility of the column in fine working order. Givens rode in the rear and would have liked to be more involved in the conversation, as it was a lonely duty riding in back with Laws, who looked more like a monster than a man, and would not speak even when spoken to. Neither could he clearly hear the conversations up front, and so, had nothing to say. Instead, Givens quietly rode along, lost in his own thoughts, taking in the scenery of the beautiful Blue Mountains and the Mauveguard Pass. Miserable to ride in silence, he took up the rear with Laws and managed the two packhorses loaded with supplies.

Kilmer abruptly stopped but not because of the hurtful teasing of Hanson and Curtz. The rest of the party stopped with him. Kilmer had stopped to look at a certain marble statue. Even Hanson, the Amalgamate, looked upon the stone statue with respect.

"Ah yes, there he is," Rhodes said. "Amtor, I remember him well."

"The best warrior on either side," Hanson agreed.

"And look"—Curtz pointed beyond Amtor's statue—"there is the statue of our very own Captain Kilmer. Captain, you are a famous celebrity!"

Just beyond the statue of Amtor, a similar statue of Kilmer stood, erected to honor the man that had saved Amtor's life, almost five years ago. It seemed that one could not be remembered without the other.

"That was a long time ago," Captain Kilmer said. "But I remember everything about that day as if it were yesterday."

Kilmer took time to remember his own private story, but unlike the talkative Rhodes, he kept it to himself. Eventually, he encouraged his horse slowly forward. The rest followed.

"We are riding with a legend," Rhodes said to Melvin, as if the boy was not already sufficiently impressed.

The column descended through the pass and Rhodes continued to reminisce about his experiences. Hanson returned to lamenting about being on the defeated side and the friends he lost. Curtz tried hard to antagonize both of them. Kilmer rode with Melvin, keeping the young recruit close to him and under his wing. In the rear, Laws and Givens were silently guarding the rear and the supplies.

"Where we are going, Captain Kilmer?" Curtz asked.

Kilmer pointed to the southeast. His silence unnerved Curtz, who was usually unflappable. He sarcastically rolled his eyes at Kilmer's reply while looking at Hanson. No one asked Kilmer any more questions after that for the rest of the day.

The search party rode until the sun was setting low in the Blue Mountains. Then Kilmer ordered that they make camp. He called for Givens to ride back to meet Lord Whitney's couriers, and to swap messages with them, and then return and bed down for the evening.

Kilmer wrote the following letter and gave it to Givens:

Lord Whitney,

My compliments. We have reached the outskirts of the Sanguine Forest without incident. We will enter it by midday tomorrow. Please continue to send couriers.

— Captain Kilmer

Givens folded the note and put it in the leather pouch hanging off his saddle. Then he saluted and was off like a bolt, thundering down the road with a cloud of dust following him.

Kilmer set a watch to protect the camp. He would take the first watch and ordered the rest of them to rest, eat, feed, care for the horses, and prepare for the next day. Kilmer would then pass the watch to Melvin, Rhodes, Hanson, Curtz, and then finally Laws. Givens was excused from this duty since he was serving as the courier.

"Why do I have middle watch?" Curtz complained. "Just when I get to sleep, I have to wake up. Hey, Laws, trade me your shift."

Laws said nothing to Curtz.

"It's just for the first night, Curtz," Kilmer told him. "I'll take middle watch next time."

The little man Curtz turned and grumbled to himself, walking past Rhodes.

"Do your part, Curtz," Rhodes told him without any trace of sympathy.

"And keep that stinking mouth shut," Hanson added just for good measure.

Curtz shook his head, while laying down in a blanket. "Amalgamates."

"Leave him alone," Laws said, speaking with a lisp because of his split lip. It was the only thing he had said since leaving Castle Odessa. Just the look of Laws chilled Curtz to the bone. He loved getting under people's skin but thought it best not to rouse a man with a foot-long axe scar across his face. For once, Curtz observed the quiet.

After about an hour, Givens came riding back with a message from Lord Whitney passed on from his courier:

Captain Kilmer,

Do your best to return before the five-year celebration next week. If for some reason, I receive no note from you in two consecutive days, I will mobilize the First Infantry to your last known location. Let me know if you need anything. Take care, my friend.
— Lord Whitney

The search party spent an uneventful night under the stars. The night was another cold one, but it did not freeze. The fire in the middle of their camp provided some comfort from the elements. The nightly watch encountered nothing to report except some local wildlife that kept a safe distance from the fire and the men.

The next day, before the sun rose, the men had a basic breakfast of bacon and eggs. They fed the horses bags of oats. By morning, the fire was extinguished and covered over. Blankets were rolled up and stuffed back in packs. They eventually mounted up and continued for another day of riding.

By now, they all knew where they were heading, even if Captain Kilmer did not tell them. The only thing out here in the direction he pointed was the Sanguine Forest. They had all heard the stories that the forest was haunted, and despite their vast combat experience, none of them had been this way before. None had ever set foot in the Sanguine.

They rode over the last of the flatlands and rocky hills of the Mid-Run Valley until, at last, they entered the forest.

"I hate this forest," Curtz said.

"I'm not much of a fan either," Hanson added.

"Are we now in the Sanguine?" Rhodes asked.

Hanson nodded. "At least it's still during the day."

"Look," Laws said, pointing to the sky ahead. "Buzzards."

Kilmer saw them too. They were circling above the forest in the distance. He had been waiting, expecting them, and had been watching for the sign of scavengers ever since they left the first camp.

Kilmer put up his hand to stop the column.

"Hanson!" Kilmer called, and the former Amalgamate came riding up. Kilmer looked back at the group, at each of the other riders.

"Laws!" Kilmer called, and the big man came forward.

With Hanson and Laws up front with Kilmer, he gave the order, "Ride ahead and look for a trail."

"Trail?" Laws asked. "What kind of trail?"

"Look for anything out of the ordinary—crushed grass, broken sticks, spots of blood," Kilmer explained.

Laws and Hanson nodded and rode on ahead.

With Hanson and Laws riding point, the column was on the move again. The deeper they went into the Sanguine, the darker it got.

"Got something here, captain." Hanson pointed to the ground near a little brook. "Looks like blood."

Kilmer looked at the signs. He agreed, something had happened here.

"I want it followed," Kilmer said. He told the rest of the column, "Spread out."

Just then, Laws stepped on a human skull, his heavy boot crushing it to pieces. "Got something here too, captain."

"What is it, Laws?" asked Kilmer, riding up.

"Human bones, sir. Look there! And there! And still more over there! Human skulls, sir. Skeletal remains. They're everywhere."

Soon, the others noticed them too.

"This place is a graveyard," Rhodes said. "Or the place of a massacre."

"I thought we just came through the place of a massacre," Curtz said, referring to Mauveguard Pass. "This must be the other massacre."

No one found him funny. Melvin felt a shiver go up his spine.

Unexpectedly, a chilling blast of strong wind blew like a hurricane through the search party. The seasoned horses, desensitized to the sounds of battle, startled and reared. Rhodes's helmet blew off as his horse reared in the sudden gale. Anything not tied down tumbled away. They all scrambled to shield their eyes while catching their falling items. The icy blast did not last long, just enough to make them feel a cold chill down to their bones. Now the horses were extremely agitated and restless. Givens tried to calm them, but even he was having no luck. It seemed the forest had turned against them suddenly. Then, just as suddenly as it started, it became quiet like before, silent and foreboding.

"Where did that come from?" Curtz said. When no one answered him, he said, "I hope that's not a sign of things to come."

"Captain Kilmer?" Melvin whispered, obviously afraid.

Melvin had found Yori's empty quiver nearby, emblazoned with Leopold's Red and Blue of the First Archer. There was no doubt it was Yori's. Shortly after Melvin's find, Rhodes discovered some arrows in the underbrush. Curtz motioned to the group, after finding the remains of a long dead and decomposed deer that had Yori's red-

and-blue arrow sticking up in its side. Givens called out and held up Yori's bow, also emblazoned with the familiar crest of Leopold still on it.

They were getting closer, Kilmer thought. After collecting themselves, they went deeper into the Sanguine. Just up ahead, a short distance from the found items of the First Archer, appeared a clearing where the vultures converged on the ground. The lively oily birds were busy thumping around on the ground, obviously feeding on something dead.

The wind shifted, and then it hit them all at once. Still at a distance, with the subtle shift in the breeze, the smell was unmistakable. The smell of death, a hot, almost sweet, earthly, rotten smell. The foul odor wafted on the wind and traveled in the riders' direction. Each of them in turn made a sour face.

"Stay here," Kilmer said, halting the column.

They stopped as he commanded. Kilmer kicked his mount and urged his horse slowly forward, alone. The smell grew more pungent, more disgusting with every step.

Up ahead, the huddled mass of black scavengers ripped at fetid flesh. Kilmer could only imagine what they were feeding on. As he neared their feathered wake, they pushed against one another, completely ignoring his presence. Their heads were stained red.

The putrid stink was now intense around him. Kilmer gave Laws a hand signal, unwilling to open his mouth to give the verbal order. Laws brought up a crossbow, and he leveled it off, taking aim. The crossbow bolt whipped ahead and found its mark in the back of one of the black birds with a *thwack*! Feathers flew as a big one dropped, and the others startled. Immediately they squawked and, one by one, they took notice of the men and hurriedly flew up to the trees or back to the skies. The vultures continued circling overhead and watching from the trees with great interest to see what these men were going to do, waiting for them to leave so their feast could start again.

Kilmer swatted a large green fly from his neck as he dismounted. The others dismounted as well, now following him. Without a word, Kilmer removed his gloves and tucked them into his leather belt. He pulled out a cloth and wrapped it around his face. The other riders silently did the same. Kilmer wrapped his horse's bridle around a tree branch, then headed on foot toward the flattened, bloodied grass. The smell was now as strong as it was going to get as Kilmer stood looking over a dead human body.

The others slowly joined him. They all gathered around and gazed down at the awful sight.

"Look at his face," Givens said in a whisper.

"Poor bastard," Kilmer said in a low tone.

Misshapen and discolored, the dead body rested on its back in the clearing. The vultures had done a thorough job of picking through its torso. The scavengers left a hollow in the man's midsection, pecked all the way down to his bony red spine.

But that was not what mesmerized the search party so. It was the scream. The abnormal overstretched look of terror frozen on the dead man's face.

"What kind of horror did this? What did he see in his last moments?" Curtz said in consternation.

Melvin commented, "Look at his eyes! What made them bug out so?"

"What kind of fear can make a man scream like that?" asked Rhodes.

Hanson asked, "Is it Yori?"

"I can't tell just yet," Kilmer said. "Let me inspect him."

The others looked away as Captain Kilmer knelt to search the corpse. All of them were privately glad that he did not order them to touch it.

Kilmer examined the corpse's stiffened left hand. He searched the third finger, particularly interested if it should still have the red-and-blue decorated signet ring of the court of King Leopold. The ring would not only prove his identity as the king's archer but would be something that the vultures would not eat. Kilmer found no ring.

He stood up and backed away.

"This is not the king's senior archer. It is not Yori. It must be his spotter. His name was Isse." Kilmer took a moment to look around the forest for clues of where Yori might have gone.

"Get the shovels," Kilmer commanded. "We need to bury him."

The others complied, and he watched them go to the horses and unpack the gear. At length, the soldiers noisily approached the body with the clanking of tools and shovels.

"Melvin!" Kilmer called, and the boy came to him. "Go find a big rock, but small enough to carry, and scratch his name on it. His name was Isse."

"Yes, sir!" the boy said.

Rhodes and Hanson started working. With considerable effort they dug the grave in the dark of the woods, through the small tree roots and the hardened gravel, with their scarfs wrapped tightly around their faces. The stink of the long-dead Isse gagged them, making their labors even harder. Givens and Curtz eventually relieved Rhodes and Hanson and completed the grave. When they were done, they climbed out of the shallow trench.

Melvin found the rock he was looking for. He took his dagger and scratched the four letters on its surface: *Isse*. He carried the stone to the grave, placing it on one end.

Laws and Kilmer took on the worst job. Producing linens, they carefully wrapped what was left of Isse's grotesque remains. Covering the body did not prevent the stench completely, nor would the men ever get that smell out of their memory.

Without ceremony, they placed his body in the grave. Afterward, they stood hot and sweaty, looking down at the body-shaped package at the bottom of the dirt hole. The sides were irregularly scraped with assorted rocks and straggly little hairs of white roots peeking through.

Kilmer broke the silence.

"Goodbye, Isse, may your spirit now be at peace."

He lingered there for a moment, as they all did, peering into the grave, looking at the wrapped body. Even though it was covered in white wrappings, they could all still remember his face, locked in that inhuman scream. There was something prophetic about him now. In the silence of his grave, he seemed to be telling them a message, giving them a silent warning.

This could be you next.

They all had an uneasy feeling.

"Fill it in," Kilmer commanded and turned to walk away. He put his hands on his hips and searched for any sign of where Yori might be. The men behind him shoveled the dirt to fill Isse's grave.

They had found the spotter, but they still had to find Yori. It would have to wait for another day, though. No one wanted to make camp in the Sanguine. Hardened war veterans rarely believed in old wives' tales of ghosts and spirits, but they had all seen Isse's face. There was a certain finality of proof in his scream. Evidence that something was out here, and none of them wanted to be sleeping when they found out what it was.

"Givens!" Kilmer commanded. "Take this note back to Lord Whitney's couriers. Do not return here—instead go to where we camped last night. We will wrap things up here and meet you there at our first camp."

Kilmer scratched out a note:

Lord Whitney,

We have found the spotter, Isse. We marked his grave with a stone in the northern half of the Sanguine Forest. We found evidence of Yori, the First Archer's arrows, bow, and quiver abandoned in the bush. The Sanguine Forest has revealed signs of a significant burial or battle here, scattered human bones en masse. Unless we find Yori alive soon, retrieving any more than these items may prove fruitless. We make for the same camp we stayed in last night.

We will continue the search for Yori in the morning.

Your servant,

— Captain Kilmer

As before, Givens folded the message and placed it in his pouch. Then with a salute, he was off like thunder.

"Pack it up, boys." Kilmer turned back to his remaining riders with the purpose of leaving the Sanguine Forest. The sky still held some brightness.

"I do not believe it is safe to make camp here. Whatever killed Isse can still be lurking out here. So, we will head north, the way we came in, back to our camp of last night. Stay alert. Especially until we get out of this forsaken forest."

The search party could not be more relieved.

She stands in the night
in the corner of her room,
and the only light that shines
through the window is the moon.

Excerpt from *The Witch's Songbook*

She grasped the darkness and the night.
She walked between them in a trail of fiery, smoky, red-orange light
— Excerpt from *The Provenance* (Chapter Six)

SISTER CHAVISE

ST. EHLONA'S ORPHANAGE,
VILLAGE OF PLUM IN THE YEAR 833 HRT
(NINE YEARS EARLIER, BEFORE YORI'S DISAPPEARANCE)

She brushed her long hair that hung down in gray curls over her nightshirt. Then she washed her face and prepared for bed. The chamber was illuminated by the soft glow of two small candles. As usual for this hour, all was quiet at St. Ehlona's Orphanage.

Sister Chavise had over the years developed an acute sensitivity for sound, particularly past nine bells. She could hear any form of muffled laughter from those who otherwise should be asleep in their beds. She had an uncanny knack for detecting audible nonsense from any room of the orphanage. Over the years, her ability only got better.

Blowing out one of the candles, she prepared to retire. After extinguishing the second candle, she expected darkness, yet there remained a rising glow. A flickering light came from outside her window. She pulled back the curtain.

A fire raged in the distance just beyond the trees on the other side of the Plum River. It came from the direction of the village of Plum, very close to where she knew the residence of the Plum family was situated. She immediately worried.

Justus Plum had been a friend of the orphanage and sometimes rode out with food to feed the orphans. His wife, Rosa Plum, would come with him and donate clothes that the children put to good use. Sister Chavise could only hope they were out of the way of the fire, safe and sound.

Concerned, she opened her window. The cold night air rushed in. Using her sensitivity to sound, she listened intently. What she heard appalled her. There were voices on the wind. At first, she could hear screaming, crying, and sounds of agony. Holding her breath, she listened ever more deeply. Soon she could hear even more. This time, the deep voices of men—strange men not from this area—shouting orders and laughing at the other screams of torment. Sister Chavise received an icy chill.

A bad wind is blowing through Plum, she thought. She knew she wanted no part of it and shut the window.

Being no stranger to magic, Sister Chavise took an anxious moment to search her room for any bad omens. Shadows formed across the stones as the fire raged across the river. For a moment, the shadows transformed into restless spirits dancing upon her walls. If it were true, if these were spirits, none came off the wall to reveal any more of themselves or their intentions. She prayed to the Goddess Ehlona.

Darius Plum floated away on the river with the other debris. Drifting on the water's current, he passed the burning village of Plum, his home in flames, and the men looking for him. Holding his face up out of the river, and his ears under the water, he could still breathe while drowning out the surrounding screams. He floated along with memories of his parents and his sweet, beloved sister, Mara. Overwhelmed by visions of their deaths, all the blood and the fire, he submerged, doubling over in pain, sobbing again.

The current of the river took him until he felt the sandy bottom scrape under him. The stones sliding across his back narrowed the channel and slowed his drift. His head gently bumped against a resting log by the calm bank of the river. He twisted to a gradual stop in the shallow water.

He lay there wishing he were dead. A few moments passed, then cold and drenched, he wearily rose to a sitting position. Shivering in the cold air, he pulled himself out of the water and onto the grass.

Far upstream, streaks of black smoke billowed in the sky, and he could still see the fire's glow in the reflections of the water. He used the cover of darkness to reach the shadows of a grove of trees. There, he found a rotting tree that had fallen over. He slid his body inside the dark tree, a slippery, smelly hole, but it would provide him with a hiding place and shelter for the night. It might keep him from being discovered by the murderers or freezing to death.

The next day dawned and Sister Maldean stood over the headmistress, shaking her awake.

"Headmistress, headmistress! Wake up, soldiers are here!"

"Sister Maldean, I'm still in my nightshirt."

"They are here right now. They are asking for you. They want to talk to you," Sister Maldean said, holding her robe for her. "Your robes, headmistress."

"I can do it myself!" Sister Chavise said, expressing her displeasure. "Tell the soldiers to wait in the kitchen. I'll be with them shortly."

Sister Chavise had once been blessed by the Goddess Ehlona herself. She had been blessed with beauty and a long healthy life. Spry and youthful in her beauty, she appeared more like a younger woman in her thirtieth year, instead of her seventieth. The Goddess had told her nothing could separate her from that blessing. So, because of Ehlona's protection, Sister Chavise had no fear of the soldiers or anything else.

As the soldiers waited in the kitchen, it took her no time at all to braid her long gray hair back into a familiar bun and get dressed in her robes. Sister Chavise had developed a strong distrust of outsiders to the orphanage; this especially held true for all soldiers. They usually represented nothing more than hard cases. They always wanted something and then they wanted more. It was her experience that soldiers never had the best interests of her or St. Ehlona's Orphanage.

Sister Chavise left her room. She locked her door, then turned and nearly tripped over Oaks, a boy of about ten years old. It surprised her to see him, as he had not been there a second ago. But that was Oaks—he was always showing up where you least expected him.

"Sister Chavise," Oaks said. "Soldiers are here. They are in the kitchen."

"Yes, Oaks. Sister Maldean told me. I'm going to speak with them now."

"Is it about the boy?"

The headmistress stopped to consider Oaks a little more closely. The boy had big dark eyes and unkempt shaggy black hair. He had come to St. Ehlona's as a mere baby, as most children do, after the untimely death of his parents. He had no other family to care for him. This was his home and always had been. Here, he had stayed for most of the ten years of his life.

"What boy, Oaks?" Sister Chavise knelt to talk to him on his level.

"I went outside last night to watch the fire. Did you know there was a fire?"

"I know." She closed her eyes and nodded. "I saw it."

"That's when I noticed the boy. He stood in the woods, hiding in the tree line. He was wet, and his clothes were tattered. He had curly red hair, I think. I waved at him, and he waved back. Then he ran away into the woods. He wouldn't come out into the open. He's too scared."

"Cold and hungry too, I would imagine," Sister Chavise said. "Oaks, I want you to go back to your bedchamber and wait for me there. And not a word of this to anyone. Just for the time being. Do you understand?"

Oaks nodded. "Especially not in front of the soldiers."

"Especially not in front of the soldiers," the headmistress repeated, standing up, hands folded in front of her. "All right, then. Now go on, Oaks, go to your room and make your bed."

"But, Sister Chavise, I already made my bed this morning."

Sister Chavise had already left and was halfway down the hall.

"Then make it again," she insisted over her shoulder. "And comb your hair."

Oaks ran his fingers through his thick hair and turned to go.

Sister Chavise rounded the corner and went down the steps, passing the long hallway leading to the kitchen. Then she stopped suddenly and felt dizzy. An oppressive feeling of foreboding passed through her senses. Maybe it was because of Oaks telling her about the sudden appearance of the boy in the woods, or perhaps the scene she saw from her window last night. She remembered the distant laughter, while the fire raged from the destruction of Plum. Or maybe it was the shadows dancing in her room. Whatever it was, Sister Chavise began to have an awful premonition.

In that moment, in Sister Chavise's mind, time slowed to a crawl. Her steps down the hallway echoed slow and labored. Her hearing intensified more than usual—she could hear each footfall echoing inside her brain. She could hear words—Sister Maldean speaking to the soldiers. They spoke in slow deep tones, but in a language void of any familiar words. What it sounded like to her was that the soldier said to Sister Maldean, "I'm going to kill you all." But that could not be right. She blinked her eyes trying hard to clear her mind.

She could see a soldier's boot, around the corner of the kitchen. As she neared the pantry, the premonition changed.

Suddenly everything was on fire; the orphanage was in flames. Sister Maldean collapsed in the corner, sabers slashing red bloody stripes into her robes, making her scream in pain. She saw dead children scattered through the hall, their blood splattered on the walls. Tables were burning, turned upside down, while broken dishes littered the floor. In the middle of the fire stood the vengeful, bloodthirsty soldiers. They were laughing at her, as she heard them before.

She looked down. A knife protruded from the center of her chest. A widening red stain grew larger and larger, until the premonition stopped.

Sister Chavise stopped short of the kitchen and supported herself against the wall until the dizziness cleared. She whispered to herself, *We wouldn't be able to stop them.*

She supported herself on a cabinet and took a deep slow breath, trying to remain calm despite her growing panic from the horrible vision.

Sister Maldean saw her.

"What was that you said, headmistress?" Sister Maldean asked from the kitchen.

Sister Chavise ignored her and confidently breezed into the room, her mind clearing just as quickly as the vision had come upon her.

Three soldiers, armed with swords and knives, were in the kitchen. Two were standing behind the table eating some potato cakes Sister Maldean gave them. One sat at the table blowing into a cup of hot tea.

"Gentlemen," the headmistress said, "an orphanage is a place for children and children's toys, not a place for weapons of war. What is the meaning of bringing your swords into St. Ehlona's Orphanage?"

They absentmindedly looked at each other, not even noticing they had carried weapons inside. One soldier sitting now stood. "My apologies, headmistress."

"Out, out, all of you. Whatever you need to say, you can say it outside," Sister Chavise said, pointing them toward the door.

"Please take some more potato cakes with you," Sister Maldean said, offering a platter of them to the soldiers.

"Food for the orphans," Sister Chavise interrupted her, intercepting the platter. "As I'm sure our brave soldiers understand. We welcome the soldiers to any food they need, but we are a poor orphanage for small children, and we all know, the more you take, the more the children will go hungry."

Sister Maldean looked down, embarrassed.

After the headmistress's rebuke, the soldiers took their leave quietly and stepped outdoors. The last snuck one more potato cake from Sister Maldean's hand with a shrug and a smile toward her.

Once outside, Sister Chavise asked them, "Now, how can I help you, soldiers?"

One cleared his throat. "Sister Chavise, isn't it?"

She nodded. "Or headmistress is fine."

"We are looking for a boy, headmistress, a boy with curly red hair, a runaway from the fire in the village of Plum last night."

"Who is this boy, and why are you looking for him?"

"His name is Darius Plum, and he's about fourteen years—"

Sister Chavise interrupted him, "Darius Plum is the son of the Head Council of the village of Plum, the Honorable Justus Plum. I know him and his family very well. I am familiar with what he looks like. What in the world would you want with Darius?"

At the mention of Justus Plum, the soldiers turned to each other with a grim smile. At last, another one of the soldiers finished, "He has run away, and his parents are looking for him. We are trying to find him, on their behalf."

"Oh my! I see," Sister Chavise said, knowing they were lying. She immediately worried about Darius and the rest of the Plums. "Well, he's not here, and I haven't seen him. But if he shows up, I will be sure to return him. His parents, the Plums, are good people, they must be worried sick. Wherever he is, when he comes to his senses, I am sure he will make his way back to them. You know how teenage boys are."

"So, you haven't seen him?"

"No, I just told you as much. I have not, and I would know because I know what he looks like. I only pray to the Goddess Ehlona that he is safe. I hope he has not gotten himself into any trouble. What is the commotion over in Plum? We've been seeing smoke coming from the town."

"A terrible fire," the soldiers smirked. "And we only wish for the boy's safety. If you see him, please hold him here for us. We will return in a couple of days."

"I most definitely will," Sister Chavise said. "On that you can be assured."

"We would be disappointed if he came here and we missed him," the soldier told her in a not-so-veiled threat.

"That would be disappointing indeed," Sister Chavise said. "Now, if you gentlemen will excuse us, Sister Maldean and I have breakfast to prepare for a lot of hungry little mouths."

The soldiers gave her a long, cold look, then slowly nodded as they turned to go. Mounting their horses nearby, they soon thundered off. Sister Chavise watched them ride away. Now she felt dizzy again.

"Weren't they dreamy?" Sister Maldean remarked, gazing after them.

"*No!* Sister Maldean, they were *not* dreamy!"

Sister Chavise turned away and hurried inside to the main sleeping room. She searched and found the young boy Oaks wandering around. Her sudden presence startled the boy.

"Oaks." Sister Chavise knelt and grabbed the boy firmly by the shoulders. "Show me where you saw the boy."

Oaks led her out past the vegetable fields, through the wooden gate, and off to the grove of trees beyond. There, they searched the grove until they found the hollow tree. Darius Plum was still there, holed up inside the slime. Sister Chavise saw him hiding. He looked dirty, wet, and cold, but otherwise unharmed. She hardly recognized him, but he recognized her. Upon seeing her, tears welled in his eyes. Sister Chavise was the only familiar face he had left. She could tell that he had been through something awful—he was not the same boy she had come to know.

Remembering Oaks was with her, she realized she had to make up a cover story to him and make it up quick.

"Why, what are you doing in there?" Sister Chavise asked Darius. "Come now, being new to St. Ehlona's Orphanage can't be that bad. We thought you ran away from us."

Oaks heard her words, and said, "You mean he's an orphan like one of us?"

"Why, yes, Oaks. The boy came here a day before the fire. But then he ran away before I got his name."

Oaks looked on with wide eyes.

"Look at you, you're all wet and cold," Sister Chavise said.

"And hungry, too, I bet," Oaks added.

"Oaks, can you run into the linen room and grab me a clean towel? That would be a big help."

Oaks nodded, and ran off as fast as he could, eager to help. Once Oaks was out of earshot, Sister Chavise pulled the child out of the fallen tree trunk.

"Darius, is that you?"

He gave Sister Chavise a tight embrace. He was shivering and crying. She had to confirm what she was already thinking.

"Darius, where are your mother and father?"

Darius backed away from her and only shook his head.

"What about Mara?"

Tears poured out of him as he continued to shake his head. "They are all dead. The soldiers killed all of them."

She embraced him again and started to cry herself. She could see Oaks now running out of the orphanage with a towel, running as fast as he could in their direction. Sister Chavise knew she had to think fast, Oaks would be there soon.

"Darius, I need you to listen to me very carefully. You can no longer say who you really are. It is too dangerous to say you are Darius Plum. You need to make up a name and make it up fast before Oaks gets here. I need you—just this one time—I need to ask you to lie. Do you understand?"

Darius looked over his shoulder and saw Oaks was almost there. He turned back to Sister Chavise and nodded. He sniffled, wiped his nose on the back of his hand, and attempted to rein in his emotions, just as Sister Chavise tried to do as well.

Oaks reached them and handed the towel to Sister Chavise.

"Thank you, Oaks. Oh, this towel is still warm." She took it and rubbed it all over the boy.

"Are you hurt?" Oaks asked him, and the boy shook his head no.

"Are you hungry?" Oaks asked, and the boy nodded his head yes.
"What's your name?" Oaks asked him.

Sister Chavise nervously stood up; she put her hand over her mouth and waited for Darius to respond.

The boy took the towel from Sister Chavise and draped it over his head. He dried his hair under it, giving himself another moment of time to think. When he removed the towel from his head, he answered Oaks's question.

"Kilmer. My name is Kilmer."

And with that, Darius Plum was now dead too.

ACT II

All the
Warnings
Were There

Running through a forest of laughing trees
The sky is getting grayer and the clouds, they fall on me
I ran down to the mountain, but don't fall over the edge!
Because you know it's a razor, and it just stuck in my head.

Excerpt from *The Witch's Songbook*

Unsure if this was a dream or reality, consumed with hopelessness,
he was forced to look upon the agonized spirit.
— Excerpt from *The Provenance* (Chapter Seven)

NO WAY OUT

THE SANGUINE FOREST IN THE YEAR 841 HRT
(FOUR DAYS AFTER YORI'S DISAPPEARANCE)

Kilmer wondered why Hollow Face had been revealing himself more lately. Even before they had left Castle Odessa, Kilmer's ghost had been appearing to him, making it look like he was distracted in melancholy. But it was more than that. In fact, the ghost had been flooding his mind all along, with scenes of another castle—not any castle, he knew, but another, a darker foreboding one. Hollow Face had been trying to warn Kilmer the whole time. The ghost's vision seemed to have started just before Lord Whitney's messenger found him overlooking the work detail polishing the Green. Then, in another appearance, Hollow Face had appeared in Lord Whitney's office, standing between him and Yori's wife, as she begged him to find her husband. Kilmer saw the ghost standing by the granite statues as the search party rode through the Mauveguard Pass, and once again nearby Amtor's cave. Later, at their first camp, Hollow Face appeared standing just beyond their campfires; the visions of the dark castle were the last thing Kilmer saw before falling asleep under the stars. All the visions had been the same: a dark castle in the deep woods. Whatever the warning was, if it were indeed the Sanguine Forest or someplace else, he felt he was getting closer.

Hollow Face had warned him like this before when danger was present, and that was the last time he saw his family alive. He had no idea what the meaning of the warning was—he only knew he had to be on guard for anything. If it troubled Hollow Face it could not be good.

Givens had left with the courier message about an hour before the search party finished packing the horses and mounted up. Then, Kilmer took the lead of the column with Melvin at his side. Rhodes, Curtz, and Hanson followed behind them and Laws took up the rear. They were ready to leave the Sanguine Forest and were headed to the relative safety of their first camp to the north, where they had stayed the night before. In the morning, they would resume the search for Yori, looking in the southern part of the Sanguine Forest.

Kilmer started to lead them away, then he stopped. Looking at the forest, the trees all appeared the same to him now.

"What's he waiting for?" Curtz whispered to Hanson. "Is he lost?"

Kilmer looked left and right, then up, then down, checking for any indication of where the sun might be. It should have been setting in the west. If he could just find where the long shadows were coming from, he could get his bearings. But the light was playing tricks with his eyes. Every shadow seemed to be pointing in a different direction. Even though that was impossible.

"Do you see that?" Curtz said softly to Rhodes and Hanson, who shared a concerned look. "I think he is lost."

Kilmer rode his horse in a tight circle to come around and continue again. Then after a while, he stopped and turned his horse to face the column.

"Does anybody remember which way we came in?" Kilmer asked them. The others seemed even less sure. Rhodes pointed that way, Hanson the other way, and Laws pointed yet a third way. No one knew which way they were going.

"Great," Curtz said. "Now what?"

Kilmer looked up, squinting his eyes, looking for the sun. It was dark in the Sanguine Forest, but not completely pitch. Some light was coming through the trees, casting shadows. But they were all mixed up, all of them pointing in different directions.

"This doesn't make sense," Kilmer said. "Let's go back to Isse's grave."

Laws in the rear would have been the closest to Isse's grave. But after turning his horse, he could not find it. They had just buried Isse, so where was it?

"Now, where did it go?" Laws asked. "The grave was here just a minute ago, wasn't it?"

They spread out, looking for Isse's grave, but no one could find it. They began doubting anything, everything, even their own sanity. A general panic set in.

"It is as if we are still in the same place, but the forest has moved on us," Curtz said. "How long have we been here?"

"It should be dark, I would think, by now," Rhodes said.

"But yet there is still light," Melvin added.

Kilmer watched for the sunset or any change in what he could see of the sky's color through the thick canopy. When the sun went down, they could travel perpendicular to the sunset. That would take them on a course north. But after what seemed like thirty minutes, the same diffused light danced in the canopy of the leaves high in the treetops and never changed. The shadows continued to dance around them.

"Wait! Someone's coming!" Laws alerted the group in a loud raspy whisper, pulling out his sword. "They are coming up behind!"

Indeed, now they all heard approaching hoofbeats. Behind Laws, they saw a rider coming toward them, kicking up dust in a charging gallop.

"It's Givens!" Laws shouted to Kilmer.

"Why is he returning?" Hanson asked. "He was supposed to meet us at the first camp."

"I don't know, but he will know the direction out," Melvin said.

Givens thundered furiously past Laws and up to the middle of the rescue party. Reaching the center, he quickly dismounted by practically falling off his horse. Scrambling from the dusty ground, he dove at Kilmer. The horse spooked, and Givens pulled his captain off by force, plucking Kilmer from his horse like a rag doll. Both he and Givens fell on top of each other. Givens started shaking him by the shoulders.

"Oh! You're alive! Thank the Gods, I found you! I never thought I would see you again."

Kilmer tried to get Givens to unhand him and back off.

"Givens! Givens!" Kilmer took control, shaking him back now. "Get ahold of yourself, man! You've only just left."

Suddenly Givens stopped and gave Kilmer a look of surprise. "What are you talking about?" he said with a confused expression. He then turned and gave each of them a puzzled look.

"What's wrong with Givens?" asked Curtz.

Givens lowered his brow and glared back at Kilmer. "I've been stuck in this forest for weeks! I couldn't find my way out, and I couldn't find anyone. I've been searching for you, for a long time, for weeks. But what did you just say? You think I've just left?"

"You did just leave us, Givens. About an hour and thirty minutes ago," Kilmer told him.

"Are you sure?" Givens asked.

Kilmer looked at Curtz, who only shrugged. He looked back at Givens. "Of course. You just left."

"No, no, no! I have been gone for days. It's been weeks. I have had to sleep in the Sanguine night after night for almost a month now."

"What are you talking about, Givens?" Kilmer asked him. "That's not possible."

Givens fell to his knees and broke down crying. His head was in his hands. "I'm so hungry, so thirsty—it has to stop! I can't do it anymore. This madness has to stop!"

Kilmer motioned to Melvin to bring food and water. Melvin dismounted quickly and knelt beside Givens.

"Take it easy, Givens. Here, drink," Melvin told him.

But before he could drink, suddenly Givens stood up. He ran to his pouch, reached in, and pulled out the note he was to deliver to Lord Whitney's courier.

"Here is the note! Here, read it! Read it!" Givens said.

Kilmer slowly took the note, hardly believing that a cavalryman as solid as Givens could crack up this bad. Kilmer unfolded the letter. It simply read:

> *Your days are gone, never to return!*
> *In Zornastic fire your soul will burn!*

"What's this?" Kilmer asked.

"Now, I didn't write that!" Givens said. "How do you explain that?"

"What does it even mean?" asked Kilmer. "Did you meet with the courier?"

Givens laughed. "I don't know. How would I know what it means? I didn't write it. I never met with the courier. I've never left. This forest is not right!"

Givens was utterly out of his mind. Kilmer did not believe any of what he was saying. Givens had to have written the note. That was the only explanation. As best as Kilmer could tell, Givens must have fallen off his horse and bumped his head. He had to be delirious. That would be the only explanation of his lost time. But it was odd for Givens, who was the best horseman Kilmer had ever known, to be this out of his mind.

Kilmer folded the letter and put it in his pocket. He encouraged Givens to drink some water and eat some bread, and Melvin helped him to sit on the ground. Kilmer turned to look at the others. The entire group stood in silence.

"From this point on, we stay together. Now, has anyone found Isse's grave yet?"

No one had.

"Well, it couldn't have just disappeared," Kilmer said. "Keep looking."

He glanced at the sky. There was no sunset, no stars, no grave, no trails, nothing to indicate where they were, or how to get out of the forest.

Kilmer could feel the heat of his anxiety. He walked a couple of feet and found a long stick. He took a dagger out of his belt and cut the tiny leaves and branches on the shaft until it was just a long, smooth surface. The others watched.

He went into a clearing and stuck the stick in the ground. He watched which way the shadows leaned. But the post gave no single shadow at all. Diffused light created four shadows—all of them surrounding the stick. None of them came from any single direction at all.

"It is not dark, nor is it light either," Laws commented.

"Is it day or night?" Curtz asked.

Rhodes and Hanson gave each other a worried look.

"Where is this light coming from?" Kilmer said.

"Are you feeling better?" Melvin asked Givens. He continued to watch over the horseman, giving him bread and water.

Givens did not say a word.

Curtz started laughing. "Yeah, Melvin, everything's great. We don't know east from west; we don't know if it's day or night. We're just marvelous, Melvin!"

Melvin looked at the others, embarrassed.

"We either stay here or pick a direction and go dead reckoning," Kilmer said. "Any ideas?"

"Are we taking a vote on it?" Curtz asked.

"Why not?" His response surprised Curtz. But it told the others all they needed to know. The truth was, they were lost in the Sanguine Forest.

"All in favor of staying here, raise your hand." No hands.

"All right, then. Let's pick a direction and go that way." All hands raised.

"But which way?" Rhodes asked.

Kilmer looked in all directions. They all appeared the same.

"Wait, listen," Kilmer said. "Do you hear that?" A low rumble came from the forest itself.

"What is that?" Hanson asked.

"I don't hear any... wait! I do hear something," said Curtz. "Yes, what is that?"

They could all hear it now—a low, reverberating sound. The rumble got louder and nearer. The sound suddenly erupted in a high-pitched wail, as a swarm of thousands of flies burst upon them like a tidal wave. Through the trees, like the blast of cold wind before, a mob of flies swept through them. The horses reared, bucking off their riders, kicking indiscriminately.

Melvin instinctively covered Givens, the two men huddling together under a blanket of big green insects. Rhodes and Hanson hit the ground at the same time and scrambled together to cover each other. Curtz and Laws ran; Curtz went in one direction, while Laws ran in the other. Both swatted the air, trying to keep the flies out of their mouths and eyes. Kilmer dropped to the ground, fending off the flies, swatting at the swirling black cyclone surrounding him.

A horse fell with a loud, high-pitched scream, choking from the flies crawling into its mouth. The rest of the horses ran for their lives. The insect's bit both men and horses, leaving them covered with welts and painful pink sores.

Hanson huddled alongside Rhodes, but he was starting to panic. He could not take the claustrophobic feeling of being covered by a thick mass of crawling, flying bugs. He stood and ran, leaving Rhodes to fend for himself against the angry horde.

The swarm dimmed the light, blotting it out of view, plunging the whole forest into darkness. The party's visibility dropped to zero, as the black torrent of flies buzzed around them.

Then, with a sudden wisp of blue vapor, the insects were gone. Dim light returned to the Sanguine Forest. Not a single fly remained.

The swarm left one horse dead on the ground, while the other horses were gone. Melvin and Givens looked up with shock in their eyes. Rhodes, just feet from them, looked just as worried.

When the flies disappeared, Laws found himself alone and separated from the group. He frantically searched in all directions but could not determine where the others were, or which path had led him this way, to this part of the Sanguine Forest.

"Kilmer, Rhodes, Curtz?" Laws said. No answer.

Curtz thought he had outrun the swarm. He had run until he felt no more flies on him. Then he stopped and looked at where he had run to. He turned, expecting to still be able to see the party, but no one was there. He was also now separated and alone.

"Hey! Where are you guys!" Curtz called out, but no one heard him, and no reply came back.

Kilmer had not run at all. He stayed put in the same place he was before the horde hit. But now he was alone too, walking in circles, trying to get his bearings, watching for any movement. He saw nothing anywhere around him. Then, he tripped and fell over Isse's grave. He got back to his feet and stared at it. Here was the stone that Melvin had found and scratched *Isse* on. Kilmer looked down, and he could not get out of his mind what the corpse had looked like. He could not help remembering the frozen devastating scream, eyes wide, his insides pecked out. Desperately he searched around again, and still saw no one, no horses, no riders, no flies, nothing but trees. Turning to peer behind him, there, standing in the shadow of the forest, a massive stone castle loomed over him. It had definitely not been there before, and seemingly appeared from nowhere.

In the distance, in front of the gates of the castle, Kilmer saw Hollow Face standing alone.

This is the castle I saw in my visions!

Now, Hollow Face had a new vision for him.

In his mind, a man in chains, savagely beaten, covered in purple and yellow bruises. He saw the First Archer inside, chained to the wall, forced to stand, covered in sweat, exhausted, thirsty, and hungry.

"Yori!" Kilmer said. Then the vision was gone. "Yori is inside."

Hollow Face stood silently in front of the spiraled domed castle. Like in days of old, Kilmer spoke his problems to Hollow Face out loud.

"My friend, there are forces here at work against me, against us, Hollow Face. There is evil magic here. What should I do?"

Hollow Face stood motionless. Kilmer blinked and pulled out his sword.

"Let us go forward, then!" Kilmer said. Then Hollow Face faded away.

With his sword drawn at the ready, Kilmer approached the castle. While still at a distance, a loud *clunk* sounded, indicating that the heavy double doors were starting to open, seemingly on their own. A yellowish glow spilled out through the dark forest. As the doors opened, the castle seemed to welcome Kilmer to come inside. Never had Kilmer felt like he was walking into a trap more than walking through the gate of the castle. But he came here for only one purpose: to find Yori. And that is what he intended to do.

He did not know where the rest of the search party was, but he hoped they were safe. He wished they could be here, but privately he was relieved that at least Hollow Face was still with him.

Getting closer to the entrance of the castle, he started to think about many things. He thought about Yori, home with his wife. He thought of Sister Chavise and Sister Maldean. He thought of yellow-and-white flowers, and his beloved sister, Mara. His mother. His father.

He had wished for many things in this life; none of them ever came true. Despite these wishes, his life had been blessed. At least so far. But walking voluntarily into a magical castle would be stretching that limit.

His boots crossed over the threshold, and he entered the castle. Once inside, behind him, the door slowly closed, then slammed shut with a heavy sound and the latch falling into place. The sound echoed away, then it was entirely quiet.

The castle had swallowed him up.

There's a new day dawning
A new beginning in the air
There's a new day, darling
And everywhere you look,
it's everywhere

Excerpt from *The Witch's Songbook*

Bells rang out from the hilltops,
announcing that the ceremony was about to begin.
— Excerpt from *The Provenance* (Chapter Eight)

PREMONITIONS, POEMS, AND PLEDGES

Sister Chavise was one of four sisters who spent the last moments with Ehlona, the Goddess of Beauty—her, Jule, Dunhi, and Catosa. Each received the blessing of Ehlona. The blessing gave them all beauty and long life.

The Goddess assured them, *nothing can separate you from this blessing.*

Each received a mandate establishing the four main orphanages. Catosa went to the west, Jule to the north, Dunhi to the east. Sister Chavise traveled south to establish hers on the outskirts of the village of Plum. All the sisters built their orphanages just as the Goddess Ehlona instructed them. They dedicated each to the memory of Ehlona, the Goddess of beauty, music, art, and love.

They were the last mortals to see the Goddess in all her legendary beauty; she gave it all away to them. After bestowing her beauty, they were the first to see what she had become. It broke their hearts to watch her become the horror of the Witch of the Great Mapes

Forest. Watching her stumble out with her crooked spine into the night was the saddest thing that ever happened to Sister Chavise, in all her long life.

Until now, as she started learning the details of the assault on Plum.

The village was in flames. The Head Council, Justus Plum, along with the other council members, were all dead. His wife, Rosa, and daughter, Mara, had been put to death by soldiers of Leopold. Public executions would follow, and there were rumors of more murders, more torture, and rape. No one was in any position to stop them. At the hands of LaNew and his Red Guard they would commit a multitude of crimes against humanity. These were the same soldiers who visited the orphanage and wanted to know the whereabouts of Darius Plum. They were not content to merely kill the boy's family and burn down the village. They wanted more.

Always more, she thought.

They wanted to finish him off and tie up loose ends. But the boy Darius Plum no longer existed now, only Kilmer remained.

Even more heartbreaking news reached her, however. Leopold had attacked the village of Umbrick and the orphanage there. Both were destroyed. So great was Leopold's hatred for the orphanage in Umbrick that he took a personal interest in destroying it. Leopold locked the doors of the orphanage from the outside. Then he set it ablaze—trapping everyone inside. Those in the orphanage perished, burned to death, including Sister Luna, the headmistress, along with all the orphans inside.

Sister Chavise remembered her terrible premonition, the one she had when the Red Guard soldiers came to speak to her and Sister Maldean in the kitchen. Before she spoke to the soldiers, she had a vision of the orphanage in flames. At the time, she thought she was just being paranoid, wild thoughts running in her mind. But she understood now that, at the very time she had the premonition, the orphanage at Umbrick was being attacked. This premonition she had was not for the orphanage in Plum but an experience of the orphanage in Umbrick. This gave her a terrible chill. She knew it could have been her orphanage, and maybe it would have been, if not for the information the soldiers searched for regarding Darius Plum. It made her shudder, knowing they could have been at the mercy of these heartless, cold-blooded killers from the beginning.

We wouldn't be able to stop them, she remembered whispering to herself.

We wouldn't be able to stop them.

It was more than she could bear.

She knew Sister Luna well, the daughter of Sister Catosa. But not as well as she should. Sister Luna was a private person, but she may have had a lot to hide. Leopold had been an orphan there since birth, and something happened to him to form such a powerful hatred. Something made Leopold feel so powerless, and desire power so much, that he took matters into his own hands and committed great violence upon Sister Luna and the orphanage. Whatever Leopold accused her of, and only he would know for sure, he had silenced their voices forever.

It would come to be known as the Massacre of Umbrick.

The destruction of the orphanage drew the attention of other powerful forces. The legendary spiritual warrior, Chen-Li, the first-born son of the Goddess of Ehlona and Heironomus, the God of Light, had pledged to be the protector of his mother's orphanages. He sensed the screams of the children, hearing them from across the Mid-Run Valley, all the way to his temple of Chen-Li high in the Gray Mountains to the east.

Chen-Li meditated until his spirit separated from his physical body. In his Li form, his spiritual form, he rocketed away from his temple across the Mid-Run Valley. As fast as lightning his spirit traveled hundreds of miles from the Temple of Chen-Li to Umbrick.

But much to his surprise, Chen-Li could not conquer Leopold's spirit. The fight ended in an impasse. Even he had to admit stalemate to Leopold.

Unable to defeat Leopold, Chen-Li comforted Sister Chavise and told her the news: that the orphanage of Umbrick was destroyed, and all that lived in it. He comforted her but could not diminish her pain. He blamed himself, as a protector of the orphanages—he did not protect the orphans in it, including the young boy who would grow up to be Leopold. They both had turned a blind eye to Sister Luna's abuses in Umbrick. Sister Chavise and Chen-Li resolved together the Massacre of Umbrick could never be allowed to happen again. Another Leopold could never be permitted.

Chen-Li turned to go back to his temple but not before he informed Sister Chavise about how Leopold had directed multiple attacks throughout the villages of the Mid-Run Valley—in Bowling, Plum, Umbrick, Darby, and Blaize. Hammerville, Olzen, and Chase. The villages were being ransacked for resources and many atrocities were being committed, with more to come.

When Sister Chavise learned the true scope of the violence, she was even more convinced she did the right thing by lying to the Red Guard when they came looking for Darius.

"Men who murder women and children do not deserve to hear the truth. There is no truth in them," Chen-Li told her.

Sisters Chavise and Maldean watched the spirit of Chen-Li shoot from St. Ehlona's Orphanage and soar back home to his Temple of Chen-Li across the Mid-Run Valley, leaving them alone again.

"I am so embarrassed that I was flirting with those animals," Sister Maldean admitted to her with tears in her eyes. "I fed them, gave them tea. Oh, Sister Chavise, I am so sorry."

"The Gods were directing your words and actions, Sister Maldean. If they had not taken a liking to you…"

"What?" Maldean sniffed.

"Well," Sister Chavise said, "they may have killed us all."

Sister Maldean burst out in tears.

"There, there. I am thankful for you, Sister Maldean. You may well have saved us all with your charms."

Regardless of their threats, the Red Guard never came back to the orphanage in search of Darius. In a couple of days, the Red Guard was on the move again, and they were not about to delay their plans for conquest over the life of a teenage boy. Instead, Leopold's Red and Blue, and the Red Guard converged and continued their drive to take over the countryside in the War of the Mid-Run Valley.

Sister Chavise left Sister Maldean in the kitchen and went out to look out for Kilmer. She saw him standing in the garden, his curly red locks falling down his face. He leaned against a hoe, not using it. He looked like he was talking to himself. The boy must have been through so much, he had only himself to converse with now. But who could blame him?

Standing in the field, Kilmer absentmindedly held the hoe. Hollow Face was there with him in the garden, but only he could see the ghost. The boy appeared to be talking to himself, when in fact he was speaking to the ghost, though Hollow Face did not have the ability to talk back. The boy asked about the fate of the invalid Kilmer. He needed to know if the real one was alive or dead.

"I know you don't want to show me, but I need you to show me. I need to know."

Hollow Face showed him nothing.

"I need to know, Hollow Face, because I am now Kilmer. I have taken his name. So, show me what happened—I need to know if he is alive or dead."

Hollow Face remained motionless, then turned to walk away.

"No! Please don't go, Hollow Face. You're my only friend now!"

The ghost stopped, then slowly turned to face the boy. Lifting its corpse-like hand he reluctantly revealed a new vision.

The images were distorted at first, as if underwater. Then the scene came into focus.

When the Red Guard discovered the crippled Kilmer hiding in the bushes near the House of Justus, with his crooked back, Kilmer tried to run away from his tormentors and shuffled toward the distant safety of the tree line. But the soldiers ran the hunchback down. He fell in the dust, then struggled to his feet and tried to run again. But he could not move fast enough, and the men on horseback easily caught him. They roughly handled him, beating him, kicking him, and pushing him down to the ground. Several of the soldiers surrounded him, stomping on him, laughing while they kicked him in the ribs and the head. All the while, Kilmer groaned in pain. Somebody produced a bullwhip and they mercilessly whipped large stripes of skin off his hunched back. His face deformed, crying in pain with each reflex from being cracked. Next came spears and knives, and then the vision was gone.

"Oh, poor Kilmer," he said, crying for his friend. "Show me the rest, Hollow Face. I need to see it."

The ghost hesitated, then the vision returned.

The captain of the Red Guard rode his horse up to the circle. This was LaNew. He dispersed the men by barking some orders, and they left him alone with the invalid. After the men were gone, Captain

LaNew drew his sword and dismounted his horse. He approached the injured Kilmer.

"I remember you! You are that cripple from Bowling I thought I killed last week. I'll correct that oversight now." LaNew thrust his sword into Kilmer's side. Then he pulled the blade out and cut him again and again, until Kilmer no longer moved. He decapitated the hunchback so he could eliminate all doubt. There would be no further question—Kilmer was dead. Not only dead, but in pieces dead. LaNew did not quit even then. He hacked at his body until he was too tired to continue further. Then, while catching his breath, he wiped the blood off his sword on what remained of the bloody torso.

"You are not surviving this time," LaNew said.

Without another look, LaNew sheathed his sword, mounted his horse, and turned to go to the town square. There, he would deal with the village leadership. He was ready to viciously overreact to any resistance he encountered.

The vision ended.

"Poor Kilmer." The boy looked down. "Thank you, Hollow Face."

When the boy looked up, Sister Chavise stood next to him, and Hollow Face was gone. Something unspoken passed between him and Sister Chavise, and spontaneously they embraced.

Later, in another private moment, Kilmer told Sister Chavise that he had witnessed the deaths of his mother and his sister, Mara, all from the river. He witnessed the burning of his father and the other council members in the town square. The only reason he survived the massacre was that he had fallen in the river just moments before the Red Guard came. After which, his house and family were rounded up and put in wagons.

Sister Chavise thought it so strange, and fortuitous, that such a clumsy accident resulted in a lifesaving event. It could be no accident, she thought. The boy was blessed and had been saved by the divine intervention of the Gods.

The boy also told her that he knew his new namesake, the disabled hunchback Kilmer, was dead, even though he never saw his actual death or told her how he knew. Neither Kilmer nor Sister Chavise would ever utter his real name of Darius Plum again. The boy had to transform fully to Kilmer. He could never trust anyone enough to reveal his true identity.

Kilmer spent the next three years at Sister Chavise's St. Ehlona's Orphanage. He made friends over those years. The youngest was Oaks, who would take personal credit for finding him in the woods. Oaks always wanted to accompany Kilmer in any adventure, like catching frogs, climbing trees, or exploring the surrounding area.

Then there was Kory, an overweight boy with blond hair, the same age as Kilmer.

He made other friends, but Oaks and Kory were his best friends.

Of all his friends, none of them caught his eye more than Darla, a small girl, with thick black hair and big brown eyes. She was two years younger than he was, but that did not matter to him, and she liked that he was older and more experienced.

Kory and Oaks did not understand it. As Oaks would often say, Darla did not climb trees, or catch tadpoles, or do anything fun for that matter. But since they knew Kilmer saw something interesting in her, they included her in their group of friends anyway. And slowly they got used to her competing for Kilmer's attention.

Kilmer, Oaks, Kory, and Darla spent a lot of time together. The boys liked to play games, like who could run the fastest—that would be Kilmer. Who could climb trees the best—that would be Oaks. Who could eat the most—that title definitely belonged to Kory. But when it came to who could write, tell stories, or compose poetry the best, there was no contest, clearly Darla won all those contests. For Kilmer did not care much which one of them was fastest, who could climb trees, or who could eat more beans than anyone else; instead, he loved to listen to the stories Darla would make up.

Once, when Oaks and Kory went down to the Plum River to catch fish, Kilmer watched them go while he sat in the grass. Darla walked up to join Kilmer, but unknown to her, he was not alone. Hollow Face was there sitting to the left of him.

Darla began to sit on the left, right on Hollow Face.

"Sit here." Kilmer patted the grass on his right side.

"Why there?" Darla asked with a smile.

"I can see you better here."

Darla shrugged and sat where he told her to. "You couldn't see me from over there?"

"The light is better on this side. The sun highlights your hair better on this side. I like to see the sun in your hair," Kilmer told her with a smile, and his words were no lie.

Darla smiled sweetly. "It's nice to see you smile. You're ordinarily so dark."

"Do I have to remind you we live in an orphanage?"

"You need to count your blessings, Kilmer. It could be worse."

"What blessings, Darla?"

"Like the time you saw sunshine in my hair. Or the time we had soft grass to sit on. Or that time I wrote you a poem."

"A poem? Really? For me?" Kilmer asked, adjusting himself to sit up straighter.

"Sure. Do you want to hear it?" she asked, holding open her little book.

"Yes, I want to hear my poem."

Darla put the tip of the pencil between her lips and smiled. She hesitated to look at the page. "No, I think not. You would just take it for granted—you wouldn't see it as a blessing."

"Darla, thank you for blessing me with your poem. Now, can I hear it?"

After a moment of thinking it over, she said, "Well, maybe I will read just a little to you."

She started.

Our love,
It's just beginning.
I can see it growing in your eyes
And all these years we've been together
But never as close as we are tonight.
Into your charms, I suddenly surrender.
I feel so disarmed but longingly remember
That our love,
Oh, our love
Is just beginning.

Darla stopped and looked embarrassed. She would not make eye contact with him.

"You wrote that?" Kilmer asked.

She nodded. "Yes, it's called 'Our Love.' I wrote it for you. For us, Kilmer."

"It is the most wonderful blessing, Darla. I love it. Thank you."

"You're welcome, Kilmer."

Kilmer, Darla, Kory, and Oaks all grew together in a special way that only orphans can. Unlike a family that had no choice to be together, orphans could choose who they cared about, who they liked, and who they loved. Over time, these four companions chose each other, and they were inseparable.

Elsewhere in the world, beyond the safe confines of St. Ehlona's Orphanage, the War of the Mid-Run Valley raged on. Leopold continued his march through the villages. But by now, the people of the villages were fighting back against him. The villages had joined forces, merging together to establish the army of the Amalgamates. Each village contributed men, materials, armor, weapons, horses, funding, and other resources to make a powerful war machine.

Over the next three years, the Amalgamates grew stronger, while Leopold could not replace his losses and grew weaker. Soon, the Amalgamates outnumbered Leopold and had him on the defensive. It was only a matter of time before Leopold, continuing in his retreat, would certainly be defeated.

The Amalgamates were being led by General Blaize Plum from the village of Haverhill.

Kilmer could not claim it out loud, but privately he knew the general was a cousin of his, a member of his family clan, and descended from the original Fortis Plum. Kilmer took a lot of pride that his family was leading the attack against Leopold.

Kilmer burned for revenge. He was not a child anymore. His body had changed—becoming taller, more muscular, and full of restless energy. He dreamed of burying a sword in his Red and Blue enemy. He longed to join the Amalgamates in defense of the villages of the Mid-Run Valley. Through the Amalgamates he could avenge the deaths of his parents, sister, and friends.

But doing that would mean breaking up the circle of friends he had made, and the only girl he had ever fallen in love with. Joining the Amalgamates meant leaving Sister Chavise and Sister Maldean. But he had to leave the orphanage someday, and soon. He was eighteen now and was considered a man. The war was as good a reason as any to leave.

Once he decided that was what he would do—leave St. Ehlona's and go off to join the Amalgamates—he had to let the others know. Darla, who was two years younger than Kilmer, had to stay in the orphanage for two more years. Unless he married her. If they were married, they could both leave, and they would not have to wait for her to turn eighteen. But then what would they do? With most every able-bodied man in military service in defense of the villages, if he did not act soon, the war would be over. He would be the only one to have a young wife, no military service, and no viable prospects of being able to support a family. He thought she deserved better than that. He thought that by going to war, he was getting the best of both worlds. By joining the Amalgamates at the end of the war, giving Darla time to turn eighteen, and gaining experience as a war veteran, he would come back to ask her to marry him. He gave this matter a lot of thought before he decided to act upon it. But once his mind was made up, his path seemed clear, at least to him.

First, he approached Sister Chavise about his plan. She listened to him patiently, knowing that it would be bittersweet to see him leave. He was special to her, after all he had been through, after all they both had been through. But she accepted his need to leave, even though his departure would be harder on her than most. But before he left, she felt compelled to give him some advice.

"Do not be so blind for vengeance that you are motivated only by hate. Your mother, father, and sister would not wish for you to throw away the opportunity that chance has blessed you with. Remember this, my dear, vengeance will not bring the dead back to life. Honor their memory by staying alive and living a good life. This is what they would have wanted for you."

She kissed and embraced him.

Next, he met with Oaks and Kory. After telling them his plans, they both enthusiastically wanted to go with him and join too.

"I'm coming with you, Kilmer. I want to be an Amalgamate too."

"You want to be a soldier, Kory?"

"I want to be part of this good cause to defend our villages. Plus, the war is almost over. The Amalgamates have Leopold on the run. I don't want to miss it. Who knows if another one will ever come in our lifetimes?"

"That's true," said Oaks. "I want to go too."

"No!" both Kory and Kilmer said at the same time. "Look, Oaks, Kory and I are five years older than you. You need to stay here at the orphanage and look after the place, just until you turn eighteen. Then if the war is still going on, you can join us. If it is not, then we will come back and get you after the war. You and Darla too."

"Yeah, but don't be gone too long," Oaks said with a tear in his eye. "Then we can all be together again."

"Exactly, Oaks," Kilmer told him. "But don't worry, we're taking you with us in spirit."

Oaks hugged them. "I'll think about you both every day."

"Now, there's just one more person I have to talk to," Kilmer said. Both Oaks and Kory knew who he was talking about.

Kilmer knocked on her door. Darla told him to come in. He found her sitting on her bed, knees pulled up, a familiar pose when she was writing in her little book.

"I suppose you're here to break the news to me that everyone else already knows? To tell me you're going to run off to fight in the war. To join the stupid Amalgamates."

"News travels fast, I suppose."

"Especially bad news. So, it is true, then? You're going to run off and get yourself killed?"

"I'm not going to lie to you, Darla. There's a war going on. People die. There are no guarantees."

"Silly me, I didn't know there were no guarantees in war. The only guarantee is not to go to war in the first place."

Kilmer remembered the fates of his father, mother, and sister. "There are no guarantees for that either."

Darla now looked directly at him. He could tell she had been crying. "I thought I was going to be your guarantee."

Kilmer sat on her bed. He could not speak for some time.

"I'm sorry, Darla, this is something I have to do."

"No, you don't. I don't understand. Why are you doing this?"

"Because I have to be Kilmer, that's why."

"That doesn't make any sense." Darla hid her eyes and started sobbing. "You will always be Kilmer. You always were, you always will be. No matter if you join the Amalgamates or not."

Kilmer could not elaborate more on who he really was.

"Kory says he is going too," he told her.

Darla wiped her nose. "At least you won't be alone."

Kilmer loved her; he wanted to tell her so. But he thought if he did, it would only make leaving harder. This was the price he had to pay.

"Goodbye, Darla." He stood up. They looked into each other's eyes for a moment. Then he turned to go.

"Kilmer!" Darla called to him.

He stopped and turned around.

"Come back to me," she said. "Just come back to me."

Kilmer nodded and walked out.

Kilmer and Kory said their goodbyes to Oaks, the other orphans, and Sisters Chavise and Maldean. They left through the gates of the courtyard. As they walked away with small bags of clean clothes and a bit of food, looking back, they saw a small crowd gathered to wish them farewell. Kilmer looked over the faces, searching for Darla, but she was not in the group. It was not until his eyes instinctively looked at the window on the second floor that he finally saw her. Darla stood behind the dark glass watching him go.

Kilmer raised his hand in a long wave. Darla slowly returned his wave, but even from this distance, he could tell she was crying. Reluctantly, sadly, he turned around slowly, not bearing to look at her anymore, knowing he might not ever see her again. Her voice kept running through his mind.

Come back to me.
Come back to me.

He would remember that voice in the most critical days ahead. And it gave him hope.

For now, though, he had to get his mind on other things. He kept his true motivations to himself, but he believed that Leopold had to be held accountable for all he did to his family. He had to pay with a life for a life. But mostly, Kilmer wanted to punish him for making a tragic mistake: leaving him alive as the only survivor. He was the only loose end of Leopold's murderous deeds in the village of Plum.

Kilmer kept his secrets and his identity to himself. He never thought he could tell anyone without endangering their lives too. He never told Kory or Oates, Sister Maldean, or anybody else at St. Ehlona's. Only Sister Chavise knew his real identity. He thought he might not ever be able to tell Darla the truth, at least until he satisfied his vengeance with Leopold or died trying.

Kory and Kilmer set off walking from the orphanage to nearby Haverhill, the rallying point for the Amalgamate army. The journey would take two days. Along the way, they met some interesting people, mercenaries from other villages, and looked admiringly at Amalgamate soldiers on patrol wearing their green-and-yellow uniforms. They listened to how the soldiers talked. The conversations centered mostly around pushing Leopold out of the villages and across the Mid-Run Valley. But sometimes they talked about bloody battles and losses that included the sacrifices of their friends' lives.

"Come on, Kilmer," Kory said. "We'd better get to Haverhill soon, or the war will be over before we get the chance to join. If that happens, how will we ever be able to live with ourselves, knowing that we missed out on the glory of fighting against Leopold?"

Kilmer did not care about the glory of fighting. He only cared about killing those responsible for killing his family.

"Just imagine, Kilmer, imagine you came face-to-face with Leopold. He had a sword, and you had a sword. Would you fight him? Could you kill him?"

"I hope so," Kilmer said. "Or else we've come all this way for nothing."

They passed the time on the road to Haverhill, feeling liberated to be on their own for the first time in their lives. They slept under the stars and dreamed about enlisting in General Blaize Plum's army. After two days, they reached the outskirts of the village of Haverhill. They had no problem finding signs showing them the way to join the Amalgamates.

Haverhill was a flurry of activity as they walked into the village. Green-and-yellow banners were flying defiantly from every market and house. The streets were lined with Amalgamate flags, flying overhead and waving everywhere. Soldiers adorned in green-and-yellow armor clanked through the streets on foot and on horseback. Men with spears, swords, shields, and arrows were part of units coming and going to the battlefields.

Wagons filled with materials rolled along in vast amounts, loaded with vats of beer, clay pots of oil, water containers of fruits and vegetables, cows, and chickens. All of this reminded the boys of chaos, but everything moved with a flair for military precision. The orphans were impressed, overwhelmed to be in the center of the resistance against Leopold.

They followed a yellow sign with a green arrow painted on it.

New Recruits This Way

They followed the arrows through the village, taking the turns as the signs guided them. Finally, they came to a little building under a thatched roof. The sign out front told them they were in the right place.

New Enlistments

Much to their surprise, no one was in line. At the window, an old man with a gray beard puffed on a pipe. He blew smoke sideways out of his mouth and nose simultaneously.

"What can I do for you boys? You here to join up?"

"Is this the place to enlist for the Amalgamates, General Blaize Plum's army?"

"It is one and the same." The man puffed away.

The two boys looked at each other.

"So yes, then?" Kory asked.

"*Yes*, yes!" the man said impatiently. "Payment in the Amalgamate army is four coins a month, and pay distribution occurs on the first day of every month. Since you are joining in the middle of the month, you won't get paid for a month and a half, until the next month after this one." The old man checked the ink level in his well. After he blew another cloud of pipe smoke, he turned the paper around to face them.

Kory stepped forward and was barely tall enough to see over the counter.

"If you're not tall enough to see the paper, son, you can't join," the old man said, looking at Kory through the top of his glasses.

"I can reach just fine," Kory said, standing on his tiptoes.

The man with the pipe considered Kory with one eye. "Not missing very many meals, are you, son?"

Kory looked at him embarrassed, stepping down after signing the paper.

"Now you look here, old man," Kilmer told him. "That's all muscle on Kory."

The old man guffawed, the smoke circling his gray head.

Kilmer signed the paper and stepped down too.

The old man turned the papers back to face him. He dipped his quill in the inkwell, filled out a couple of vouchers, made a few signatures, and stamped the papers hard with an ink stamp, making it official.

"Now raise your right hand—I need to swear you in."

The boys raised their right hands.

"Repeat after me," the old man cleared his throat. "I, state your name."

"I, Kilmer."

"I, Kory."

"Do this day pledge my allegiance…"

"Do this day pledge my allegiance…"

"To the Amalgamate forces of the villages of the Mid-Run Valley…"

"To the Amalgamate forces of the villages of the Mid-Run Valley…"

"And when called upon to do so, give my life in its defense."

"And when called upon to do so, give my life in its defense."

"And if I betray the forces I have pledged to defend…"

"And if I betray the forces I have pledged to defend…"

"Then, may I be put to death."

"Then, may I be put to death."

"Congratulations, boys. You are now soldiers in the Amalgamate army. Now, take this stamped voucher over to that building there and get your standard issue."

"Standard issue?" Kilmer asked.

"Well, son, you ain't going to war dressed like that, are you?"

After doing what the old man told them to do, they received their standard issue of Amalgamate uniforms adorned in green and yellow. They were fitted for swords and trained quickly in how to use them. They soon settled into their lives as soldiers.

More training followed—how to march, how to follow orders, how to use their shield, and how to dig fortifications. There was a lot of digging fortifications. They were trained how to attack with spears, swords, knives, and hand-to-hand combat. They were taught how to use their hands and feet, knees and elbows, anything. All the necessary skills to be killers.

After a couple weeks of training, they were anxious to put their newfound skills to use against the accursed Leopold Red and Blue.

In short, Kilmer and Kory were ready for blood.

In the darkness
The storm passes away,
And the mortician
Limps along the way

Excerpt from *The Witch's Songbook*

Crawling backward, kicking over piles of papers,
anything to get away from the reanimated dead man.
— Excerpt from *The Provenance* (Chapter Nine)

THE MOST PERILOUS DAY

The Sanguine Forest in the Year 841 HRT
(Four Days After Yori's Disappearance)

LAWS

Laws found himself separated from the main search party. Now alone in the Sanguine Forest, he was on his own, a position not entirely unfamiliar to him. In every battle he had ever been in, which were many, once the chaos of fighting started, every man had to take care of himself when swords started swinging. And if anybody could take care of himself, it was the hardened warrior Laws. His face bore the evidence of that—his diagonal facial scar, cleaving his lips in two from the nearly fatal battle-axe wound. The weathering of his face made his skin look like the cracked leather of alligator hide.

He pulled his sword and did not call out, knowing it would give away his position. Using the trees as cover, his heavy boots crushed bones underfoot as he moved. As he scrambled behind the natural foliage, he felt guarded on the left while scanning the forest to his right. Laws did not see any of his comrades from the search party, nothing but the endless depths of the dark forest.

He took a deep breath calming, himself. He had been in worse positions before. He reminded himself he was a very large man with a giant sword, and as long as he had it, he was the most dangerous thing in this forest.

But still, things were happening here that he could not explain at all. The feeling present unnerved him, the confusion, the loss of direction, Givens' loss of time, the sudden appearance of the horde of flies, rotting skulls, the bones all around. None of this could be natural, and Laws already had a superstitious fear of anything he could not put his sword through. This forest had bad magic, and he wanted no part of it. Quite frankly, this place scared him.

Very faintly, he heard a woman's voice, feminine singing. He tried to locate where the sound was coming from. The singing got clearer and closer.

> *Your days are gone, never to return!*
> *In Zornastic fire your soul will burn!*

"My, my, my. What have we got here?"

The demon Langula slithered from behind a tree. Laws saw her but had trouble understanding her. Her skin was blue, she had long black hair with horns protruding from her head. Her body was one of a voluptuous woman on her upper half, but down below her waist she was trailed by a serpent tail that slithered in the wet leaves behind her.

"What a beautiful man. Perfectly delicious. Absolutely demonic."

Laws looked at her and became immediately confused. He could only understand her upper form and was transfixed by her beauty. He did not even lift his sword to defend himself.

He blinked. "Lady, what are you doing out here? Are you lost? Do you need help?"

The demon laughed and continued casting her seduction spell.

"What marvelous scars," she said, coming nearer. Touching his face, she ran a black fingernail lightly across the scar, across his face, and down to his mouth. "I have never seen such delectable lips. Oh, they are most wonderfully scarred, the flesh of them, split in two. What manner of wound is this? Did a sword do this to you?"

"An Amalgamate battle-axe," Laws told her.

"And what did you do? Did you run?"

"No. I didn't run. I stayed. I killed that man."

"How did you kill that man?" she asked, her curiosity piquing with his tale.

"I tackled him, pinned him to the ground, then strangled him with the axe handle. Until I broke his neck with it."

Langula laughed. "How delightful. Oh! What is your name?"

"L-Laws," he said.

Langula deliberately put her hand on his sword; she brought the blade up to her face to gaze upon her dark reflection. Ever since her master had destroyed all the mirrors and reflective surfaces in Castle Orlo, she now enjoyed looking at herself, more than ever. Seeing herself for the first time in quite a while, she made soft cooing sounds like that of a dove. Laws did nothing to stop her.

She glided her hand from the sword to his wrist. Then slowly she put a squeeze on, penetrating her dark fingernails deep into the muscles of his flesh. She progressively increased her grip until he dropped the heavy sword. It hit the ground with a ponderous thud. He hardly took any notice.

Wrapping her coils around his waist, her eyes mesmerized the salty veteran. She constricted him, pulling him tighter to her, until he could not move. Throughout it all, he could not find the power to resist.

Langula drew closer to him, her face touching his. In a passionate hunger, her black lips searched for his. She found the opening of his cleaved lips and longingly kissed him deeply. Enjoying his warmth, her scaly tail wrapped tighter around his waist in a twisting, constricting coil, drawing them together. Their bottom halves were pressed tighter against each other. Her spell pulled him deeper into her, as she ran her hands across his chest and biceps. He breathed heavily and she unbuttoned his shirt and ran her hands over his scars. Keeping her head on his chest, lightly kissing his wounds, she felt his pounding blood through his veins underneath. Her silver eyes flashed in desire to get at that blood, sensing the pulsations throbbing through him.

Then, another hand emerged from out of the darkness, and it touched him from behind. Laws felt the third hand caress the side of his scarred face, at the same time bending his head to the side, exposing his long neck. Sharp claws colored in yellow-and-brown spots accompanied Langula's caress, as a second pair of silver demon eyes peered over Laws's shoulder. This second demon revealed fangs and placed an open mouth on the tender spot between the bulge in his shoulder and neck. With only a slight grimace from Laws, the new demon bit into his flesh with an audible crunch.

Langula continued to guide Laws into what she desired, and he could not resist her. Together the two demons moved upon Laws in a dance of bloodthirsty urgency.

The spotted demon tugged, tearing out a large muscle and chewing on it, spilling blood out of its demon mouth and down Law's chest. Under Langula's spell, Laws did not realize the second demon's presence, despite the pain of having his flesh eaten alive.

At length, Laws rapid breathing escalated to ecstasy, then he collapsed, held powerless in Langula's coils. But she was not ready to surrender control of him. They were far from done. Greedily, her mouth opened and covered his bicep, and then she too bit into him deeply.

Langula pulled against the muscle of Laws's bicep, as the other demon quietly maneuvered to the other side of his neck to get at the other fleshy part. But then, something was wrong. Langula squirmed, increasingly aggravated, although she did not know exactly why. She released his bicep and opened her eyes. She realized a light had been shining, and continued to shine, directly into her eyes. She had not noticed it before, but now the entire forest looked brighter. She uncoiled from Laws, leaving him trembling behind some trees, as she slithered a distance away looking up through the trees.

"Come with me, Monticello," she told the other demon. Together they moved into a nearby clearing and searched the canopy overhead for the source of the unnatural light. Standing fully upright on her serpent tail, she investigated the treetops.

That was when she saw it. A new bright star. She knew its meaning, and immediately recognized what it was. She seethed with anger upon seeing it and gave it a hateful hiss.

"We must warn the master."

She slithered away quickly with the other demon. They left Laws on the forest floor where he collapsed in the litter of human bones.

CURTZ

When the horde of flies hit him, Curtz had reacted in the only way he knew: he ran. But as fast as he was, Curtz could not outrun them. Flies still caught him. They got in his ears, eyes, nose, mouth, and everywhere else. Their welting bites made him run even faster. But Curtz escaped being entirely blanketed by them, unlike the rest of the search party.

When the flies disintegrated in the blue mist, he did not even notice. He was too focused on getting away. At some point, he thought he had outdistanced them. He stopped and swatted the imaginary ones off his ears and spit them out of his mouth, but they were all gone. Then, he got down to scratching his wounds. The flies were behind him now, but he remained alert for any sign that he should dart away again if he thought they had come back. Curtz realized he had not only run away from the flies, but he had run from the party too.

Then he had an attack of conscience. Equally as devasting as the flies, he felt terrible. He had left his companions behind. He worried about the others; if they were hurt, or if he could help them. But more, he wondered what would they think of him for running away? Would they say he was a coward because of a few flies? He had an even bigger problem: he had abandoned his commanding officer. Kilmer would be well within his authority to reprimand him. He had to go back. He had to find them and do whatever he could to help regroup.

"Captain Kilmer! Rhodes! Hanson! Laws! Melvin!" he called out as he walked back. Over and over, he listened to his voice echo through the darkness of the trees. No response came. Just the reverberation of his own voice.

Captain Kilmer had handpicked him for this mission primarily because of his speed and athleticism. But Curtz had a quick wit too. He was smart enough and thought quick on his feet, although many did not give him credit. There was a reason for that, however. Most of the time he just looked for ways to irritate people. He knew what made people tick, and he could use it against them, if nothing else for his amusement. He had always been the shortest in any group and that gave him something of an inferiority complex. So, he used his wit and his speed, and they could never catch him. Curtz was way too fast for any of them, but now had to rely on his wits.

The forest was quiet, bathed in dull shadows. Diffused light shone above through the leaves, making it hard to determine if it was day or night. After calling for help again, he scanned the forest for anything he could see that might prove useful. Curtz started taking mental stock of any resources available.

I have a lot of trees, he thought.

What do you do with a lot of trees? he asked himself.

"Of course!" he finally said out loud. "You climb them."

In his youth, he climbed a lot of trees. But these trees would be tricky. They had tall featureless trunks before any branches started to form. Luckily, he had climbed their type before, and he knew how to go about it.

Sheathing his sword, he chose one to climb. Gripping his arms around the trunk, he pulled up his feet. Alternating his weight between his arms and legs, he slid himself higher up the trunk, like a human caterpillar. He managed to crawl up until he could reach the lowest branches. Once these came into range he climbed them, as easy as climbing a ladder. The higher he went, the more of the Sanguine Forest he could see. He could see the graves and the bones and the exposed skeletal remains on the ground below. Still, he saw none of the search party. He continued climbing and as he did the sky was getting brighter, even though he felt as if it should be the middle of night, but maybe he was confused, and it was still day after all.

He climbed until he emerged above the canopy. The entirety of the Sanguine Forest stretched out before him. Poking his head around the leaves at the very top, the first thing he saw was a bright star illuminating the night. This was a new star that had turned the night into day. Curtz had never seen anything like it—it defied explanation. Instinctively, he knew that this star could not be the work of the illusionary magic of the Sanguine Forest. It was far too big for that. This was a new star, indicating something of cosmic proportions. He could not help himself and marveled a moment. He knew it had to be the sign of something he would never likely see again. This was the work, or mischief, of the Gods.

After a moment of admiration, his mind got back to the business at hand. He used the brightness of the star to see the surrounding area. Curtz could see the entire Sanguine Forest, the Gray Mountains in the distance, and even the opening of the Mauveguard Pass. With those landmarks he could determine his location. His bearings returned. He knew which way he wanted to go toward the Blue Mountains, and now he knew which direction: northwest, that was the way home.

He climbed down out of the canopy, using gravity to help descend quickly. He was still high on the tree, when he saw dark movement on the ground below.

"Kilmer! Rhodes! Hanson! Laws!" he called out.

RHODES AND MELVIN

As the horde of flies attacked them, Rhodes and Hanson huddled together near where Melvin and Givens hunkered down as well. Shortly after Hanson broke and ran, the flies disintegrated into a sparkling blue mist. Then, they were gone.

After they disappeared, Rhodes crawled to Givens and Melvin. He kept close to the ground—instincts ingrained from his military training. He wanted to keep a low profile, to protect himself, not knowing what was going to happen next. He reached Melvin, and the still delirious Givens, and they crouched together.

"Where's Captain Kilmer?" Rhodes asked, scanning the trees. "Did anybody see him?"

"I only saw flies," Melvin said, spitting out a few dead bugs.

Givens had gotten worse, as if his mind was rotting away. After the swarm, he could barely function. He hung his head low and drooled.

"What's wrong with Givens?" Rhodes asked.

"Givens! Givens!" Melvin shook him, but the man did not respond. "I don't know what's wrong with him."

"Wait here!" Rhodes quickly crawled over to the dead horse. The beast lay on its side with terror-filled blue eyes frozen in fear. This had been Curtz's horse, but it was dead now. Rhodes rummaged through the saddlebags. He found a rope and came crawling back to Melvin and Givens. Rhodes stood up and unwound the rope.

"Here, take this," Rhodes said, giving one end to Melvin. He tied the other around his waist. "Tie yourself off, then tie off Givens. We will not get separated again."

The inexperienced Melvin nodded and did whatever Rhodes asked of him. Melvin felt better knowing the old veteran was taking charge in Kilmer's absence. Hopefully, they would soon all be reunited. Together they wrapped the rope around Givens's shoulders and armpits, making a harness, then tied himself to the rope in the same way.

"Keep the rest of the slack with you, Melvin. Let's go look for the others. We are all going to leave this place together." Rhodes pulled a long dagger out of his boot, then came over to help Melvin with Givens, who was babbling like a child. He could barely walk under his own power.

"This way." Rhodes pointed with the dagger. "This was where I last saw Captain Kilmer. We will dead reckon on this heading, in this direction, until we find someone or come to the end of the Sanguine Forest. Agreed?"

Melvin nodded. He did not argue. Any idea was better than not having one at all.

Rhodes and Melvin got on either side and helped drag Givens through the forest. But they saw no sign of Captain Kilmer.

Melvin heard a voice call out.

"Listen!" Melvin said in a whisper. Soon Rhodes heard the voice too.

"Is that Curtz?"

"Curtz? Curtz?" they both shouted.

Curtz continued searching for any evidence of the identity of the darkened shapes he saw from higher up.

As Rhodes and Melvin kept calling for him, Curtz skirted down the trunk, into their view, and closer to the ground.

Finally, Curtz saw them, and he could tell it was Rhodes, Melvin, and Givens.

"Hey! Rhodes! Melvin!" Curtz yelled and flailed his hand. "Hey! Am I glad to see you two!"

"Curtz?" Rhodes shouted up the tree. "Curtz! Is that you?"

"Oh, Curtz, I'm so glad we found you," Melvin said.

Curtz jumped to the ground in a cloud of dust, breaking some old, bleached bones that were piled there on the ground. As Rhodes, Melvin, and Givens reached him by the tree, Curtz saw they were tied together with a rope. "Why are you tied together?"

"So nothing can separate us again," Rhodes told him.

"Smart. Good idea, Rhodes," Curtz said, patting Rhodes on the back. "I climbed above the canopy of the trees to see the forest as it is. I know the way out. Where are Kilmer and Hanson?" As Rhodes gave him the update, he looked at Givens. "What's wrong with him?"

"Not sure," Melvin told him. "He can walk a little, but just barely. We need to get him out of here."

"Where's Captain Kilmer?" Curtz asked. "Have you seen him?"

They told him they had not; Laws and Hanson were still missing too.

Curtz told them, "I know the way out. We need to go northwest."

"Agreed. But which way is northwest?" Rhodes asked.

"It's that way," Curtz correctly pointed with an open hand.

"You sure?" Melvin asked.

"Absolutely," Curtz said. "When I was above the canopy, I got my sense of direction back."

"What do we do about the captain, Hanson, and Laws?" Melvin said. "We can't just leave them."

"We have to think about this," Rhodes said. He took a minute to look the situation over. "We are not an effective fighting force anymore. We are splintered and separated, our gear is gone, our horses are gone. Givens is wounded, and Captain Kilmer, Laws, and Hanson are missing."

They all looked at Givens, who smiled moronically at them after recognizing his name.

"What we need to do is retreat and regroup," Rhodes said. "Melvin, you and Curtz take Givens out of here. I'll stay and go back to look for Captain Kilmer, Hanson, and Laws. Go back to that camp of last night, the camp to the northwest. I'll be along shortly with the others as soon as I can find them."

"No, Rhodes, I'll search for them," Curtz said, then pointed to the others. "You take Givens and Melvin out of here. You go that way."

Curtz motioned again with the flat of his hand in the direction they should follow. "You got that? Do not deviate from this directional path. Dead reckon that way, keep it straight, and you'll get to the camp to the northwest where we were last night."

"Are you sure, Curtz?" Rhodes asked. "What are you going to do?"

"I have a sense of direction now, Rhodes. And now that I know it, I won't get lost. I'll find the captain and the others and bring them out. But listen, if you don't see me by morning, send Lord Whitney's army to find me. Just in case."

Rhodes acknowledged Curtz's plan by patting him on the back.

Curtz went on, "That is the best we can do right now. Get Givens and Melvin to safety."

"Fine, Curtz, but if we need Lord Whitney's forces, I'm coming back in with them, and nothing you say can stop me."

"Whatever happens, Rhodes, don't let Melvin or Givens back into this forest once you get out. Get them both back to Castle Odessa."

"I will," Rhodes told him, and Curtz turned to go. "Good hunting, Curtz."

"And Rhodes?" Curtz stopped again. Rhodes turned to look at him. "I don't want you to be surprised, but a new star is shining in the night sky. It's a bright one. So bright it is turning night into day. That's why the shadows were going crazy when Kilmer tried to get his bearings. It's why we got lost."

"A new star? Thanks for letting me know," Rhodes said, wondering if Curtz had lost his mind like Givens. "See you soon, Curtz."

"Melvin, you take care and watch out for Givens." Curtz quickly turned and faded into the mist in his search for the others.

After Curtz had left, Rhodes and Melvin picked up Givens and turned to go, still tied to one another.

HANSON

Hanson was huddled against Rhodes as the horde of flies came upon them. Rhodes dropped against Hanson, bringing their bodies as close together as they could, in an effort to shield them both against the swarm.

Without looking, they heard the screams of the horses over the loud buzz of a thousand wings attacking them. Despite the horses' suffering, there was nothing they could do. In the darkness, they could only cling to each other.

Shortly after, Hanson began to panic. He could feel the weight of the flies massing on his back, his arms, and the side of his face. The buzzing became louder as they wiggled into his ears. Wherever they landed, they bit, and his body stung from hundreds of simultaneous welts. Hanson thought he was going to die. As more of the flies covered them, Hanson became more claustrophobic. Squirming, he frantically tried to shake off as many of them as he could, but nothing was working.

Rhodes lay beside him, clutching him tightly, not moving at all.

"Hanson!" Rhodes shouted over the noise. "Stay down, Hanson."

Hanson had felt this hopeless once before at the Battle of Mauveguard Pass, when he was forced to march uphill, in the rain, in the mud, and ordered to attack an enemy that had taken cover behind hardened fortifications. It was a suicide mission. All that day, his friends were slaughtered by spears, arrows, and swords. The fear was returning to him.

He wanted out, he wanted to run; he needed to run. He knew Rhodes would be left exposed, but he knew his chances of getting away from the flies were better on foot than lying here letting them crawl over him.

Hanson abruptly rolled away then ran. Rhodes immediately felt his absence, and the side that Hanson vacated was now exposed to more of the flies. They quickly seized the opportunity and attacked the additional exposed parts of his body. Rhodes wanted to call out after him, but when he tried to shout, he received a mouthful of flies. Spitting them out, he could only lay there alone.

Hanson struggled to his feet and ran as fast as he could, swatting the air, swatting himself, trying to get away from the flies. He ran through the painful bites, carrying away those huddled stuck bugs that stayed connected to him in thick black masses. Trying to brush them away, he had more of them pursue him as he ran.

Just as quickly as the flies appeared, they disappeared in a sparkling cloud of blue mist. Still in a panic, Hanson did not realize they were gone, and continued running as fast as he could, not knowing or watching where he was going. Abruptly, he fell and sank knee-deep in gritty mud. He noticed the flies were gone, but now he could not move his legs, and he was stuck in a deep watery mire. Worse yet, he was slowly sinking deeper.

The mud swallowed his hips and worked its way up to his stomach and he continued sinking. Desperately reaching for something to grab, but there was nothing—no rocks, or vines, or bushes, nothing that would help him get out of the mud or slow his descent.

"Help me, help!" he screamed. The mud rose to his neck and it showed no sign of slowing or having a bottom. Continuing his descent, he soon realized he would go under and be lost, never to be seen again. The worst part was that no one would ever know what happened to him.

So, this is how it is all going to end, after everything I've been through? He never thought he would go like this, drowning in a bottomless pool of muck.

Running out of time, the first splash of mud went into his mouth. He angled his head upward as the gritty muck covered his ears. He struggled against it, stretching his neck trying to keep his face above the surface of the mud. Taking quick sporadic breaths, he did not know which one would be his last. Finally, the bog dragged him under.

Below the surface, Hanson's eyelids started to burn in red ovals from the lack of air. Desperately, he clung to life, grasping wildly upwardly through the bog for something, anything, to help get him back to the top. That was where he had to get to fast, back to where the cool air was. Yet he felt himself sinking further into the swill, sucking him down. His lungs bursting for air.

Then his hand, the only part of him still remaining outside the mud, did feel something. Something solid brushed against his fingers. He latched onto it as a reflex, he clung to it, grasping and pulling against it with all his strength. His hand clenched a rope! He held onto it tightly. The rope tightened from a power not his own. It boosted him up through the gritty soup to break the surface.

He opened his mouth wide, breathing in a lungful of cool air. With mud in his eyes, he could barely make out a dark figure on the other end of the rope. This was his savior.

"I got you, Hanson!"

It was Curtz! He leaned back with each pull on the rope from the safety of the bank on solid ground. With each pull, he dragged Hanson closer to the edge of the mire. He had the rope wrapped around his waist and leaned back dramatically with each heaving pull. "I've got you. There you go!"

After Hanson breathlessly crawled to safety and rolled out upon solid ground, the mud reverted back into hardened ground again. The two men collapsed on the bank, breathing heavily from their efforts. They both blinked their eyes looking at the hardened stone, which had been a deep suffocating bog just a moment ago.

Despite the transmutation of the mud to stone, Hanson was ecstatic to see Curtz.

"Oh, thank you, Curtz! Thank you! You saved my life!"

"This is some powerful magic!" Curtz said, looking at Hanson. As they gazed at each other, they began to laugh, a release of nervous energy. Soon, laughing hard, both of their booming voices burst forth in the surrounding forest, echoing in their laughter.

"How did you find me?" Hanson asked, covered in dried mud.

Curtz picked up Hanson's sword and handed it to him.

"I found your sword nearby," Curtz said. "Then when I looked at the bog, I saw a hand that was missing a sword. Isn't that just like an Amalgamate though? Leaving your sword lying around without a hand."

They both could not help laughing and relaxed their heads back on the ground, savoring that, at least for now, this danger had passed. They continued to laugh without a care.

"I am so glad I found you though, kid," Curtz told him, laughing some more, and patting his arm.

"Me too, Curtz, me too." Hanson patted his arm back.

Rhodes and Melvin had to drag Givens, who could no longer walk, his feet plowing behind through the underbrush. They continued their northwest trek. Along their way, in the misty distance, they saw a horse. Rhodes handed Givens to Melvin and untied himself.

"No, no, don't untie from us," Melvin pleaded in fear.

But Rhodes dashed off anyway to retrieve the horse. As it turned out, it was his own, at least the one he rode into the Sanguine, the one with his own gear. Rhodes led it back to Melvin and Givens and they laid Givens across the horse. Rhodes helped put Melvin on too, then he led the horse by the bridle for a little over an hour, until at last, the darkness of the Sanguine Forest gave way to the spaciousness of the Mid-Run Valley. Almost immediately the oppressive feeling was gone. The first thing they noticed was the new star, just as Curtz had told them, shining brightly, bursting forth in a radiance above them. Curtz was not crazy after all.

"It turns out he was telling the truth," Rhodes said. "I thought he might be seeing things like Givens."

"Me too," Melvin agreed. "Unless we are all under the same spell and this is the same vision."

Rhodes did not want to dwell upon that. He had enough to worry about for now. They continued northwest until they reached the campsite from the night before. They established the largest bonfire they could, as a signal, stoking it up higher to help their companions see where they were. Melvin tended to Givens, while Rhodes stood at the edge of the camp, looking back at the Sanguine Forest, occasionally staring at the shining new star. Nearby his horse grazed on wild grass.

"I could go back in," Rhodes said.

"Don't do it, Rhodes," Melvin told him. "Wait here for the night to pass as we agreed with Curtz. If he doesn't come back by morning, then the army goes in. Until then, give him a chance."

But just then, Rhodes saw a person stumbling in the distance, coming out of the Sanguine Forest and heading their way.

"Somebody's coming!" Rhodes said, trying to identify the dark figure. "Who is that? I can't make them out."

Rhodes squinted.

"Is it Captain Kilmer?" Melvin asked, his hand on his sword. At last, the light of the star helped to reveal the person's identity.

"It's Laws!" Rhodes shouted. He ran toward him, and when he got to Laws, the big man collapsed in his arms. His clothes were torn and tattered. His body was cut and bloodied.

"Laws, what happened? You are wounded! Where is your sword? Who did this to you?"

But Laws did not, or could not, speak. Rhodes heaved the man up upon his broad shoulders with a great deal of leverage and carried him back to their campfire. With Melvin's help, they gently set Laws down beside Givens.

"What's wrong with him?" Melvin asked.

"I don't know, maybe the same as Givens. Just try to get him to eat and drink something. Don't let him go anywhere."

"What are you going to do?" Melvin asked.

Rhodes didn't answer. He ran to his horse and mounted it.

"I'm going to get as close to the Sanguine without going in," he shouted, then he rode away making noise and calling out their names.

"Kilmer! Curtz! Hanson! We found Laws!"

He did not have long to wait. Soon two men came riding horses out of the Sanguine, leading a third horse with no rider. It was Curtz and Hanson! They had found each other, and three horses before they reached the forest's edge.

"I found mine, but it's dead!" Curtz said sarcastically. "And by the way, you owe me a rope, Rhodes."

Rhodes laughed with relief and welcomed them. Together they rode back to the northwest camp. Under the new star, Hanson eagerly told his story of nearly drowning in the mud if not for Curtz saving his life.

"Well, we got out," Curtz said. "But still no sign of Captain Kilmer anywhere."

When they reached the camp, they dismounted. Curtz looked at Givens and Laws. "Are those two going to live?"

"I have no idea," Melvin shrugged. "I'm not even sure what is wrong with them."

"Those two are wounded," Rhodes said. "And we're missing some horses. But maybe most important: what happened to Captain Kilmer?"

One by one, they all shook their heads. They acknowledged Kilmer was still missing, and their relief turned into something morose.

"This is not good," Curtz said. "What will King Leopold think of us for losing our commanding officer?"

"Well, I, for one, am not going back without him," Rhodes said. "We are not leaving here without Captain Kilmer."

Rhodes, Curtz, Melvin, and Hanson all agreed. Laws and Givens said nothing. The Sanguine Forest had rendered them barely conscious.

I've been throwing away everything
that means anything to me.
I've been crawling on my hands and knees
I hear the whispering, but can't you hear my plea?

Excerpt from *The Witch's Songbook*

In the cemeteries, new tombstones went up
almost daily at an alarming rate.
— Excerpt from *The Provenance* (Chapter Ten)

MAUVEGUARD PASS

ON THE BATTLEFIELDS OF THE MID-RUN VALLEY IN THE YEAR 837HRT (FIVE YEARS EARLIER, BEFORE YORI'S DISAPPEARANCE)

The Amalgamates shipped Kory and Kilmer out one morning by horse-drawn wagon on a bumpy road. They shipped out with other recent trainees heading west. Their destination was unknown, but they were going in the direction of the front, somewhere around the vicinity of the village of Conner, one of the latest of Leopold's conquests, in the north of the Mid-Run Valley. General Blaize Plum had been gathering forces to counterattack Leopold for the past month.

They rode along for days, joining with wagons of other new recruits. Finally, they stopped on the outskirts of Conner. They filed out and were ordered to report to the general's formation.

This had been the moment Kory and Kilmer had long waited for, to see the general close up, and to fight for all the villages of the Mid-Run Valley under his command.

Along the way, they passed some casualties of the war strewn in the road, dead bodies, soldiers who had passed before them stacked up in the grasslands. Some in bloodied uniforms of red and blue, others in the Amalgamate green and yellow, but all of them were just as dead, lying in heaps and clumps in death.

Kory had never been this close to the enemy or death before. His first look at Leopold's Red and Blue was also the first time he had ever seen a dead body. He watched mesmerized while the death wardens stacked more of the dead men in rows. For Kory, seeing the dead was a revelation of the seriousness of their situation. The sight reminded him that this war was a profoundly serious contest. And the war was nowhere near being over.

But this was not the first time Kilmer had seen Leopold's fighting men or the dead. He had seen them before, in the village of Plum—a sight he would never forget and still haunted his dreams. There he saw the Red Guard and a host of the dead, which used to be his friends and neighbors. He did not mind seeing these dead now.

Next came the walking wounded, the casualties, the men bravely wearing the same green and yellow uniforms of the Amalgamates. They stumbled by the new troops, blind and in bandages, with wounds and missing limbs, covered in blood.

These scenes sickened Kory; seeing them was sobering, but Kilmer needed no such reminder.

"Come on," Kilmer told Kory, encouraging him to keep marching.

Ahead was a fiery field, partially covered in flames and black smoke. This was where the Amalgamate troops were forming. Kory and Kilmer were given orders to hurry and fall into the line.

"What's happening now?" Kory asked. "What are we doing?"

"We are going to meet the enemy."

"We are going into battle?" Kory asked. "Now?"

"Yes," Kilmer told him. "Stay close."

The first time they saw General Blaize Plum he wore golden armor adorned with emerald fabrics and flanked alongside other officers.

He appeared mounted on an enormous black warhorse also armored in matching green-and-yellow armaments. The warhorse he called Ruboru and was the largest, most fearsome horse the boys had ever seen. Ruboru reared on the general's command, and the troops gave a whooping shout. It all looked like a glorious painting come to life.

"I wish Oaks was here to see Ruboru," Kory whispered to Kilmer while they stood in formation. Kilmer nodded but did not say a word. Just the thought of Oaks made him think of Darla, and he wondered if he would ever see either of them again.

"Amalgamates!" General Blaize Plum shouted. "Today is our time. At your hand, we strike back for the Mid-Run Valley. We strike to liberate the village of Conner and take back what this mad dog took from us. Make the Red and Blue pay for their war atrocities! You will become the weapons of our vengeance! Remember Conner! Remember Plum! Remember Bowling!"

Remember Conner!
Remember Plum!
Remember Bowling!

This became their war cry.

The general removed his sword from its scabbard, lifting it high, and gave the order, "Forward to the fight!"

The column lurched forward, like a giant snake crawling across the land. The Amalgamate column was a magnificent force of nearly thirty thousand soldiers. Swords, shields, and spears glinted in the sun.

It was such a beautiful day—overhead, the sky was blue, the temperature warm. Kilmer and Kory nervously held their spears at the ready with sweaty hands, marching in the column with all the others.

Soon, powerful eruptions exploded around them, as heavy stone projectiles heaved dirt skyward and blasted flesh to twirling pieces. The sounds of explosions and screams pierced the air equally.

After the projectiles, enemy troops appeared, through the black smoke in front of them armored in red and blue armor. Without so much as a fight, Leopold's men were running, retreating before the power of the Amalgamates.

Then the order was given to charge!

The whole column, including Kilmer and Kory, accelerated, running at the enemy. Kilmer and Kory stayed together, but Kory ran slower than Kilmer did, and Kory had to try harder to keep up with him. They came to a conflagration in front as Leopold's forces ignited explosive traps they left behind for the Amalgamates. Many of their fellow soldiers up front erupted into flaming, thrashing, burning dolls. Yet Kory and Kilmer continued running past these poor souls, knowing they were as good as dead.

Then, leaping through the flames, the Red and Blue counterattacked, completing their trap. The Amalgamates' front line lurched forward to clash into them. Kilmer and Kory continued running fast toward the point where the sound of battling iron clashed together. Ahead, they could see the front lines surge in deadly fighting with the enemy.

With a loud scream Kilmer launched himself upon an unsuspecting enemy soldier wearing the Red and Blue. The man only had time to widen his eyes to see death coming, as Kilmer cleaved his sword into the man's face. Kory screamed as well, swinging his weapon wildly but striking nothing.

Kilmer pulled his sword out of the man's face with the heel of his boot, then turned it on another's neck in one smooth motion. Blood splattered into Kory's face with a surprising splash of gore.

Kilmer reared back, narrowly dodging a spear that almost ran him through. He released his sword and grabbed the shaft of the spear, fighting for control of it. The enemy pulled sharply, tugging it out of Kilmer's hands and making him fall forward. Looking up, Kilmer saw the soldier pulling the spear back to make the fatal plunge into his side. Kilmer held out his bare hands screaming, knowing the lethal blow was coming.

The enemy's eyes suddenly widened, as a sword ran him through. He looked down in shock to see a blade exiting out of the front of his chest. Blood splattered across Kilmer's face in a bloody explosion. It was Kory, coming to Kilmer's rescue!

Kory put his foot on the man, then withdrew his sword out of the man's back. The man fell on top of Kilmer, dead. Kilmer pushed the corpse away as Kory held out a hand and helped Kilmer back up.

Leopold's army had been overcome. The trap had killed a lot of good Amalgamates but the counterattack had not been effective. Leopold's remaining forces were now being pulled from the field in retreat until all of them were gone. Leopold was on the run again.

A cheer rose from the Amalgamates. They had been victorious. They had liberated Conner, just as the general said they would. Today they had become the instrument of vengeance!

Kilmer and Kory embraced. Now in relative safety they laughed and released their nervous energy. The battle was over, they both survived, and they were successful. They had their first taste and were battle tested. Now they had the experience of killing men, and just how horribly decisive and lethal war could be.

Afterward, the field was littered with the dead, strewn across the field in smoldering heaps and bloody remains. Gravely wounded soldiers of Leopold were executed in the field. Those that could be healed were helped. Those that surrendered were taken away as prisoners in chains. Dead bodies were thrown into the black smoke of the fire.

With blackened faces, both Kilmer and Kory watched the bodies burning. Glad it was not them.

In the year that followed, Kilmer and Kory fought in more battles, liberating more villages from Leopold. The Amalgamates liberated Madison, Wildlane, and Sudbury. Leopold could no longer be the conqueror of unsuspecting villages. The resistance of the Amalgamates grew stronger, and General Blaize Plum was on the offensive. Now Leopold had to contend with the Amalgamates as the aggressors in this War of the Mid-Run Valley that he started.

Leopold's forces were suffering losses every day that reduced the army to just under thirty thousand tired and hungry men. But the Amalgamates were growing. With each liberated village they grew stronger and were in pursuit of the Red and Blue with forty-five thousand well-armed, well-fed men.

In the quiet times, Kilmer missed Darla. He thought of her all the time and wrote letters to her on a regular basis.

Dearest Darla,

Still the war drags on, it seems to be only a matter of time before an Amalgamate victory. If we could just corner Leopold the mad dog, we would outnumber him, and then this war would be over. We have pursued him to the Blue Mountains. Leopold mistakenly has come here, and now he has nowhere to go. Their backs are against the mountains. The end seems near. I hope to see you soon, and to kiss your lips again. Tell Sisters Chavise and Maldean that Kory and I are well and give them our blessings, as we know they are saying their prayers for us. Also, tell Oaks that General Plum's horse is named Ruboru, and is really something he must see someday. We will see you all soon.

— Love, Kilmer and Kory

Kilmer had no way of knowing this would be his last letter home.

The night before the Battle of Mauveguard Pass, Kilmer awoke in the middle of the night, with Hollow Face standing over him, looming in the darkness.

He whispered, "You scared me!" Kilmer's heart beat fast.

"What are you doing here? Do you want to show me something, Hollow Face?" The ghost nodded. Kilmer knew that Leopold's army had nowhere to go except for the Mauveguard Pass. Therefore, the Amalgamates could corner and destroy him. It would be the end of the war.

So, why was Hollow Face appearing to him now?

"Go on, show me what you must."

The ghost hesitated. It made a sweeping motion with its hand, and a vision flooded Kilmer's mind. The scenes were of war, death, fire, and blood. This was not unexpected, but then he saw himself covered in blood. He saw Kory lying there dead—killed and lying in a puddle of blood. He saw a large man on a black warhorse dressed in Red and Blue and yet, he was not the enemy. The vision became veiled in darkness, then a symbol appeared: a crescent moon inside a silver circle. Kilmer saw himself again, but this time he was not in the uniform of the Amalgamates but was wearing the armor of Leopold's Red and Blue.

Then the visions were gone, and with them, Hollow Face was gone too. This vision of Kory disturbed him the most. Kilmer crawled to the next blanket over, where Kory slept. He shook him awake.

"Kory! Kory!" Kilmer said in a whisper until he woke him.

"Kilmer?" Kory asked still half-asleep. "What is it? What's wrong?"

"Kory." Kilmer did not know what to say. "Are you sure you want to do this tomorrow?"

"What are you talking about? Tomorrow is going to be the battle that ends this war. We are going to win."

"But Kory, I'm worried. I'm scared, Kory. Maybe we should get away from here, away from Mauveguard Pass."

"You want to run? After all these years, Kilmer, you have always encouraged me. Maybe it's my turn to encourage you. Be brave now, Kilmer."

Kilmer hesitated. "It's not me I'm worried about."

"Me? You're worried about me? Kilmer, we've been through so many battles together. No one knows how it is going to go. If it's my time, then all I can do is fight, fight the best I can. That's all any of us can do. If we fall tomorrow, Kilmer, just know that as for me, this has been the greatest adventure of my life, and I have you to thank for that. Whatever happens when the sun comes up, at least we can say we did it together, you and I."

The two looked in each other's eyes for a moment.

"I love you, Kory," Kilmer told him.

"I love you too, Kilmer. Try to get some sleep."

Kilmer laid back on his bedroll. But he could not stop thinking about the vision. Next to him, Kory slept peacefully, as Kilmer only stared at the stars.

The morning crept up to shine its light. The fog rolled in, and dew descended upon them like a blanket of ice water. Kilmer had not slept a wink, and the night passed quickly. Soon the others awoke to a drizzle, and dismal rain clouds came rumbling in.

With the morning light, the order came for them to get into their formations.

The Battle of Mauveguard Pass was about to begin.

Once assembled, General Blaize Plum spoke to his forces numbering forty-five thousand. "Amalgamates! Today we have pursued our enemy to the Blue Mountains. They have nowhere left to run, nowhere else to turn, and we outnumber them two to one. The initiative is in our favor. Today we will deal the last strike to Leopold and break this rebellion for good. Break them for Conner! Break them for Plum! Break them for Bowling! Break them forever!"

A loud cheer went up as the general finished. It had been a long bloody war, and today they were ready to end it. General Blaize Plum gave the order to move out, and the column moved toward the mountains.

"Kilmer? What do you think the general will do with Leopold after the war?"

"Hang him, I suppose."

"They should burn him at the stake," Kory said.

"Yeah," Kilmer agreed.

The column kept moving in pursuit until at last they came to the bottom of the Mauveguard Pass, a low-lying area cut between the cliffs of the Blue Mountains. The Amalgamates gave the order for the column to halt, while the general assessed the situation.

Just then, the drizzle turned to rain.

Kilmer, Kory, and all the others looked up the pass and could see what the general could see. The Red and Blue waited for them there at the top of the pass. The beginnings of a castle and other surrounding fortifications were unexpectedly there. Leopold's forces cowered behind them. Kilmer could see the general looking over maps, only imagining the conversations of his leadership.

A fellow soldier spoke up. "Here we are, and there they are. We have the advantage of superior numbers, and they have the benefit of position."

"Do you think we're going to attack, Kilmer?" Kory asked him.

Kilmer did not even look at him. "Yeah, we're going to attack."

No sooner did the words leave Kilmer's mouth than the order was given to march forward. Forty-five thousand soldiers in the column started to move up the muddy uphill incline of the Mauveguard

Pass. Their feet squished the wet ground, turning it to sloppy, slippery mud. The column stayed in line as best they could, as troops slipped and fell. Those that fell in front of the column caused a rippling effect throughout the line.

"Kilmer, something doesn't feel right," Kory said.

"Stay brave, Kory."

"I should have listened to you last night. We shouldn't be here. Maybe we should have run away when we could."

"Be quiet, Kory. We are here now."

Suddenly, the air darkened as archers launched the first volleys of arrows overhead, and they blotted out the sky as they arced toward them.

"*Arrows!*" the front line screamed, and the entire column stopped and shifted their shields over their heads. The arrows slammed into them from far overhead and found their mark in the reserve numbers behind Kilmer and Kory.

"They shot long," Kory said, relieved.

"They won't make that mistake twice," Kilmer told him. Another volley came whistling in from overhead.

"*Arrows!*" they screamed again. This time they slammed into the front lines. Kilmer and Kory put up their shields and defended themselves as the missiles landed.

Kory screamed! An arrow lodged itself in his upper thigh. Kilmer tried to give aid, but the column was pushing them along from behind.

"I can go on," Kory said. He continued to march despite his pain. He was not the only one hit, but kept pressing on, slipping up the hill, an arrow sticking out of his thigh. Some others were not as fortunate and lay dead in front of them, so that they had to step over them.

Kilmer watched Kory carefully. The boy had blood spilling down his leg. Tears started to well up in Kilmer's eyes remembering the vision Hollow Face showed him the night before.

Continuing up the muddy hill, they could see the Amalgamates ahead slam into Leopold's front line of spears.

Kilmer and Kory stepped through mud and over dead bodies, inching their way toward the sound of battle. They could hear commands from the Red and Blue leaders on the other side. They were close enough to hear the voice of Leopold himself.

A swell of enemy soldiers rushed out to attack with a shout from behind their stone fortifications. They came running downhill like a wave, thousands of them, attacking the Amalgamate forces. Leopold's army surged forward, pushing the Amalgamate line back, while at the same time, the Amalgamates own soldiers were pushing forward from the rear. With their front line in retreat, but having nowhere to retreat to, and the back of the column continuing to advance and push the front up the hill, Kilmer and Kory were squeezed inside a deadly vise.

Metal struck against metal, shields bent, the screams of the dying reverberated throughout the Mauveguard Pass. Kilmer and Kory had little room to swing their swords, and they were being thrust upon broken spears ahead, pushed from behind. Death raged all around them.

An enemy soldier leaped into their line swinging his sword wildly; the blade hit Kilmer on the head with its broadside, nearly knocking him out. Kilmer wobbled.

Men on both sides fought for their lives. They clashed bravely and brutally. Kory fought on through his wound, and the dazed Kilmer could barely lift his sword. Amid this close quartered battle the inevitable happened. Kory gave a wail, a scream of agony as a sword thrust into his side. The wound went deep. Kilmer saw what happened and leaped into the air with a war cry in defense of his friend. Clumsily, but violently, he came down upon the neck of the man that held the blade in Kory. Kilmer slashed with his sword and flayed two, then three, enemy soldiers. With blood dripping down his face, into his eyes, Kilmer used one arm to lift Kory, dragging him away to the north side of the pass.

As the struggle continued all around them, Kilmer and Kory fell backward, landing in a deep puddle of water, a runoff from the sudden rain. It was filled with mud and supplied with a fresh current of blood. Kory let out an agonizing scream as the arrow in his upper thigh snapped off. Kilmer splashed a few feet away. The wound on the top of his head continued to leak crimson rivulets down his face.

Kilmer could taste the coppery blood as it ran into his mouth. Everything looked surreal and artificial, looking at the scenes of death all around him, as if in a hazy dreamlike state. He watched swords hacking at flesh, men suffering horrific wounds, cleaved heads, arms, and legs littered the battlefield, dead soldiers impaled upon spears.

They both sat in the water, Kilmer in a daze as Kory held his side and bled out, writhing in pain. Neither of them could walk, neither could fight anymore. Their faces spoke grim volumes.

The Amalgamates were losing the day. Their superior numbers, their forty-five thousand troops, were in the process of defeat at Mauveguard Pass.

"Kilmer?" Kory cried out, grasping his side. "I think I'm going to die."

"Be still, Kory, you'll wake Sister Chavise. You know she can hear anything," Kilmer said, blood running down his face. "I can see Hollow Face again, Kory. He's standing here with us, at the edge of the water. I see Mara crying; she dropped her flowers. Dropped them in this blood."

"You're not making any sense," Kory cried out. With tears in his eyes, he gave him a confused look. "You have blood on your face."

Kilmer raised his hand, touched his face. He saw the blood. "Her pretty flowers."

Even in the confusion of his mind, Kilmer recognized the real enemy riding up to them. Walking through the flames, he saw the face he could never forget. It was LaNew! Captain of the Red Guard. The man who killed his family. He had ridden his horse up to the bloody pool.

LaNew saw them, stopped, and dismounted. He wielded a heavy war hammer and approached Kory lying in the puddle.

"Well, well, well. What have we got here? Look at you. You are a real fat one, aren't you? I bet I can pop you like a pimple." LaNew raised the hammer over his head.

Kory screamed and lifted his hands up in defense. The hammer smashed into his arms, breaking them into unnatural positions. The bones had snapped and were sticking out of his skin. Kory screamed in pain.

"Stop it!" Kilmer shouted to LaNew. "He's already dying! Can't you see that? Leave him alone!"

LaNew ignored Kilmer and raised his hammer again. He brought it down once more, this time on Kory's chest, breaking his ribs. A rush of air came forcibly out of his lungs in a hollow scream.

"No!" Kilmer cried. "Kory!"

"Eh? What's this?" LaNew turned to Kilmer, now holding the hammer waist high. He looked in his direction. "Don't you worry, after this next swing, I'll have something for you too."

No, no, no, Kilmer cried. *Oh, Kory! Please don't be dead!*

LaNew raised the hammer again and brought it down squarely upon Kory's head.

Blood spattered on LaNew's face. He left the hammer sticking out of Kory's skull, then let the handle fall, splashing down into the puddle now stained with Kory's blood. LaNew took a deep breath.

"Phew! Who knew swinging that would be so much work? I'm not a young man anymore," he said. "And so, I must treat you all old-fashioned, like." LaNew reached into his uniform and pulled out a long knife. Stepping over Kory's body, he walked through the water toward Kilmer. LaNew grabbed Kilmer's curly hair with his free hand and maneuvered behind him.

"I can't decide if your hair is red or just covered in blood."

Behind Kilmer, LaNew pulled him up by the hair, stretching his neck, then placed the sharp blade to his throat.

Just then, a large man came riding up on a black horse. Before LaNew could make the cut, the big man shouted.

"LaNew!" he called out.

LaNew looked up, startled to see Amtor.

"Leave that one for me. I need him to collect some intelligence. Gather your Red Guard and meet me back at the fortifications."

LaNew released Kilmer with a forceful push into the bloody water. Kilmer's head came to rest just inches away from Kory's. Finally, he started to come to his senses again.

"What makes you think there is anything intelligent about this one? You just want a little fun for yourself, Amtor?" LaNew laughed, as he splashed out of the pool.

Amtor? Kilmer had heard the name before. Even in his delirious state, he knew Amtor was Leopold's Minister of War, the second in charge. He had authority second only to Leopold himself. Kilmer wondered what Amtor wanted with him and why.

Amtor dismounted and walked to meet LaNew. "Well done, LaNew."

LaNew approached him, slowly moved very close, then whispered in his ear, "Make him suffer." With one last look at Kilmer, he walked to his horse, mounted, and rode away.

Kilmer could not look at Kory. His friend still had LaNew's war hammer in his head. No question, he was dead for sure. Kory was dead.

After LaNew rode away, Amtor walked into the puddle. The water rose to the top of his boots. Approaching Kilmer, he helped him up and out of the water, assisting him to his warhorse.

"Here, let me help you." Amtor gave him some linen. "Apply pressure to that head wound, it will stop the bleeding."

Kilmer did what he was told, while Amtor helped guide him behind the cover of some rocks. Once there, Amtor lowered him to the ground, then assisted him with the bandages.

Amtor said, "These bandages might give you some relief from the fighting as the men can tell you are wounded. But if I were you, I would get out of those Amalgamate greens before someone else from the Red Guard takes a special interest in you."

"Thank you," Kilmer said, still dizzy from his head wound. "Why are you helping me?"

"This war is over; we cannot be enemies any longer," Amtor told him. "What is your name?"

Kilmer looked confused at the question. He had to answer carefully but could not remember what name to use. Was he Darius or Kilmer?

"You do have a name, don't you?"

At last, it came to him. "Kilmer."

"Well, Kilmer, I see there is a cave here behind us. Once you get out of those greens—" Amtor was interrupted suddenly as an arrow pierced his knee. He screamed in pain. Another arrow flew by his face, while another one lodged itself deep in his shoulder.

Kilmer searched the cliffs where the shots came from. There he saw archers in green and yellow bearing down, notching and aiming another round of arrows. The archers were not aiming for Kilmer, they were after Amtor.

Grimacing in pain, Amtor scrambled backward into the narrow opening of the cave. Another arrow struck deep into the ground as he pulled back his hand. Sliding across the rocks, he scooted himself deeper into the cave. Then suddenly, he disappeared into the darkness with a loud rumble.

Kilmer scrambled into the cave and saw that only a few feet back, Amtor had fallen into a deep crevasse, a hole in the cave's floor. Kilmer carefully approached the crumbling edge of the crevasse, watchful not to fall in himself. He could see the big man lying on the bottom, alive but badly hurt, about thirty feet down.

Turning from the hole, Kilmer rested against the cave wall. He was coming to his senses even more now, the wooziness fading; he was able to gain his wits about him again. The vision he had the night before was all coming true. He took a moment to cry for Kory, remembering his last moments before LaNew killed yet another person he loved.

The large man who had fallen into the hole would perish there. But then Kilmer thought again. For some inexplicable reason, Amtor saved his life just mere moments ago. If it were not for this man, Amtor, LaNew would have slashed his throat. As he pondered this, a weak voice called out from the depths of the pit.

"Help. Please help me."

He heard the agony in the voice down below calling for aid, his voice barely above a whisper. Kilmer thought even more. He knew the Amalgamates were in defeat. What was it that Amtor told him?

If I were you, I would get out of the Amalgamate greens before someone else from the Red Guard takes a special interest in you.

Kilmer looked up and the ghost was standing in the cave with him. Kilmer looked at Hollow Face.

"What should I do?"

This time, for the very first time, Hollow Face did not fill Kilmer's mind with a vision. This time, he materialized in the mortal realm, and with flesh lips under his deep hood, spoke audible words.

Stay alive. You have changed before. You can do it again. The ghost spoke in a low reverberating hum, barely discernible to his ears but understood in his mind.

Hollow Face faded away into the rain. Kilmer knew the ghost was right. With the dread LaNew unleashed on the Amalgamate survivors, to stay alive, he must change his colors. Plus, a disguise would help bring him closer to the vengeance he swore.

For Justus.

For Rosa.

For Mara.

For Kilmer the crippled beggar.

For Kory.

For all of them.

After Hollow Face vanished, Kilmer quickly struggled to take off his uniform. Once down to his undershirt, he scrambled out to the mouth of the cave, briefly pausing to look for any sign of assassins, but he saw no one.

Nearby a Red and Blue soldier lay dead on the rocks. Kilmer frantically tore the armor off the poor soul. He put his head through the breastplate, taking what he could off the corpse to complete the disguise.

Hollow Face appeared again. He pointed to Amtor's big black warhorse. The horse ignored the surrounding battle, standing motionless waiting for his master to return, as he had been trained to do.

Hollow Face pointed to Amtor's saddlebag with a spectral finger, then the ghost faded away again.

Kilmer rushed to Amtor's horse. Opening the saddlebag, he rummaged through the papers and other things. Ultimately, he found a coiled rope. After grabbing the rope, he turned and saw Kory's body in the water.

"Oh Kory," he said out loud. "I'm so sorry."

With the rope, he scrambled back behind the rocks in front of the cave. Kilmer slid on his back into the darkness. He approached the hole again ready to throw down the rope, but then he hesitated. Amtor was part of the same army as LaNew, the same force that killed his family, killed his friend Kory.

Why should I help him?

Hollow Face returned in sputters. The ghost repeated his earlier words.

Stay alive. You have changed before. You can do it again.

Kilmer wrapped the rope around his waist, then tied one end around a rock to help him steady it. The other end, he held in his hand for a moment. Kilmer heard the voice again, even more weakly this time.

"Help me, please!"

He dropped the rope in the hole from above. Then he stuck his head over the opening to look down into the crevasse. As he did this, he lost his bandages in the process, and he watched them as they floated down into the crevasse. Kilmer's eyes followed his bandage down the hole and saw Amtor lying at the bottom of it. But Amtor was not alone. Down at the bottom in the darkness was a corpse wearing a black robe, adorned with a crescent moon in a silver circle emblazoned upon the corpse's chest. Just like in his vision, the same symbol, like some priest from another time.

Amtor saw the rope dangling in front of his eyes and reacted. "Kilmer!" he shouted. "Oh, thank the Gods. Thank you."

"Grab the rope! Can you loop it around your body?"

"Yes, yes, I think so. Give me a second," Amtor called up. "Ready!" he added, once completed, giving the rope a couple of tugs.

Kilmer loosened the rope around the rock and as he pulled, he wrapped, stretched, and wrapped again. Amtor was much heavier than Kilmer, but the boy was strong.

After a tricky but gradual effort, Amtor could reach the top of the lip, and Kilmer steadied the rope around the rock with his foot, carefully helping Amtor out of the hole. Grabbing the big man by his belt, Kilmer pulled him away from the rim of the hole, to safety away from the pit. The two collapsed on top of one another.

"Oh, Kilmer! Thank you, thank you." Amtor patted Kilmer.

"You would do the same for me," Kilmer told him. "We are no longer enemies."

"We are safe now," they both said. "We are safe."

Help me, help me, help me, help me, help me
Wake up from my nightmare.

Excerpt from *The Witch's Songbook*

They know when they are being observed.
— Excerpt from *The Provenance* (Chapter Eleven)

THE DUNGEONS OF CASTLE ORLO

THE CASTLE ORLO IN THE YEAR 841 HRT
(FOUR DAYS AFTER YORI'S DISAPPEARANCE)

Kilmer turned slightly as the heavy wooden doors slowly closed behind him. He kept his sword in front to lead the way, then walked cautiously into the glow of the castle. Inside was a large entryway with two curved stairways, one to the left and one to the right, that led to the same landing above. Below the upstairs balcony, between the stairways, an archway led to a set of double doors. Dirt and grime blackened the floor but in some small patches under the filth and around the edges, he could see the fine marble of the original stone. Torchlight provided the yellow glow coming from sconces positioned evenly on the walls and landings.

He took a torch off the wall and continued ahead. Entering the darkened space just beyond the archway, he stopped to listen. Beyond the double doors he heard the remote sounds of distant bangs and drips, with the occasional rattle. None of the sounds were immediately threatening. He opened one of the double doors under the balcony. Through the darkness of the antechamber in front of him, he could see inky shapes of silhouetted candelabras, cabinets, chairs, and tables. Detecting unknown movement in the darkness, he could not precisely locate its source. The room looked too gloomy and now became too quiet. He cast the torchlight ahead of him illuminating the chamber in flickering shadows. With a sweep of the torch several passages appeared leading away from the antechamber.

A draft brought the smell of rot to his senses. The castle was old and dark, musty, and the cold air smelled of moldy, disgusting things.

Kilmer's ghost appeared.

"Which way should I go, Hollow Face? Show me where Yori is being held."

Hollow Face faced the steps and pointed down.

Kilmer moved past the ghost to look down the darkened stairs— his torch revealed a flight of worn stone steps curving down, out of view into the pitch-black below. Spiderwebs framed the corners of the walls.

As he scanned the stairway with his torch, a blue light emerged into his view, coming out of the gloom below. Rounding the corner and coming toward him, a ball of blue haze the size of a human head floated up the steps, trailing a wispy tail of vapor behind it. As he watched, the mist transformed itself into a ball of energy with the form of a human face. When the thing saw Kilmer, it opened its mouth and screamed in a bone-chilling shriek.

As if in replay, many more screams wailed in concert throughout the castle. They came from other rooms, up the stairs, through the doors, out of the cabinets, and through the ceiling. As the howling cries continued, more balls of energy appeared from everywhere, all converging on Kilmer. Hollow Face stood motionless, not reacting to the shrieking spirits.

The first and closest face screeched in anger, or agony, then rushed through him. He could do nothing to prevent this. The spirit penetrated his body, then breezed out from behind him, coming out of his back. Immediately Kilmer's stomach turned. He got dizzy and thought he might be sick as more of the translucent spirits rapidly approached. They violated him again, repeatedly and at will, inhabiting his humanity just to briefly feel the warmth of living flesh once more.

The spirits of the vengeful dead are coming to life, Hollow Face told him.

Kilmer had unintentionally awakened the dead. A feeling of anguish came with the souls entering him. He could feel their pain, the torments of a thousand priests who killed themselves in this castle. These were the remnants of their poor souls, those that found no peace in death. Their untimely and violent deaths turned them into these vengeful spirits of the dead. Now awake and materialized, they despised the living. They detested being disturbed and sought to enact their revenge. Kilmer found himself surrounded by scores of these spiraling materialized faces, floating through the room in blue spheres with streaming wispy tails, all screaming in agony.

A strong gust of wind blew and the torches flickered out one by one. Darkness descended throughout. Kilmer held his sword uselessly against the angered spirits. Some circled him before penetrating his body, others shot mercilessly directly through. He vomited on the floor. He felt weak, his power draining away, his energy ebbing out of him.

In the dark, he crouched, as the spirits streamed through the chamber, calling out, screaming, crying, still tormented from the pain of taking their own lives under the Zorn's spell. Streaming blue lights raced around the room, providing the only light Kilmer could see. They created a cacophony of noise and swirling activity as they disturbed the furniture, rattled the walls, and opened and closed doors. Heavy footfalls stomped in the darkness above him. He could hear music playing and voices singing the ancient Zornastic chant.

Your days are gone, never to return!
In Zornastic fire your soul will burn!

Finally, he heard his name being called out. Not the name he had assumed, when the Red Guard murdered his family, but his real one.

Darius Plum!

When the spirits entered him, they had penetrated his mind, as well as his body. They read his thoughts, knew his memories, understood his intentions, and now they realized who he really was. He had always been sensitive to spirits of the dead, but now, beyond his control, these vengeful spirits connected with him. Hollow Face stood in silent testament and watched the vengeful spirits do that which was necessary.

"I can't run from them," Kilmer said to his ghost. He got to his feet in the darkness, despite his sickness. The spirits had not hurt him, even though they could have. He tried to understand them now. He felt they wanted him to know their truth. He could feel the panic of the priests, the pain, the screams of the dying, and the deaths that stole their hope of living. There was nowhere to run, nowhere to hide from the massacre of the Zorn's Grand Command, of the forced suicide. Under the Zorn's spell, they did the only thing they could do—they obeyed by taking their own lives.

The vengeful spirits sent him visions and feelings from the scene a long time ago:

For hours, death reigned as the Zornastic priests cut, sliced, and poisoned themselves. They ended their own lives just as the Zorn's Grand Command ordered them to. They died in this castle on the floors, over balconies, down the stairs. Bodies of the twenty thousand priests collapsed in piles one on top of the other. They considered it a privilege to do their master's will, demonstrating their unwavering loyalty.

The visions faded. Seeing the lives of these spirits, and how they came to exist, he was not frightened of them anymore. He pitied them. All those poor souls, twenty thousand of them, loyal priests of the Zornastic Order, commanded to take their own lives by the scorn of Hazor the Zorn.

Satisfied that Kilmer now understood, Hollow Face lifted his arms with a sweeping motion, and the fellow spirits were dispelled back to where they came. The silence returned, no more screams, or shouting, or banging on the furniture. Just as fast as the spirits had manifested, they disappeared, in wispy jets of blue. The torches sparked back to life. The yellow glow returned to the chamber. And Kilmer picked up the torch he had dropped earlier.

Kilmer needed a moment to collect himself and recover. Then, he continued down the stone steps, trying to ignore the foul air, until he reached the bottom. There, he continued through a darkened corridor, wondering which of the pathways to take. Hollow Face glided along with him, without making contact with the floor. The ghost lifted his arm to the left and Kilmer knew that was the way he needed to go.

Hollow Face stood by and watched as Kilmer entered the stone archway past him.

Kilmer made his way through another dark passage, down the steps of the circular stone stairway, descending in total blackness.

He extended his torch in front of him and cautiously followed the cobwebbed way down.

Along the way, he encountered skeletal remains of long-dead Zornastic priests. Corpses adorned in black robes still grasping the daggers that plunged into their former bodies with skeletal fingers. The symbol of the crescent moon inside a silver circle was emblazoned upon their adornments. He had seen this type of black tunic and silver circle before, at the bottom of the pit where Amtor fell during the Battle of Mauveguard Pass. Here there were many of them. He continued downward until he reached the landing below. Sounds of dripping, and the occasional ring of metal chain sounded lightly. Black moldy grease and bloodied dirt covered everything here. The smell was that of concentrated and rotten death.

A long hallway led from the stairs. Kilmer lifted the torch higher. Three more skeletons came into view, long-dead priests, piled together in the hall. The torch revealed more corridors that led to dungeon cells.

"Yori?" Kilmer called out. "Yori!"

Kilmer heard a soft noise, the slight rattle of chain. It came from up ahead on the right. He pressed on, continuing to call for Yori. He listened for any reply and followed what appeared to be moaning.

Elsewhere in the castle, the Zorn was in the highest part of the tower when Langula and Monticello reached him. The Zorn was looking out of the tower at the star brightening the night. Langula reached the top of the stairs, and the Zorn hardly noticed her.

"Her star has come!" Langula said.

"You think I can't see that?" the Zorn said. "Of course, I have seen her star. Everybody in the world can see it."

"What do you want to do?"

"Kill every newborn baby living in the world today," the Zorn said with a fire in his yellow eyes. "But that is a bit too impractical, isn't it?"

The Zorn turned to face Langula. His skeletal face reflected the light of the new star. "I have allowed Leopold's Captain into the castle. He is searching for the king's archer. I cannot allow him to leave here alive."

"What of the others in the search party?" she asked. "Are they still in the Sanguine Forest?"

"No, I have played with them long enough. I confounded them, separated them, and finally attacked them."

"Attacked them how?"

"With a horde of flies," the Zorn said with an exhale, indicating his boredom. "But then I let them go. It makes no difference. They are doomed anyway."

"Monticello and I seduced the large one with the scarred face."

"I thought he'd be the one you'd pick," the Zorn said. "Scarred flesh fascinates you."

"I collected his essence; I will use it to fertilize others."

"You do that. I'll deal with our guest downstairs."

The Zorn pushed past her, disappearing into the darkness of the tower. Langula and Monticello were left staring up at the star and all that it meant.

Kilmer turned the corner into one of the cells, following the soft moans. Upon entering and lifting his torch, he saw a man, naked, bruised and bloodied, chained to the wall in a standing position. The man had been beaten severely and looked to be barely alive.

He was chained by his wrists at a height that would not allow him to do anything else but stand. If his legs got tired, he would have to support his weight from his wrists. The steel constraints around his wrists were kept slightly loose, so they would slide and scrape across the bone of his arms, which were now skinned and bleeding. Each time he shifted his weight, they dug in more, causing him extra pain.

Beneath the prisoner, a square notch had been cut into the stone floor. Inside the square notch sat an enormous gray egg lined with purple veins, sitting in dark fluid. The fluid looked to be blood dripping from the prisoner into the notch below.

Kilmer rushed to the prisoner and examined him. He had met Yori before and knew what he looked like. However, this man had been beaten so badly he was an unrecognizable pulp. Kilmer had to examine the ring finger like he previously did with Isse. There was no ring, but Kilmer detected a pale band of skin where a ring might have been, if worn for some time. Kilmer removed his waterskin and gave the prisoner a drink of water. But in his condition, a short sip was all the man could swallow.

"Slow, go slow. Don't drink too much. My name is Kilmer. What is your name? Who are you?"

"Kilmer?" the man said. "I know you."

"What is your name? Can you tell me your name?"

"Y-Yori!" the man shouted. "I am Yori, First Archer of the king."

Kilmer had found Yori! He gave him another sip of water. He flashed his torch around the room. There was a small table with a wooden box on it. Looking into the box it only had oddly shaped metal tools in it. But beside it, Kilmer found a key on a brass ring. Kilmer grabbed the key and turned to set Yori free.

But unexpectedly, the key launched out of his hands, skidded across the floor, and splashed into the black fluid of the square notch holding the strange egg. At the same time, his sword also dropped on the floor with a loud clang. His body trembled, the joints in his arms and legs stiffening. His muscular coordination failed, and his movements slowed to a crawl. Then, he became paralyzed and could move no more.

That was when the Skeletal King appeared. He stood by the cell's archway without contact to the floor, then drifted into the chamber with fading skin stretched tight across his face like a cadaver. His eye sockets were large and hollow, containing the yellow orbs that formed his small circular eyes.

Kilmer could not move except his eyes in their sockets. Yori screamed in fear, avoiding the Zorn's gaze, and began to cry.

"Thank you for accepting my invitation to Castle Orlo," the Zorn said to Kilmer. "I so seldom have guests these days." The Zorn moved across the cell. "You will have to excuse me for being a rude host and not attending to you sooner, but something came up."

He spoke as he maneuvered himself in front of Kilmer's eyes. His gaze generated fear in the hearts of men. Kilmer could not breathe while looking upon the face of the scorned one, Hazor the Zorn.

"Now, let's see what we have here." The Zorn placed his cold bony fingers alongside Kilmer's temples. There was nothing that Kilmer could hide from him now, as the Zorn scanned the memories of his mind.

"Oh, I see you are full of deception, I like that. And fear of being revealed for your true self. You are so full of anger and vengeance. You lost somebody close to you, at the Battle of Mauveguard Pass, a friend. Well, all of you mortals lost someone at Mauveguard Pass; that much is not uncommon. But wait, what is this I see? Now, here is something interesting. By the Gods! You saved Amtor's life? My, you are special. You helped him out of a deep cave, and… wait, what's this?"

Suddenly, the Zorn startled. "At the bottom of the pit, you saw my symbol. The symbol of the Zornastic order? Could it be? Is this just coincidence or are you something truly special?"

The Zorn floated over to Yori and pushed two bony fingers inside his wounds. Yori screamed in pain. The Zorn pulled his fingers out with an excessive amount of blood on them to use as paint. He plied the blood to draw a crescent moon inside a circle on the dirty stone wall.

Then he pointed to what he just painted. "This is my symbol of the Zornastic Order. You have seen this symbol before, yes? The dead priest at the bottom of the pit, yes? You saw this symbol. He was my missing priest. He had something of mine in his possession. Something very important to me and I want it back. Do you know of what I speak? Do you know what I lost? Speak!"

Kilmer could not speak.

A little shamefully the Zorn realized. "Oh sorry!" he said, waving his hand and releasing Kilmer from his paralysis. Kilmer dropped to the floor.

"I don't know what you are talking about," Kilmer said, crawling away.

"Where is it?" the Zorn shouted, getting nearer.

Kilmer's silence incensed the Zorn.

"*All this time I've waited for a sign*! And on the same day, I have seen both Ehlona's star and a sign of Soothsayer! My magic dagger! *On the very same day!*" the Zorn screamed at them at the top of his lungs. "This cannot simply be a coincidence. This is an act of the *Gods!*"

The Zorn composed himself and took a deep breath.

"Why are they always trying to confuse me?" the Zorn said. He rubbed his face with his hand. "The Gods are always trying to confound me."

"I've come for the king's archer only. Let us go," Kilmer said. "Let me take the archer home."

"Hardly. I'm not done with him yet, and I haven't even started on you."

The Zorn cast another spell. From his fingers a wave of energy enveloped Kilmer. Just a simple spell really, but the ball of energy that hit Kilmer knocked him out like a stone. The magic rocked his head back and he fell unconscious upon the cold stone floor with a thump like a bag of coal.

The chamber went dark.

Everything turned black.

ACT III

Of Feasts

& Stars

No more time spent thinking about my younger days
I got a bad chill creeping down my back and through my legs.

Excerpt from *The Witch's Songbook*

She looked away in disgust and never looked back at the child.
— Excerpt from *The Provenance* (Chapter Twelve)

PIT OF DEATH

ON THE BATTLEFIELDS OF THE
MID-RUN VALLEY IN THE YEAR 837 HRT
(FIVE YEARS EARLIER, BEFORE YORI'S DISAPPEARANCE)

Pierced by two arrows, one deep in the shoulder and another to the knee, Amtor pushed himself farther back against the walls of the cave, attempting to be a smaller target for the assassins outside. With an unexpected loud crumbling roar, the rocky floor below him broke apart and collapsed under his weight. Frantically he grasped for anything to stop his slide into the steep-tilted descent of the pit. Finding no purchase, the hole swallowed him up and he disappeared, leaving a dusty, rubble-filled cloud behind. Slipping over the edge, he fell through the vast opening in the darkness, with the rocks and rubble.

Kilmer did not see what happened, but when he looked up, he was all alone in the cave. He heard the rumble of the dislodged stones but missed seeing Amtor fall. He was too busy holding the bandages as a pressure dressing to the wound on top of his bloody head. Hearing the crashing rocks now, he blinked and wondered where the big man went. Seeing he was now alone, he tried to remember if he had always been alone, or if someone had been in the cave with him just a moment ago; he really could not be sure about anything. After being struck hard in the head, Kilmer was suffering from delusions and had been seeing phantoms. Some were imaginary, some were not. But the cloud of dust in the air indicated that something had just happened, for real.

In the dark pit, Amtor fell for a full three seconds. He fell for so long his body rotated in the opposite direction. He struck the bottom hard in a violent splintering of shattered bones. His leg, ribs, wrist, and arm all broke in multiple places. Both of the arrows, in the shoulder and knee, snapped off, leaving just the iron tips remaining deep in his body. He winced in agony and would have screamed in pain if not for the fall forcing all the wind out of him.

Back on top, Kilmer looked into the brightness outside the cave. He saw Amtor's assassins dressed in their green-and-yellow uniforms, indicating they were all part of the Army of the Amalgamated Villages of the Mid-Run Valley. They came out from their concealments and moved through the rocks, holding their bows and quivers. As they moved across the pass, they ignored him because they could tell from his uniform they were on the same side. Kilmer turned away from them and considered the large hole in front of him. He leaned forward to look over its edge.

Not only did the fall knock the wind out of Amtor, but it forced all the remaining rotten air, those built-up gases, out of the hollow cavities of the decayed corpse he landed on. The bottom of the pit lay thirty feet straight down from the edge of the lip. The fall could have easily killed a man as big as Amtor, if not for the dead body that was already there that cushioned his fall. Giving way under his impact, Amtor crushed the corpse flat.

Outside the cave, the battle of Mauveguard Pass raged. Every second that passed, men—some of them his men—were still suffering and dying very violent deaths. Yet, before the fall, the day had been in favor of the Red and Blue, indicating a probable end to the war—the war of the Mid-Run Valley. And here he lay at the bottom of a hole.

In the darkness of the deep pit, Amtor had to remain conscious to stay alive, but he was losing slices of time. The pain washed over him in waves causing him to black out. Never knowing if the next wave of pain might be his last, he struggled to concentrate, forcing himself to take whatever actions he could to improve his dire situation, as well as keep his mind alert and occupied.

He fumbled with his right hand, one of the only parts of his body still operating, for the tinderbox he kept in his uniform. Retrieving it and spilling out its contents, he worked the flint one-handed to create a spark. He had worked this flint a thousand times before but never had it been so difficult as this, under these conditions. Fortunately, his familiarity with the device gave him the confidence and dexterity needed. Soon he had a flame and applied it to the small broken candle's wick. A warm orange glow lit his darkness.

Immediately, the ivory skull of the corpse gaped back at him. The sudden collision that pushed out the remaining gases forced the jawbone open in a lingering forever scream. One eye hole was dark and empty, but the other still had a waxy milky eye in it. The dead eye blankly stared at Amtor and seemed to speak to him.

You will soon be like me! You will soon be with us!

Amtor's head fell forward as another wave of pain hit him. His forehead came to rest on the dead man's face, crumbling the dry, dead flesh of the corpse's nose. Then he passed out momentarily.

Amtor was a large man, with a solid muscular frame, until the assassins' arrows and the impact of the fall broke him down. As His Majesty's Minister of War for the Army of the Red and Blue, he was the most powerful man in all the Kingdom of Odessa, second only to King Leopold himself, a position with immense power, yet down here lying at the bottom of the pit unconscious, he and the long-dead corpse seemed to be equals.

In his painful slumber a vision appeared to him. He saw a vivid red sky framed by two mountain peaks. The colors of the sky indicated that change, a transition, was happening, whether it was dawn or dusk did not seem to matter. The dream gave way to a misty fog where the red light shone through it in dusty beams. Amtor detected motion in the center of the light. He felt as if he were not alone, someone was with him, even down here in the bottom of the pit. The shape transformed into the image of a woman, a beautiful woman, with long blond hair falling in curls past her fair shoulders. Dressed in a flowing white dress, she held a lyre and stepped through the mountains, walking toward Amtor in his dream. Coming closer to him in jerky intervals, as Amtor fought against unconsciousness, she leaned close to his face. She was so close to him now that he could see her tender blue eyes. Through her ruby lips the vision spoke to him.

Do not fear, Amtor, the Goddess Ehlona will protect you.

He opened his eyes, and the beautiful face was replaced with the decayed skull of the screaming dead man he landed on. Yet through the rot of the corpse, he thought he could smell the faint odor of something sweet, something like… sandalwood.

The light of the broken candle still glowed, revealing the reality of his situation. The dream was pleasant but upon waking, waves of pain shot through him again, reminding him of the urgency to find a way out.

He searched the bottom of the pit. There was no immediate way out, no other tunnels or crevasses, just the sheer walls and rocky bottom. He lay among the dislodged rocks and the dead body.

He searched himself, anxious to pinpoint the source of his pain and to stop whatever bleeding he could. He had puncture wounds in his shoulder and knee from the broken arrows. His left arm was broken and twisted into an unnatural position. Just seeing the damage made his head swoon and he felt like passing out again. Instead, he cried out in pain.

"Help," his voice crackled. He coughed out some blood. "Help me!"

He considered the corpse next, hoping to find something, anything, that could be useful. The body was draped in a black garment. A torn and stained emblem, a silver circle with a crescent moon sewed onto it, was emblazoned upon its chest. This corpse looked to be a member of some sort of ancient sect or priesthood. Amtor ran his only good remaining hand along the corpse to search him. At the same time his hand felt cold steel, the light of his candle glinted gold upon the walls. Amtor pulled a knife out of the corpse's belt. This dagger appeared to be fashioned from solid gold, and its reflection in the dim light lit Amtor's face.

Suddenly the rotten hand of the dead priest clutched his wrist, reluctant to give up the dagger. Amtor looked at the bony hand with its shreds of torn flesh that gripped him upon his wrist. The corpse quickly sprang up, its moldering face coming close to Amtor's.

Your days are gone, never to return!

In Zornastic fire your soul will burn!

But then, Amtor opened his eyes again, realizing that another wave of pain made him pass out momentarily. The corpse still lay in death. Amtor's hand was free, still gripping the golden dagger, bringing it closer to his weary eyes. He knew the value of such an artifact, and to him, it appeared priceless and invaluable, but worthless at this moment. He let out another grimace through his pain, his own survival being foremost in his mind. He could not hold on to it and let it drop in front of him.

He managed another shout. "Help! Help me, please!"

Shouting sent pangs of pain like lightning through his torso; from the blood in his mouth, he knew his ribs were broken too. He lay his head upon the weathered silver circle on top of the corpse and closed his eyes.

The corpse sat up, more slowly this time, and kindly spoke to him now.

You are never going to get out of this pit, you know. You and I will become one. We will be together for all eternity.

"Tell me, corpse," Amtor asked, "did we win? Up above out there. Was our side victorious?"

You lost as all the others have.

"Am I dead?"

Yes, you are dead, like all the others. You just don't realize it yet.

"You lie, ghost. I don't believe you."

Then you lie to yourself, Amtor. There is no way out of here, out of this pit of death.

"No, I will get out of this."

Why bother fighting it? Come, rest, join me in death.

"I am not like you. I will not sleep in death tonight."

Such a pity.

Amtor woke again, a rope dangling in front of his face.

Unsure if he was still dreaming, he rolled onto his side to look up at the top of the pit. There, he saw a face looking down at him, a man with a bandaged head. The bandage suddenly fell off and floated down to him. Amtor could see the curly red hair.

"Kilmer! Thank the Gods! Kilmer!" It was the Amalgamate boy he had pulled away from certain death just moments ago. Saved from the sadistic blood rage of LaNew, the murderous captain of the Red Guard.

"Can you wrap the rope around you?"

"I think I can. Wait!" Amtor picked up the golden dagger and put it inside his uniform. Then, he gave the rope a couple quick tugs after wrapping it around his waist. "Ready now!"

As Kilmer heaved Amtor against the rope, the big man looked down. He had left the broken candle burning on the ledge below in the pit. He saw the black-adorned corpse sitting up watching him leave. As Amtor moved higher up the wall in jerking intervals, the dead man casually lay back down and got himself settled into a still position, as if he were going to sleep, in the disposition Amtor found him. There, he would remain for all eternity.

Turning his gaze upward, Amtor watched the opening of the pit come closer. Leaving the dim light of his candle farther below, the open air and the daylight streamed in brilliant beams from the opening above. There, the Goddess Ehlona appeared to him again, arms outstretched, smiling reassuringly.

Welcome back to the land of the living, she said to Amtor. She was the most beautiful image he had ever seen. But the closer he got to daylight the farther and dimmer she became.

At last, Kilmer latched on to Amtor's wrists and managed to pull the big man to shoulder level on the rim. The vision of the Goddess faded completely now from Amtor. Coming out of the darkness, he blinked the hallucinations away, his focus squarely on his own rescue, desperately attempting with all his remaining strength to come out of the hole. Kilmer pulled Amtor's waist out, and Amtor managed to swing his only remaining functional leg over the drop.

With a final pull from Kilmer, the two fell on top of each other. Once free from the pit of death, Amtor and Kilmer deliriously laughed, thanking each other and telling the other they were safe now.

The next thing Amtor remembered was opening his eyes outside the cave. Kilmer had dragged him out of the mouth of the cave and laid him down on a patch of soft grass. Amtor saw that a wagonful of the wounded had ridden up and stopped by him and Kilmer, who set resting, nursing his own head wound.

"Is that Amtor?" a man with his arm in a sling stood up in the wagon and asked. The rest of the wagon reacted despite their wounds.

"This man"—Amtor pointed to Kilmer—"this man saved my life. He is a hero."

By now, Kilmer had shed the green and yellow of the Army of the Amalgamates. He was now wearing the uniform of King Leopold's Red and Blue. Kilmer, ever the chameleon, a changeling, whenever necessary to save his life. It was an action suggested to him, before Amtor's fall into the deep pit by his ghost. Now, Amtor was hailing him as a hero to the crown for saving the life of Leopold's Minister of War.

All in the wagon hailed Kilmer as the hero he was. Then, Amtor's eyes rolled back in his head as another wave of pain caused him to black out.

When Amtor opened his eyes again, the Goddess Ehlona stood over him, smiling with a reassurance that nothing could possibly hurt him anymore. His pain did, in fact, seem to be gone, replaced by hallucinations of the Goddess of Beauty.

I have a plan for you, the Goddess told him with a whisper inside his mind.

Despite the seriousness of his wounds, he had never felt so alive with a feeling of love. Then, the face of the Goddess faded away into a human face, a real one, but this face was just as beautiful and full of love. She hovered over him and touched him with healing powers.

"There, there, Amtor, you've been through a lot, but you are safe now. I will take care of you with the love of Goddess Ehlona."

"Who are you?" Amtor asked with a coarse throat. With foggy eyes, he continued gazing into her face, so beautiful and unforgettable, waiting for her reply.

"I am Gilglad, a healer from the Temple of Valor, and you have been cast in the spell of my love. Now rest your head back and relax."

Her hands emitted electric green energy—healing magic—brought about by her all-encompassing love and empathy for him. Her power relieved him, and his pain dissipated in distant waves. She slowly, but deliberately, inserted two fingers in the slash made by the arrowhead lodged in his shoulder, but Amtor barely noticed. Her fingers worked deeper inside him causing a displacement of blood inside the wound to overflow, as she searched for the tip of the arrow. Absorbing his spilling blood with a fresh linen, she wiped him clean along the way.

But Amtor could only consider Gilglad's beauty, touching her long brown hair with his free hand. Distracted with the job of retrieving the arrowhead, she hardly took notice. But then, she gave him a quick look in his eyes, a warm gentle smile, as if she really did not mind his touch. She was a beautiful woman with bright green eyes. Gilglad and all the other healers were dressed in black and red, supposedly to mask the blood smeared on their clothes, and this indicated to opposing forces that they were not combatants—not life takers but life sustainers.

The war was over. There was no more fighting, no more killing. Both the Amalgamates and the Red and Blue were either already dead, dying, or helping each other live. Amtor had eyes for nothing except Gilglad.

"Please don't leave me, Gilglad," he told her.

"I won't leave you," she replied.

"Stay with me."

"I'll stay here with you, my love." Gilglad pulled the sticky arrowhead out of the gaping wound in his shoulder with two fingers. It came out with a sickly sucking sound, reminding Amtor of the time he stepped on a fat toad under his heavy boot. Gilglad quickly hid the arrowhead, wrapping it in a bloody linen, to keep him from seeing it. Despite the pain, Amtor felt suddenly relieved to have the thing free from his body. The painful pressure was gone, and now only the pain remained.

"Will you kiss me?" he asked her.

Gilglad gave him a glance, wiped his blood from her hand, then stroked his deep chiseled, heavily bearded face. Her green eyes came close to his now. Without a word she slowly leaned forward and pressed her lips upon his. Delicately moving in their magic, a pure emotive electricity sparked between her lips and entered his body.

"If I never live another day, I have kissed an angel," he told her.

She rose slowly from him with a knowing smile. Then ran her fingertips across his wide chest, lower to his waist, down further still inside his thigh, eventually settling in the place where the wound in his knee needed her immediate attention.

"By the Gods!" exclaimed Amtor.

Another crackle of green energy came from her touch and suddenly the pain in his knee was merely a dim memory.

"I am going to make you better," Gilglad told him, as she penetrated her fingers into him once again, overflowing another wound in order to retrieve the broken arrowhead. "But for now, you should sleep."

With her left hand she reached up and touched his forehead. A wave of emerald force dimmed his view and sent him off dreaming again.

By the gods, he whispered again from the depths of his slumber.

Dangerous woman put your arms around me

Love will be your master

Testing all the best of me.

———◆◆◆———

Excerpt from *The Witch's Songbook*

If the Cosmic Creation is involved,
it will end in a most amazing resolution.
— Excerpt from *The Provenance* (Chapter Thirteen)

DEMONIC EGGS

The Castle Orlo in the Year 841 HRT
(Day One of Kilmer's Captivity in Castle Orlo)

Kilmer awoke and found himself chained to the same wall as Yori. Iron chains constricted his wrists. He had been stripped of all his clothes and his weapons were taken. Yori was unconscious but still alive. Kilmer could take some solace knowing that he was successful in finding the king's archer and found him alive; at least that part of this mission was complete. But his rescue was not going well at all. There could be no worse place to be than this.

Opening his eyes, he scanned his surroundings around the small cell. In their current predicament, the cell seemed larger than it really was. A drain, no doubt to allow the drainage of blood, guts, and whatever comes out of a person being tortured, was in the middle of the floor. A table stood by the far wall, with a wooden box on it. Kilmer already knew what was in it—torture devices and tools for causing pain. He wanted no part of that box. A single torch burning in a sconce, through the archway and out in the hallway, made the dark shadows dance.

He looked over at Yori and saw blood, black and oozing, coming out of his mouth. Kilmer observed his blood flowed into the square notch cut below him in the floor. The notch held a large oval object that looked like a dirty egg, marbled with purple veins. The egg sat in a puddle of bloody black ooze that dripped from Yori's body. He was incubating the egg.

A similar square notch below Kilmer was empty. He started to pull against his chains, but they secured him solid. If he were able to pull on them for a thousand years, he could never break loose.

Since paralyzing him, the Zorn was nowhere to be seen. The Skeletal King could take his time, tormenting them at his leisure. But thankfully, according to his outburst, something else had happened. He said he had other matters to attend to. Something about Ehlona's star and a sign of Soothsayer, but Kilmer had no idea what he meant.

Hollow Face appeared in front of him.

"Hollow Face," Kilmer said. "I have really done it this time, my friend. I fear I've doomed us both. I'm afraid it will get worse before it gets any better. I'm so thirsty."

Hollow Face floated closer. At length, the spirit reached out, showing him a vision, not of what would happen, but an image of an ancient scene.

Kilmer's head hummed in the familiar way and his sight became dim, as he received the vision the ghost projected upon him.

It started bright and beautiful, from an age not long remembered. A time, when the muscle-bound redheaded God Heironomus stood in an empty field of luscious tall grass alongside a long bend in a distant river.

"Oh, something pleasant," Kilmer told the spirit. "Thank you for showing me something pleasant, Hollow Face." But Hollow Face slowly shook his head. No, he indicated there was something more to this vision, something he was missing, something more than what

Kilmer had yet seen. Kilmer relaxed his mind, watching with heightened interest as the vision continued.

Heironomus turned and a human being came into his presence, a dark-haired man with a long, flowing mustache extending nearly a foot on either side of his face. The man dropped to his knees and spoke to Heironomus.

"Oh, great one, praise to you. I am Your Majesty's humble servant."

Heironomus stopped long enough to give this man some attention.

"I do believe I recognize you. Yes, you are Fortis Plum. What do you desire with me, man?" Heironomus asked, marveling at his boldness.

"Oh, great Heironomus, I ask your blessing."

"Of course, long life to you, Fortis; go with my blessing." Heironomus turned to go.

"Wait! Oh, great Heironomus, please hear me."

Heironomus, a little impatiently, turned to face him once again. "You know it is a sin to waste the time of a God. Especially the God of Light, Fortis."

"Oh yes, forgive me, great Heironomus, and thank you. Thank you for your blessing of long life. However, my prayers go unanswered. The blessing I request was for this land—this very piece of ground under our feet, here, by the great bend of the river's waters. Please give me your leave to settle my namesake in this land by the river, and I will create a village for future generations of Plums. One that I can establish to forever worship and serve you. Oh great Heironomus."

"Forever worship and serve me?" Heironomus considered him for a moment. "You know you are very bold, Fortis. Never before have I been asked for such a blessing by mortal man. Nor ever before have I given a blessing such as you ask."

"Forgive my boldness." He bowed low.

"Yet I admire you for it. The boldness of your spirit favors you. Even as tedious as I may find it now. I have foreseen the future of your family Plum, and the consequences in bestowing on you what you seek. I see prophecy unfolding in it. You and your generations that follow may yet serve a pledge to me. I will grant you what you desire, but it comes at a price. A cost that will affect not just you, but all your future generations to come. A steep price to pay for all the unborn Plums to bear for what you ask of me now."

"Only as you will, Your Grace. I pledge forever to your service."

"Are you quite certain, Fortis? A pledge to my service forever is what you desire?"

"I will pledge all future generations of the Plum name."

"Then pledge that you will ask me for nothing more and admonish my enemies as your enemies. And I will grant you what you desire."

"I am your servant, oh great Heironomus. I pledge service to you as you have said. I will burden you no more, and your enemies will be my enemies, throughout all generations of my family. Forever."

"I see. Very well then, Fortis Plum, having your pledge so stated, I bless you with more than I have ever blessed any other mortal. Your boldness has a future part yet to play, a prophesy to fulfill, aligning your destiny with my own. To keep your pledge, I grant you with extended life. Even after you outlive your physical body, your spirit will continue to live on through generations of time, to oversee the future of your family. To mark this pledge in their flesh, they will have the stamp of my likeness upon them; every surviving male child will have the curls of my amber hair. This shall be the mark of our pledge upon them, so they will know of what you have done this day. I grant you this land, Fortis, and the waters of the bending river to be yours, to be forever known as you name them." Heironomus put his thick hands upon Fortis's shoulders and a blue energy enveloped him in a bolt of sulfuric crackling. "Now rise, Fortis Plum, stand, as my faithful servant."

"I am humbled, great one," Fortis said. He breathlessly stood, with tears in his eyes and his hand over his heart, glowing outwardly from the magic freshly cast upon him. A change had occurred. Deep inside he felt it. "Thank you, my God, I thank you."

"Tell me, what will you name this land, Fortis?"

"In honor of the future generations that must bear this burden, and for all future generations, I simply call this place the village of Plum."

"And the waters?" Heironomus asked.

"One and the same," Fortis said. "Plum will be its name, and it will flow for a thousand years through the village."

"A village and a river, both named after the Plums," Heironomus laughed. "Well enough! A blessing to you and all your future generations." Heironomus turned and went his way. Fortis did nothing to attempt another word to him, according to the conditions of the pledge. He stood alone on the ground now his, the land of his desire, marked with the power of his name.

The images faded away in blurry waves inside Kilmer's mind, and then, the vision was gone. His thoughts cleared and the glow of the dancing shadows in the torchlit dungeon returned.

"You are the living spirit of my ancestor, Fortis Plum?" he asked Hollow Face.

"*Beware*," the ghost spoke again in a human voice, pointing to the archway of the cell. "*The demon, she comes.*"

Just as the ghost faded from view, Langula slithered into Kilmer's cell on her serpent's tail. She stopped in the cell and giggled over the two men hanging naked in chains, gently biting her finger. Her eyes scanned them up and down, and she laughed to herself.

"It's always so exciting to have fresh men in my life," she said. Slithering up to Yori, with a long blue finger, she lifted his head. Her tail caressed around him, smearing blood across his chest. Seeing the blood on her tail, she gave Kilmer a glance and licked herself clean of it. She smiled at him, savoring the taste.

"A woman gets lonely. I've gotten accustomed to the archer's taste. But I have been craving something new, something fresh."

She slid over to Kilmer, and he tried to avoid her gaze.

"Oh, I like that."

She backed away from Kilmer and stood in front of the square notch under Yori. She plunged her hand deep into the filth, into the black ooze, up to her elbow. Cradling her egg, she carefully pulled it out of the slime. She delicately caressed it and held it close to her breast, as she spoke.

"Our new creation, born only for one purpose: to grow into the greatest plague upon humanity. More than all the priests of the Zornastic Order combined. Monticello was beautiful, but this one will be mine, created in the image of my wickedness."

Kilmer shivered at the thought. She carefully sank the egg back into the black fluid, returning it to incubate in the blood. When she submerged the egg, the black water rose in the notch. She carefully rotated the egg inside its nesting place. Kilmer could not help but watch. He saw the egg responding to her touch, changing color from purple to blue, and he could see something resembling a serpent slithering against the walls inside.

"It is almost ready," she said. "The essence of the big man with the scarred face will help it come along sooner."

Big man with the scarred face?

Kilmer looked startled. "Laws? What did you do to him?"

"I did nothing he did not enjoy," Langula said. "Thoroughly."

"Where is he?"

"Why would you think I care? I got what I wanted."

"Is he still alive?"

"I did not have the time to kill him, if that is what you mean. If he does still live, that poor man. Can you imagine what he must be going through?"

Langula coiled herself with her tail around the notch, her egg, and even Yori himself. Then upon the paler underside of her softer scales, a pore opened, and liquid spewed out. A milky essence gushed out of her and onto the egg. After the deposit, her tail uncoiled around the egg and Yori, and allowed his stream of blood to continue down into the notch, adding to the black fluid fertilizing it.

Kilmer once again tried to look away but could not help watching what Langula did next. The demon contorted herself into another tightly wound coil, this time in front of him. Her lower half covered her human upper half as she settled into a tight circle. Her eyes peered through an opening in the loops between her serpent coils. Her silver eyes sparkled at him, as her body heaved and convulsed in pulsating rhythms. At length, Kilmer watched in horror. Heaving repeatedly an opening widened inside her to form a large white almond shape, like that of an eye. But it was not an eye, it was another egg coming out of her. She pushed the egg, a new one, a fresh one, out. She heaved and pulsated until the slippery egg was almost free. Then, her two blue arms reached carefully through her coils and she delicately secured the egg in her clawed hands as it finally slipped free from her. The opening from where the egg came closed immediately in a reflexive tightening.

She uncoiled herself. The effort left her weak. A look of weary delight lit her face as she held a new demonic egg. She carefully placed the egg into the empty square receptacle below Kilmer's feet. After resting it there, she backed away, keeping an eye on her new creation with the pride of a new parent. Slowly she looked up at Kilmer.

"Now it is your turn to contribute," she said, slithering closer. "You can't play hard to get anymore."

She approached quickly and gave him a deep kiss. He could not resist. Their bodies pressed together, and he could smell her. She smelled of musky acacia wood; it smelled foreign, exotic, but not unpleasant. Her scent, an illusion that appealed to men, could change depending on what stimulated her victim's pheromones the most.

Kilmer knew it was wrong, but she beguiled him beyond his ability to resist. He became lost in a wilderness of a forbidden private desire. Langula used her demonic instincts, she knew the hearts and desires of men. She knew what they desired and gave it to them in order to take whatever she wanted. She had the magic to be any man's darkest fantasy. Kilmer kept telling himself it was wrong. It was wrong, but he was trapped in Langula's seduction spell.

She laughed when she felt him convulse and he trembled in aftershocks of ecstasy. Backing away now with what she wanted, she gave him no more. All Kilmer wanted was her, to have her continue. But the farther she moved away, the more her spell wore off, until the fantasy left him completely, leaving his mind in torment to return to the stinking reality of the dungeon and the shame of what he had just done.

She tended to her new egg, applying his newly gained essence to it. The egg reacted to her touch and turned shades of red and violet.

"Now we'll need some of your blood," she told him. Her silver eyes flashed in a demonic stare, cold and menacing. She fell upon Kilmer as quick as a cobra and slashed his stomach with four sharp claws. Ruthlessly cut open with deep slashes in his gut, Kilmer grimaced in pain. It happened so fast he neither had time to bleed nor to feel the pain immediately. But upon looking at his wounds for a moment, he could see the deep slashes across his stomach were clean.

A moment later, upon his next breath, the pain hit at the same time the blood gushed out of the four slits in his flesh.

The blood spilled out of him, down his body, splattering the new egg, collecting in the square notch, pooling around it.

Yori, who had been unconscious until now, started to revive. He woke briefly and spoke weakly.

"Oh no. Not you too, Kilmer," Yori said.

The demon laughed, feeding off the collective fear of both men. But still, she was woozy from the labor of pushing out another egg, and she turned to go. She left them hanging on the walls of the cell. But before she left, she gave them one more indignity. She extinguished the torch in the hallway, bathing them in utter darkness.

She slithered down the corridor, away from their cells. Out of their view, she couldn't help stopping and listening momentarily.

At length, she heard Kilmer scream. That was what she waited to hear. Langula smiled, then disappeared up the stairs.

It's so good to be with you again

Having you so close to me again

Holding you in my arms so near

And not to fear the things we feel.

Excerpt from *The Witch's Songbook*

Just seeing her from a distance, they would run for their lives.
— Excerpt from *The Provenance* (Chapter Fourteen)

GILGLAD'S HEALING LOVE MAGIC

THE VILLAGE OF HOMESTEAD IN THE YEAR 841 HRT
(MONTHS BEFORE THE BIRTH)

The golden dagger stayed with Amtor but haunted his nights. A series of weird visions conflicted his dreams. Visions of the Goddess Ehlona intermingled with strange swirling yellow eyes, silver-eyed demons, black raven-like priests, and bright glowing priests with shaved heads and banded red topknots. It was like a war going on inside his head.

Gilglad had made a series of horizontal cuts in Amtor's broken arm that she intermittently inserted fingers into to repair and straighten the bone. Inch by inch, day by day, she worked her way down the breaks, fusing the bone together with the healing energy of her touch. Gliding her fingers inside the grooves of skin, she reached deeply inside the tissue until she touched the splintered bone, then emitted a crackle of emerald energy that flashed under his flesh and that part of the bone was set. Amtor only felt some pressure from her touch but no pain.

All the while Gilglad whispered to him, "Our love with the Goddess Ehlona will make you whole again."

Amtor was in a state of euphoria, despite his wounds, as Gilglad brushed against him, always in contact. He could smell the clean fragrance of honeysuckle in her long brown hair, the warmness and softness of her skin.

"I have never felt this way," Amtor told her. "I have never loved anybody else, as I have love for you."

"Shh, my darling, just breathe." Gilglad slowly slid her fingers out of the incision in his arm, then poured clean water on her hands. She washed them delicately, then dried them on a fresh warm white linen cloth that had been heated by the sun. Amtor watched her, fighting the urge to touch her, aching from his pounding heart. With her instincts, she clearly understood his desire and only wished to love him, relieve him, to release him from any and all of his sufferings. Carefully avoiding his injuries, she knew just where to lay her body upon his that would maximize their pleasure and comfort without hurting him. Her head lay in the small of his neck as she lightly felt his heart beating. She laid soft kisses upon him there and she felt him tighten a strong arm around her delicate shoulder. Her hand ran down his body, knowing exactly where the broken painful parts were and avoiding them. Much to Amtor's surprise there was plenty of him that still worked and could be capable of feeling pleasure with her touch.

"This is good for you," she whispered, as her touch aroused him. "Our love will heal you."

Night after night, day after day, Gilglad nursed Amtor's wounds. His left arm was the most damaged and needed the most work. He had two ribs broken too, crushed in the fall into the pit of death. His right leg and ankle had twisted and snapped, which needed straightening and fusing together. But the deepest wounds were where the two arrows penetrated his shoulder and knee; these extended to the very limits of Gilglad's small fingers, and she repaired them as well as she could. They both knew that only time could heal them the rest of the way, if they ever fully healed at all.

The change in Amtor surprised him. He had been a man of war his whole life. From his early upbringing in the streets of Hammerville, an orphaned son of a prostitute, he did whatever he could to hustle and fight to scratch out his humanity. The Gods blessed him with an enormous body, a hulking and muscular frame. He was always the biggest, the largest, the fiercest fighter of all, bested only by one man: the tall skinny boy who would later become King Leopold. But now, a foreign feeling beset him on all sides, like the siege works of an enemy combatant, one for which he had no defense: love. This small woman who found him nearly dead in the Mauveguard Pass had changed him. She was all he could think about now. The thought of returning to Odessa, and King Leopold, seemed as far away in his thoughts as his reach of the moon.

Amtor booked passage for them in an ambulatory coach. It was painted in black and fitted with red velvet seats cushioned and padded. It would take them toward their destination. They decided to settle in the little peaceful village of Homestead, a small town situated in the uppermost northern part of the Mid-Run Valley, just a bit south of the beginnings of the Great Mapes Forest. There, Amtor and Gilglad would live together, eat and sleep together, eventually becoming man and wife. There in the surroundings of the giant Mapes they would laugh and love together and plant their stake in the hopes of having children someday.

Because of Amtor's position as King Leopold's former Minister of War, the costs of having a home to retire to was not a problem. He had amassed a fortune in plunder, enough to build his own castle. Yet Amtor did not desire a castle or mansion for him or Gilglad, instead he wanted only a small cottage with some frontage to walk and nurture. Gilglad planned to plant a flower garden with spices and herbs and vining plants. It was what they wanted, and that is precisely what they set out to do.

Time passed and their happiness increased. Not just for their home and land in Homestead, but mostly for each other. They became intensely attuned to what the other was thinking and feeling. Attuned also to what the other wanted and needed.

Amtor made a good partner for Gilglad. He was patient and kind, yet sturdy and powerful, even in his weakened condition. He gave her someone to tend to, which was firmly in her wish to heal and love through the powers of the Goddess Ehlona. And Gilglad was Amtor's healer, friend, confidant, and lover. With her, he would wish for none other. Even in his sleep, he dreamed of her.

Yet, in his dreams the Goddess Ehlona appeared to him often, standing in front of swirling beams of light, reddened by the setting sun. She always held her arms wide open in an embrace of love, lightness, and beauty.

"Can you feel it too? Her presence in dreams?" Amtor would ask Gilglad. "I wonder why it is, that the Goddess Ehlona appears to me in my dreams?"

"Yes, her presence dwells inside me as well. Not just when I sleep, I feel her in my waking hours too. She seems to be getting closer."

"Yes, me too," Amtor confessed. "I feel as if…"

"As if something is about to happen?" Gilglad finished his thought.

"Yes, I wonder what it could mean?"

The little cottage was a flurry of activity for the king's men, carpenters, soldiers, bricklayers, fence builders, roofers, painters, and woodsmen. All labored at His Majesty's expense to complete the work on Amtor's home. While they finished, Amtor and Gilglad stayed in a large tent less than a mile away from the construction site.

Sometimes when Amtor was alone, he would pull out the golden dagger. Its gold face shimmered magnificently in a reflection of superb craftsmanship. Strange though, Amtor thought, occasionally the dagger would give off a light green sheen, a sparkle of sorts, like an emerald wave spiderwebbing over it. Amtor had held plenty of gold in his hands before, mostly plundered from the villages of the war, but he never saw such a thing as this golden dagger. It looked so refined, so special, almost... dangerous. The blade had a melancholy about it. Amtor could not help thinking that some would kill for it, some had most likely already died for it. He wrapped it in a soft leather wrap and placed it in a small hole covered with a heavy stone. And though he knew his better fighting days were past, he kept his sword, as well as a light battle-axe, within arm's reach all the time. If someone wanted a fight he would give it to them, more than enough. He would not be caught unprepared.

Gilglad opened the flap of the tent and came inside. She noticed his weapons, the sword and scabbard on the bedpost, the handle of the battle-axe leaning on the wall. She only felt comforted, more secure by them being in his reach, and said nothing to discourage the practice. She felt safe with Amtor. And now, she felt something else entirely with him.

"Gilglad, finally! I have missed you. Come to me, my love."

Gilglad looked happy and beamed with a smile. She stepped lightly, nearly floating, over to where Amtor lay naked in his double wide cot, covered over with warm soft sheepskin.

"Oh, Amtor! The Goddess Ehlona has truly blessed us so!"

"Oh? The Goddess has blessed me to you, and us with each other?"

"Yes, yes, that, and more as well. A little one stirs inside me. I feel it. I am going to have your baby, Amtor!"

"Oh, such great news! So blessed we are!" Amtor laughed. "There are dreams plenty enough for all of us. All three of us now."

Leaving the tent the next morning, Gilglad almost tripped over a large wicker basket filled with fruits, vegetables, clay pitchers of cold clean water, and beautifully woven fabrics of gold, white, yellow, and blue. All the gifts, the basket, and the surrounding grounds were covered with flowers, chrysanthemums of purple, white, orange, and yellow, the fragrance of which pleasantly filled Gilglad's senses.

"Amtor, there is a basket here," she turned and told him. "It looks like someone left us a gift."

"A gift? Maybe the workers? Certainly thoughtful if they did, but I can't imagine why, and why now?"

Gilglad looked, scanning the surrounding area.

"Is there a note?" Amtor asked.

Gilglad bent down and rummaged through the basket. "No, no note. But what a nice surprise, and on the morning after I told you I am expectant with our child."

Imperceptibly to Gilglad, the large trees in the surrounding area began shifting ever so slightly.

Gilglad brought the wicker basket into their tent and when the flap closed behind her, large sections of the Great Mapes disassembled into particles, a flurry of golden orbs spun wildly through the branches, unable to control their delight in hearing the news.

The baby was coming.

I consider you my friend, one I can rely on

We share the laughter, and a shoulder to cry on

I'm only living to make every moment last

Because I'd do most anything not to make it go so fast.

Excerpt from *The Witch's Songbook*

The creatures were recognizing and honoring her as their supreme creator,
and as their God, they worshipped her.
— Excerpt from *The Provenance* (Chapter Fifteen)

KILMER'S GHOST

THE CASTLE ORLO IN THE YEAR 841 HRT
(DAY OF KILMER'S CAPTIVITY: UNKNOWN)

Darkness, nothing but total darkness. He opened his eyes, and it was no different than having them shut. Kilmer hung in chains. He had no idea how long he had been hanging there, what day it was, or if it were day or night. He grimaced in pain, burning from his wrists having to support his weight. The iron restraints dug into the bones of his arms, ripping at his flesh. Spasms from his stomach wounds throbbed in pain from where Langula had cut him. Every breath shot waves of agony through him. He could not see it, but death, blood and filth were all around him. The smell of it permeated these dungeons under Castle Orlo.

As Kilmer woke, he searched his mind for reason. He could not remember how he got here. He remembered he was on a mission but could not remember what it was. Why could he not remember?

He heard a distant scream down one of the darkened hallways. Maybe the scream came from another prisoner being tortured or killed elsewhere. Or maybe, as Kilmer remembered, it could be the vengeful ghosts. Those poor restless specters seeking out their vengeance. He remembered their torments. Then he remembered more.

Memories of the men of the search party started to come back to him: Rhodes, Laws, Givens, Hanson, Curtz, and who was the last one? Melvin, the youngest. The overweight kid who reminded him of Kory. Where was he now? Was he safe? He wondered. Were any of them alive or were they dead? Or were they being held as prisoners like Kilmer?

By remembering the names of his men, he remembered why he was here.

"Yori?" he whispered in the darkness.

A chain rattled to his right. He could hear faint breathing beside him. Finally, he heard Yori moan, trying to speak.

"Kilmer?" the voice said.

"Yori? Yori?" No answer came back now. Kilmer knew time was running out for Yori, but soon, they would both be dead.

He heard another scream and turned toward the sound. But it was too dark to see anything. His first reaction was to call out. But then, he thought better of it. Maybe being alone in the dark was better than the alternative. He adjusted his feet to relieve some of the pain on his wrists.

"We are prisoners of the Zorn," he whispered, hoping Yori could hear him and understand. "I remember his hideous face. And that blue demon, she hurt me." He could feel a wave of intense pain from where she cut him.

Kilmer heard Yori moan beside him. He was still alive. For now.

"Kilmer?" Yori said in a soft whisper. "Help me. Please, Kilmer, help me."

Kilmer did not know what to say. He could not help anyone while in the same chains as Yori.

"It will be all right, Yori," Kilmer said. "Help is coming. Stay alive, Yori, hold on."

Kilmer tried to focus his eyes in the dark. He tried to make out any shapes he could. The outline of the chamber, its arched entrance, came into focus and was getting progressively lighter. His eyes were not getting used to the darkness, torchlight was nearing. His heart began to pound.

"Yori," Kilmer said. "Someone is coming."

"Oh no, no," Yori said, crying beside him. "No more pain. Not again."

The light was growing brighter, but he could not hear any footfalls coming closer. Maybe that meant Langula was coming back slithering on her tail. He felt a bead of sweat run down his spine.

He startled as the Zorn himself appeared instead. He rounded the corner with the torch under his face, casting shadows that made him look even more chilling. His appearance took Kilmer's breath away in fear. He tried to look away, but helplessly chained to the wall, he found himself forced to face forward or else it put a new pain upon his wrists. The Zorn stood looking at Kilmer for a long moment, not saying a word, although Kilmer could hear his heavy breathing through his exposed nasal passages.

Why is he hesitating? Kilmer thought.

Yori was conscious and crying again. He hung limply with a fearful expression. For the first time, Kilmer could see the extent of Yori's wounds—he was in bad shape. They both trembled involuntarily, both from the cold and the fright.

The Zorn lit the torches in sconces. Warm light flooded the room in flickering golden patterns, hurting Kilmer's unconditioned eyes. The Zorn turned to face the prisoners.

"Langula will not be joining us," he said, then knelt to inspect the two large eggs submerged in dark fluids below the prisoners.

He stood and spoke again. "She exerted herself earlier and is currently resting. However, I get restless and bored without her. So, I thought I would pay you both a visit. I thought you might… entertain me for a while."

The Zorn reached into the wooden box on the table and took out a metal cutting tool bent into a strange angle. He held it up and repeatedly opened and closed it in front of them with loud snaps.

"My mother's star, the Star of Ehlona, is shining overhead. Of course, you might not have been aware of that down here in the dungeon. But trust me, it is." The Zorn cradled the cutting tool with both hands and took a deep breath. Then continued his thoughts, "You know what that means, don't you? Well, it can only mean one thing. My mother has returned. Just when I thought I had rid the world of her, this cosmic foolishness saw fit to send her back to me. What a joke!" He shook his head. "No, more like a bad dream."

Then, he paced the room and continued, "The Gods are trying to deceive me. They always confuse me with their mixed signals. Did the witch's prophecy not say that only when I am at the height of my power will the star appear? So, is this true? Am I at the height of my power? I destroyed my Zornastic Order, thinking I may have been close to peaking with an army of twenty thousand. I thought if I did not destroy them, then I might invoke her star. Yet, at the height of the Zornastic Order the star did not shine. So, I had them all killed. And now? Now that I have no army of priests in place, the Star of Ehlona appears? What have I missed? I must be overlooking something."

The Zorn lifted the tool and tapped it to his lips lightly while looking at Kilmer, and then he used the tool to point. "And then you appear. And the Star of Ehlona shone at the same time. Maybe that is just a coincidence?"

The Zorn approached Kilmer very close to his face. "Problem is, in my business, I can't afford to believe in coincidences."

Kilmer stared wide-eyed at him in fear. He could not avert his eyes from the Zorn's face. He could not even blink.

"You! You have something to do with this," the Zorn scowled. "Somehow, in some way, you are responsible for the appearance of the Star of Ehlona. I have condemned tens of thousands of people to death, and never, not once, have I ever cared to ask for the name of any of them.

"But for you, I will make this one, single, exception," The Zorn moved even closer. "Who are you? What's your name?"

All Kilmer could do was tremble with his mouth open, frozen in a silent scream.

"Who are you?" The Zorn waited for the information he wanted.

"Your name?" he repeated, more slowly this time.

Kilmer stared into the Zorn's dark eye sockets and could only see death. His two yellow eyes swirled deep inside their depths. Kilmer managed to close his mouth and licked his lips. Blinked his eyes in a flutter. In his mind, he could not remember what his name was anymore.

Who was he really? Was he Kilmer or Darius Plum?

"My-my name is…" Kilmer could not comprehend what name to give him. Or which name would have significance to the Star of Ehlona. Should he say Kilmer or Darius Plum?

"Well?" the Zorn asked impatiently.

"My name is Kilmer."

The Zorn gave him a questioning look, then backed away, revealing to Kilmer that Hollow Face stood in the corner of the cell behind the Zorn.

"Kilmer?" the Zorn puzzled. "That means nothing to me. Not a thing. Why have I never heard of you before? What could be missing?"

The Zorn turned and tapped the metal instrument on the wooden table. "Unless, of course, you are lying, and your name is not really Kilmer, and you are someone else."

Then the Zorn stopped in his tracks and slowly turned to face the corner of the cell.

"What is this?" The Zorn saw Hollow Face. "Who are you?"

The Zorn spoke directly to Kilmer's ghost—no one except Kilmer had ever seen his ghost before. Could it be the Zorn could see him too?

"Another guest?" The Zorn turned to look at Kilmer, then back at the ghost. "I see. It is not you that I need concern myself with, but your ghost."

Hollow Face spread his arms and the chamber erupted in a blue swarm of vengeful spirits. Screaming faces of pained specters, these long dead Zornastic priests, attacked the Zorn in mass. Overwhelmed by the concentration of vengeful spirits, the Zorn was taken by surprise by hundreds of tormented souls invading his body all at once. They caused him to lose his balance and he fell to the floor. Once down, the spirits continued to pound into and through him. He screamed but a scream more in fury than in pain.

Kilmer and Yori watched helplessly with wide eyes as the Zorn came under attack. Over and over again, the suicidal spirits of the Zornastic Order awoke from the grave bent on revenge.

The Zorn struggled through the ghostly attack to his feet. Then in a vicious sweep of his arms he sent streams of purple energy crackling throughout the chamber. After casting his magic spell many of the vengeful spirits spun dizzily into his hands like water going down a drain. The tormented screaming blue faces of energy absorbed into the Zorn until they were gone.

"That was refreshing," the Zorn said, looking and sounding revitalized by devouring the spiritual energy of the vengeful spirits.

Hollow Face dropped his arms, as the Zorn turned to face him.

But before the Skeletal King could collect himself any further, Kilmer's ghost swept across the distance separating them, and Hollow

Face disappeared into the Zorn's body. Now two spirits inhabited the one body, and they engaged in combat for spiritual control.

Hollow Face was attempting to possess the Zorn!

The Skeletal King's yellow eyes rolled back and changed in color from swirling yellow to pale white as the two spirits clashed. He doubled over and hit the floor again, quivering and convulsing as the internal struggle raged.

"Hollow Face!" Kilmer shouted.

After a moment, the Zorn stood with his back to the prisoners. The fight for inhabitance of the Zorn's body was over. The Skeletal King turned to face the prisoners.

But the Zorn's appearance had changed. His face was no longer that of the Skeletal King. Instead, it had changed to a dim luminescent face of a human, the face of a man, with dark hair and a long flowing black mustache. This was not the face of the Zorn anymore at all. Kilmer recognized that the face the Zorn wore now was the face Kilmer recognized of his ancestor Fortis Plum! Hollow Face had won the battle for habitation!

Fortis spoke through the Zorn's throat, "Darius! You don't have much time. The Zorn is powerful, I cannot hold him for long. Free yourself and Yori, then run, quickly now, go!"

"*No!*" the Zorn growled. His skeletal appearance reappeared again. He reached to grab Kilmer. But a startled expression pained him, and the spiritual battle continued. They wrestled again inside the same body. The Zorn's face shifted back to Fortis once more.

"Hurry, Kilmer! I'm not sure how long I can hold him," Kilmer's ghost said. Fortis controlled the Zorn's magic now, and out of his hand, purple energy crackled. With the Zorn's magic, Kilmer's shackles opened. His hands were free, and limply dropped to his sides, numb and useless.

With another beast-like growl, the Zorn appeared again as he took control of his own body. "What is this? How is this happening? I am Hazor the scorned! I am the Zorn!"

As the struggle continued, the faces changed rapidly in succession between the faces of the Zorn and Fortis Plum. Appearing again and stabilizing, Fortis shouted. "I am Fortis Plum! And you will yield to me by the power of Heironomus the firstborn God of Light!"

Kilmer hurried to gain feeling in his arms, shocked to hear his ghost speak those words. He knew he had to get the blood flowing to his hands. Yori looked on in disbelief.

The Zorn's face changed several more times between the Skeletal King and the long mustached ancestor of the Plums as the two struggled in front of Kilmer and Yori.

"Kilmer, is this real?" Yori said. "What is happening?"

"We are getting out of here, Yori," Kilmer told him. His arms were still numb but he dropped to his knees in front of Yori and plunged an arm into the sickly black fluid that incubated Langula's demonic egg. This is where he had seen the key drop, if only it were still there. The black liquid was putrid and thick. His hand frantically searched the bottom feeling for the key. His hand brushed against the egg; each time he felt it shift as something inside perpetuated living motion just under its surface. Yet he could not find the key.

The Zorn's appearance continued to change rapidly. First Fortis then back to the Skeletal King. Shifting to the Zorn's face, he grabbed Kilmer by the neck, choking him from behind. Kilmer brought his hands out of the fluid, splattering the black stuff as he tried to pry the Zorn's skeletal fingers from closing his airway. The sickly fluid splashed into his mouth staining everything he touched.

The battle for the Zorn's body continued, and Fortis appeared again. Released from the choke hold, Kilmer coughed out putrid ooze and struggled for air. He recovered quickly, plunging his hand back into the dark blood, his free hand rotating the egg to search under it. At last, he found it and pulled the key out of the dark slime.

The Zorn's face was flashing between the two straining combatants. They could all feel the power of Fortis was starting to dwindle.

"Hurry, Kilmer," Yori told him.

As the Zorn struggled in the torchlight, the slimy key went into the lock of Yori's chains. The left shackle popped open, and Yori's arm dropped lifeless to his side. The Zorn heard the lock open and spun to look. Kilmer moved to the other side, quickly opening the right shackle. When the locked popped open, Yori fell free into Kilmer's arms.

"Kilmer!" Fortis shouted. "My power is fading fast. If I never see you again…" Fortis wanted to tell him more but did not have time to finish the thought. The Zorn's face now appeared. Kilmer gave him one last look, wrapped his arm around Yori, and dragged him out.

The two slipped and slid on the blood and gall in their bare feet. They ran out of the chamber, leaving the Zorn to battle for control of his body with the ghost of Fortis Plum. Each time the Zorn appeared in control, he pursued the prisoners. But then Fortis regained control, keeping the Zorn at bay as best he could.

After Kilmer exited the torture cell, he immediately regretted not destroying the demon's eggs. But he was not going back, afraid for his life—escape was his only concern. Kilmer continued to drag Yori down the dark unfamiliar corridors.

Through the darkness of the castle, the two raced as fast as they could. Desperately searching for the way out, watching for any sign of Langula or her new spotted demon, they did not have any idea about how to navigate the castle.

Back in the cell, the tide of the battle turned and the Zorn resumed greater control of his body.

Yori and Kilmer were lost inside Castle Orlo, not able to find the passage out. They raced around every corner, expecting at any time to run into the Zorn, Langula, or some new horror. The vengeful spirits were moving all around them and passed the two men in wispy blue streaks that formed the faces of long-dead tormented souls. But the spirits did not attack them, instead they floated around them deliberately. They were allied in purpose and gathered in a single passageway to give Kilmer a sign. The vengeful spirits took pity on them, as Kilmer had expressed for them, and they wanted to help Kilmer and Yori find the way out.

Kilmer instinctively followed the Vengeful Spirits. Whenever the corridor led to a choice in their path, a chamber or hallway, that branched into multiple passageways, the spirits showed which way to go. They followed the paths where the spirits guided them. Stumbling along, they turned left, then right, up the stairs, around the corners, through the doors, and across antechambers.

Until eventually, Kilmer and Yori crashed through a door, collapsing one on top of the other in the bright light of the Sanguine Forest. The vengeful spirits could only guide them, they themselves could not leave. They were imprisoned within the walls of the castle where they took their own lives.

Kilmer guessed the same spirits that led them out of the castle continued to harangue the Skeletal King, slowing his progress, and distracting him from intercepting them. But here in the Sanguine Forest, Kilmer knew the Zorn still held the upper hand.

Kilmer picked Yori up off the ground. Yori was finding some new strength after gaining his freedom. The men supported each other and moved through the forest as fast as two severely wounded and naked men could. They ran as straight as they could in one direction.

Kilmer kept looking back, expecting the door of the castle to burst open with the Zorn in pursuit of them. But when he looked back, the castle had disappeared. It was gone, as if it were never there in the first place.

They continued to run, fearing an attack at any moment. They fell, picked themselves back up, then ran some more. With bare feet, they ran across the sharp bones of exposed corpses, until their soles were raw and bloody. They ignored the pain, because they knew that if they could not get away, the demons would exact more suffering in more extreme ways through the Zorn and Langula. They ran as if their lives depended on it.

They fell again, and this time they landed at the foot of the Zorn's boots. They knew they were too weak to resist him. All they could hope for, after their escape, was that he would just kill them outright, instead of torturing them slowly. Either way, they were as good as dead.

Then a man knelt beside them. They looked up from the ground and saw that the boots in front of them were not the Zorn's at all. These were the dirty leather boots of a large man wearing the armor of the Red and Blue, King Leopold's infantry! Armed with a large broad sword, the soldier knelt beside them and inquisitively considered the two naked men.

"Hey!" the soldier shouted. "I have something here!"

Others quickly came running. Shouting came from all directions. Kilmer and Yori nervously searched for any signs of the Zorn, or Langula, a swarm of insects, or any other magical tricks. But then more and more of the Red and Blue soldiers unsheathed their swords forming a defensive perimeter to protect the two wounded men.

"What's your name?" the soldier asked.

"My name is Captain Kilmer, this is Yori, the king's First Archer."

"We got him! We found Captain Kilmer! And he's got Yori too!" the soldiers called out.

Soon a whole company of Red and Blue infantry encircled them with swords drawn in every direction; the soldiers delicately picked up the men, and carried out a retreat, out of the Sanguine Forest.

"Captain Kilmer! Captain Kilmer!" One of the soldiers forced his way through the spears and swords. It was Rhodes! "We've got you, Captain Kilmer—you are safe now."

"Oh, Rhodes! Praise the Gods!" Kilmer said.

"We knew you were alive!" Curtz and Hanson rushed through the guards as well. "We never gave up on you!"

"Please get me out of here," Kilmer told them. And get him out of there is just what they did. No fewer than a thousand soldiers of Leopold's First Red and Blue infantry came into the Sanguine Forest to find Captain Kilmer. Lord Whitney sent them in, after two days with no contact, just as Kilmer predetermined through the couriers.

Forming a human bucket brigade, they escorted and assisted Kilmer and Yori out of the Sanguine Forest under an heavily armed escort. The infantry men, acting upon the stories of Curtz, Hanson, and Rhodes, took no chances in getting out of the Sanguine Forest. Being passed along through the brigade, the troops added their congratulations, patting Kilmer and Yori as they were carried through. Once the rescue party passed, the brigade cautiously collapsed in on itself, retreating safely within the ranks returning to the Mid-Run Valley. Outside the Sanguine Forest, horse-drawn wagons waited for them. The infantry men gently put Kilmer and Yori in. Rhodes, Hanson, and Curtz rode with Kilmer. The men's nakedness was covered with warm blankets, and healers attended to their wounds. Kilmer and Yori received warm bread, meat, vegetables, and cakes, cool water, wine, and stronger drink, whatever they wanted.

Then, the wagons started to move on the long uphill road back to Castle Odessa.

"What do we tell them?" Yori asked Kilmer. "I wonder if anyone will believe what we have been through. What if they do not believe?"

"We will make them believe, Yori, at least the truth as we can comprehend it. We will make them believe."

Yori asked, "What do I tell Lara, my wife, about, well, you know… what we were forced to do in there?"

Kilmer looked at Yori, remembering his own encounter with the demon Langula. "I do not know, Yori. I never want to speak of that."

He looked at Rhodes instead. "What happened to the others? Melvin, Laws, Givens? Where are they?"

"Givens lived," Rhodes said. "But something happened to his mind. I fear he may have gone insane."

"And Laws?" Kilmer asked, remembering what Langula said about him. "Is he alive?"

"Laws isn't right either. But yes, he's alive," Curtz said.

"And Melvin?" Kilmer asked, fearing the boy was dead.

"Melvin is in better shape than the rest of us," Rhodes said to him. "We got him out of the Sanguine Forest. He wanted to come back in to look for you, but we wouldn't let him, once we got him out. He was very concerned about you though."

"Thank you for watching out for him, protecting him," Kilmer said, relieved to hear no harm had become of him.

"We sent him back with Laws and Givens," Hanson said.

Kilmer said, patting them, "I'm glad all of you made it out."

"I can tell you this, Captain Kilmer," Curtz said. "I'll never go back into that forest again."

The company forced a laugh.

The wagons rocked all night without stopping. Different riders took turns driving until they reached the Mauveguard Pass, and then on to Castle Odessa.

"Look!" Yori said. "The Star of Ehlona."

Above them, the star shone in beams of light. Despite what they had all been through, they gazed at the star as a new wonder.

Kilmer did not speak but looked upon it. He rested his head back to get a better view and rest. His thoughts drifted to Hollow Face who he now knew was his ancestor Fortis Plum. Kilmer wondered why he could never see it before. Kilmer would always remember his face, the long black mustache, and the fact that Hollow Face had saved his life, twice now. He wondered how Fortis could overpower the Zorn for control of his body. But most of all he wondered if he would ever see him again.

"I wonder whatever happened to Isse?" Yori said just then, breaking Kilmer's thoughts. He was thinking about his own friend.

Kilmer knew Isse's fate. But after looking at the others of the rescue party, an unspoken word passed between them. They did not have the heart to tell him currently. They would tell him someday, but not today. What they had been through was sufficient for now.

Kilmer looked at his men of the rescue party and smiled. Then let his eyes close. They all took the liberty of showing their affection for him. One by one, they took turns patting their hands on their commanding officer. In turn, he reached up and touched each of them back.

Now they could all go home.

Just like a bright bolt of light from the blue

Like a change from things that are suddenly new

Today it's me, but tomorrow it could be,

It could be you

Excerpt from *The Witch's Songbook*

They are heartless, cold-blooded killers.
— Excerpt from *The Provenance* (Chapter Sixteen)

EHLONA'S MESSENGER

THE VILLAGE OF HOMESTEAD IN THE YEAR 841 HRT
(THE NIGHT OF THE BIRTH)

Gilglad was starting to show in her pregnancy. She continued to nurse Amtor's wounds, but he began objecting more and more. He wanted her to stop worrying about him and start focusing on caring for herself and their unborn baby.

One morning when Amtor limped out to the kitchen, he saw Gilglad sitting in a chair looking out the window. She seemed tired, as if she had not been to bed or slept at all the night before. She did not seem to notice Amtor as he shuffled in, a fact that he picked up on.

"What are you doing, did you sleep last night?"

Gilglad turned to look at her husband without a trace of recognition. She appeared exhausted. Then, his presence brought her back to her senses and suddenly her face brightened in expression. Finally, she spoke.

"Oh, Amtor, a most amazing thing happened to me last night."

Without a word, Amtor sat in a wooden chair. The worry on his face comprised a look of confusion mixed with curiosity.

"I was sitting in the nursery, thinking of having the baby, when a messenger came to me."

"A messenger?"

"Yes. An angel, a spirit from the Goddess Ehlona herself. She came to me in shining light, like the orange-and-purple fire of a glorious sunset. She came walking out of beams of glowing mist." Gilglad started to cry in her joy. "She was so beautiful."

Amtor sat in silence and let her go on.

"And she gave me a message. She said, 'Do not fear. For it is the spirit of the Goddess Ehlona that sleeps in your womb tonight. You have been chosen as the vessel to carry her reemergence into this world. Oh, glorious day!' Then she nearly blinded me with beams from her eyes of beautiful spinning colors. Then the messenger disappeared."

"Did this vision say she was the Goddess Ehlona?"

"No, no, she didn't have to. She didn't say that exactly, but I knew. I never saw her before, but I knew. I knew it was her."

"What did she look like?"

"Flowing blond hair, full and vibrant. Eyes bright blue filled with light. Lips shining like scarlet ruby. She was dressed in white robes, adorned in gold bracelets. A crown of golden entwining leaves graced the top of her beautiful face. She glowed, Amtor, she radiated a brilliant golden light."

"Did she say anything else?"

"She told me I would be blessed for being the vessel. She told me she already understood my heart and she did not have to ask me of my desire. She already knew what I desired more than anything, and soon she would come to me again.

"Then, with that, she smiled. And then she was gone."

Amtor looked down at his large bare feet, while Gilglad stared off above him, still remembering the Goddess's visit.

"It seemed so real," Gilglad said. "Could it have been? I so want it to be."

"It was real," Amtor told her.

"How do you know? How can you sound so certain?"

"Because it happened to me too."

"The Goddess Ehlona appeared to you last night as well?"

"No, not last night. In the bottom of the pit. She came to me in the crevasse at Mauveguard Pass. She reassured me I would make it out alive. And I did. Then I saw her once more."

"When?"

"When I looked upon your face for the first time. I lay in the grass in Mauveguard Pass. I had escaped the pit, but I knew there was a chance I might not live much longer after that. When I opened my eyes, it was your face that leaned over me, but it was the face of the Goddess Ehlona that my eyes saw."

Gilglad stared at Amtor with shock. "Why have you never told me this before?"

"Like you, I didn't think it was real either. I thought I was seeing things, being so close to death. But now, after the same vision appeared to you too, I know something involving the Mother Goddess is real, and it has something to do with you."

"With us, Amtor," Gilglad corrected him.

The night before Gilglad went into labor, the Goddess Ehlona appeared to her again. As she slept beside Amtor, the entire room was bathed in emerald light. The spirit of the Goddess Ehlona came to prepare Gilglad for what was to come.

The Cosmic Creation is sending my spirit back to the world, and you have been blessed as the vessel.

In her dream Gilglad spoke to Ehlona.

"Mother, you are inside me now. You've been in my womb for many months. You fill me with your blessing."

My blessings to you are yet to come. But beware, Gilglad. There are dark forces that will try to kill you. When the boy turns four, my blessing will come upon you.

"A boy? You will come back to this world to grow to a man?"

There are many enemies, and you have strength like no other. You are the one that can wield my power. You must.

"I will do whatever the Mother Goddess asks of me."

What about your husband? Will he be strong enough?

"Amtor is the strongest man I know. The strongest I have ever seen."

Your blessing will take its toll on him. But through his wounds you will find strength. Remember that, through his wounds you will find strength.

"I will remember."

Tomorrow my spirit will enter the world through you, and vengeance will be mine.

"Let it be so, Mother. Your will is my desire."

The Goddess Ehlona burst into a thousand green particles and the room got dark. Gilglad warmed herself with her cold arms. As soon as the spirit of Ehlona dimmed, the baby moved and shifted in her womb. Gilglad smiled and spoke to herself out loud.

"Oh, the joy that crowns me with the greatest blessings of the Mother Goddess!"

Amtor stirred, opened his eyes, and looked at her.

"What did you say?"

"Oh, Amtor! Tomorrow is the day."

Goddess or not, when the labor pains came, the birth was a normal and a natural one for Gilglad. She felt everything as would any other woman. For seven hours, she labored in waves of increasing discomfort and strain, as three midwives assisted her in her time of need.

Outside the cottage, Amtor nervously paced the grounds. He sharpened his axe on the grindstone no fewer than a dozen times. He chopped wood, he collected water and kindling. Anything to keep his mind off what was happening in the cottage. He stayed as busy and preoccupied as he could until the light of day started to get hazy.

But then, instead of getting darker, tthe sky burst into color and became lighter, a new light suddenly rushed forth in the night sky. Amtor expected long shadows at dusk, but instead, he looked up and noticed the new bright light in the sky. At first, he thought it was the moon, but then no. It was too small to be the moon. A new star shone.

At the same time he noticed the star, he heard a baby cry from inside the cottage. His child had been born. Amtor heard the cries and knew it was a boy. A son. He knew this because Gilglad told him so, that the Goddess Ehlona had told her. The Goddess Ehlona had come back into the world as a male child.

A midwife burst out of the house, the open door revealing an emerald glow inside. The woman held a small package, wrapped in clean fresh white linens. She approached him with the bundle and handed his son to him.

"You have a son, Amtor," the midwife told him. "You are certainly blessed this day."

"A son," Amtor repeated, taking the bundle into his strong arms ever so gently. "A son."

"What will you name him?" asked the midwife. It was the custom of the time that the husband name the child immediately after the birth. The sooner the better, as the providence of the Gods determined that good blessings would follow the child named soon after its birth.

Amtor remembered what Gilglad had told him. This was not only their son, but this child, was the spirit of the Goddess Ehlona, recycled and renewed and sent back into the world. But for now, it was just a normal baby, weak and helpless as any other baby born to any other woman.

He looked at the baby in his arms, then the star in the sky, and mused to himself, "A son, A star. A son of a star. Astar. The child's name will be Astar."

I've learned to pick myself up off the ground

And I've learned to let those words,
sail right through me now

I've learned to stand, without your hand

And I'm never going to fall down again.

Excerpt from *The Witch's Songbook*

Come to me, child, and I will give you everything you ever wanted.
— Excerpt from *The Provenance* (Chapter Seventeen)

THE KING'S CELEBRATION

THE CASTLE ODESSA IN THE YEAR 842 HRT
(SIX DAYS SINCE THE STAR OF EHLONA)

The scene was surreal. The wagon came rolling through the entrance of Castle Odessa. Celebratory banners of red and blue flew in the breeze with the word *Odessa* emblazoned upon them. Garlands of red and blue flowers decorated the arches, the towers, and the surrounding grounds. Sitting in the wagon, Kilmer, Yori, Rhodes, Hanson, and Curtz rocked back and forth seeing how the castle had transformed in anticipation of the king's celebration.

Almost five years had passed since the Battle of Mauveguard Pass; the final decisive battle between the Amalgamates and Leopold's Red and Blue. The resulting surrender of General Blaize Plum and the Amalgamates forces brought about an end to the war. Leopold finally achieved his objective, control over all the villages of the Mid-Run Valley, from the Gray Mountains to the east to the Blue Mountains to the west. His reach included all the shipping and trade routes on the Endless Seas.

"Leopold is celebrating the five-year anniversary of his Kingdom of Odessa," Hanson said.

"It's your kingdom too, Hanson," Rhodes said.

Hanson guffawed. But Rhodes was not offended. They all knew Hanson had served on the losing side, as an Amalgamate, and was still sore about Mauveguard Pass, even after five years. No one could blame him for being bitter. Rhodes knew had he been on the losing side, he would have been too. Hanson had a right to his opinions. After the past week in the Sanguine Forest, he had earned the right to say whatever he wanted.

The wagon rolled into the lower reaches of the castle and then came to a stop. Stripped of their clothes at Castle Orlo, Kilmer and Yori were draped with white linen bedsheets to hide their nakedness. An extra blanket covered Yori to keep him warm. A large portion of Kilmer's sheet was stained with blood, from his stomach wounds, the place where the demon sliced him open with her claws. Yori was weak and had several wounds also staining the linens covering him with streaks of blood.

Rhodes and Hanson gingerly helped them out of the wagon. The wisecracking Curtz remained in the wagon, tired, and uncharacteristically quiet.

"Yori!" a voice cried out. Lara, Yori's wife, came rushing to him. Her arms wrapped around his neck, showering him in hugs and kisses welcoming him back home. Lord Whitney walked behind her.

Yori looked over at Kilmer, remembering what they had done with the demon. They shared a concerned look, a single thought, that passed wordlessly between them. Its meaning was not lost on Kilmer. How could Yori, how could any of them for that matter, go back to normal life after all they had experienced in the Sanguine Forest and Castle Orlo? All the men of the rescue party who walked into the Sanguine Forest were coming home different than when they left. This was especially true for Kilmer, Laws, and Yori who had fallen under Langula's seduction spell, another burden not all of them knew. Yori had been seduced into unholy infidelity with a demon that used his essence to breed a brand-new evil.

Kilmer gave him a reassuring nod. But the look in Yori's eyes said it all. He could not even pretend to be happy knowing what he did.

"Oh, Yori, you're safe now! You're alive, and you're safe!" She continued to cover him with affection. "Oh darling! You're bleeding, you're so weak. But you're home now, I will take care of you."

The healers were quick to come on the scene with stretchers. They helped Yori onto one and whisked him away with Lara following close behind. They stopped only long enough to allow Yori to accept a quick word of praise from Lord Whitney as he passed. Yori was finally home.

More healers came with more stretchers. The next stretcher had come for Kilmer, who stood slightly bent, holding his arms defensively around his midsection. But before he was put on the stretcher, he wanted to stand to receive Lord Whitney.

"Thank the Gods you're safe, Kilmer!" Lord Whitney said. Lord Whitney helped him stand, as the redheaded Kilmer grimaced, quivering in pain. "You saved Yori! Not only did you find him, but you also brought him home. You saved his life!"

"I had my doubts," Kilmer said. "We were all nearly killed."

"I deployed the First Infantry to the Sanguine Forest when you missed two letters back to me. You had a smart idea to establish couriers and a mitigation plan."

"I thought for a moment that the Sanguine Forest would confound the entire First Infantry too."

"We sent one thousand soldiers into the Sanguine Forest. I had no doubt of what we were up against."

"The Zorn revealed to me that he had the entire Zornastic Order put to death, over twenty thousand men. I was afraid that one thousand men wouldn't be enough. I will tell you more about what happened someday. But not right now, if you don't mind."

Lord Whitney agreed.

"I see the castle is readied for the fifth anniversary of His Majesty's coronation. Forgive me, but I've lost track of time. I haven't missed it, have I?"

"That's understandable – no, the celebration starts day after tomorrow."

"I wouldn't miss it for the world," Kilmer told him.

Kilmer turned and saw Melvin. The boy came running to him and moved as if to hug Kilmer, but then hesitated, unsure if it was appropriate. He took Kilmer by the arm and patted him on the back instead.

"I'm so glad they found you and got you out of there. We are all lucky to be alive," Melvin said.

Kilmer nodded. "What about Givens and Laws?"

"They made it out. They are in the infirmary. Still not sure what is wrong with them," Melvin said with a shrug. "But something is— they are not responsive."

Kilmer did not say he knew what happened to Laws, because the source of his information was the demon Langula. Kilmer remembered watching Givens lose his mind in the Sanguine Forest suffering from illusions.

"Thank you for taking care of them, Melvin. You don't know how much it means to me that all of you are safe. Especially you, Melvin."

"I came out without a scratch, thanks to Rhodes and Curtz. They watched out for me like a couple of old hens," Melvin said with an awkward laugh.

"Good, Melvin, that's good." Kilmer laid back on the stretcher that had been waiting for him. He pointed to the large bloodstain around his stomach. "Now, if you'll excuse me, Melvin. I would like to see the healers and get some rest."

"Yes, of course." Melvin backed out of the way and let the healers do their work. Kilmer gave him a nod. They carried him away past Melvin, past Lord Whitney, past Rhodes and Hanson.

On his way to the infirmary, Kilmer looked back and saw Curtz still sitting in the wagon by himself. He had a faraway distracted look, the same look Givens had. But then, Hanson extended his hand to help Curtz out of the wagon, and he immediately sparked back to life. Maybe, he thought, it was just his imagination about Curtz.

Kilmer laid his head back and sleep took him, as he drifted off in exhaustion. He managed to stay that way through the healers medicating him and disinfecting and cleaning his wounds.

After many hours of sleeping, he awoke to a voice from the doorway.

"That is quite a wound," the voice said.

Kilmer noticed all the healers scurrying away. He turned to look. King Leopold stood in the doorway. He wore his blue uniform with red trim, a thick black cape made of bear fur and a solid gold circlet of oak leaves crowned his head. The king walked to Kilmer's bedside. He held a ribbon of bright red and blue in his hand.

Kilmer nodded. "Your Majesty."

Leopold smiled at him. "Are you in much pain?"

"Some cuts, across here, but I will recover, Your Majesty."

"Well, I don't want to disturb your rest. The Gods know you deserve it. But I wanted to come in person and express my gratitude to you. It is the least I could do since you undertook this mission to rescue my First Archer. I understand this is not the first time that I have come into your debt. You have distinguished yourself before on behalf of the kingdom, not once but twice. The day you saved Amtor, my Minister of War at the Battle of Mauveguard Pass. For that you were promoted to captain. A leadership position?"

"I saved him because he saved me first," Kilmer said.

Tears were welling up in Kilmer's eyes, not because of the king's words, or the memories they aroused. But because this was the first time he had ever seen King Leopold in the flesh. He cried because he had always sworn to kill Leopold, and now, in his weakened condition, he could not.

But here, standing within arm's reach, was the man responsible for LaNew, and the deaths of his mother, Rosa, his father, Justus, his sister, Mara, his friend Kory, and the poor beggar, Kilmer. He scanned the room for a sword, a knife, a dagger, anything he could use to inflict his revenge. But Kilmer had lost his sword in the Zorn's castle, and no weapons were kept in the infirmary. His eyes trailed down Leopold's body to his sword. But the king's legendary agility was something not to be tested.

"So I helped Amtor when he needed me to," Kilmer finished saying.

"You went into the Sanguine Forest to locate my First Archer Yori. You found him and returned him alive. You did not lose a single man of the search party, even after facing some powerful dark magic in the forest. How did you do that?"

"We got separated. A swarm of flies hit us. Givens went mad."

Leopold listened to Kilmer intently, trying to make out the story. But then Kilmer stopped talking, too weary to speak. He feared he was not making any sense anyway.

"Well, you have been through a tremendous amount, and I owe you a huge debt of gratitude. I thank the Gods that you got out of there, wounded, but relatively safe. I want to commend you for your bravery. It is your kind of leadership I value. I want to give you this."

And Leopold bent down and laid a medal upon his pillow. "This is Odessa's highest award for bravery, merit, and leadership."

Kilmer looked at Leopold in his eyes as the king continued.

"It is called the Medal of Heroism. I recognize your achievements with our highest award. You set the standard for bravery and loyalty, Kilmer, you set it high."

"Thank you, Your Majesty," Kilmer said.

"And I want to do more," Leopold said, walking to the other side of the bed. "I am going to promote you to the rank of colonel. If you feel well enough, I would like to officially present you with the Medal of Heroism and the promotion during the celebration this week. But if you don't feel up to it…"

"I'll be there, Your Majesty," Kilmer said. The words echoed in the room. There was something about the king, something unexpected. He did not seem the sadistic killer, the dark lord character, of Kilmer's dreams, as he thought he would be. The king could be inspirational, even charming. He laid his head back.

King Leopold saw he needed rest. "There, there. You take care," the king said. He touched him on the shoulder. "And again, thank you."

After saying this, King Leopold walked out just as casually as he had come in.

Kilmer thought he could get a new sword and strike him down during the ceremony in front of all Odessa. But then, something inside him thought again. If it were not for King Leopold's Red and Blue, specifically Amtor, he would have been killed by LaNew at Mauveguard Pass. If not for Lord Whitney sending in Leopold's First Infantry, he and Yori would have been slaughtered in Castle Orlo. The king had mentioned that Kilmer had distinguished himself twice to Leopold's kingdom. But was it not also true that Leopold had saved his life twice now as well? That kind of behavior did not seem like the actions of a sadistic killer.

Plus, was it not the king himself who ordered the death of the villain LaNew for his atrocities?

But what did it all mean? He had never felt so conflicted. He was living a lie as Kilmer. He had no home, no family. He did not know if he would ever see Hollow Face again. Then, he was humbled by Leopold's surprising generosity. This king was a mystery to Kilmer. He decided to curb his vengeance for now and wait and see. Plus, he was too weak to do anything about it now anyway. He would have to be in top physical shape to take on an intimidating and experienced warrior like Leopold. For that, he would have to be on his best game. Revenge would have to wait.

Kilmer convalesced for two days, as much as he could. His white bandages were still bleeding through and needed to be changed with fresh ones every couple of hours, but his pain was manageable. The healers cared for him, fed him, kept him hydrated, and made him walk several times a day.

On one of these daily walks, he entered Yori's room. Lara was there, never leaving her husband's side.

"How is he doing?" he asked her quietly.

"He's eating and drinking some, but he sleeps a lot."

"Well, he's been through a lot."

"What happened out there, Captain Kilmer? He will not tell me. I feel he is keeping something from me. Why is he protecting me from what really happened?"

"I have no answers to give, Lara," he said. "He cannot tell you because it is still too fresh. It still hurts. Give him time."

Lara touched Kilmer's hand. "At any rate, thank you for bringing him back to me. That is all that matters."

"He loves you very much, Lara." Kilmer nodded and turned to go. "You are lucky to have each other."

She lowered her head and kissed Yori's hand.

He walked down the hallway farther and went into Laws' room. The big man lay there with his eyes open. Kilmer knew why Laws could not shut his eyes. He knew what he saw when he shut them, because Kilmer saw it too. The lingering effect of the encounter with the demon. Something that seemed to be getting worse, not better, over time.

"Laws?" Kilmer whispered to him. Laws only continued to stare at the ceiling, a bandage on his shoulder, split face and cleaved lips. "You're home. You are safe now."

The big man muttered something under his breath. Kilmer listened.

Marvelous scars.

Absolutely demonic.

Kilmer frowned. "I'm going to check on the rest of the men now. I'll be back to check on you later. Laws?"

But Laws made no response.

Kilmer left his room and continued down the hall of the infirmary. Looking in on Givens, Kilmer saw him sitting in a chair, babbling to himself, drooling down the front of his shirt. A healer spoon-fed him broth for lunch. They treated him as they would a young child.

What could have happened to him? Kilmer wondered.

It just did not make any sense. Givens went into the Sanguine Forest an expert cavalry horseman. He was the best. He came out of the Sanguine Forest with his mind utterly destroyed.

Kilmer returned to his room.

In a day, it would be time for the king's celebration. Kilmer was feeling rested, a little better, but not altogether normal. A light unexplained buzz kept circling in his head. He could not shake it.

Horns rang out, signaling the beginning of the king's celebration on the Green of Castle Odessa. Groups of brightly dressed guests sat at tables on the extensively polished parade grounds, inlaid with green limestone. The summits of the surrounding Blue Mountains provided a stunning backdrop in the distance. Archers and infantry stood with red-and-blue banners between the Spears of Leopold. They marched in a procession entering the Green and posting on the front railing. The castle's towers behind them overlooked the activities as silently standing sentinels.

A choir of young singers shuffled in. The young girls dressed in red and the boys in blue. They sang a song in beautiful harmonies:

> *You don't know where you're going*
> *Frozen, stuck in time.*
> *It's coming down to this moment*
> *You leave the world behind*
> *When your heart is empty and*
> *Your soul refused to die*
> *Catch a breath, breathe again*
> *Breathe again.*
> *Before you say goodbye.*

As the singing ended, the double green doors of the castle parted, and King Leopold emerged onto the Green and took his place at the table of honor to tremendous applause. The ovation carried on for several minutes; no matter how many times he waved, acknowledging the large crowd, they continued to honor him with resounding cheers. He remained standing throughout this demonstration, then the king spoke an introduction.

"Please welcome General Blaize Plum," the king introduced his former combatant.

The crowd erupted in more applause as the two previous enemies came together and shook hands at the middle of the stage. General Blaize Plum, his hair completely gray now, stood straight and waved at the rousing ovation with all the mannerisms of a well-heeled aristocrat.

The two men shook hands again and passed some quiet words between them to thunderous applause. Once former enemies at the Battle of Mauveguard Pass, these two men of war found each other's support for a renewed call for unity and peace. The former general of the Amalgamates sat at Leopold's table of honor.

Five years ago, General Blaize Plum surrendered the forces of the Amalgamates to King Leopold. The prevailing thought that day was that there would be many executions, especially hangings, of the commanding leadership of the Amalgamate military forces. But once again, Leopold shocked the world. The only executions the king ordered were for his own Red Guard for war atrocities and its sadistic leader, the villain LaNew.

In peace, King Leopold promoted enduring unity. The Amalgamates and Leopold's Red and Blue merged into a larger fighting force for the new Kingdom of Odessa. Once enemies, they were now formidable allies.

Another twenty minutes of applause ensued. Once the raucous crowd quieted, then it was time to introduce Lord Whitney. The tall and lanky noble came out waving to the crowd, now aroused again. Even more cheers erupted when he stopped and saluted both the king and the former general.

Next, Kilmer was introduced. He came out dressed in a clean set of freshly pressed Red and Blues, walking out onstage slowly and at an angle due to the soreness in his abdomen. He was helped to the stage gingerly by Rhodes and Hanson. Because of his wounds, he saluted as properly as the damage to his body would allow. King Leopold returned with a smart salute and personally helped him to his chair, waving off the others nearby. Kilmer grimaced as he slowly sat at the table of honor with the two other members of his search party.

King Leopold asked Lord Whitney to read the citation. Lord Whitney rose, cleared his throat, and began to read the unscrolled words.

"For meritorious heroism during the Battle of Mauveguard Pass resulting in the daring lifesaving rescue of His Majesty's Minister of War—" Lord Whitney had to stop as he was interrupted by applause for Amtor, who could not attend. When the applause abated Lord Whitney could continue reading from the citation again.

"And for the recent search and rescue mission into the Sanguine Forest, rescuing the life of Yori, His Majesty's First Archer—" more applause.

When it faded away, Lord Whitney added, "Yori could not be with us today, as he is recovering in the infirmary."

He then finished reading the citation. "In recognition of his fearless leadership, bravery, and heroism, the Kingdom of Odessa bestows this award on Captain Kilmer, the recipient of King Leopold's Medal of Heroism."

The crowd broke out in applause again.

Captain Kilmer struggled to his feet. Then Leopold came to him, pinning a larger version of the Medal of Heroism around his neck for all the king's celebration to see. Kilmer shook hands with Lord Whitney and saluted the king smartly.

Leopold addressed the crowd himself. "We are honored and fortunate to have Captain Kilmer as an example of leadership for our Red and Blue. Therefore, today I grant Kilmer the title and rank of Lord of the Realm in the Grand Combined Army of Odessa. From this moment on, he will be called Lord Kilmer. Congratulations!"

Kilmer was now a lord, equal in title and rank to Lord Whitney. The choir of singers began to sing again:

> *The miles and miles that time allows*
> *Spinning faster away*
> *Flying through the universe*
> *Across the Mid-Run plain*
> *Farther than a gentle touch*
> *I clasp my hands to pray*
> *For the strength to be strong again*
> *And belong again*
> *When we say goodbye.*

When the singers finished, the horns were raised and sounded again. Once they finished, an army of food servers burst through the double doors with trays loaded with all types of cooked meats, crisp vegetables, fresh fruits, wine, and beer. The king spared no expense. Once the food was served, this quieted the crowd to a murmur, and an orchestra played relaxing music to dine to. Private conversations at each table took place but softer now.

King Leopold and General Blaize Plum spoke together, while Lord Whitney and Lord Kilmer joined the conversation at the main table. They ate and drank, laughed, and told war stories remembering their fallen comrades.

"Captain Kilmer!" a voice shouted out above the music.

"Captain Kilmer!" the voice shouted again.

No one knew where the voice was coming from. The murmur of the crowd hushed as the guests heard the voice calling out for Kilmer but could not locate it.

The voice rang out again. "Captain Kilmer! Where are you?"

People scanned the Green to determine where the voice was coming from, thinking it all just part of the celebration.

"Look up there!" a female guest gasped, rising from her table, pointing skyward. Then, a general scream rang out, as more people stood up, gesturing to the highest tower. The orchestra stopped playing, as the guests at the celebration gasped and looked. The attention of the main table of honor now peered curiously toward the towers.

"Captain Kilmer! I can see the way out of the Sanguine Forest. I can see Rhodes and Givens. And there's Melvin."

It was Curtz! He had climbed out of the arched stone window to stand on the roof of the highest tower some two hundred feet above the Green. Behind him the Star of Ehlona shone in the daylight.

Curtz laughed, holding the pinnacle of the highest tower's lightning rod. He was pointing to the star. "I can see the Star of Ehlona. That's why we got lost, Captain Kilmer. The light from the star confused us. But not anymore. I found Hanson. I pulled him out of the mud. I saved him, Captain Kilmer!"

A strong breeze blew through his blond hair as he laughed hysterically. He loosened his grip on the lightning rod and lifted both arms as if in victory. He was gazing outward at things only he could see, visions that remained invisible to the rest of the world. Curtz was reliving the Sanguine Forest.

"Stop that man," the king commanded. He signaled for a cadre of troops to scamper up the tower immediately.

"Come down, Curtz," Kilmer tried to call out, but his wounds prevented him from shouting. All he could do was shake his head. "No, Curtz, no."

"Captain Kilmer! Where are you?" Curtz said. "I know the way out now. Don't worry! I know the way out!"

With that, Curtz launched himself off the roof of the tower.

Collective screams and gasps rang out from the guests, accompanied by the sound of dishes breaking and tables turning over.

Curtz fell for a long time, his body getting smaller as it picked up speed. Tossing and turning, he fell behind the two-hundred-foot drop to the Green and continued plummeting down the three thousand feet of the Blue Mountain. Finally, his body disappeared behind the castle. But there could be no doubt of the outcome.

The Honorable General Blaize Plum and Lord Whitney caught Kilmer as he collapsed backward. Rhodes and Hanson immediately left to go find Curtz. The rest of the celebration attendees either screamed or held their hands over their mouths in horror. The formation of soldiers ran wildly in chaos to do something, anything. Some of the king's guests got away as fast as they could, giving in to the fear of seeing something they could not understand.

The king turned to go, escorted by his security detail. He was safely ushered inside Castle Odessa. Before the king walked inside the double doors, he paused to look at the choir of young singers. The young boys and girls held each other, shielding their eyes. They all had tears streaming down their faces. This angered the king more than anything else.

The five-year celebration of his reign was over.

Tonight, I stare at the night sky.
And all I want is you.
The bright light of the face of the moon,
somewhere I know you can see it too.

Excerpt from *The Witch's Songbook*

He calls them priests of his Zornastic Order, and he himself, the Zorn.
— Excerpt from *The Provenance* (Chapter Eighteen)

THE STAR PROPHETS

Some people were born to watch the stars. They believed every cosmic event signified a message from the Cosmic Creation. These were called the Star Prophets, and their profession was as old as Human Recorded Time itself. Pre-dating the Era of the Gods, these people traced back to the primitive people of the world who watched and waited for any sign in the stars to foretell a change in the times to come.

It was the Goddess Ehlona who organized them, establishing the Star Prophets as part of a subset of her Acolytes of the Temple of Valor. They charted star alignments, assigning values to their physical qualities to help explain the meaning of these cosmic events. As one of the original gods, Ehlona's explanations helped the world understand what they saw in the skies, what they witnessed in the past, and what they would see in the future.

The Star Prophets had in their possession a tome of star lore, a thick book called the *Constellation Volume*. As writings of the

Goddess of Ehlona, these volumes became the sacred texts of the Star Prophets. In this book, cosmic activities, along with their definitions, meanings, and values were prophesized by the Goddess.

These early people used stones from the ancient world to build observation platforms on three corresponding mountaintops in the Mid-Run Valley, each with a different view of the sky and each with a copy of Ehlona's *Constellation Volume.*

Centuries later these observation platforms still existed, and Chen-Li continued the tradition of the Star Prophets as a subset of his White Eminence. They were a select group of intellectuals, handpicked by Chen-Li, based on specific abilities, such as mathematics, geometry, intelligence, and of course, astronomy. Assigned to mountaintop observatories, each group of Star Prophets had a different view of the sky. They spent their lives pouring over their star maps and reading the charts of ancient lore.

The Star Prophets wore the familiar white robes of the White Eminence, like the rest of the order, but distinguished themselves with a light blue sash worn around the waist. The Order of the Star Prophets was one of his highest priorities, based primarily on the warning the witch gave him:

> *When you see the sign in the sky, it will tell you that the Zorn, your brother Hazor, will be at his strongest. There can be no mistake of it, the entire world will see it.*

For casual observers this was not the most exciting work and could border on downright boredom. After many years of watching the heavens with no appreciable activity, the many generations of Star Prophets found another more gratifying purpose to their charts and numbers: fortune-telling. They did this for payment, and the signs they looked for were called the dynamic signs.

The dynamic signs. These were the signs that would influence the lives of human beings, based on where the stars were in the heavens, and the slightest tug they exerted on the fabric of daily life. They could foretell if a merchant's new business would succeed or fail if he started at a particular time. There were star alignments for love and marriage—another for childbirth and children's names. They could prophesize when to go to war and when best to sue for peace.

The villagers were superstitious and considered the Star Prophets before embarking on any important events in life. And for this, the Star Prophets charged a nominal fee; it only cost a metro or two. These were the events that filled the coffers of the Star Prophets. And over time, it developed into a lucrative business, as well as something interesting for them to do to pass the long evenings.

Then there were the static signs. To say they were unusual and uncommon would be an understatement. They were exceedingly rare. Static signs determined the activities of the Gods. When a static sign appeared, it meant the Gods were up to some mischief. The static signs presented a change condition of the gods and human beings alike. They were difficult to understand, impossible to predict. They were the primary reason Chen-Li kept the tradition of the Star Prophets waiting and watching. Static signs were so special, a once-in-a-lifetime event. And as long as the Star Prophets existed as a subset of the White Eminence, no static sign had ever been recorded. There was even some talk that they did not exist; that the *Constellation Volume* was the work of fantasy of what became of the witch's depraved mind.

Gia was young for a Star Prophet, recently selected from a wide field as a replacement for the much older Sister Worley, who retired at seventy-seven years old. Sister Worley had spent her life telling fortunes reading the dynamic signs, and as previously stated, without ever seeing a single static sign. As Sister Worley's replacement, Gia spent her days and nights on the mountaintop with Sister Chastain. She was an elderly Star Prophet, like Sister Worley, who had been watching and waiting for something to happen for over ten years.

Gia was a short woman with a wide frame, with cropped black hair and large round glasses. She was exceedingly good at geometry, coming from a long line of mathematicians. Being new to the Star Prophets, she was very diligent in doing her work in the traditional sense, meaning she scanned the heavens and looked for static signs, taking little to no interest at all in what she considered to be the controversial prophecies of fortune-telling.

Sister Chastain favored the more profitable dynamic signs and walked into the observation chamber with a thick stack of papers. The observation chamber sat at the very top of the observation deck, open to the outside air. A large telescope was placed in the middle of the observation deck, and Gia settled in a padded chair scanning the daytime sky with the telescope. As Chastain came in holding a stack of papers, Gia pulled back from the telescope and put her glasses on.

"It's cold out," Sister Chastain said, putting the stack of papers down on a table and pulling her hood over her head. Chastain blew on her hands, then looked at Gia and stopped.

"Gia! Come now. Why waste time with observations during the day? You know you can't see anything while there is light. Come, we have work to do. I swear you are lazy."

"I am not lazy, Sister Chastain. I'm only doing what I should be doing. And also, what you said is not true! I can see Cygnus clearly during the day."

"But what good does that do? Cygnus is not going anywhere."

"I hope not," Gia told her. "What have you got there?"

Sister Chastain continued to blow into her hands. "Requests! Requests!" she said impatiently. She picked one up.

"Here, a request from a farmer regarding the best dates to plant his crops. And here is another. A lady wants to know if she should buy a goat."

Gia shook her head, took off her glasses, and wiped her weary eyes. Then, looked through the telescope again, an action that did not go unnoticed by Sister Chastain.

"I brought you your half of them, Gia."

"That's only half of the requests?"

"This is your half. Actually, there are a bit more in my half."

"Then that's not half," Gia said.

"Don't be condescending, Gia. You are very bright, but no one likes a… This half does not represent two equal halves in number—they represent equal halves in time. Your half is equal to the amount I think you can handle in the same time it will take me to do mine, since I know you are not too well versed in the dynamic signs. And I can do them a little faster than you can."

"Is that important?" Gia put on her glasses again and looked at Chastain. "Are we here to guess about when to buy goats? Or to look for the more important signs of the Gods, like our master Chen-Li wants."

"You are so young and naive, Gia. We provide an essential service to our communities."

"A service you provide from the kindness of your heart, Sister Chastain?" Gia asked.

"Why shouldn't we charge for our labors?" Chastain asked her. "And our time?"

Gia did not reply but turned away.

"I see," Sister Chastain said. "I know you are inexperienced with these requests, but I will leave them here with you. If you find the time to read them, please do. If you need help with any of the dynamic signs or their definitions, I'll be glad to help you. If you can break away from Cygnus, I will come back later and take on your half."

"Thank you, Sister Chastain," Gia said, still looking in the telescope. Then she stopped to look at Chastain before she left. "I will get to them. You have my word."

Sister Chastain nodded and repeated, "It's cold out." Then she turned to go.

Gia knew that they had waited for static signs that never came to pass through many generations of the Star Prophets. The older ones would pass the work on to the younger ones without ever seeing any signs of the Gods. Those Star Prophets would retire or die, and whether they spent their retirement penniless or in comfort depended not on the static signs, but the more profitable dynamic ones. But regardless the cycle kept going. Generation after generation passed on the knowledge of the signs. And on it went.

Gia and Chastain answered all the requests by foretelling fortunes with their knowledge of the dynamic signs. This was not hard work for either of them. The alignment of stars, planets, tides, and weather patterns were a simple but time-consuming process. They responded back to requests about planting crops, raising livestock, starting businesses, and falling in and out of love. Gia privately thought it was all rubbish, but as she knew, that was the expectation of being a Star Prophet. And for the time she wasted on dynamic events, she received one or two coins for each. After a month, she had a bag full of metros but less and less time on the telescope scanning for static signs. Imagine the embarrassment if a real static sign was missed because of time spent telling a farmer when to buy a goat. The thought was unbearable.

Gia would often sleep during the day to keep watch at night. She looked through the telescope during the day too, but she agreed with Chastain that the best time for stellar observations occurred at night.

Gia answered some more of the requests, then put away the rest of them, as it became too dark to read, and it was getting too cold to care about them. She sat in the dark and poured herself some hot tea, and scanning the sky without the use of the telescope, just with her naked eye.

As she blew into her tea, a light blue tint illuminated her face. She saw it first in the cup. Briefly, she wondered why her tea looked so blue. Then she noticed her hands looked blue as well. She nearly missed it, but the dim light was coming from the stars, a comet of blue in the sky.

She thought rapidly. A blue comet? A blue comet was a static sign! Could it be?

She stood up, quickly dropping her cup; it broke into pieces on the observation deck's stone floor, but she didn't care about that. Frantically looking through the telescope, she located the comet and confirmed what she suspected—it was a blue comet. She ran to the library and pulled out the thick, dusty book, the *Constellation Volume*. She licked her fingers and frantically searched for the right page.

Blue comet, blue comet, where is it? she repeated while turning the pages. At last, she found the page she was looking for.

> *A comet will appear, blue in color, to indicate the birth of the Supreme Historian.*

"*A static sign!*" Gia excitedly shouted out loud. She continued to read the volume.

> *The Supreme Historian, the boy who cannot forget, representing a heavenly gift from the Gods, will be born. A male child who never forgets will be sent to the world to serve the Gods as the Supreme Historian. All his senses will have acute memory*

recall. He will remember everything including his birth and will
remain unerringly lucid throughout an unnaturally long life.

Gia closed the large volume.

"The boy who never forgets," she said, looking up. "The Supreme Historian."

Racing back to the telescope, she tracked the comet through the sky as it got closer to the ground.

Where is it going?

She grabbed her torch and tried to light it. Between the cold and her nervousness, her hands were shaking, and she had trouble working the flint tinder. Ultimately, she got the torch lit and quickly set the beacon on top of the observation chamber to burst into flame. Gia looked again through the telescope. The blue comet was speeding toward the ground.

Where is it going to land?

"*Sister Chastain! Chastain!*" she shouted while keeping her eye on the telescope. "*Wake up! The blue comet! The boy who cannot forget! The Supreme Historian! Get up! Get up!*"

Gia impatiently looked at the distant mountaintops where the other Star Prophets were located in their observation platforms. She was checking for any sign that they saw her beacon. But nothing, no sign returned from any of them.

She briefly worried that she was overacting. What if she was wrong?

"Come on! Come on!" She nervously fidgeted. She took turns tracking the comet and looking for a beacon response from the others.

Just then, Sister Chastain burst through the doorway in her nightshirt.

"Gia, you'll wake the Gods! What's the matter? I thought you were falling. Why is our beacon lit?"

"Look, look, look!" she said, backing away from the telescope. She hurriedly encouraged her to the telescope. But neither of them needed to look through the telescope anymore to recognize the blue comet now. It illuminated the entire night sky, bathing the Mid-Run Valley in a blue glow.

"Is that what I think it is?" Sister Chastain asked.

"That's a blue comet, yes!" Gia said, finishing Sister's Chastain's thoughts. "A static sign! It's the static sign of the blue comet!"

"Did you look it up in the *C-Volume*?" Sister Chastain asked her. The *C* stood for Constellation.

Gia acknowledged she did, cursing herself for closing the book on the page. She searched for the page again. But before she could find it, a shining light returned from the mountaintop of another observation platform.

"Look there!" Chastain said. "They answered back! Their beacon is lit!"

Gia squealed in delight. "That means we have geometry! Thank the Gods! We have geometry!"

With another observation deck detecting the comet, it not only confirmed Gia's findings but could also provide a triangulation to locate the precise location of the comet once it landed on the ground.

Sister Chastain could not believe her eyes! She had spent over ten years without ever seeing a static sign, taking over from many others who had not seen any either. Now she realized not only was this a once-in-a-lifetime event, but she trembled to think that the Gods were at play in the world and what it meant.

"We can find it!" Gia said. "Oh, Sister Chastain, this is big!"

They watched the comet approach while making their mathematical calculations. As the comet neared the ground, it increased in both speed and brightness.

Finally, it struck, and a white dome of light flashed in the Mid-Run Valley. After the light burst, darkness returned. And Gia quickly scribbled the coordinates.

Gia and Chastain looked at each other with their mouths wide open.

"He's here," Gia told her. "He's here."

"Who is here?" Sister Chastain asked.

"The boy who cannot forget," Gia told her. "The Supreme Historian."

Then Gia burst out into excited laughter and embraced Sister Chastain, who awkwardly hugged her back.

As the sun rose, Gia packed her bags. Having no sleep, she was off to the North Mountain to discuss the sign with the Star Prophets there.

"If they took the same measurements I did, we can triangulate the location of the comet's descent and find the location of not only where the comet landed, but according to the *C-Volume*, it will take us to the boy who cannot forget, the Supreme Historian himself."

"What should I do?" Sister Chastain asked, feeling woefully underprepared compared to Gia, despite her longer tenure.

"Get word to Chen-Li that a static sign has occurred."

Chastain nodded and embraced Gia now. Gia was equally ecstatic with her gesture.

"Thank you, Gia," Sister Chastain told her.

Gia smiled at her. Then she left for the North Mountain full of excitement.

It took her the better part of the day to get to the North Mountain Observation Chamber. The Star Prophets Glover and Tomar were nearly as excited. After some initial greeting and eagerness, they rapidly got down to business.

Glover was on telescope duty the night of the comet. He saw Gia's beacon at the same time he saw the blue comet. Gia was so glad not only that she saw the comet but that he lit the beacon in response to hers. The other Star Prophet observation chambers on the corresponding mountaintop had not even been aware of the comet. They would have to answer to Chen-Li for that. Even though scanning the skies for static signs was their primary duty, only Gia and Tomar saw it when it finally occurred. This was the wisdom of Chen-Li from the very beginning.

Gia was just so glad that she had another observation to produce the geometry.

Tomar produced his calculations and Gia spread hers out. Together they found their estimates were done well and mathematically accurate. They quickly got to work applying the geometry to their calculations. So well-practiced they were in this that they produced a location in no time at all.

"Here!" they both agreed and stamped a location on the map rolled out over their table. "This is where the Supreme Historian, the boy who never forgets, was born."

Gia grabbed her bag.

"Are you going there now?" Glover asked.

"Yes, of course I am. Do you want to come with me?"

"I wouldn't miss it for the world," Glover said.

They said goodbye to Tomar, reminding him to tell Chen-Li about the signs, and where they were headed—just in case anything happened to Sister Chastain—and their whereabouts immediately. They were heading for the village of Conner.

"Good luck, you two," Tomar told them with a smile. With farewells and excitement, they all embraced. Then Glover and Gia left immediately for the Mid-Run Valley.

When they departed the Northern Observation Tower, they had no idea that only six months later the Star of Ehlona would appear, another static sign and another once-in-a-lifetime event. It was going to be a very short but hectic six months.

The Gods were in motion in the world again.

I memorized my lines
I really played my part
When it was my time to shine
Why wasn't I the star?
It should've been me in those lights.
I could've been the one.

Excerpt from *The Witch's Songbook*

Seduction and manipulation are your most powerful spells.
— Excerpt from *The Provenance* (Chapter Nineteen)

AN OLD FAMILIAR CROW

Leopold turned away from the celebration and stormed into Castle Odessa without a word. The rest of his guests gathered in small groups or scrambled away in different directions—the topic of conversation on everybody's mind was the suicide of Curtz.

Leopold was quickly escorted by his security detail into the castle. They walked him down the castle's corridors, where he stopped abruptly before ascending the stairs. He turned to address them.

"Go find the body and put him in the infirmary. Then, report back to me."

The detail saluted and turned to go.

Leopold walked up a series of winding stairs alone, up the castle's main tower to his private chamber three hundred feet above. He walked into his room; this was just one of many of the king's chambers. This one furnished him with whatever comforts he might need: a thick cotton bed, overstuffed couches, leather chairs, a large hand-carved desk, a stone fireplace. He walked through the chamber, opened the window, and leaned against it. He could not have asked for better weather for his celebration, or a worse outcome.

Looking down, among the streaming red-and-blue banners, he saw the Green. Small groups of people still huddled around the ruined festival. Overturned tables, broken dishes, food splattered over its reflective Green surface—his celebration in shambles. Looking up, the Star of Ehlona shone brightly despite the light of day. Below, the Blue Mountains stretched to the horizon. Even farther down, his men searched among the rocky crags, looking for Curtz's body, laboring through the peaks to find him.

It was not until a day later when the crows helped the search. The recovery teams followed the scavengers, reaching the spot where the crows huddled.

At last, a soldier cried out, "I found Curtz! Here he is!" *What is left of him*, he whispered under his breath.

Leopold answered a knock on his private chamber door. The soldier reported they had found the body. "Your Majesty. The body of Curtz has been recovered to the infirmary."

Leopold looked down at the floor upon hearing the news. He thanked the soldier for the message and closed the door.

Then, before he could turn away, Leopold heard a voice behind him.

"Leopold!" a crow cawed.

An old familiar crow had perched on the open window of his chamber.

"Leopold!" the crow cawed again.

Leopold touched the scar that never healed on his cheek—remembering that he once encountered another talking crow, a giant human-sized one in the woods outside Hammerville. A lot had happened since that first encounter. Yet the scar left by that first crow never healed. This was no ordinary crow.

"The little orphan has grown to be king. You have done well for yourself. Just as I said you would."

Leopold said nothing, he just stood there, looking at the bird, and simmered.

"Do you realize how well you have fulfilled my will?" the crow asked.

"Your will?" Leopold said with a scoff.

"My father was the—" the crow started to say, but Leopold interrupted him.

"I care not who your father was," Leopold told the crow. "I follow no one's will, but my own."

"That is where you are wrong, King Leopold. Very wrong. That is not even your name; I gave you that name in the forest of Hammerville, when you were just a poor and unknown orphan, destined for the hangman's noose. But after I gave you a name, a name of power, just look at all you have achieved since."

"It was just a name, crow."

"Was it?"

"What difference can a name make?"

"Excellent question. Like the name of the man you honored at your celebration?"

Leopold thought for moment. "You mean Lord Kilmer?"

"Is that his real name?"

"Did you name him too, Zorn?"

"No, I didn't. But is Kilmer his real name, or is it just the name he took, one that originally belonged to a homeless beggar, a hunchback?"

"Do not speak falsely to me, bird."

"You murdered the real Kilmer, King Leopold. And instead, you left the only heir of Justus Plum alive."

"You weary me with your riddles, demon crow."

"Don't you see, mighty one? Kilmer is really the missing surviving son, Darius Plum, son of Justus Plum. The son of the man burned alive during your conquest of that village. Darius Plum and Kilmer: they are one and the same."

"So what? Why would I have a care about that?"

"Because, my liege, do you think this boy, whatever he calls himself, does not ache for revenge, to avenge the death of his family with your blood? Mark my words, the boy will kill you someday."

Leopold was silent and turned his back in thought.

"That is, unless you kill him first," the Zorn said. "Finish what you started, king."

"This man named Kilmer—you are scared of him. Why?" Leopold asked. "Why do you want me to do your dirty work? You had the chance to kill him yourself. He was a prisoner in your castle. Why didn't you kill him then?"

"If we work together..."

Leopold interrupted the crow again. "We do not work together, Zorn. I told you: I follow no one."

The crow spread his wings, then like lightning, flew into Leopold's chest. A fight to inhabit Leopold's body ensued. Leopold's eyes rolled back in his head, and he fell to the floor. Leopold tried to resist the Zorn as he had resisted Chen-Li the same way many years ago, when he tried to take over his body. But this time, the Zorn made short work of him, and took control.

The Zorn explored Leopold's thoughts without any resistance. But the crow was just proving a point and did not linger inside Leopold for long.

When the Zorn exited out of the body, he returned control back to Leopold, and flew to the window to take his place as the crow again. Leopold slowly recovered, laying on the floor of the chamber. He wiped his nose on his sleeve and looked at the crow.

"Just a harmless demonstration. To show you I can have you any time I want, and you cannot stop me. Remember, you owe everything to me: your power, your kingdom. It is all because of me, and it will be me that you will obey."

"No, Zorn. That's where you are wrong. Whether I received power from you or the Gods themselves. I am still King Leopold. I did not ask you for anything, or any such power. If you gave me anything, you did it willingly. You gave it to me of your own accord. And a gift so given is mine to command. The power is mine alone!"

"For now. But remember, when no one else would do anything for you, only I knew of your potential."

"I knew of my potential long before you ever did."

"You only needed my power to accomplish great things."

"We will never know what I would have become on my own. You are coming to me now because you need me to remove Kilmer for some reason, because you cannot? Now after all these years, you show up pleading for my help. Why? Why didn't you do it yourself when you had the chance? When he and my First Archer were your prisoners?"

"Tread carefully, Leopold. Your climber, Curtz, the one now lying dead in your infirmary, he could not free himself from my spell. What of the others? Just because I have released them as my prisoners does not mean they are free. They will never be free. You have seen the Star of Ehlona, the blue comet of Aberfell. Can't you feel it? The Cosmic Creation is in motion, attempting to right the balance. Do not find yourself on the wrong side of history, Leopold."

Leopold laughed at the crow. "You are scared! That is a weakness. Reason enough for me to go my own way."

"You have been warned, Leopold," the crow said. "Do not disappoint me."

Your days are gone, never to return!
In Zornastic fire your soul will burn!

Then the crow flew out of reach. Leopold watched him circle the castle, then disappear alongside the other crows. Swooping down the Mauveguard Pass, the Zorn flew away. Leopold stood at the window, thinking about what the crow had said. Finally, he turned from the window.

"Guard!" Leopold shouted.

The king's guardsmen arrived outside his door.

"Bring Babbit to me." Leopold ordered.

Soon Leopold was laying on his bed with his dog, Babbit the Magnificent, a black furball with brown eyes, a long tail and one sharp ear and one folded in half.

I think better with you by my side.

Babbit looked at Leopold and wagged his tail.

Running all the events through his strategic mind, Leopold and Babbit thought together and planned on what their next move should be.

High overhead, the Zorn, in his crow form, soared alone through the Mauveguard Pass. The crow glided to a landing about halfway through. It landed on the head of Kilmer's statue. Then hopped down through the rocks, exploring the opening of the cave where his magic dagger, Soothsayer, was discovered. Looking down into the steep hole, thirty feet below, the crow could see the remains of a skeleton wearing the familiar crest of the Zornastic Order, the familiar black crescent on a silver circle laying at the bottom.

The magic dagger came here to rest long ago. Looking at the skeletal remains of the Zornastic priest, in life just a fourteen-year-old boy by the name of Nantz, the Zorn knew there was nothing else of value here anymore. But he felt that he needed to see the place firsthand, the place that escaped his detection for so long. Now, the pit was merely the final resting place of the bones and the decayed uniform of the boy Nantz and his now defunct Zornastic Order. He left the cave and took to the air again, back to the Sanguine Forest.

Once inside Castle Orlo, the crow materialized back into the Skeletal King. The black oily feathers were replaced with his corpse-like features and crooked crown. He walked the dark halls of the castle, with a few renegade feathers trailing behind, leftovers from the magic spell of the crow. As he walked along, the vengeful spirits of the Zornastic Order reacted to his presence. They materialized in screaming faces, still tormented by their untimely deaths as if it had just happened fresh. A few of the vengeful spirits bounced off the Zorn's body, or circled him like a swarm of wasps, waiting for the right time to strike. They unleashed horrible screams of pain and anguish, moaning through the corridors as he passed. He ignored them as best as he could.

The Zorn navigated back to the dungeon, looking for Langula. She was not there, but he checked on the demonic eggs floating in the murky black fluids. Entering the same place where Kilmer and Yori once hung, he could see the eggs were intact, with two new prisoners chained to the wall as adequate substitutes. Like the other prisoners before, they bled upon the demonic eggs, incubating them in their sickly fluids. Both prisoners cried, pleading for their freedom. The Zorn ignored them both and turned to go find Langula.

Back outside in the Sanguine Forest, at the ground level of the castle, he could sense Langula's whereabouts. He made his way outside Castle Orlo where the ground was wet and foggy. Between the wicked trees of the haunted Sanguine Forest, he found her standing in the fog, looking down at the ground. She stood over a little grave, that of Isse, the spotter of Leopold's First Archer.

The Zorn approached her. "What are you doing here?"

"I have been manipulating the thoughts of the search party. The one Leopold sent inside the Sanguine Forest. Especially the dreams of the big man, my scarred one. I have been controlling them all, giving them visions, false realities, dreams of suicide, and suggestions to do the same."

"Why give them visions instead of just commanding them to kill themselves?"

"What's the fun in that, Zorn? I enjoy their emotions. I love playing with them, possessing them, letting them go, possessing them again. The tension is erotic to me. I come to them in their dreams, in the middle of the day, whenever they least expect it."

"Take care you do not play with them too much. Not with these men. You should have killed them all by now. Do it, while you have the chance. But why are you out here in the fog and not in the castle?"

"I found a fresh grave, here look."

"They buried the archer's man here in this grave."

"He was the first feast for our Monticello." Langula remembered.

"Where is he anyway?" The Zorn asked.

"I sent him to the nomad camp."

A silence came between them. Finally, Langula spoke.

"What a waste. Why do the mortals put their dead in the ground?"

"I don't really know," the Zorn said. "I don't understand it myself. They plant their dead like seeds the way we plant our eggs. Only while our eggs produce life, their graves produce nothing. Purely sentimental. Just one of their many weaknesses."

"Our next eggs will hatch soon. Then we will have two new demons."

The Zorn heard her, and knew she meant to please him. But he was not pleased by anything at this moment. His words about weakness reminded him. He could not stop thinking about Kilmer's ghost. How he lost the battle of control for his own body. That was a critical shock and weakness for the Zorn, a weakness he did not know he had. The struggle for control that took place between him and Kilmer's ghost was something new and unexpected. Nothing like that had ever happened to him before, and he wanted to know why. Leopold was right about him; he was scared, wondering about the power of Kilmer's ghost.

But he kept these concerns to himself. Langula did not need to know that he had lost control of his body, or that he had been temporarily possessed. There was no reason to tell her. She could not possibly understand what the Zorn himself did not. He felt things were getting out of control, in ways he could not predict anymore. And he worried about the future. The Star of Ehlona, Aberfell's blue comet, and now Kilmer's ghost, they all scared him. And he was not used to being the recipient of fear. It felt foreign to him.

The Zorn mumbled something to Langula, "I look forward to whatever your new demon will look like."

"We will know soon enough," she said with a serpent's hiss.

Not a minute too soon, the Zorn thought.

The stars are finally starting to show through

*Down the miles and miles of road
my life may go through*

So, I'll leave it up to you, my friend, to pull me through

'Cause I'd do most anything, just to be with you.

Excerpt from *The Witch's Songbook*

As he slept, the first shovel of dirt landed on the prisoner's face.
— Excerpt from *The Provenance* (Chapter Twenty)

SIGNS OF THE GODS

THE TEMPLE OF CHEN-LI IN THE YEAR 841 HRT
(SIX MONTHS PRIOR TO YORI'S DISAPPEARANCE)

The scouts of the White Eminence saw the beacons at two of the observation platforms. So did others. Soon the word spread throughout the villages of Odessa and Mid-Run Valley, from the Gray Mountains in the east to the Blue Mountains in the west. The southern towns surrounding Port Harbor to the very ships at sea spread the word that the Gods had gifted humanity with the boy that never forgets. The Supreme Historian had come.

As for Chen-Li, he was working on fixing an old problem. While traveling in his spiritual form he had his limitations, especially for gripping, carrying, or anything else requiring his physical form, including attacking when necessary.

In his home, he practiced his gift of separating from his physical body. Across from him, a paper target resembling a human form leaned on a straw bale. After relaxing deep in meditation, the room illuminated from a golden light. Eventually, he rose, levitating off the floor and into the air. After several more minutes, the top of his head stretched slightly. With the usual *pop*! a dulled version of his spirit shot out of the top of his head and floated above, hovering in the air. He had done this countless times before, but this time, he concentrated his spirit to strike the paper target with solid hands. But he had no luck. Every time he tried, he passed harmlessly right through the target without so much as the smallest tear. He kept trying, increasingly frustrated with his efforts. Maybe it was impossible after all.

A scout entered. He calmly saw Chen-Li's spirit flying around the room separated from his levitating body. The scout bowed his head and gave him the news.

"Master, Star Prophets in the north and south observatories have lit the fires of their beacons. Indicating they have detected a static sign in the stars."

"At last," the news stopped Chen-Li in midflight. "Which one? What static sign did they see?"

"No confirmation yet, Your Majesty, but word is, it is the blue comet of the Supreme Historian. The boy who cannot forget."

Upon hearing the news, he immediately floated toward his scout. Unnerved, the scout nervously asked. "Will you be going there, master?"

"I will send my Li in the morning, after I rest," he told him. Noticing the look on his scout's face, he added, "I just hope the sight of my spirit does not frighten the daylights out of the Star Prophets."

The next day, Chen-Li when separated from his body once more, a dull form of himself rose through the ceiling, and his spirit soared away. Past the Temple of Chen-Li, his journey would take him through miles of the Gray Mountains. Through the imposing risers of sharply angled limestone rock, the jagged hills called the Fangs, that sat like giant teeth protecting his mountain home. Exiting the mountains, he soared across the Mid-Run Valley as fast as the wind.

He reached the base of the southern mountain observatory. His Li shot up the steep hillside up to the top. He entered the observation platform by materializing through the stone wall. When he emerged on the other side, he did so right in front of Sister Chastain, she startled and dropped several papers out of her hands in shock.

"Sorry I scared you, Sister Chastain," he said to her in a voice that sounded distant and altered.

"Oh my goodness, it is you, Chen-Li!" Sister Chastain said. "You almost stopped my heart!"

"We have seen the beacons, what sign has caused you to light them?"

"A static sign," Sister Chastain said, then thought better of it. "It was Gia actually. She should get the credit."

Sister Chastain pointed to the exact page, now marked with a blue ribbon, in the *Constellation Volume*. "Here, in the CV. The blue comet. The static sign indicating the arrival of the Supreme Historian. The boy that never forgets!"

"A gift from the Gods. A sign the Cosmic Creation is in motion! Where is Gia? I want to commend her," Chen-Li scanned the area.

"She is not here," Sister Chastain averted her eyes from Chen-Li. "She went to the northern tower to calculate geometry."

"The northern tower? The Star Prophets, Glover and Tomar, are there? I will go there next," Chen-Li said. Then, almost as an afterthought, taking a moment, he turned back to face Sister Chastain. "Thank you, Sister Chastain, you have done great work here. You have provided a glimmer of hope for all of us. Well done, Sister."

With that, Chen-Li disappeared through the wall, floating through the stones of the observation chamber again, and was gone. He left Sister Chastain with a smile that she had done something good.

Outside of the tower, he was off like the wind again, sailing high across the Mid-Run Valley, leaving a trail of white vapor weaving through the mountaintops.

When he reached the southern mountain, in the same way he appeared to Sister Chastain, he emerged through the wall of the northern observation platform. The Star Prophet Tomar had his back turned and did not see him materialize behind him.

"Excuse me, Tomar?" Chen-Li said.

Tomar jumped, then turned to find Chen-Li floating in the chamber.

"Do not be alarmed. It is me, Chen-Li."

"My goodness, you gave me a fright."

Chen-Li was getting used to apologizing often for his sudden appearances. "I didn't mean to scare you."

"You are here about the blue comet? Gia saw it first. She was at the southern platform. When she lit the beacon, Glover was on telescope. He saw her fire first, then scanned the sky to see why she had lit it. That's when we saw it too! The blue comet! The first of the static signs."

"The Blue Comet: the Supreme Historian."

"Yes, exactly. Just imagine, a person who can never forget."

"Where did the geometry lead them?"

Tomar produced the map on which they worked their triangulation. "We calculated, here, in the Mid-Run Valley. He was born in the village of Conner; this is where he is. Glover and Gia are already heading there."

Chen-Li studied the map; he knew the area. Then he looked up at Tomar. "You did well, Tomar. Thank you."

Then, Chen-Li blasted through the wall of the chamber. Tomar's hair tousled when Chen-Li left, and he watched the spirit depart through the wall with a smile.

Trees and landscapes swooshed past Chen-Li again in a flash, his spirit making its way to Conner. The village was a sleepy little hamlet to the north of the Mid-Run Valley. And when he arrived there, he was floating in front of a humble cottage sitting alone, a thin plume of smoke rising from its chimney. The door to the cottage was open, and already several people stood in and around the building. Chen-Li glided to the ground and stood before the house.

He drifted close to the door and looked inside. He observed Gia and Glover standing in front of a cradle. Behind the cradle stood a man and a woman; these must be the proud parents, arm in arm, smiling with pride. He could have floated through the wall, but weary of scaring anyone else, he chose to drift through the open door. The father nodded to Gia when Chen-Li entered.

She turned around and saw him. Chen-Li could see she was holding a baby.

"Chen-Li! Isn't it wonderful?" she said, speaking as proudly as if she had given birth herself.

"Is this... the one?" Chen-Li asked.

"This is the one," Glover said. "The Supreme Historian. His mother and father, Norwa and Barclay."

"Hello, have you given the child a name?" Chen-Li asked the father.

Barclay answered, "We have named the child, Aberfell."

"Aberfell," Chen-Li repeated. "May I hold him?"

They looked at each other and laughed. Then Chen-Li realized. He was in his Li form. He must have forgotten. He had no hands to grasp or hold anything, especially not the baby. He quickly corrected his previous question.

"Someday, I meant. May I come back and hold your baby some other day, at another time?"

"Of course, you can," Norwa said with a little laugh. "You honor us. Come back anytime."

"But you might have to stand in line," Glover said. "I'm sure all the Mid-Run Valley will want to do the same thing."

Gia was beaming. She held the child and whispered things in the baby's ear, knowing that no matter how old she got, or how old the baby got, Aberfell would never forget what she said now. She whispered to the baby about her hopes and dreams. That was the appeal of Supreme Historian. He would remember whatever Gia, or anyone else, said. He would remember Chen-Li in his spiritual form who first asked to hold him with ghostly hands.

As word of the Supreme Historian spread quickly through the Mid-Run Valley, Glover's words turned true. People traveled from all over to see him and whisper things into the baby's ears. They confided in him, telling him secrets they wanted kept, their hopes, fears, predictions, and knew nothing would never be lost. In some way, speaking to Aberfell was the common villager's way of a permanence beyond their lifetime. A chance to be remembered.

The mind of Aberfell was an endless void to be filled. Even though he could not yet speak or walk, he would remember everything.

Years later, Aberfell would reveal that he remembered his birth. He would remember his time in the womb; maybe even further back than that. Into a time before his conception, into the Cosmic Creation itself, when he was just part of a wispy cosmic fabric. True or not, Aberfell would neither confirm nor deny. As he aged, he became more and more secretive.

But for now, the Mid-Run Valley celebrated the birth of Aberfell. The Star Prophets were in near euphoria from their once-in-a-generation discovery of a static cosmic sign come true. Gia rose to celebrity status in the minds of people everywhere. Aberfell's parents, Norwa and Barclay, were also celebrated in high regard for bringing the boy into the world. Even Sister Chastain profited from the discovery, never having so many requests to read dynamics charts and scry the fortunes of others in the working class—she made a fortune.

Chen-Li went back to his temple, focusing on his training to materialize his hands in his Li form. It took him six months working both day and night to learn how to manifest his spiritual hands into pure concentrated energy. By focusing his energy on his fists, he eventually learned to turn them into red glowing fire. Keeping his energy concentrated, he shot like an arrow toward the paper target across the room. This time, his fists of energy struck the training dummy, making it explode into an eruption of straw and torn paper shreds. At first it startled him, but he had established a new skill of spiritual materialization.

This was an exciting time for Chen-Li. Within a relatively short period of time, only six months, his Star Prophets had discovered the Supreme Historian. Then, he mastered spiritual materialization. He could not imagine things could get any better.

Pleased with himself, he walked up to the balcony of the temple and took in the fresh night air. But something seemed different, a light was shining. The hour was late, past ten bells, but he looked up at a bright sky. Walking up the stairs to the temple, he stood on the balcony. That's when he saw the new star.

He needed no Star Prophet, no *Constellation Volume*, to know what this star was, and what it meant. This was the second static sign, and the one he had been waiting for most anxiously. Six months after the blue comet, a second, even more important, once-in-a-generation cosmic event happened. He was now gazing at the Star of Ehlona. This was his mother's star. Its appearance was a sign indicating her return from the Cosmic Creation. She was coming back into the world. A sign for all to see, just as the Witch of the Great Mapes predicted years ago. This star was the reason he established the Star Prophets in the first place. It brightened the entire Mid-Run Valley and cast eerie shadows throughout the mountains and forests. Chen-Li could see that all three of the Star Prophets' beacons were blazing. As improbable as it was, a second static cosmic sign was upon them.

The Star of Ehlona.

As he stood there looking at it, bells started ringing in the surrounding villages. He leaned forward upon the temple's railing to get a better look. Somewhere out there, the soul of his mother, Ehlona, the Goddess of Beauty, had returned.

Chen-Li turned and noticed that the Dragonbreath Mountain, with the ever-present cloud on top of the summit, was reacting to the star. Lightning flashed through the cloud, illuminating the summit. But this lightning was unusual in colors of blue, gold, red, yellow, green, and purple.

The Timmutes were celebrating the sign of their creator's return.

Elsewhere, King Leopold leaned against his railing in Castle Odessa.

"How many newborns are there?" Leopold asked Lord Whitney.

Lord Whitney at first shrugged, looking at the Star of Ehlona. "Maybe five hundred a day. That would be an estimate. It could be more, maybe less. A lot, regardless."

"Scattered all across Odessa," Leopold said almost to himself.

Lord Whitney nodded, wondering if it was a comment or a question. "Yes, Your Majesty. All throughout the land of Odessa."

"Can we determine where this child, this spirit of Ehlona, will be? What do you recommend, Lord Whitney? How would you find her?"

"We could send out scouts," Lord Whitney said. "We could look for the ones born this day. I'm sure others will be looking too."

"How long would that take? A year?" Leopold asked.

"Maybe we could do it in eight months."

"Would you be able to recognize the child, if they found her?"

"Positive confirmation?" Lord Whitney said nothing for a long while. "I am afraid it would not be so obvious, until the child was grown and started to reveal itself. Otherwise, we would have to wait and see."

"Then, that is what we will do, Lord Whitney. Wait and see."

"Yes, of course, Your Majesty."

Chen-Li and King Leopold were not the only ones watching. The whole world saw the star and knew what it meant. All of Odessa understood that something of the Gods just happened, something of cosmic significance had just occurred. It thrilled some, terrified others. But after the initial surprise of seeing the second static celestial sign, most of the world rejoiced.

The scorned Hazor the Zorn watched the star of his mother too. He was not afraid, and he did not rejoice either. For him, it was time to get down to business. He had to find this child, this manifestation of his mother, and kill her. He could not allow her to grow into her power. Because this time, she would be out for vengeance.

And the balance be damned.

Every time you die, a hero is born

Every night you spend so far away from your home

Every time you dive in crystal blue lagoons

Every time you cry over lost balloons.

Excerpt from *The Witch's Songbook*

Look upon me for the last time.
For if I ever see you again, I will kill you. Balance be damned.
— Excerpt from *The Provenance* (Chapter Twenty-One)

SELF-DESTRUCTION

THE CASTLE ODESSA IN THE YEAR 842 HRT
(ONE MONTH SINCE THE STAR OF EHLONA)

B*ump! Bump!* Lord Whitney watched the man's boots knock into the wall. *Bump! Bump!*

Laws was hanging by the neck. The rope, looped around a wooden ceiling beam, stretched and groaned under his dead weight.

Bump! Bump! His left boot hit the wall occasionally as his body twisted on the frayed rope. *Bump! Bump!*

"Is that him? Is that Laws?" Lord Whitney asked the guards. He could not be sure. His face was swollen and blue, hardly recognizable with his tongue swelled and sticking out. Dead for some time, rigor mortis had already set in. He likely killed himself the night before, but no one knew for sure how long he had been hanging there. Lord Whitney saw the scars on his face, his cleaved lips, confirming it was Laws.

Bump! Bump! There was no note, only the sound of his left foot hitting the wall. *Bump! Bump!*

"Cut him down!" Lord Whitney commanded.

Climbing to the top of the horse stall, a guard tried not to look into the milky white eyes of Laws, but it was hard not to, as he was so close to the dead man's face. To release him from the rope, the guard pulled out his knife, shouting to another, "Grab his legs."

The other guard hesitated, afraid of what was happening. Word was spreading that this suicidal tendency was a contagion of evil magic brought back from the Sanguine Forest. Not just for the search party, but also for a percentage of the thousand men that went into the forest to rescue Kilmer and Yori. This deathly trend had been infectious.

Yet the other guard did as he was told. He held his breath and held the big man around the waist. With the bottom half secured, the guard above applied a sharp knife against the tight bristles of the rope, bursting it in two with the slightest touch. The dead man's weight dropped full and heavy upon the man at the bottom, and they carefully managed to lower his body to the ground.

First it was Curtz at the king's celebration, now Laws—both by self-destruction. Both had gone into the Sanguine Forest. Now both were dead by their own hand. As many of the others were.

The body of Laws was covered over with a horse blanket and left lying in the straw, as they waited for the death wardens to bring a wagon to come and take him away. Until then, only Law's pale arm poked out from under the cover of the blanket.

Lord Whitney escorted the remains back to the infirmary where Laws had escaped the night before. There, they placed him beside Curtz. Two members of the search party dead, along with the others, struck down by madness.

Melvin appeared in the infirmary. He looked in shock at the covered remains of his comrades on the metal table.

"The evening check found his bed empty," Lord Whitney told Melvin. "They conducted a search but couldn't find him until they discovered him this way."

Lord Whitney backed away from the dead men. He softly spoke to him.

"How are you feeling, Melvin?"

"You mean, am I suicidal?"

Lord Whitney turned and considered him briefly.

"Well, are you?" he asked. "Will you be next? Or will it be Hanson, Rhodes, or Givens? Maybe Yori? Even Lord Kilmer, perhaps?"

"Lord Kilmer? Has he been having nightmares too?"

"So you admit it, then. You are having nightmares?"

Melvin looked down. At last, he said trembling, "Horrible ones. So much blood. Enough to swim in. All that death, makes you just want to…"

"Makes you want to join them?" Lord Whitney asked.

Melvin put his face in his hands and sobbed, unashamed. Lord Whitney put his arm around him.

"It will be fine, Melvin," Lord Whitney said. "We should check on the others."

They went down the hallway of the infirmary and looked in on Givens. His disconnected demeanor was like that of a child laughing in madness. Mindlessly, he sat in a rocking chair, talking to himself and giggling manically. Lord Whitney shut the door and walked down the hall.

Yori was not so lucky. They had to keep him sedated. He had attacked Lara upon awaking from his dreams. He was having hallucinatory visions, as if he did not see her face at all, but someone or something else.

"Langula! Get away from me, you demon!" he screamed at her, thrashing and pulling her hair violently. "Don't touch me, I swear I'll kill you!"

He scratched and ripped at his face, trying to tear the flesh from it. When Lara tried to stop him, he attempted to tear the flesh off her face instead. Healers rushed in and held him down, making him drink a strong sedative. Finally, he fell asleep again, but to what kind of dreams they sent him was anybody's guess.

Lara insisted, "This is not my Yori. I did not recognize the look in his eye; he was somebody else. Not my Yori."

Suddenly Melvin grabbed his head.

"Melvin? What's wrong?" Lord Whitney asked, helping him to a chair.

It did not take long to clear his head, and Melvin nodded that he would be fine. "These things have been happening to me more frequently in the past day or two. I don't have to be asleep anymore to have the nightmares."

The two walked together through the castle and made their way to the soldiers' barracks, looking for Hanson and Rhodes. They first went to find Hanson, and soon stood in front of his door. They knocked but received no answer.

But Hanson was there.

Inside, he was lying on his bed, wide awake, his eyes open and staring at the ceiling unblinking. His mind was tormented with visions of black-garbed priests complying with the Zorn's Grand Order to take their own lives. The visions revealed the anguish of their self-destruction, the cutting, the stabbing, the choking. The cries of twenty thousand priests ending their own lives. The visions made him feel as if he were dying. He could feel the eyes upon him, the pressure, the expectation that his turn had now come.

He never heard the knock on the door.

"Are you sure this is Hanson's room?" Lord Whitney asked Melvin.

"I'm sure of it," Melvin said, then shouted, "Hanson! Hanson! Open up! It is me, Melvin. I am here with Lord Whitney. Let us in!"

But Hanson did not hear Melvin.

He was dimly aware of holding the razor in his right hand. Lifting the thin metal blade, he pulled it across his body. He felt no pain as he applied its sharp pressure to his arm, pressing down then pulling across, cutting his flesh from his inner elbow toward his wrist. A thin line of pink traced the slice in an opening of skin. He took a breath, then the thin line burst forth a steadily oozing trail of bright red blood.

While Hanson cut into his veins, Lord Whitney tried the door-knob—locked.

"Let's summon the quartermaster," he said. "He will have the master keys to all the rooms."

As the blood began to soak into the bed from Hanson's left forearm, all he could think of was the sensation of drowning in the mud of the Sanguine Forest. Switching the bloody razor to his sticky left hand, the bloodied one, he gashed another long slice down his right arm, in the same manner. Soon blood erupted from that arm too.

As Melvin and Lord Whitney waited for the quartermaster to come with the key, they walked a short way down the hall to Rhodes's barracks room. Knocking on his door, they had better luck.

Rhodes opened the door. But he looked tired and weary. Behind him the room was dark from having the shade drawn to shield him from the bright light of the day. The three men shared a curious awkward look at each other, causing the ever-perceptible Rhodes to question them.

"Something happened? What?"

There was more awkward silence. Then Lord Whitney frowned and told him, "Laws is dead."

Rhodes acknowledged his words with an unemotional and silent nod. "How? When?"

"He hung himself," Lord Whitney told him. "Last night sometime. We found him this morning in the stables."

"What of the others?" Rhodes asked.

"Hanson is not answering the door," Melvin said. "Have you seen him lately?"

"Not since last night," Rhodes said, looking down the hall at Hanson's door. "But here's the quartermaster walking down the hall. I'll ask him to unlock the door. Hopefully he's just sleeping."

The three men went to meet the quartermaster at Hanson's door.

Hanson's sight grew dim. He let out a slight gasp as he slipped under the mud in his mind, the quagmire of his vision. Once under the surface of the mud, he fell rapidly deeper. The laugh of the demon tormented him as he sank deeper into blackness.

Just then, the quartermaster unlocked the door, and they were all shocked to see what Hanson had done.

He lay in his bed, head up, eyes closed, face pale. He looked as if he was sleeping peacefully. His arms were stretched out before him, with channels of blood flowing in drizzles like rivers. The bed was saturated in blood and dripping on the floor. The razor that he used to open his veins was still in his left hand.

Lord Whitney and the quartermaster froze in shock; Melvin gasped and turned away. Only Rhodes was quick to act. He rushed into the room to attempt to save Hanson's life. Instinctively he grabbed a towel and swept to Hanson's side. Trying to stop the bleeding, Rhodes checked him for a pulse. He found a faint heartbeat, but it was dim and shortly after, it faded away altogether.

"Hanson! Hanson!" Rhodes shouted, shaking him. Hanson's head moved to-and-fro with no expression, just lifeless. He tried desper-

ately to revive him, but his wounds were too deep to stop the bleeding. Hanson's face had turned to pale white.

Three white sheets. Three dead bodies in the infirmary: Curtz, Laws,
and now Hanson joined them.

"What is happening to us?" Melvin asked. "We can't stop it! I wish
we had never stepped foot inside the Sanguine Forest!"

Lord Whitney and Rhodes looked at each other. Nobody seemed
to have any answers. Then a voice spoke out behind them.

"We need help." It was King Leopold. He had come up unseen
behind them. The men turned to see His Majesty walk into the infirmary. Leopold looked at Melvin and saw his tears and his panic. He
placed his hand on the boy.

"We need Chen-Li," he said.

"Your Majesty," Lord Whitney greeted the king with a low nod.
Rhodes and Melvin bowed quietly in unison.

"Our men have been exposed to a force against which we have no
knowledge or power to deal with," the king said, pacing the floor.
"This can only be the magic of the Zorn." Leopold looked at Melvin
and Rhodes. "Yori is not himself. Givens has been overcome with feeble-mindedness. The rest of you are having visions and nightmares,
and you need help. Lord Kilmer, and all the members of the search
party, need Chen-Li's spiritual magic. I fear it is our only hope."

The king approached the bodies on the table. The white linens were
stained in blood. King Leopold spoke as he looked at the bodies for
a long time. "He will know I am right. If help does not come soon,
I fear what will happen to the rest of you. It is already too late for

Curtz, Laws, and Hanson. Chen-Li must come to our aid, in our hour of need.

"Enough!" King Leopold said, defiantly turning away from the dead. "We can only break the spell of the Zorn with a more powerful one. There is only one person I know that could do that. The only person that would possibly have that kind of power: Chen-Li. We must go to his temple and request that he come here."

Lord Whitney looked at the three dead bodies. "That will take weeks, my lord."

Leopold patted him on the back. "I think you know what we are up against. Send a detail of messengers right away. Send them to the Temple of Chen-Li. Request Chen-Li himself. He is a good and caring man, maybe the master priest will help us. Until then, keep Givens, Kilmer, and Yori under guard at all times, and keep them sedated. Confine them to their beds, use restraints if necessary."

Then, the king looked at Melvin and Rhodes, and said gently, "That goes for you too. It's for your own good."

Melvin nodded looking down with tears in his eyes, and slowly walked with Rhodes to a group of healers in a room in the back of infirmary. Soon, they were drinking a concoction that sedated them. As they fell asleep, the healers carefully restrained them to the infirmary beds.

Givens babbled incomprehensibly when the healers came. He gave no resistance, drank the same sedative cocktail, and was soon asleep and restrained like Melvin and Rhodes.

All five men—Givens, Melvin, Rhodes, Yori, and Kilmer—were put in a deep sleep. Confined by leather straps, buckles, and locks securing their wrists and ankles, soon all of them were sleeping, resting peacefully or having vivid nightmares and struggling against their restraints. Only they could speak about what horrors awaited them in the dark dreams of the Sanguine.

That very hour, hoofs thundered down the Mauveguard Pass to make their way across the expanse of the Mid-Run Valley heading to the Temple of Chen-Li to request the aid of the only man that could possibly help them.

King Leopold turned to leave, but before he went, he had one more command to give. He spoke quietly to one of his guards.

"Find out anything you can about Lord Kilmer's background. See if he has any family, anyone special to him. Anyone that can come to him in his hour of need. Look around the village of Plum. Report back to me what you find."

With a crisp salute, the guard acknowledged his orders, then nodded low and turned to go to the village of Plum.

The day after, Curtz, Laws, and Hanson were interred into the catacombs of Castle Odessa. Extensive military services were held in their honor, with King Leopold presiding over their interment.

Howling at the moon, grasping at your very soul
After his bite your life is not in your control.

⸺ ⁘ ⟨●⟩ ⁘ ⸺

Excerpt from *The Witch's Songbook*

The Star of Ehlona would shine again, and her soul would return.
— Excerpt from *The Provenance* (Chapter Twenty-Two)

THE BIRTH OF MONTICELLO

In the Sanguine Forest, strange footprints and slither marks tracked through the mud leading away from an open grave. The grave of Langula's first malevolent demon child now lay empty. This was the place Langula placed the first of her demonic eggs for incubating. After fertilizing in the black fluid back in the castle, the egg grew like a seed in the ground, until the demon could claw its way up and out of the earth. Two more fresh graves lay open, ready to receive more of her eggs.

Inside Castle Orlo, the Zorn stood beside Langula to witness the birth of a new generation of demons. In front of them on a table, lay a putrid form, covered in stringy black fluids and slime. Langula took an oily rag and smeared some of the dark filth away. The Zorn stood slightly behind her with a clean linen up to his exposed nasal cavity.

"It smells so bad, it stinks," the Zorn said. He watched as Langula peeled a thin black membrane from the body. The Zorn kept his distance as Langula removed the thin sticky substance.

"It does not stink," she said and continued to wipe away the blood and mucus.

The form on the table twitched. The body was in the form of a male shape and rested naked in the fetal position. The thing coughed and choked as it spat dirt and bile from its mouth.

Blinking its silver eyes, slowly the form rolled to stretch, exposing its masculine parts in the nude. Seeing the thing move, Langula licked her lips as she continued to wipe the body. The skin of the freshly born demon began to come into focus.

"Are those spots?" the Zorn asked.

"There, there," Langula said, assuring the creature, then backed away from the table. She took the Zorn's arm and interlocked it with hers. "Those are glorious spots."

"Why is he spotted?"

"I think his spots are magnificently demonic."

"You think everything is magnificently demonic."

"Mortals will fear him even more with his spots."

The creature had come to a sitting position now on the table.

"What shall we call him? What will be his name?" Langula asked the Zorn with building excitement. Neither could avert their eyes from him. The Zorn pushed past her and strode forward to face the demon. The newborn stood unsteadily on its feet. The two figures looked at each other face-to-face. The Zorn lowered the linen from his decaying face allowing the demon to see him more clearly. The Zorn's yellow eyes swirled in their dark eye sockets as he studied the creature. In return the demon stared back at him without any hint of fear.

"Am I to understand that there is not a drop of my blood in this creature?" the Zorn asked Langula.

"Not a drop," she said. "This one was created from a collection of different reproductive materials, including some from Amtor."

"Amtor? Leopold's former Minister of War?"

"One and the same. I first visited him searching for Soothsayer, but now I visit him just because it excites me. He is such a … large man."

The Zorn considered the creature more. It had deep reddened eyes where they should be white and possessed no life behind their blackness, unholy dark and bland. His hair hung wet and dark. Its sinewy build was athletic and muscular. The creature breathed in deep rapid breaths as his sharp fangs protruded under his black lips.

Breathing out hot fetid vapors, the Zorn could not stand the smell of it. But he needed to judge the fabric of this new creature.

"He is a stinking heap," the Zorn said after an involuntary gag. He turned away and placed the linen back to his face. "Monticello will be his name."

"Monticello. He will strike fear in the hearts of men as he serves our bidding," Langula said.

"Yes, but until then, keep him away from me. Right now, he disgusts me."

"Monticello, the first of the Vampiric Demons," she gushed. Langula wrapped her tail around the new demon then drew herself closer.

"Hail to the Zorn," she whispered to Monticello. "Say it."

Without looking at her and keeping his eyes steadily fixed on the Zorn, Monticello spoke.

"Hail to the Zorn," he repeated. He breathed out another wave of hot vapor that found the Zorn's skeletal nasal passages, making him gag again. "Hail the Master."

Langula giggled and ran her tongue across Monticello's face. A string of black slime formed between her tongue and his face, but she seemed happy and enjoyed it. Running her hand down Monticello's chest, she traced her sharp black fingernails gently down the middle of his stomach. Then, breathing in his ear, she explored him even lower. She fondled him for a moment, running each of her fingers slowly between his legs, before giving him a firm grip.

Monticello did not understand his arousal but turned his attention away from the Zorn to stare at Langula. With her other hand, she touched his face, wiping the hair from his eyes. Her serpent's tail crawled up Monticello's wide muscular back. They stared at each other with an intense look as the Zorn silently watched with interest. Monticello had not yet developed a sense of humor, or an equivalent emotion to react to how she touched him. She giggled in delight and released him.

She went over to a box of clothes and rummaged through the stolen fabrics. Langula dressed him in black pants and an orange shirt with frills around the neck and puffy sleeves. She helped dress him, and then, Monticello stood in clean, luxurious fabrics, a completed creation, a new vampiric beast. Ready to terrorize the surrounding countryside. His work would begin immediately.

"You must be hungry. Tonight, we will feed," Langula told him, anxious to introduce Monticello to a finer appreciation of his inherent abilities to hunt and quench his appetite for blood.

The Zorn, Langula, and their new spotted demon Monticello disappeared into the darkness. The three of them left Castle Orlo to explore the surrounding Sanguine Forest. Roaming the area, they looked for any living creature that Monticello could feed from immediately.

"You will find that human blood is the most fulfilling to your body and satisfying for the hunt," Langula said. "But since none dare come into the Sanguine Forest, we must improvise your first meal.

"People know better than to come here, they do not dare, especially after sunset," Langula continued. "They know these woods are haunted, and they that go in are never seen again. But there are some nomadic camps to the south, who instinctively know of us through their superstitions. Soon they will know of you too."

"Listen," the Zorn said. "Something is coming." The sound of crunching leaves and branches was getting louder.

Suddenly, leaping through the bushes, a deer hurtled toward them.

"There!" Langula pointed, and Monticello closed the distance in a blinding flash. He fell upon the deer's neck, knocking it over, making it scream as the demon's fangs sank deep into its jugular.

Monticello drank the blood out of the deer, guzzling it down like a thirsty man in the wilderness drinks from a cool spring. Langula and the Zorn walked up to watch.

"Look at him, my love," Langula said to the Zorn. "There is an arrow in this deer. That means hunters are near."

The arrow was brightly colored in the Red and Blue fletching of King Leopold's First Archer. The Zorn searched the direction the deer came from.

"I'm thinking we may have company in the Sanguine tonight, Langula," the Zorn said. "They must not be too far behind. Let's give them a welcome, shall we?"

Monticello looked up, the deer now drained of fluids, the demon's eyes sparkling above the bloody smears across his face. He wanted to taste more.

"I believe this belongs to the king's archer," the Zorn said, looking at the arrow. "If this is the king's man, we may want to put him to better use than just a meal for our newborn demon. But if there are two of them, you can have the other one, Monticello."

Soon the Zorn sensed the presence of mortal men in the forest.

"You two stay hidden; I will draw them out."

Langula and Monticello became invisible by hiding low to the ground, while the Zorn walked openly through the woods.

Soon two roaming hunters appeared in a clearing to the south of the Sanguine Forest, tracking the blood trail of the deer.

The Zorn cast a spell and a jolt of fear pulsed like a smoke ring in an ever-increasing circle around him and through the forest. It moved through the darkness like a ripple on a lake.

Fear struck the hunters and they maneuvered themselves behind a bush for a sense of the false protection it would give.

Glowing eyes emerged from the surrounding Sanguine Forest, as Langula and Monticello spied on them. But they did not attack yet, they watched and listened, and waited for the Zorn's signal.

"Shall I attack them?" Monticello asked Langula.

"Not so fast. No, I have another idea."

"What is it?"

"Watch the master play."

The hunters peeked over the bushes and saw the Zorn walking ahead of them through the Sanguine. He turned to face them, and the hunters ducked out of sight once again behind the bush. The Zorn bent down, and toward them, opening his ghastly mouth wide. With a burst of blue-and-silver magic, he vomited forth wave after wave of cockroaches. They hit the ground on spindly armored legs that rushed the hunters behind the bushes. Langula and Monticello laughed heartily. The hunters now under attack from the cockroach swarm could not hear their laughter. Instead, they jumped from the bush and began running, each in different directions.

The Zorn saw them run and stood up straight after vomiting the cockroaches. He pointed a bony finger at the skinnier one. This one liked to run and was more afraid than the other. The Zorn cast another spell, an orange beam of magic light, hardly perceptible to mortals, grabbed ahold of the fleeing man and pulled him with a slight deviation to the left. His magic worked as a funnel, like a gravity drain, causing him to think he was running in a straight line, while in fact he was being pulled ever so slightly counterclockwise back to the source, back to the Zorn.

While the Zorn waited for the man to make his way back to him, he motioned to the others to move on the First Archer. Langula and Monticello stalked him tree to tree.

The running man finally realized he had run in a circle, returning right back to the Zorn. The man fell and the Zorn approached him. But the Zorn hesitated and got some amusement by allowing him to look upon his face. The last thing the doomed man's eyes saw was the terrifying skeletal face of the Zorn coming closer to him. The Zorn lifted his hands and drained the life from the man, as the man's face widened deeper in terror and then froze that way in death.

Elsewhere, Langula and Monticello surrounded the king's First Archer. The Zorn left the drained body of the runner and approached the archer who had hidden behind a tree. Langula watched from one side of him, Monticello on the other. The Zorn spoke to the archer, asking him to come out from hiding. The Zorn waved his hand, and Castle Orlo materialized into view with its spiraled towers and domed ceilings behind him.

Then Langula slithered upon the archer, who backed away from her only to bump blindly into the demon Monticello. With his senses overwhelmed, the archer collapsed into Monticello's arms unconscious.

Langula sang:

> *Your days are gone, never to return!*
> *In Zornastic fire your soul will burn!*

They dragged the archer to the castle. But then, Langula stopped. "Zorn?" she asked.

The Zorn turned to her.

"You promised," Langula pouted.

The Zorn stood there a moment without expression. Then he and Langula took the archer off the hands of Monticello. Released from his burden, the new demon ran like lightning to the body of the other man and sank his fangs deeply into his fatty torso. He tore a large piece of bloody, fatty flesh from the dead man, licking his lips and fingers.

It did not take more than a few moments until Monticello had his fill of the flesh and entrails. Fed and bloodied, Monticello sped to catch up with Langula and the Zorn before they reached the gates of Castle Orlo.

All four of them entered the castle at near the same time. The heavy thick wooden gates shut with a loud bang. Then, the castle was gone, leaving the half-eaten corpse of a man and a deer drained of all blood.

On the very tip of the red-and-blue arrow, a single cockroach crawled down the shaft toward the shriveled heart of the deer, and the Sanguine Forest was quiet again.

Overhead a buzzard circled.

I need a change of scenery,
A little bit of different things every day
It feels like I've been here too long.
I've got to keep moving on.

Excerpt from *The Witch's Songbook*

Something was happening to him. He was changing; he knew it.
— Excerpt from *The Provenance* (Chapter Twenty-Three)

THE FIRST WIVES
OF CHEN-LI

THE TEMPLE OF CHEN-LI IN THE YEAR 842 HRT
(FOUR MONTHS SINCE THE STAR OF EHLONA)

Priests of the White Eminence patrolled these lands. Around the Temple of Chen-Li, the warrior-priests were ever watchful for signs of the Zorn or his demon. On patrol, adorned in their white overgarments, three priests of the watch assembled on a windy hilltop, just a few miles before the Last Outpost of the East. Mounted on uneasy horses they scanned the distance in the grayish gloom. Along with watching the rain sweeping across the Mid-Run Valley, they could see riders approaching from out of the west over the hills.

These were the riders of Leopold coming toward them.

"Now, who are these people?" one of the priests questioned the others.

"Are we under attack?" another asked, blowing into his hands in the cold drizzle of rain.

"I only count three. Not much of an attack if that is their purpose. But just in case, you'd better ride back and report to the sergeant-at-arms. Tell them we've got riders approaching out of the west. They should send out another patrol. Go!"

"Yes, sir!" the guard said and thundered away, privately happy to be leaving.

The patrol deliberately stayed on the hilltop silhouetting themselves so as to be more detectable. The riders rode hard across the valley. But then, as they neared the patrol, slowed to a trot.

"Well, now that they've seen us, might as well go meet them," one priest said to the other.

Soon, they covered the distance between them, and stopped short of each other. The priest raised his arm in both a salute that welcomed as well as halted them. The riders addressed the patrol.

"Hail, White Eminence! King Leopold sends his compliments to the Temple of Chen-Li!"

"Hail, riders of His Majesty's Red and Blue. Welcome to the lands of Chen-Li. Please state your purpose," the priest said, lowering his hand and considering the riders with an inquisitive look. The other priest nervously patted the pommel of his sword.

The riders wore the familiar red-and-blue armor, broad swords, and one held the king's banner of the kingdom of Odessa. The riders looked at each other briefly. One eventually spoke for the group.

"King Leopold sent us to the farthest reaches of his kingdom to request assistance from your master, the honorable Chen-Li. We are in need of his help."

The priest recoiled slightly at the mention that the temple was a part of King Leopold's kingdom of Odessa. The prevailing thought was that the Temple of Chen-Li was sovereign. "Chen-Li is not in his temple at present. But you are welcome to wait for him there and enjoy his hospitality as his guests."

The riders of Leopold abruptly reached for their swords. The priests of the White Eminence tensed slightly, carefully watching their actions. The riders unfastened their sword belts, disarming themselves and freely handing their weapons over to their escorts.

"Thank you for your master's hospitality," the rider said to the priest.

The priests relaxed and kicked their horses forward to accept their weapons. Once collected, the warrior-priests of Chen-Li turned toward the east.

"Please follow us. We will escort you to the temple of Chen-Li." The patrol of the White Eminence moved ahead with the riders' swords lying across their laps. The riders looked at each other and spurred their mounts to follow them.

As they passed through the high peaks, the riders could see other patrols of the White Eminence waiting for them to pass through, watching them from the hilltops. Their horses sauntered up the path past the patrols. Soon the riders got their first look at the Temple of Chen-Li.

These riders were soldiers, all veterans of the war, each having served and fought in the west. But this was the first time they had ever come farther east than the central Mid-Run Valley. As the temple revealed itself over the hills, it was an impressive sight for them, one they would not soon forget.

The temple rose over a hill to the east, nestled on top of the first series of uplifting peaks, called the Fangs, bright and brilliant white with fluted marble columns and sharp slanting eaves.

The riders followed the priests up a gradually zigzagging path, plodding safely up the first summit. Still below the temple they began to hear voices, reverberating shouts of combat training echoing off the surrounding hills. The party reached the final trail leading up to the temple with no fewer than a dozen more priests joining them along the way. Winding up the last marble paths, they passed ever higher, under more watchful eyes from stone parapets, more guards armed with crossbows. Squads of foot soldiers lined the roads now, standing at attention armed with long pikes. They rode under the archways and entered the temple, growing even more impressed and intimidated.

"Seems like these priests are itching for a fight," one of the riders whispered.

"Let's not give them any reason for one today," responded the other.

It was clear that despite the political boundary, Chen-Li ruled this area.

"Soldiers of King Leopold, welcome to the Temple of Chen-Li," a priest said to the riders, approaching them with open arms.

Drawing their horses to a stop inside the temple grounds, priests in white robes dutifully reigned in their horses. Still others adorned in white garments took the weapons from the patrol, securing them out of sight.

"Gentlemen, your weapons will be safe and will be returned to you upon your exit from the temple. Until then, enjoy your stay," the priest said. "You will be well taken care of by the First Wives of Chen-Li."

"First Wives of Chen-Li?" the riders asked the priest while dismounting foamy horses.

The priest stopped what he was doing. "Chen-Li has many wives. They hold a revered position within the temple."

The riders looked at each other with raised eyebrows, sufficiently impressed.

"How many wives does Chen-Li have?"

"Twelve at this time." Myra appeared dressed in blue robes with Tyla at her side dressed in gold. They approached the riders of Leopold with an air of confident grace.

"Welcome to the Temple of Chen-Li," Tyla said.

"We are honored by your presence," Myra said.

"Please come with us!" they said as more of the First Wives approached.

The First Wives led the way and invited the riders to walk and talk with them. They passed through the grounds of the temple, past the disciplined lines of priests practicing rigorous martial training. The riders stopped to watch as one hundred priests all punched in unison accompanied by a loud shout. Hearing a distant command that came from somewhere unseen, they pivoted to face the opposite direction. After their turn, with a sweeping motion of their arms, they followed through with another straight-arm punch, and another resounding shout.

"Impressive," one of the riders said. "How many are there?"

"Today, one hundred priests are what you see here—these are all the children of Chen-Li. But in total well over thirty thousand priests of Chen-Li live and train here," Myra told him.

The riders gave each other a concerned look.

"Is this your first visit to the temple?" Tyla said.

The men nodded. "Very impressive."

They continued walking into the depths of the temple. They were led to a comfortable chamber away from the training area. A space had been prepared where they could relax and talk comfortably in private. Or so they thought. In the Temple of Chen-Li there were always unseen eyes watching and ears listening.

Several more of Chen-Li's priests and First Wives brought fresh fruits, vegetables, cooked meats, soft crusty bread, light sweet cakes and other pastries, along with pitchers of cold mountain spring water, as well as pomegranate juice. Folded fresh linens were provided, and hot water was poured in bowls for the men to shave, clean, and refresh themselves from such a long ride.

The riders were equally impressed and grateful for their gracious reception. They washed their hands and faces and consumed as much food and drink as they desired. Then they relaxed comfortably in the hospitality provided by the First Wives of the Master Priest. Chen-Li was a man they knew to be fabled and feared, having powers of both spiritual and physical, but the hospitality of his First Wives was impeccable.

Under ordinary circumstances, Leopold's riders could get used to this pampered treatment. But they were here on the orders of their king. They were on a most urgent important mission.

"We appreciate such a gracious reception. And we are most grateful for the First Wives. But how long must we wait for Chen-Li?" asked one of the riders of the Red and Blue. "We come to you with an urgent request from the king himself."

"How long have you been traveling?" Myra asked them.

The riders told the priests and First Wives that they had been riding on the trail for a week, riding as fast as they could to request Chen-Li's assistance as a matter of life and death.

"Life and death? We are all intrigued. What can Chen-Li do to assist His Majesty?" Tyla said.

"We have had, of late, a rash of suicides among our ranks. Men of the crown are dying by their own hand. They suffer from a condition, a malevolent presence, that is tormenting their minds."

"What has happened?" Tyla asked.

"During the five-year memorial celebration of King Leopold's rule, one of these men climbed the highest tower in the sight of all the guests. Then leaped to his death."

"How terrible," Myra said.

"Another one of these men hanged himself. While yet another opened his veins with a razor. One man has been stricken with feeble-mindedness and is at present catatonic. There were others. They all suffer from visions that confuse them and influence harm upon themselves. All of them have one thing in common—they all went into the Sanguine Forest. There, they encountered powerful magic. Now, nightmares overcome them. We are powerless against this kind of dark magic."

Another rider spoke up. "We are asking for Chen-Li's help, to save the lives of many innocent others that escaped the clutches of the Sanguine Forest, only to find they are prisoners of a darker power."

"These dreams occur even in their waking time," a third rider added. "And maybe worst of all are Lord Kilmer and Yori, the king's first archer."

"Lord Kilmer and Yori?" Myra asked. "What about these men?"

"They were held captive in Castle Orlo," the rider said.

"The Zorn!" Tyla shared a look with Myra.

The rider nodded. "They were kept inside Castle Orlo for days and tortured."

"And they escaped the clutches of the Zorn?" Tyla asked.

"They did, but they need Chen-Li's help; if he cannot help, then I'm afraid there will be no hope for them, they will be the next to die."

"I see. Thank the Gods for the wisdom of King Leopold to send you to us," Myra said. "However, Chen-Li has gone on another errand, but I am confident the First Wives can help."

Myra and Tyla joined hands, sat cross-legged on the floor, and began to meditate. The soldiers looked at each other puzzled. The rest of the First Wives stopped in silence and fell to their knees. An infectious hush fell throughout the room.

After a few minutes, the women began to emit a soft glow, illuminated together in brighter tones of gold and blue. Shortly after their bodies slowly lifted from the floor. The soldiers stared wide-eyed, afraid to make a sound.

Tyla's head elongated slightly, and with an audible popping sound, a light golden specter appeared. The spirit leaped out of her physical body and floated there above her head. A moment later, Myra's spirit exited her body, casting a pale blue light. Without words, the two spirits of Myra and Tyla held hands, then gave a brief nod to the riders before vanishing into the ceiling. Then they were gone but left their physical bodies floating in meditation in front of the riders.

The soldiers were startled, not believing what they had just seen. One of the First Wives, holding a water pitcher, turned to the riders of Leopold and filled their empty cups.

"They are now with Chen-Li hundreds of miles away," she told them.

All of the First Wives continued their duties making the riders of Leopold comfortable in any way they could.

Across the miles of the Mid-Run Valley, the two spirits of the First Wives flew. Sensing Chen-Li's location they traveled to the village of Conner. They swept down into the humble home of Barclay and Norwa, the birth parents of Aberfell. The house was crowded with people inside and out to see the Supreme Historian.

The First Wives found Chen-Li holding Aberfell in his arms, speaking to him, while sitting in a rocking chair. When the spirits of Tyla and Myra materialized overhead, Chen-Li knew something had happened. It must have been something urgent for his two First Wives to come all this way to join him in their Li forms.

Chen-Li stood and addressed his wives.

"I was just telling Aberfell about my time in the Great Mapes Forest, about the witch, and the creation of the Timmutes."

"But he is still just a baby," Myra said. "Does he understand your words?"

"He does not understand the language of my words now, but unlike other infants, his memory will keep the words and wait for the vocabulary to understand them. Until then, my words will remain with him in his memory. When finally his learning of the language catches up, he will remember everything."

Then he looked at the spirits above him. "Even this interruption by you, my First Wives. Your sudden appearance will never be forgotten."

"My apologies, my husband. We have had visitors that bring an urgent request to you," Tyla said. "A matter of life and death, otherwise we would not have disturbed you."

Chen-Li looked at Aberfell. "Speak the request out loud, so that the child will hear it too, and remember."

"Three riders from His Majesty, King Leopold, have ridden from Castle Odessa to request your assistance," Myra said in the hollow voice of the spirit.

"Some of King Leopold's soldiers entered the Sanguine Forest and they barely escaped," Tyla told Chen-Li, her voice quivering. "But they did not truly escape. Not long after, three of them killed themselves, and the rest are incapacitated, suffering from visions of death by their own hand. The king fears they will all destroy themselves. They are requesting your help."

"Two of them, Yori the king's First Archer and Lord Kilmer, were held captive in Castle Orlo," Myra told them.

"Castle Orlo? Then, my brother's curse is upon them." Chen-Li handed Aberfell to his mother. Norwa accepted her child back, and in turn, gave Aberfell to another of the many outstretched arms in the crowd. They, too, wanted to tell the child things he would never forget.

"See that?" Chen-Li said, motioning to the baby in someone else's arms. "We all want to have a chance at immortality. Our histories remembered. This is what Aberfell represents for humanity. This is our generation's opportunity to have a part of us live forever."

Chen-Li turned to the spirits of his First Wives floating above him as blue-and-gold specters. "Go back to the temple. Prepare a cadre of ten priests to travel with you to Castle Odessa. The Zorn's plans, whatever they are, must be stopped. I will set off for Castle Odessa soon after you and will meet you there."

"You are not coming back to the Temple of Chen-Li?" Tyla asked.

"No, I will leave for Castle Odessa from here," Chen-Li told them. "You will get there before me, but you know what to do. You have my full trust and confidence."

"As you wish, husband."

Like a strong wind, the blue-and-gold spirits were gone. They raced back across the Mid-Run Valley toward their home at the Temple of Chen-Li.

Hearing this news, that his First Wives relayed, disturbed him. Chen-Li knew the Zorn well enough to realize that he only made visible what he wanted to be seen. There must be another purpose he did not want Chen-Li to focus on. He was not sure what that purpose was, but he was sure it was not good. First things first though. These men, the ones that survived the Sanguine Forest, must be spared from the Zorn's grasp and be given protection from their self-destruction.

I've been cheated, I've been lied to,

Mistreated, and been led blind through

alleyways and miseries, and games that weren't played fair.

Excerpt from *The Witch's Songbook*

In one fluid motion, he instinctively reached for the hilt of his sword.
— Excerpt from *The Provenance* (Chapter Twenty-Four)

ALLIANCE OF FLESH EATERS

SOUTH OF THE SANGUINE FOREST IN THE YEAR 842 HRT
(THREE MONTHS SINCE THE STAR OF EHLONA)

Nadya ran for her life as fast as she could. Tripping over the under-brush, she fell only to rise and run again. Through the woods she went stumbling but not stopping even though thorns entangled and cut her. Her nomadic garments of orange and black were torn and her skin bloodied by the sharp broken branches. She frantically broke through it all in a desperate flight to get away from the thing that followed her.

She came bounding out of the dark trees and into a bright clearing. Collapsing on a white wooden fence, beyond she could see the burrowed garden that nestled before a little thatched roof house. A torch provided a warm light in a sconce by the door. It was a welcome sight to illuminate the darkness. Hanging on to the wooden fence post, she looked behind her, trying to catch her breath.

For a moment she thought she had lost him. But after a couple of breaths, her heart fell into her stomach. The shadow walked into her view once again.

It was a tall man in a long coat wearing a fancy hat and heavy boots. He slowly appeared in the tree line behind her. Below the rim of his hat, Nadya could see shining eyes burning red like two small embers. This was no ordinary man. His strength, his speed, and his power were not possible for something human.

Her escort from the nomad camp, her champion and lover, had just been brutally murdered in front of her. Podno came with Nadya to protect her, but no one could protect him. This thing that followed her viciously disemboweled him. This thing of no mercy and super-human strength. But Nadya did not have time to think about what had just happened to Podno. The thing was after her now.

"Help!" she screamed, still clinging to the fence post.

The torch went out. Nadya turned to look. The villagers extin-guished the light. No matter what happened, this household would not get involved. The land was flooded in darkness once more.

Turning back to look at her pursuer, the thing had gone. Ner-vously her terrified eyes scanned the darkness.

Suddenly, the thing was right beside her.

Nadya screamed again.

In a heartbeat, she lost her grasp on the fence as she was whisked away. Now her hands grasped the shoulders of the man-thing. He carried her away with no effort at all. For Nadya, everything became a blur, streaming past her in the darkness, rushing by, as the wind whipped through her long black hair. Trying to understand where she was going, the blurs were trees rushing by her and streaming lights speeding past. She did not want to be touching the thing, but her momentum forced her to. At first, she was unaware she was touch-ing it because of the sudden burst of speed, but against her better judgment, she clung tightly to him to keep from falling. They were going so fast she did not want to become detached now, no matter what waited for her later.

The thing moved at inconceivable speeds. His power was immense. His neck, covered in dark curly hair, was bursting with sinews of muscles and veins. On his skin were yellow-and-brown patches of discoloration.

The night air continued rushing by her until it changed to an oppressive darkness. She felt she was falling, yet she and the thing stayed locked together. They were going down, under the ground, feeling as if they were going beneath the world. Without end and without bottom, they continued to the left, then to the right, twisting through a labyrinth of smoky underground passages.

They abruptly stopped. Then Nadya was alone. She came to a stop, landing hard on her backside, upon a cold stone floor. She knew her landing was not as hard as it could have been. She could have been splattered upon the rocks, but instead she was placed there. Lying in utter darkness, she heard a faint and distant drip of water into water. Behind that sound, a slow and shuffling footfall. She heard other noises too, then realized they were echoes in an expansive space.

A small spark of flame bathed the underground chamber in yellow light. The man had his back to her as he slipped the torch back into a single holder. Nearby were bones, human skulls, and ribcages. He kept his distance from her as he prepared another torch. It illuminated a large stone chair, a throne, which sat in the middle of the room.

More bones were lying around, she noticed. She tried to scoot away from them, only to discover she had come nearer to others that lay closer to her. The large cavern seemed to go on forever in the dark.

Satisfied that the chamber was adequately lit, he turned to face her, and she got her first unimpeded look at him. His face was spotted yellow and brown. A collection of red-and-black facial hair formed a scruffy red beard. His bushy eyebrows were colored black and orange. His heavy boots echoed when he walked through the chamber. Flipping back his coat, long and purple, revealed a white shirt and black pants.

Despite how he had brutally dispatched Podno, so vicious and violent, he had not a smear of blood on him. He removed his short, brimmed hat that held a tiny yellow feather in its band, revealing a head of long curly multicolored hair. He had a thick nose with wide nostrils, deeply lined features on his face and creased cheeks. His boots scraped to a stop, as he rested his clawed hand on the throne in the center of the cavern. His amber eyes considered Nadya lying on the floor. Then he spoke to her in a clear full voice.

"I want to be clear. I need you to completely understand, so there can be no question of who we are, what we can do, and what we want from you. My name is Monticello. And this is my brother, Grim." He motioned with his hand to her right.

She had thought they were alone. But then she noticed that another stood right beside her. Before she could react to this other presence, Grim attacked her like lightning. With deadly precision, Grim launched himself upon her, piercing his fangs into the front of her neck. Her head snapped backward from the force as Grim went to work on either side of her Adam's apple, intending to rip it out.

Her chin had no choice but to rest upon his curly black hair. She could only breathe through clenched teeth as he punctured her throat. She could not resist him, and he quickly overpowered her with incredible strength.

"Grim, leave her!" Monticello shouted. "We need to come to an understanding." Monticello casually moved to sit on the stone throne and covered his mouth with his hand to conceal his amusement at his brother's actions upon her.

Grim released her and she fell to the floor. Nadya quickly brought her hands to her throat, examining it for damage. The one called Grim stood up and backed away, licking the blood off his lips.

"I want her," Grim said, flashing his red eyes at Nadya.

"You give a man a fish and you feed him for a day," Monticello said. "Or you teach him to fish and you feed an entire village."

"What?" Grim asked, looking over at Monticello. "You and your nonsense."

Still, the red demon backed off.

"Nadya?" Monticello whispered. "Nadya, can you hear me? Are you listening?"

It took a moment for her to sit up, still holding her throat, although they had her complete attention. Grim paced around the cavern like a tiger in a cage, face red. The demon had a large barrel chest, a thick wide nose, and a short but powerfully sturdy frame.

"You should not have attacked her. Give her a moment to collect herself," Monticello said to Grim. They gave Nadya a few moments to recover from the red demon's attack.

Monticello rose from his cavern throne. Patiently, he walked closer.

"It is important to know, we respect you. I respect you." Monticello pointed to Grim. "We are not the blood drinkers some have called us: Vampiric Demons. We are not blood drinkers, we are flesh eaters, make no mistake."

"Speak for yourself," Grim said. "I like blood."

"Forgive him, Nadya, he is the youngest of us."

"Young and impetuous, Grim. You are a perfect demon," a third voice said somewhere from the darkness.

Nadya turned to look. She had just started to breathe again. She turned to her left and saw yet another demon walking out of the shadow into the light. This one was blue.

"I am the demon Frost, the middle born."

She scrambled away from Frost, not realizing she left behind a puddle of urine.

"I resemble more of our mother Langula than either Monticello or Grim," said Frost, the tallest of the three. His hair was flowing white in long wisps that angled upward. His skin possessed a light blue tint, and his lips were a darker blue. Frost's eyes were not red like the other two—they were silver of the brightest hue.

Frost wandered to where Nadya had just been, then his feet stopped abruptly short of puddle Nadya left behind. Interrupted by seeing the urine, he knelt and pressed a finger into it.

"Monticello is right, you know," Frost said, licking his finger. A grin slowly formed on his face, revealing sharp ivory fangs on the top and bottom of his teeth. He closed his lips around his finger, and slowly pulled it out. Then he stood over her. "We are not blood drinkers."

Grim could hardly manage his excitement. As Frost walked away from Nadya, Grim rushed to the puddle.

"What we are," Monticello said, still trying to make his point to Nadya, "are the demonic."

Grim laid his palm in the puddle. Then swiping his red tongue across his palm, savored it. He licked his lips.

"We feed on everything mortal," Grim said, giving his palm another lick. "But mostly human flesh, muscle, and bone."

"What you have already seen is what we have allowed you to see," Monticello said. "We are stronger than you, we are faster than you, we can be more vicious than you. But make no mistake, we are not as barbaric as you."

Grim went to the puddle again, for another palmful of Nadya's urine.

"Well, most of us," Monticello said, watching Grim lick his palms. "Now that we have achieved a clear understanding of who we are and what we are capable of, the next and last step, is to develop an understanding of what we want from you."

"We have been watching you. You are Nadya, queen of the southern nomadic tribes," Frost said. "Are you not?"

"I am not who you think I am," Nadya said, rubbing her throat. "I am not the queen. Podno is… was, the king of the Nomads of Spiron, the nomads of the south. At least he was, before you killed him. I was not his wife, not the queen. We were lovers."

"Your truthfulness is refreshing," Frost told her.

"Ill-advised though," Grim said, rising from the wet floor that had now seeped through the porous stone; he joined his demonic brothers. "If she is not queen…"

"No, not at all, Grim," Frost said. "It is better for her to speak the truth now, instead of telling us lies. She cannot do anything without our help, and she cannot get our help with lies. In her truth, she spares us time and effort. Plus, what does it matter anyway?"

"That's right. Maybe you are not the queen of Spiron at present," Monticello said. "But you can be, you will be. With our alliance, and the power we will give you, they will respect and honor you."

"And they will fear you," Grim said. "Because they fear us."

Nadya looked at her hand, caked with sticky blood, her blood; blood she had been smearing across her neck. Her neck hurt and it still oozed from the puncture holes on either side of her windpipe. She could tell the bleeding was slowing now, starting to clot. They had hurt her, but she would not bleed to death here in this dark cavern, at least not from Grim's first attack. But she worried there might be another.

As if reading her thoughts Monticello spoke, "If you say the right things, you will yet see the light of another morning."

"What would you have me do?" Nadya asked.

"One body a month," Monticello told her, holding up a single finger. "A payment. A simple concept, really. We want you to make enemies in Spiron."

"Political enemies," Frost added. "People who stand in your way of power."

"Then," Monticello concluded with a shrug, "hand them over to us."

"We'll take care of them," Grim said.

"Send more than one body a month if you like. That's fine, we will handle as many of the tribe as you wish. But you must understand us perfectly clear—" Monticello held up one finger. "It must be no less than one body a month from your tribe, without fail. Every month."

"And for all time, there will be no end. This will be considered your power to the mortals," Frost stated. "With this type of power, no human would ever dare oppose you."

"Go to the tribes and declare yourself queen," Grim said. "They'll fall into place. Or they will die."

"Either way," Monticello said. "It's more for us. You will find you have little problem ascending to the top of the nomads. But once there, remember the tally must remain: one body a month. How you do it is your choice. Now, do we have a complete understanding and agreement?"

"What if I say no?" Nadya asked.

"Most unwise," Monticello said sitting back. "Then we will go to the next in line after you and give them the same opportunity we have just given you. They will take it."

"And that's good for me, but not for you," Grim added.

"Then I do not have a choice," Nadya said. "What happens if I miss a month?"

"Then we kill the whole tribe, including you, in one night," Frost told her. "It would be such a waste for all."

"So, you completely understand, then?"

"I understand. When do the payments start?"

"In thirty days, one month from tonight. On the first eve of the new moon. We do not need anything else to eat tonight."

Nadya cried, "You ate Podno?"

"Did we eat Podno? No, not yet."

"That will be later tonight," Grim said.

The laughter echoed down the cavern tunnels. Nadya, still holding her neck, nearly collapsed, fighting back tears.

"Now, as long as we have an understanding," Monticello spread his hands, "you are free to go."

Nadya looked up slowly. "But I don't know where I am."

Just then, as before, her body involuntarily left the ground. The sensation of flying overcame her. In the darkness everything was hurling by her again, just as it was when she was taken from the little farmhouse less than an hour ago. Her stomach seemed to fall, and felt heavy as the demon carried her upward. They passed the sulfur fumes, through the zigzagging corridors of the maze that was their subterranean home.

Frost had replaced Monticello this time. His blue demon skin shone in the moonlight as eventually the two of them burst back out into the open night air. Fresh air filled her lungs, a feeling of crispness returned, without the stink of the dead. Frost carried her through the grayness in passing blurs and streaming lights. She had the faintest impression that they were going farther than where she was taken.

They stopped abruptly. When her senses cleared, she was in one of the canvas wagons back home in Spiron. Still in the demon's arms, he lay her gently on her bed. Nadya suspected there was more of a message in the way he brought her all this way. Nadya wanted to crawl away, but he held her powerfully and prevented it. There, he looked at her for a long moment. The dim lantern's light in the wagon silhouetted his features in darkness. Nadya, still unsure what may happen, froze in Frost's grasp. Time seemed to stand still.

At length, the blue demon spoke, "Remember, at the end of each month, one sacrifice from the tribe of your choosing. Do not disappoint us."

He continued to linger over her until Nadya silently nodded. Then, with a sudden rush of wind, he left. The lanterns leaped from the canvas walls and went out, and Frost was gone. He left her in the dark, objects fell off the canvas walls, and papers spiraled down in the wagon's interior. But at least the demon had gone.

The unholy alliance had been sealed in blood.

Well, I loved you
But I just couldn't show you
I can't be hurt, not that way
So, let me take you
Let me love you
A second chance to not fade away.

Excerpt from *The Witch's Songbook*

The chanting started to fade away,
as there were fewer of them every minute that passed.
— Excerpt from *The Provenance* (Chapter Twenty-Five)

A SECOND CHANCE

The Castle Odessa in the Year 842 HRT
(Six Months Since the Star of Ehlona)

Darla sat in a wooden chair, looking at herself in a mirror, with her big brown eyes. She had developed a sad look these days as if all happiness seemed to have abandoned her. She brushed her dark hair, trying to ignore her surroundings at the orphanage. Being over twenty years old now, she could leave St. Ehlona's Orphanage whenever she wanted. But since it was the only home she knew, she stayed there after her eighteenth year to help the sisters at the orphanage, and also because she had nowhere else to go.

That was not the main reason she stayed. The main reason was in case he returned. Kilmer had been gone over seven years now. Darla did not know if he was alive or dead. His letters abruptly stopped. Her hope had been strong that he would return. Even now, that hope was more of a fantasy she replayed over and again in her imagination. Yet, she found she could not let him go.

The war between the Amalgamates and Leopold's Red and Blue had waged for two more years since Kilmer and Kory had left the orphanage. Now it had been nearly five years since the end of the war. News circulated in bits and pieces throughout the area, occasionally reaching the orphanage. At first the news reported that the war was nearly over; that the Amalgamates would be victorious. Then news came that General Blaize Plum had Leopold cornered in a mountain pass to the west, named Mauveguard Pass. Back then, it was a place very few had heard of. No one knew that Mauveguard Pass would be the stuff of legends, but now everybody knew and talked about that awful place. Then, fearful rumors circulated that General Blaize Plum and the Amalgamates had been shockingly defeated and surrendered to Leopold's forces. Afterward, Leopold had declared himself king and established the Kingdom of Odessa. His rule over all the Mid-Run Valley was complete.

This was fearful news. Leopold was considered a cold brutal killer, but just when they thought the worst, the orphanages received supplies, more food, more resources than ever before. A brutal and bloodthirsty Leopold had changed to a benevolent monarch.

The first year Kilmer and Kory were gone, she used to worry about them, and she still did. But after the second year of war, her worry lessened. In the following years, her concern turned to hazy memories of things she was not even sure about anymore. She wondered if these were not false memories—if they ever even happened at all. She had perfected a memory of him, remembered sitting in the grass, composing poetry, kissing him, and holding each other.

She was now twenty-two, and she had changed from a child to a woman. Yet she cherished memories of her time with Kilmer and what might have been. Life seemed incomplete without knowing what happened, and about the whereabouts of her boys: Kilmer and Kory. She did not even know if they were still alive. But in her dreams, it seemed they were.

Sister Chavise would not send her away. Darla knew someday she would have to strike out independently. She would have done so already, if she had closure, an idea of where she wanted to go, or what she wanted to do. She only knew she wanted to be with Kilmer, to find out if he still lived, and find out if he even cared about her anymore. But going into the seventh year with no message or news of his whereabouts, it seemed that one of two outcomes was clear: either he did not care about her at all, or he was dead.

She turned from the little oval mirror and grabbed a sweater. A couple of younger orphans ran by her. They were going up the stairs giggling, as she was going down. They passed somewhere in the middle when Darla slowed, thinking she heard men talking. Walking into the large kitchen, she was startled at what she saw. Her heart jumped.

Sister Chavise was holding a conversation with soldiers of Leopold's Red and Blue. Certainly, she thought, they were bringing bad news of Kilmer and Kory. After seven years of waiting, this was the moment she had been dreading. She knew the soldiers brought news they were both dead, she just knew it.

Sister Chavise turned to Darla with an odd expression.

"Darla! Come here, I want you to meet Captain Tanner, a cavalry soldier of King Leopold."

Darla was taken aback. She suddenly felt weak. But the captain looked pleasant enough.

"Captain Tanner," Darla greeted him politely with a nod, taking a moment to catch her breath and trying to calm her heart.

"What's this all about?" Oaks said, suddenly appearing, walking right past Darla and coming into the kitchen. He had no fear at all. Oaks was eighteen years old now, tall and thin from the growth spurt he had had in the subsequent years since Kilmer's and Kory's departure.

The soldier gave them both a smile.

"You must be Oaks. Sister Chavise has told me all about you."

Darla turned to go.

"Darla! Wait," Captain Tanner said. "I came here especially to meet you."

Darla stopped and turned. Captain Tanner walked between Oaks and Sister Chavise.

"How old are you now?" the captain asked.

Darla said nothing, but Oaks did not hesitate.

"I turned eighteen almost a year ago."

Captain Tanner nodded approvingly. "And what of you, Darla?"

"Darla was eighteen a few years ago, Captain Tanner," Sister Chavise said. "But she decided to stay on here at the orphanage. She's been such a blessing; I hate the thought of seeing her go."

"Am I going somewhere?" Darla asked.

Captain Tanner smiled, then looked at Sister Chavise. He focused back on Darla.

"His Majesty, King Leopold, sent me here personally to ask if you would allow me, let me, escort you to Castle Odessa."

Darla gave a slight giggle and shrugged in disbelief. "King Leopold asked you to escort me? Are you sure you have the right person? I mean, I do not know him. He does not know me."

"He does know you, Darla."

"Why? Am I in trouble? What did I do?"

Captain Tanner laughed. "You did nothing wrong, I assure you. I received orders to come here and escort you to help a mutual friend. I think you know him. His name is Lord Kilmer."

"Kilmer? He is alive?"

"Yes, he is alive. But he has been sick for months. King Leopold thought if you accompanied me to Castle Odessa, you might be able to, well, save his life. Give him hope, a reason to live."

Darla looked at Sister Chavise. The sister nodded in agreement with Darla's excitement.

"Well?" Darla asked, searching in her eyes for answers.

"Go to him, he needs you."

Darla looked flustered. "I don't think he needs anything from me. How come… I mean, he stopped writing? What can I do? What do I bring? Do I need anything?"

"No, Darla," Captain Tanner said. "We will take care of any needs you might have courtesy of His Majesty, King Leopold. All we need is you."

Darla rushed to Sister Chavise and embraced her in a hug for several long moments, then gave her a kiss on the cheek. She thanked the sister repeatedly, even as she was being led out of the orphanage by the captain.

"Captain Tanner," Darla stopped abruptly. "Is this real?"

"It is. I wish I could promise that everything will be fine, but I can't. Kilmer is very sick. But I do promise you that while you are under the care of King Leopold, nothing will harm you."

"What is wrong with him?" Sister Chavise asked.

"He is lost in his own mind. The king suspects that a familiar face, like yours, and his love for you, could be the only thing to help save his life."

"His love for me?" Darla began to cry.

Sister Chavise came to her and placed her hands on her shoulders.

"Go now," she said, nodding her approval. "Save Kilmer, fight for your dreams."

Darla nodded and wiped her eyes. Without further word, Captain Tanner whisked her away out the door. He took her to a waiting horse-drawn wagon. There, they both stopped in their tracks, surprised to see Oaks already sitting in the wagon.

"Don't look surprised, you two," Oaks said. "As soon as I heard Kilmer's name, I was in."

Captain Tanner supported Darla by the shoulders and turned to look at Sister Chavise who stood in the doorway of the orphanage. Sister Chavise clasped her hands and gave him an affirmative nod.

"Go ahead," Sister Chavise said. "Take him along with you. He would only give me grief, knowing that an adventure with Kilmer was waiting and he couldn't be in on it. He would be impossible otherwise."

"We will keep him safe, Sister Chavise."

Oaks smiled approvingly.

Captain Tanner helped Darla up the floorboards of the wagon. Then, he climbed up himself. The other horsemen with Captain Tanner rode up beside him. They would be riding in defense of the little wagon, protecting them on the orders of the king.

Captain Tanner snapped the reins on the backs of the horses and the wagon rolled down the path away from the orphanage. The rest of the horsemen spread out in strategic positions to the front, back, and sides of the wagon.

After a few feet, Darla turned around to look back at St. Ehlona's Orphanage. She saw Sister Chavise waving goodbye. She didn't know it, but this would be the last time she would ever see her.

Word had spread among the orphans; they, too, stood outside and waved at her, wishing them the best of luck.

"This must be how Kilmer and Kory felt when they left almost seven years ago," Darla said.

Oaks, with moist eyes, turned to look back too. "We are seeing what they saw and feeling what they felt."

They turned to look at each other.

"I'm so glad you came, Oaks," Darla said.

"I couldn't let you face it alone. You're my best friend."

She hugged him.

"Say, Captain Tanner," Oaks said. "Why did you call him Lord Kilmer?"

Captain Tanner rocked with the wagon's rolling down the rocky path. "Because he is a lord. Back in the Battle of Mauveguard Pass, Kilmer was a hero. He saved the life of Amtor, King Leopold's Minister of War. Amtor was the second highest-ranking person in His Majesty's kingdom. He was awarded the rank of lord in the Red and Blue army and given title, wealth, and lands. Your friend Kilmer is a remarkably courageous man. We are lucky to have him, and you are lucky to know him the way you do."

"Wait a minute, did you say the Red and Blue? Not the Amalgamates?"

"There was a rumor about that. A rumor that Kilmer was originally an Amalgamate. But in the end, King Leopold did not find it relevant. The fact remained Kilmer still saved Amtor's life when he could have just as easily killed him. That doesn't sound like the work of an enemy."

Oaks and Darla gave each other a confused look.

"What about Kory? Where is he?"

"Sorry, Mr. Oaks," Captain Tanner said. "I know nothing about this Kory you ask about."

Oaks stared ahead in his thoughts, worried for his friend. Darla did as well. But finally, Oaks broke the silence again, as he was always known to do.

"Lord Kilmer, huh? That has a nice ring to it, doesn't it, Darla?"

"I just want him to be alive and well. To me, that's all that matters."

"Yeah, but he will be, and he is still a lord. If there is any better way to be, I don't know what it is."

"You are ever the optimist," Darla told him.

"What's an optimist?" Oaks asked.

"The opposite of a pessimist," Darla said.

The wagon continued to rock westward, flanked by mounted guards, into the Blue Mountains, and on to Castle Odessa.

"Captain Tanner?" Oaks turned to the captain. "What's a pessimist?"

Captain Tanner smiled and gave him a sideways look. "The opposite of an optimist."

The captain and Darla smiled at each other, and Oaks looked frustrated, as the wagon and the guards rolled down the road toward Mauveguard Pass and Castle Odessa.

The Star of Ehlona shone overhead.

I looked into the gambler's face

He's a lonely man, in a crowed place

When the wheel started spinning in time.

"Just one more drink," he said,

Right before he died.

Excerpt from *The Witch's Songbook*

After many hours of terror-filled screams, the sounds gradually began fading away, to a final dreadful quiet.
— Excerpt from *The Provenance* (Chapter Twenty-Six)

FEAST OF THE DEMONIC

CAVERNS BELOW THE SANGUINE FOREST
IN THE YEAR 842 HRT
(SEVEN MONTHS SINCE THE STAR OF EHLONA)

Every month that followed, when all the land was at its darkest, on the first day of the dark cycle of a new moon, the sacrifice of the Nomads provided a feast for the demonic. With the alliance in place, the flesh eaters specified that the sacrifice must be provided every month, without fail, or the wrath of the demonic would be invoked upon the entire tribe. That was the bargain, one living sacrifice per month. Anything less would be considered a waste of sweet, delicious human flesh. In this task Nadya, now the reigning queen of the Nomads of Spiron, was diligent.

Nadya saw to it how the Spirons would select their monthly sacrifice. At first, she took it upon herself, handing over those derelicts of their society, those that no one would miss: the outcasts, those that committed crimes against the tribe, those who were not well liked. They would not be missed. But then once these obvious selections were gone, the decisions became more difficult, more heartbreaking.

Selections had to be made of those who would be missed, and not only missed, but those connected to the tribe: functionally, financially, and emotionally. So, she moved to a system of selecting lots.

A representative from each of the twelve tribal families came together on the night of the full moon to select a stone for their tribe. The stones would be examined for authenticity by several witnesses, then all placed into a black satin pouch. Eleven of the stones were colored white, these were called the benevolent stones. One was colored black and was called the sacrificial stone. When selected, the black sacrificial stone indicated which family would present a sacrifice from their own tribe. That tribe's sacrificial selection would be the sacrifice for all the tribes of the Nomads of Spiron. This sacrifice would become the flesh of the unholy feast to feed the hunger of the demonic. In exchange, the rest of the tribe would endure another month of safety. Safety within the tribe, safety from the demons, but also, safety from all other threats.

For the tribe selecting the sacrificial stone, the walk home was a sad and lonely one. That tribe was now considered cursed and contagious; that tribe and all its members were to be avoided by the other tribes. They were forced to consider what they had done, what sin they had committed, to invoke the sacrificial stone, and why the gods had cursed them.

In this process, it was common knowledge, that if the family chosen by lot did not provide a sacrifice on their own, the rest of the tribes would come and take the first one they could find. But regardless, each tribe was responsible for coming up with their own way, within their family clan, to select their sacrifice.

Sometimes, the sacrificial family would have a volunteer to be the sacrifice. This was someone who valued their loved ones over their own life. But more often than not, a selection had to be made. Some clans chose their elders, reasoning that they had had an opportunity to live a long life. Other families picked their youngest, reasoning by their short lives they would not have the knowledge of fear, along with parents who resolved that they could still have more children, to replace their accursed ones. Others, valuing one gender over another, would select the males for sacrifice, sparing their women. While others burdened it as a curse only to their female members.

But however the decision was reached individually by the clans, the sacrifice had to be sent to the demonic every month without fail for the good of the entire tribe. As tragic as the sacrifice was, the long-term benefit resulted in the survival of the tribe. In time they would find they benefited more by having the sacrifice than not having it. The alliance with the demonic would most certainly not have been the worst they could have done, and they reasoned that on a monthly basis, someone would have died anyway. Overall, the sacrifices pruned out the weak of the tribe, and made those remaining even stronger.

But still, somebody had to die.

When the night of the new moon came, the condemned dressed in plain sackcloth and were given a strong concoction to dull and numb their senses. So, when the feast began, the consumption of their flesh, they would be as disconnected from their pain as possible. The demonic had no objections regarding the sedation. The sedatives had no effect on the demonic and didn't change the taste of the meat.

Inside Castle Orlo, Monticello and his brothers, Frost and Grim, prepared the sacrifice for the feast. Tonight, an elderly man shivered in the darkness, as the sacrifice; he was brought into a room dimly lit by a multitude of candlelight. The old man was shuffled through the cavern by the demons with surprising respect and adequate concern for his advanced age. He did not make a sound as he stepped quietly in his bare feet. Looking over the room with big wide eyes, he faltered occasionally, only to be held up by one of the demons who reassured him, *everything will be all right.* Delicately he was led to a room with a large table in the center. The demons helped him sit, removed his sackcloth, swung his legs up, and laid him down. Once the old man was naked and flat on the table, they secured his hands and feet with leather straps connected to posts situated in the four corners.

The old man's eyes widened as the feast started. He watched fearfully as the demons circled him, then began ripping through his torso with their sharp claws and tearing through his entrails with sharp teeth. The old man screamed, writhing in pain, despite the sedative. But only for a moment. Then it was over.

His blood ran out of him, down little channels notched along the sides of the table. Gravity filled the notches with streaming blood cascading along at an angle in fluid unison, dropping through waiting round drain holes located at the end of the table. These drains funneled the old man's blood through curved pipes and out to an open tap, where it flowed in dark crimson into waiting golden chalices. Once sufficiently filled, the tap was closed to save the rest for later. Then the demons savored his blood, drinking it in the fancy cups.

Langula came out from the dining area, licking the blood from her fingers. Monticello was close behind her. They both approached the Zorn, who sat back in his throne after enjoying his own meal, consisting of the life force of the old man, the newly deceased sacrifice, that flowed into him as a renewing spiritual energy.

Langula spoke to him, "Have you any news of the Ghost Man?"

The Zorn flinched at the mention of it. He still remembered losing the battle for control of his own body and spirit. It still scared him. For the first and only time in his life, he had been subjugated in possession. It represented an unfamiliar subordinate position and unwanted experience. An experience he remembered bitterly.

"You do mean Kilmer, don't you?" the Zorn shouted at her. "His name is Kilmer! Not to be forgotten. Not Ghost Man! But you knew that already, didn't you?"

Langula gave the Zorn a naughty grin. She looked delighted to invoke his emotion. Noticing this, the Zorn responded.

"You take every opportunity to torment me, to mock me, just like the filthy demon you are. The only spirit I have ever feared was Kilmer's ghost. This spirit of Fortis Plum, blessed by my father's enemy, the God Heironomus, the only thing that has ever demonstrated power over me."

"This will not do," Langula said. "What do you intend to do about it?"

"I have already transformed into my crow form and paid a visit to our King Leopold. I told him the true identity of this man Lord Kilmer. That his name is not Kilmer at all, but rather it is Darius Plum, the only surviving son of Justus Plum, the Head Council of the village of Plum, a descendant of Fortis himself."

"Who told you this Kilmer is really a descendant of Fortis Plum?" Monticello asked.

"No one. As the ghost Fortis Plum was roaming through my memory, I was roaming through his. During the times I gained control, I was in the mind of Kilmer's ghost. There I learned the story of Fortis Plum, the blessings of the god Heironomus, bestowed upon him to live beyond his physical body forever. Fortis was an instrument of insurance for Heironomus, like my father's castle in the clouds was to me. Heironomus saw to it if anything ever happened to him, he would still have a living link to a rogue power to rival his brother, my father, Hexor the God of Darkness. Fortis Plum was an insurance policy for Heironomus. The power of Heironomus trumped my power and my control."

"All of that was revealed to you by Kilmer's ghost?" Langula asked. But Hazor ignored her.

"After the seed of deceit I planted grows in Leopold's mind, I know what the outcome will be. Lord Kilmer will die at King Leopold's hand. Leopold could never abide being lied to. Plus, it's just bad business to leave loose ends like Darius Plum live, no matter what he is called. He left a single child of his enemy alive. A child whose family he was responsible for killing, leaving Lord Kilmer with so many reasons for revenge. For this reason alone, it is enough to drive the king to action. And by action, I mean killing this man and sending his damnable ghost, Fortis Plum, to oblivion."

"This must be done, if it is so important to you," Langula said with a hiss.

"This unforeseen event has the potential to blow up everything. Don't you understand? The Cosmic Creation is desperate. I am the most powerful I have ever been, even more so now than when the Zornastic Order was alive and at its strongest. For as long as Leopold is king, and with my ability to control him? I have indirectly conquered... the entire known world!"

Back at the table, Frost and Grim picked through the scarlet bones.

ACT IV

The Ungrateful
Child

Give me one good reason
Why my skin feels like its freezing,
Like a body in the morgue.

Excerpt from *The Witch's Songbook*

Something bad happened here, he could tell; something was wrong.
— Excerpt from *The Provenance* (Chapter Twenty-Seven)

YORI IS DEAD

THE CASTLE ODESSA IN THE YEAR 842 HRT
(EIGHT MONTHS SINCE THE STAR OF EHLONA)

Five months had passed since he was put in a coma of sedation. Now, Kilmer felt a warm softness on his cheek. The feeling gently moved across his forehead, slowly across his face, then back to his cheek. A feeling more gentle, more pleasant, more caring than the healers.

Opening his eyes, he thought he saw an angel standing over him. A hazy shape wiped his brow with a cool damp cloth, speaking soft words to him. Dim in his eyesight, silhouetted against the glow of the distant torchlight, shadows darkened the angel's face. But Kilmer found her voice oddly familiar.

"Kilmer?" Darla whispered. "Come back to me, Kilmer."

He blinked his eyes, his vision clearing. A face emerged from the shadows, and he could make out her long dark hair, her soft delicate mannerism. He recognized that Darla was with him.

She leaned closer and kissed his cheek, leaving a pleasantly clean scent of honeysuckle behind when she withdrew. After her kiss, their eyes met.

"Darla? Is that you? How did you find me?"

Darla did not say a word but let out a strange laugh. Her laughter became maniacal, and the smell of honeysuckle changed to the rotten smell of filth. The same stench Kilmer remembered from Castle Orlo.

Darla had changed in appearance too. Her skin turned to dark blue, her fingers capped with black sharp claws. Darla was gone, and in her place, he saw the demon Langula. Her black lips stretched across ivory fangs under silver serpent eyes. She reached out with her coiling tail and wrapped it around him.

Kilmer kicked at her as the demon got closer. Still, he could not escape her grasp. She held him firm, struggling to push out another demonic egg from her scaly coils. The egg landed on his chest slippery and wet, and covered in the stink of her black blood. The egg grew bigger, larger, until it suffocated him.

He screamed and the demon's face faded away and the face of Darla returned. Kilmer realized Langula had never been there in the first place. There was no egg. He laid on the bed breathing heavily, in panic, a frantic look in his eyes. His lips quivered and he tried to speak but was incoherent.

"What's wrong, Kilmer?" Darla asked being pulled away by the healers. "It's me, Kilmer. It's Darla!"

"Darla!" he kept repeating. "Are you real? Are you real, Darla?"

More healers rushed into the room and threw a blanket over him. One of the healers applied drops of a strong-smelling liquid into a cloth and placed it over his nose and mouth. Kilmer breathed in the vapors deeply and the sedative overpowered him. His eyes rolled back. He relaxed and fought no more as he started to go under. Tightening the straps restraining his arms and legs, the healers made sure he was tightly secured.

Kilmer drifted once more into his vivid dreams.

He was back in the Sanguine Forest riding his horse through the fog in the trees. Curtz and Laws were there with him. They halted, so that Hanson could ride up to join them.

"I thought you were all dead?" Kilmer asked them.

"We are as alive as you," Curtz told him.

"Where are Melvin and Rhodes?" Kilmer asked.

"They will be here soon," Laws told Kilmer. "First Rhodes, then Melvin."

Kilmer insisted again that Curtz, Laws, and Hanson were all dead.

"Hanson, you were the last to die, and the last to join us in this dream."

They will be here soon, Laws said again in a haunting voice. *I already told you so.*

Now the three of them looked as they did in death. Curtz sat on his dead horse, the one that had choked on the swarm of flies, its eyes colored in a milky hue of death. Curtz's skull had burst open, his face covered with blood. Laws' face was purple, his lips blue, his neck stretched and broken. Hanson looked pale his forearms covered in blood that dripped upon the ground.

But you are not supposed to be here, Laws said. *Not yet.*

Kilmer came out of his dream. It had been days since he was last conscious.

"I'm here with you," said the voice of Darla. "I've been here with you the entire time."

His lips were dry and parched, and he had dark circles around his eyes. His voice was weak as he spoke.

He licked his lips and asked her, "Do you know about Kory?"

"Kory?" she asked. "No, what about him?"

He started to cry. "I couldn't protect him. I knew he would die at Mauveguard Pass, but there was nothing I could do about it. The ghost was right."

Kilmer sounded delirious.

"You don't ever have to talk about that again, Kilmer," Darla told him.

Kilmer wondered if he was getting confused again.

"Are you real, Darla?"

"Yes, Kilmer, I am. And I am really here with you."

"How can I be sure?"

"Remember Oaks? He came with me. You remember Oaks, don't you? No phantom would know about him."

"Oaks?" Kilmer smiled. "Darla?"

"I'm here," she said.

"I was saved by a ghost. But the demon, she poisons our minds, clouds my thinking… we never came out of the forest," Kilmer said. "We never escaped. We are still there in the Sanguine Forest. With her."

"With who, Kilmer?"

"A demon attacked Laws. She made him do things."

"A demon?"

Kilmer heard wicked laughter from the demon Langula but only in his mind. He passed out again, continuing to dream.

This time in his dream, he kicked his mount, urging his horse forward. Searching the sky above, he could see circling buzzards. Up ahead, the scavengers were already on the ground, huddled in black masses. But these were not birds any longer, they were black feathered demons, with red eyes, feasting on the flesh of a dead man. The birds stopped feasting when they saw Kilmer coming. They scattered away as he approached. Then he could not see them anymore, but he heard them squawking in the distance, as if mocking him in his own language from afar.

They said, *Murder, death, blood, folly.*

Innocence, horror.

Kilmer tried his best to ignore them, dismounted and walked toward the bloody grass. Gazing down on the awful sight, he saw a dead human body. Misshapen and discolored, a vast hole was visible in the man's torso, pecked by the feathered demons all the way down to his crooked blood-red spine. The body's mouth was stretched abnormally wide in a frozen expression of terror. Kilmer had seen this face before, on Isse. But this time it was not Isse.

"Look at his face," Curtz whispered behind him.

"Aye," Kilmer said softly. "Poor bastard."

But looking upon the face of the body, it was not Isse. It was Yori, the king's senior archer, hardly recognizable now in death.

"Wait," Kilmer said. "This is supposed to be Isse, not Yori."

Is it really? Are you sure? the broken-necked Laws asked.

Does it matter? asked Curtz with his busted, broken head. *Both of them are with us now.*

But it was the pale Hanson who raised a bloody arm and warned him, *Run away, Kilmer. Run far away.*

Kilmer realized a new presence with them. He looked up and saw Yori, not as Kilmer remembered him, but as a ghost. He stood in a pale translucent glow. He looked sad as he gazed down upon his former mortal remains. He turned a confused eye toward Kilmer, as if reaching out for answers.

"Yori, my friend," Kilmer whispered. "I am sorry, but you are dead, and I am dreaming."

The ghost looked at him puzzled.

Kilmer asked, "Do you remember anything of your death?"

The ghost did not answer, just gave a quizzical look.

"Yori, tell me what happened, and I-I swear to you, I will avenge your death."

Still no response.

"For your family's sake, think and remember."

That seemed to rattle the ghost profoundly more than his current thoughts.

Lara, my wife. The ghost acknowledged his wife's name, looking into Kilmer's eyes with deep sadness.

"Yes, Yori. That's right. Lara will be well taken care of. She will be provided for, until you both can be reunited again. What happened to you, Yori? Remember and tell me."

The ghost of Yori screamed in growing alarm and kept screaming for long moments. Lara appeared and tried to calm him. But Yori only became more agitated and screamed more. He clawed and scratched at his face, pulling at it, tearing the flesh under his eyes, ripping it off his skull. Deep bloody wounds appeared on his face. Yori tore away his skin until his appearance underneath turned into the face of the Zorn, complete with swirling yellow eyes.

Then he turned to attack Lara, tearing the flesh away from her face. And beneath her skin revealed the demon Langula.

The vision stopped, and then melted, burning away.

The scene replayed and started over.

Kilmer and the ghost of Yori, now in full ghostly form, face intact again, stood calmly beside him by an open grave.

"How is this possible, Kilmer?" Yori's ghost now asked.

Kilmer replied, "I don't know, Yori."

Yori pointed. "Be prepared, Kilmer. We are not alone. Evil is here with us. I'm not sure how much longer I will be allowed to stay."

"Aye, my friend, I feel it too. Something is wrong in this place."

"Beware, Kilmer, I fear for your soul."

The ghost dissolved, and the apparitions of the dead Curtz, Laws, and Hanson approached Kilmer again. They carried a dead body wrapped in burial cloth. All four of them gently lowered the body into the grave. After, they stood looking down into the hole.

"Who was this we just lowered into this grave?" Kilmer asked them. But no one said a word because they were all gone. Kilmer was standing alone.

He looked down into the grave again. He did not see the twisted remains of Yori anymore. Instead, he saw the bodies of Curtz, Laws, and Hanson. All three dead at the bottom of the hole. He felt a presence and looked up to see who was standing with him now, but he only saw the Sanguine Forest turning into a bright white light.

Kilmer woke with a startled reflex. Opening his eyes, he came out of the horrible dream, realizing that he had been trying to raise his hands, but two healers stood on either side of him holding down his restrained arms. Initially resisting them, coming to his senses now, he stopped struggling.

Darla was at his bedside. She had been watching him sleep restlessly for many days and nights. She talked to him softly, wiping his brow as he was covered in beads of sweat. With a cool towel, she patted his forehead. Kilmer, grateful for her merciful act, spoke.

"Yori is dead," he said. "I saw his ghost. It spoke to me."

The healers and Darla shared a look.

Moments before he awoke, Yori had died in the next room.

The healers sedated Kilmer once again, and he fell into that place of deep dreams again.

We bought a silver dream
Then tarnished it to green
Father walked away
When we turned our backs to stay.

Excerpt from *The Witch's Songbook*

He had turned from life; he was changing into something else.
— Excerpt from *The Provenance* (Chapter Twenty-Eight)

THE SEVENTH SON
OF FORTIS PLUM

THE VILLAGE OF PLUM IN THE YEAR 741 HRT
(HUNDREDS OF YEARS IN THE PAST)

Fortis Plum had a long life but not necessarily a good one. It was true his life was filled with prosperity, adventure, and intrigue. He settled in the land blessed to him, establishing the village of Plum as a premiere trading post for commerce in the Mid-Run Valley. The Plums supplied goods and services to all the other villages. The town he established was the hub of all trade, making him a very wealthy man. Plus, he had become the patriarch for all future generations of Plums. All in all, he was a man to be looked up to.

The God of Light, Heironomus, had given this land to him, but it came at a cost. He was blessed with what would be an unusually long life, one foretold to span time, even after the death of his physical body. Heironomus's words seemed like a blessing at the time. But Fortis did not realize what the extent of a long life would mean, or the curse it would bring.

Centuries ago, to set the balance straight the God of Darkness cursed Fortis's long life with crushing melancholy. No matter how successful the village of Plum became, the trade it generated, or the prosperity he garnered, nothing could brighten his demeanor and tragedy seemed to haunt him.

Fortis had seven sons. Strong youthful boys that were the pride of their father's eye. But he never had two of them living at the same time. Every time he would sire a new son, the former one would die. The first six all succumbed to tragedy, illness, or madness. Fortis had to dig two of their graves and bury them, the other four were lost, missing to misadventures. Their absence broke his heart. Their deaths gave him a failed sense of any chance of lasting hope, that all the wealth in the world could not fill. Until in the end, only one son remained that grew past adolescence.

Fortis had long prepared for a time when his own physical body would begin to fail and break down. Just as it had been foretold to him that his spirit would live on, he expected that to happen eventually. What he did not count on was that before he crossed that dark threshold of death, that he would be haunted by the ghosts of his dead sons. Their visions forced upon him the memories of happier days unfulfilled and would ultimately drive him to deep depression. The depression developed into a madness.

Even through the worst of conditions, his public image was protected by those who loved him, his wives and daughters. They were free from the magic of the Gods and shielded him from prying eyes through the decades. People of the Mid-Run Valley viewed Fortis as the village founder, the bold entrepreneur, who courageously established the village of Plum, and made it what it was. But those who were close to him knew that the man's mind had broken and twisted years ago from a series of tragic events to his six sons.

Then, on his deathbed, he had suffered enough. In the year 741 HRT, after having just passed his 260th birthday, he longed to live no more in this world. His legendary long mustache now lay gray and limp down the sides of his cheeks, and he was confined to his bed with his eyes staring out blankly at the unseen phantoms of his dead sons swirling around him.

Only his one remaining son, his wives and four daughters, attended to him in his hour of need.

"Do you see them?" Fortis asked his son. "Can you see the spirits of your brothers?"

"We cannot see what only torments you," they told him. The family gave each other looks of concern. They could not see the spirits of Fortis's dead sons. But they believed he could.

Oh! How tormented his mind must be!

His son squeezed his hand and leaned forward to kiss his forehead through the beads of sweat that formed on his brow. He was running a fever. Fortis looked at his son already fifty-seven years old himself. He spoke to him.

"My son, you are the only one remaining. I am sorry this burden must fall to you. You are the last male child of the Plum family. You must carry the curse of this family with you now."

"I will, Father. I will bear this burden for the family's sake, so no other will have to."

"There's a good lad," Fortis said. "We will see each other again."

"Oh, Father, I will look for you." The son lowered his brow on his father's hand.

"Yes, my son. We will intersect throughout all of time with all the other surviving sons of every generation of Plums."

"Then let it be so, Father, let it be."

"As for you, I give you my blessing of long life, and ask that you keep the memories I have given you, that you forget nothing. This is my blessing to you, my son, my dearest son."

With those words, life escaped Fortis Plum and he slipped from this life to the other.

But unseen to the others, his last son saw the spirit of Fortis lifting up into a streaming tunnel of swirling light. His body transformed from its worldly prison of flesh to boundless energy. Rotating in circles, in all directions, becoming unfathomable, undetectable. Then he was gone from the world.

A series of violent collisions rocked Fortis as he hit barriers, walls that normally allowed the dead through with access to the next world of the dead and the unborn. But instead of letting Fortis through, it blocked him from neither continuing into the Cosmic Creation, nor letting him go back to the life he came from. Trapped somewhere in the middle of two worlds, captured by a strange gravity allowing him only the slightest wiggle in between these realities. There, he floated, tumbling lengthways, as just one lone solitary man against the backdrop of a vast universe. No spirit before him had ever been so utterly isolated. This was the cost of his curse he had to endure.

Back in the mortal realm, his body lay on his deathbed, expired and lifeless. The cry rang out when he breathed his last. His only remaining son backed away from the body, knowing that the man was gone, but the spirit remained nearby somewhere. He scanned the room, searched through the emotional wails of Fortis's surviving widow and daughters. But it was he, the only surviving male heir, that bore the curse now. And he was scared.

Fortis, trapped between the worlds, was detained in some dim place, forced to observe the timelines of men, but without any direct involvement. He could see the past; he could see the future, but he had no say in it. He had no voice, no way to communicate the warnings and the dangers ahead. He tried to speak but could not.

In the days that followed his physical death, he floated over his own grave as the family buried his worldly remains in a plot of land that would later become the Plum family cemetery. Two of his dead sons were already interred there, the other four were lost, either to the Endless Sea, in caves below the mountains, or carrion for the wild beasts of the Mid-Run Valley.

It was raining the day of his funeral. The wind blew chilly cold for the mourners, although in his ghost form unseen, his spirit could not feel it. The oblong coffin, made of rich acacia wood, highly polished and stained in amber, containing his body was lowered into the grave. The ropes were held by men of the town's council, all owing Fortis for their fortunes. His only surviving son watched the casket lower into the darkness of the grave. Fortis stood among the mourners watching silently as the dirt was shoveled in, falling into the grave, landing and spreading upon the amber casket. He saw their tears, felt their emotions and grief. Sadness and despondency filled his spirit. Not grief for himself, because his spirit had lived on, but for those remaining who did not understand. Also, he grieved for those not yet born to whom he would someday be sent to. Before the grave was entirely filled, Fortis left his funeral. He traveled through time turning the page to another era.

The next phase he entered was years later. Fortis could see the destiny in his son's future, knowing what he would become, in this life and in the next. He appeared to his son throughout his life but could not speak the words of the future to him. He could only show him shadows of visions, not yet realized.

His son was frightened by the ghost of his father. Frightened that the specter did not speak, and that the ghost forced visions into his mind. The visions shown to him the most were of a blue comet descending upon the world, and landing in the Mid-Run Valley. A cosmic event of significant proportion. But he did not understand what the ghost's vision meant. He could not understand at the time. But would come to understand it years later. And he would never forget.

The seventh son lived to be one hundred and two years old, the blessings of a long life extended to him by his father. He lived until the year 786 HRT, then just after his last birthday, he closed his eyes and passed on from this life to the Cosmic Creation. But the seventh son would not die as most would, and he lived on, like his father. Later he always considered the year of his death, as his birth. Because after this, he changed into something else.

Upon leaving the world, the spirit of the seventh son became a part of the rust-colored world of the Cosmic Creation. There, he always remembered his former life, as he was the seventh son of Fortis Plum. In his current form he found he could remember everything. He spent the next years in spirit visiting other sons of the Plum family as his father did for many generations. Watching and waiting for something to happen, something in his destiny he knew was coming.

Then, he felt himself leaving for life again. He lifted from that rusty sphere of the netherworld modulated within a blue comet. He was on his way to being born again. On the night it happened, his comet lit the world of the entire Mid-Run Valley, alerting the Star Prophets of the first static sign in a lifetime.

He opened his eyes again, he saw faces, Norwa and Barclay, his new mother and father. He came back into the world as a normal infant, a baby that could not talk, or walk, wholly dependent upon his new parents. He remembered seeing Gia and Glover next—the Star Prophets who first saw the blue comet. There were others too, a lot of other people. He even remembered being in the arms of the spiritual warrior Chen-Li. All of them whispering secrets to him, and he could remember what they said. Actually, he could not forget, even if he wanted to. He was born the boy who cannot forget. The Supreme Historian.

He remembered Fortis, his brothers, his previous family, everything. He could remember his time of renewal in the Cosmic Creation, travelling in the blue comet, his birth in the village of Conner, everything. And he would continue to remember everything, just as his father, Fortis, blessed him. Even as his father continued to walk in spirit forever in the world.

But later in this new life, after hundreds of years of remembering and not forgetting anything, he resorted to wrapping his head in linens, so as not to experience anything new with his senses that he would remember. He longed to forget. He would even long to die eventually.

But why was this happening to him? For what purpose had he been cursed?

His new parents, Norwa and Barclay, named him Aberfell. This was his true name, the same name Fortis had given him back in the year 684 HRT, and the only name he ever had. Whether they had been programmed or influenced by the Cosmic Creation to give him that name, he did not know. But something must have happened to them to name him by his familiar name.

He thought, *I am Aberfell, the Seventh Son of Fortis Plum.*

I always was, and will always be, Aberfell.

I wonder, does it all come back again.

Yes, I wonder, will it come to me in the end?

And I wonder,

If I'm ever going to come this way again?

Excerpt from *The Witch's Songbook*

Why should I fear you? I have never seen a bird like you before.
Nor will you ever see one like me again, the crow answered.
— Excerpt from *The Provenance* (Chapter Twenty-Nine)

THE BROKEN PIECES

THE CASTLE ODESSA IN THE YEAR 842 HRT
(NINE MONTHS SINCE THE STAR OF EHLONA)

Chen-Li sat on a thick rug on the stone floor of the infirmary. He sat cross-legged and meditated. His First Wives, Tyla and Myra, joined him and meditated along beside him. The hall was quiet, except for occasional restless sounds in the distance.

Lord Whitney, Darla, and Oaks stood in the doorway of Kilmer's room in the infirmary nearby. Standing along with them were two of the king's couriers and four healers. All watched and waited in silence.

Kilmer was asleep, no doubt having bizarre dreams again. Strapped to the bed rails by his wrists and ankles, he struggled against them in a sweaty nightmarish battle.

Tyla and Myra began to illuminate in their respective colors of gold and blue. The small audience stood outside the door to witness Chen-Li's First Wives radiate colored light. What happened next mystified them.

Tyla levitated off the floor, rising higher in her cross-legged meditation. Immediately after, Myra rose off the floor too. Following Tyla, she hovered up into the air with a slight unbalanced wobble.

Excited whispers and gasps came from the witnesses in the hallway. Then, they all let out an audible gasp as Tyla's head elongated, popped, and out came her dulled golden ghostlike spirit. Her spirit lingered over her body, swimming in the air, waiting for Myra to join her. Soon, another pop could be heard, and Myra's blue spirit joined her overhead. Both of their bodies still floated in meditation.

The two spirits of the First Wives circled momentarily, then there came a flash, and both of their spirits plunged into Kilmer's chest, making him arch his back and gasp loudly for air. The crowd outside the room gasped, as his pupils rolled back, revealing his eyes as two almond shaped golden blanks.

Darla swooned, then fainted. Lord Whitney caught her and supported her as the healers rushed to her side. They gave her room to breathe, dabbed her face, and fanned her.

Oaks wobbled with the color removed from his face but endured it.

Kilmer relaxed peacefully back into his bed. The spiritual struggle over, he was at peace once again.

The First Wives joined together inside Kilmer's body. For the first time in months, the battle against the magic of the Zorn was joined.

Kilmer seemed to wake in his infirmary bed, but his body no longer belonged to him. Soon, he was free to get up, and he walked to the door. But upon looking back, he saw his body still in bed fast asleep, still secured by the wrists and ankles in leather buckles.

"Am I dreaming?" he asked.

Yes, you are dreaming, a distant voice said in his mind.

"Who's there? Who said that?"

Hello Kilmer, my name is Tyla. I am one of the First Wives of Chen-Li. I am here in your mind with you, but I am not alone.

I am here with you too, Kilmer. I am Myra, another one of Chen-Li's First Wives. We have come a long way to help you.

"Where are you? I cannot see you."

Our physical bodies are there. Kilmer was aware she wanted him to look at the foot of his bed. He observed them, sitting cross-legged on the floor, Tyla and Myra levitating in a trance.

"I feel very strange," Kilmer said. "I've never felt like this before."

Nothing can harm you here, Tyla told him.

With our help, you have left your body, said Myra. *We are controlling your spirit. The process can be quite disorienting if you are not familiar with it.*

"Why are you doing this to me?"

To help you. You are being controlled through what you think are nightmares, Tyla said.

"I have been having horrible nightmares."

No, not nightmares. You are being possessed by the demon Langula, said Myra. *She can torment you whenever she wants. It gives her amusement. She is toying with you, showing you images of death to feed off your emotional response.*

She uses madness, forcing hallucinations, causing you to want to kill yourself. Her power holds sway over you. We are here to cure you of this, and drive this demon out, but it will not be easy, Tyla said. *Alone, you are powerless against her magic.*

Kilmer looked at the First Wives' bodies levitating off the floor.

We have been with you for weeks. We have seen much. We know you, know what you know, what you have been through, Myra told him.

The dead have appeared to you, telling you about their deaths, Tyla added. *Encouraging you to join them. But this is not part of the demon possession. You have a great power to communicate with spirits of the dead. You've had this power a long time.*

"Am I going to kill myself?"

Not if we can help it, Myra said. *You are not facing this demon alone. We are with you.*

"What about Melvin and Rhodes?"

They are nearby, they are sedated. They are safe.

"Are they still alive?"

Yes, they are well so far.

"And Yori?"

Yori is dead. He has passed over to the Cosmic Creation. But you already knew that.

"How long have I been sedated?"

Over six months.

Kilmer considered not having any memory of the lost time.

"I am thirsty."

No, you're not. You are in your spiritual form. Your thirst is merely a reflex, a fragment of memory lingering from your physical body.

A drink is being prepared for you. This drink will not quench your thirst but cure your disease.

"You said you have seen much. What have you seen?"

You have an interesting and terrifying past you keep hidden behind unpleasant memories. But there are pleasant ones as well.

"What pleasant memories?"

Memories of a girl.

Memories of Darla.

"You know about Darla?"

We know everything about you.

"Do you know who my parents were, and what happened to them?"

Yes, we know about Justus and Rosa Plum.

"Does Leopold know?"

No, and we do not intend to tell him. Trust us, Kilmer. Your secrets are safe with Chen-Li and his First Wives.

You are a strong man, Kilmer. You are to be greatly admired. We have never met anyone like you. You are blessed with your spirit, Hollow Face. Who is really Fortis Plum.

"Hollow Face? You know about him too? He sacrificed his life to save me."

Do you not know that a ghost cannot die?

"Hollow Face is… still… alive?"

You cannot kill what does not live. Behold!

Just then, Hollow Face materialized to the spirit of Kilmer. The spirit was weaker, fainter, harder to detect. But the ghost floated into his view.

Kilmer's ghost pulled back his hood, exposing the long mustache from under it. It was the familiar face of Fortis Plum.

Darius, the Zorn took all the energy I had in the struggle that weakened me. I needed to rest. I only appear to you now because it is easier to appear spirit to spirit. I still cannot cross from the spiritual world and enter the mortal realm of man, as it takes more energy than I currently have. But I have not abandoned you. I will never abandon you. Someday I will return to continue to be with you for the rest of your life. You will never be alone.

Kilmer started to cry. "I am so happy you are safe. I thought I lost you."

I have told you, Kilmer, a ghost cannot die, Tyla said.

I am sorry, my sister, Myra interrupted, *but Langula can sense us now. She knows she has no power here.*

Chen-Li opened his eyes, coming out of his meditation. He reached out in front of him and grasped the hilt of the sharp knife. Lifting it, he placed it on a vein in the area just below his elbow. He applied pressure and a stream of blood ran in a rivulet down his arm. His blood was allowed to run into a glass container. Steadily the tube filled with the blood of Chen-Li.

With the container full, he abruptly spun the knife with a flourish of motion, placing it lightly on the floor in front of him. He produced a small but thick swab of linen from his belt. With his free hand he applied steady pressure to his self-inflicted wound, then bent his elbow to further stop the bleeding.

Two healers rushed in. One carefully lifted the tube with Chen-Li's blood, while another produced a smaller tube to extract a more negligible amount of the blood into. Once a sample had been secured, the larger container was fitted with a cork precisely made to fit and sealed airtight. It was whisked out of Kilmer's room. Other healers received the blood and consulted with each other in the hallway.

Darla was beginning to revive; the healers gave her cool water to drink. Oaks continued to fan her, absentmindedly, but his attention was drawn away to the activities inside the room.

The smaller tube of Chen-Li's blood was poured into a concoction of pomegranate juice. The healer stood by Kilmer, holding the glass and looking at Chen-Li.

With a nod, Chen-Li spoke, "You can remove his restraints now."

Two more healers rushed in and unbuckled the leather cuffs that secured his wrists and ankles to the bed frame.

"The demon will try to stop us now. But with Myra and Tyla inhabiting the space she would ordinarily try to possess, she has been banished from his body."

Chen-Li stood and walked past the bodies of his First Wives levitating above the floor. The healer backed away from the bedside to give the master priest room to work.

Kilmer's eyes slowly opened, as the spirits of the First Wives encouraged him to wake. Chen-Li slowly, gently, laid his hands on Kilmer.

"Can you sit up?"

Kilmer nodded. With Chen-Li's help, he came to a sitting position.

The healer placed the juice into Chen-Li's hand as he reached back for it, then he brought the cup forward.

"Drink all of this. Don't worry, it is not unpleasant, it's good."

Kilmer grasped the cup with both hands. He drank all the liquid in hefty gulps, not spilling a single drop until the glass was empty.

"There," Chen-Li smiled. "Good."

Chen-Li's blood in the glass immediately negated the Zorn's influence from Kilmer and inoculated him against the possession of the demon Langula.

"The spell is broken," Chen-Li told him. "You can rest peacefully now, Kilmer."

"Am I free?" Kilmer asked him. "Can I finally come out of the Sanguine Forest?"

Chen-Li nodded. "The First Wives will stay with you a while longer, to assist with any lingering effects."

Upon hearing this, the audience in the hall erupted in cheers and applause. Chen-Li looked at Darla and motioned for her to come to Kilmer.

Darla rushed in and held him, much to his surprise.

"Is this real? Are you real?" Kilmer asked. "Is this really happening?"

He embraced her. He could smell the sweet fragrance of honeysuckle in her hair, just like in his dreams and memory. But this time, it was lasting and real. Darla was real.

No more demons. The bad dreams were gone, and the good dreams could now come true.

My love is in you
So deep inside
You know it touches your heart
And it fills your time

Excerpt from *The Witch's Songbook*

He smashed the bottle on the ground
with a growl as beer dripped down his chin.
He was ready for a fight.
— Excerpt from *The Provenance* (Chapter Thirty)

AFTER THE POSSESSION

THE CASTLE ODESSA IN THE YEAR 842 HRT
(ELEVEN MONTHS SINCE THE STAR OF EHLONA)

For the next few months, Chen-Li and his First Wives stayed at Castle Odessa as guests of the king. They continued the care of the survivors of the search party. Each of them was carefully attended and inhabited. The First Wives and Chen-Li protected them during their nightmarish possessions with Langula. The remainder of Chen-Li's blood was prepared, and each of the infected men given the same concoction. One by one, over the next few weeks each of them slowly returned to normal. None of them wanted to harm themselves, or others, anymore. Chen-Li's blood slowly cured them, releasing them from the power of the Zorn and Langula that held sway over all that went into the Sanguine Forest.

But the cure did not come in time for all of them. Curtz, Laws, Hanson, and Yori, and of course, poor Isse would be counted among the dead. Five deaths in total. Men who went into the Sanguine Forest and, in a sense, never came out.

King Leopold held a public ceremony officially recognizing and appreciating Chen-Li and his First Wives for heeding the call for assistance. They came quickly, dropping their own interests, and stayed over a long period of time, several long months. Ultimately, they produced a miraculous cure as only Chen-Li could.

King Leopold presented him with a golden plaque, pledging friendship between Castle Odessa and the Temple of Chen-Li. The plaque was warmly received by Chen-Li and the First Wives.

Soon after, they bid farewell. In the morning, after the king's ceremony, they departed with well wishes. They set off to go back to the Temple of Chen-Li under a mostly ceremonial escort of a dozen mounted troops of King Leopold's finest cavalry, brightly adorned in the colors of red and blue.

Over time, and with the infusion of Chen-Li's blood, Givens' feeble-mindedness subsided, and he returned to his former self, back to the man he was prior to entering the Sanguine Forest. The blood of Chen-Li removed the malady that Givens, thankfully, had little memory of. He suffered no long-term effects of the madness that had consumed him. The last thing he remembered was riding his horse straight out of the Sanguine Forest, but he just ended up riding in a circle. That event never sat well with him in the following years. As an experienced horseman, it was hard to accept he would be capable of riding his horse in a circle and get lost in the woods. For the rest of his days, Givens knew that some powerful form of magic had been cast upon him. A spell to circle him around back to the starting point like a door into a different reality. When others heard his story, it scared them, that such magic would, or could, exist. People believed his story, but what the truth was, whether it was feeble-mindedness, or some inter-dimensional doorway, may not ever be known. All agreed, however, that powerful magic and the Sanguine Forest should be avoided at all costs.

This problem of the Sanguine Forest bothered Lord Whitney. He embarked upon a mission of ridding the world of it. But for the first time in his life, one of his undertakings was a disaster. He deployed a large military force, and they headed off to systematically set the Sanguine Forest on fire and burn it down. For the task, Lord Whitney assembled four thousand men, all armed with fire accelerators, oil, kerosene, alcohol, pitch, and a variety of other flammables. However, every time the men tried to burn the forest down, the forest fought back.

The men tried to apply simple torches to the trees, but strong gusts of wind would blow them out. Next, they poured oil as accelerant upon the base of the trees, but before they could set them ablaze, they were attacked by swarms of hornets. Soldiers would get lost and never be found. Men had accidents and were setting each other on fire with regularity. Their wagons were exploding with the combustible liquids in them before they could use them to burn the forest. No matter how carefully Lord Whitney planned, one calamity occurred after another. The campaign was a disaster. Finally, for the safety of his men, and what was left of the task force of four thousand, Lord Whitney gave the order to retreat to Castle Odessa, leaving the Sanguine Forest intact and unharmed.

"It's just unlucky there," Lord Whitney reported back to the king. But Leopold knew better.

"Leave it, then," the king said. "By my decree, send out the word: the Sanguine Forest is a forbidden area."

The decree spread out far and wide.

Yori had been through the most. He had survived a variety of terrors, of which any one of them could have been the one that killed him. He survived the Sanguine Forest, even though his partner Isse did not. He survived an encounter with the demon Langula, although Laws had not. She drained his blood and seduced him to fertilize her demonic eggs, and he could never bear to tell his wife about it. He survived sadistic torture at the hands of the Zorn. He escaped vengeful spirits, the Sanguine Forest, and demon possession. After all he had been through, he was fortunate to die in a soft warm bed back at the castle with his wife Lara to hold him.

For the rest of her life, Lara would be taken care of by King Leopold and the Kingdom of Odessa. She lived out the remainder of her days in comfort, but she always remembered Yori dearly in her heart as the love of her life.

Kilmer and Lara never discussed again the details of Yori's torments in Castle Orlo.

Langula had possessed them all and had been in control of their thoughts and dreams, and all the survivors had considered taking their own lives. She amused herself by tormenting the men in turn, first one of them, then moving on to the others. She delightfully succeeded in influencing Curtz to leap off the highest tower, Laws to hang himself, and Hanson to slice his wrists. But she wanted more—nothing could satisfy her voracious lust for death.

Rhodes thought he would be next. He had vivid fantasies about leaning into his sword and allowing it to run through him. He resisted as long as he could, but he was losing the battle. Just at the right time, King Leopold ordered them sedated and confined to bed, an action that saved lives. If not for the king's order, Rhodes would have done it, run himself through, killing himself. He trembled to think how close he had come. After his ordeal, Rhodes wanted to continue serving in King Leopold's Red and Blue infantry. Over the years he flourished, at length promoted to the high rank of colonel. He was right to his men and tough as nails as the consummate soldier.

Out of all the men, Melvin was the least affected. Maybe it was because of his youth. He thought it was because he was the weakest and did not present an adequate challenge for the demons to demonstrate their power. Had he been more experienced, if his willpower were more robust, they could have considered him more worthy of their attention. As it was, his weakness turned out to be his strength. It made him invisible to them. That was not to say that he was untouched by Langula's beguiling. He was not. In the end, the feeling of powerlessness affected him the most. He suffered survivor's guilt, a sense of insignificance, a feeling that he never wanted to experience again. Melvin was the last to drink Chen-Li's blood. Afterward, he swore he would never be powerless again. He resolved through hard work, to hone his fighting skills, emulating the most professional soldiers, and pledging to make the most of the life given to him.

Curtz ended up being the best of them. He was the primary reason the search party did not die lost and was responsible for getting them out of Sanguine Forest; They all owed him their lives for the actions he took back in the Sanguine. Melvin later thought that was why the demons targeted Curtz first. When he climbed that tower during the king's celebration, he was not climbing what he thought he was. To Curtz, he was still in the Sanguine Forest climbing above the trees to see over the canopy. In his mind, he was breaking the spell of whatever confusion the Zorn had cast over them. Curtz was the best of them, the hero.

Laws was mentally crushed, thoroughly seduced by the demon, his senses overloaded. A war-hardened soldier, Laws had seen many terrible things. He had survived awful things done to him. But when the demon breathed her curse in his face, he was not prepared for it. He was the strongest of them all physically, but emotionally he was easy work for Langula. His fear of magic would be the end of him. The demon compelled him to put his head through that scratchy rope just to escape the memories of what Langula and Monticello did to him.

Hanson had loved life the most. But he had already tasted defeat serving in the Amalgamates. Losing the war had always been a sore spot with him. It provided the necessary wedge the demon needed, as he ran, separating himself, in isolation from the rest of the group. When he sliced his wrists, he was attempting to demonstrate his courage and strength, just like the courage of the suicidal Zornastic priests. The demon had convinced him he could become whole again, indicating he possessed the strength and willpower to demonstrate his strength through opening his veins. Through blood, he would finally be equal to King Leopold. But it was all an illusion.

Then, there was Kilmer. The commander of the search party. The Zorn and Langula had other plans for him. They did not want to kill him. They planned to keep him alive for years to bleed him for more demonic eggs. As the vengeful spirits would witness in the dank stinking prison cell, they would bleed him dry. The demons planned on toying with him, giving him a life of prolonged torture. They even had Langula seduce him to help reproduce new demonic eggs.

All of it would have been a foregone conclusion, if not for Kilmer's ghost. The spirit he called Hollow Face, the ghost of Fortis Plum long blessed with life beyond this world by the original power: Heironomus, the God of Light. So blessed by Heironomus, the spirit of Fortis Plum had power over the son of Hexor. The ghost of Fortis Plum was a cosmic anomaly but possessed a greater control over the Zorn. Kilmer's ghost had sacrificed itself so that Kilmer may live. Otherwise, without Kilmer's ghost, Yori and Kilmer both would have been doomed. Even after their escape, it seemed that doom would follow them to the grave anyway. If not for Chen-Li, the only son of the God Heironomus, and the power of negation through his blood, their doom would have been complete.

The Zorn sat in his Castle Orlo and contemplated Kilmer's ghost.

Kilmer was reunited with Darla, the only girl he had ever loved. Ultimately, Darla and Oaks learned about Kory's fate—wounded and killed at Mauveguard Pass, cruelly dispatched by none other than LaNew, the sadistic killer and captain of the murderous Red Guard. Exactly how LaNew dispatched Kory was not something Kilmer ever discussed, and Darla and Oaks had never asked. They did not need to hear the morbid details.

Oaks joined the king's horse cavalry of the Red and Blue.

"I'm going to be a horseman," he said.

Kilmer gave him his blessing, knowing that with his title of lord, he could be sure that Oaks would be assigned to him.

There, Kilmer could keep him out of trouble.

Everything was going right for Kilmer, and he planned to ask Darla to marry him. He never wanted to be without her again. The question for him, was when and where?

But for her part, Darla still had some unanswered questions that she intended to explore.

We stand and dance in place.

You touch my face while the music lingers on.

How can I fight what's right?

And the feelings that I've had for so long?

Excerpt from *The Witch's Songbook*

His clothes blazed, his flesh roasted,
his body struggled against the bindings.
— Excerpt from *The Provenance* (Chapter Thirty-One)

THE WEDDING CONFESSION

The Castle Odessa in the Year 843 HRT
(Twelve Months Since the Star of Ehlona)

There was one matter that still needed clearing up.

"Why did you stop writing me? Why did you just disappear from my life?" Darla asked Kilmer. "Do you know what you put me through? I thought you were dead. Both you and Kory."

"I know, I'm sorry. I am so sorry."

"But why did you do it?"

"Because of my lies. I've lived my whole life with lies. Even now, I have so many of them. I don't know how to wash them away. I don't think I'll ever be clean."

Darla considered him. She could plainly see he had been a turncoat, someone who changed sides to save themselves. She looked both ways before she spoke, ensuring no one could hear them.

"Why don't you tell me? I'm on your side. Trust me. Come clean with me."

But Kilmer looked away.

"Are we in danger?" Darla asked. "I think I have the right to know."

Kilmer looked at Darla now. "I will, I promise. But let me do it in my own time. When the time is right. Then I will tell you everything. For now, it's best if we wait."

Darla nodded. Instinctively feeling an undercurrent of danger, she felt he was only keeping silent to protect her. So, she accepted it and would not push. At least, not for now.

Kilmer was feeling better. Free from demon possession, happy to be himself again, but doubly happy to be with Darla. They spent their days and nights together. As he recuperated from his ordeal, he showed Darla all around the beautiful scenery and grounds of Castle Odessa, and all the wonders it had to offer, which were many. They walked to the tops of the towers looking out over the Blue Mountains. From the highest vantage point, they could see the Wilds, the native strip of flatlands where the tribal hunters roamed, and the coastline of where the Endless Sea started.

He showed her the large rooms where the king held banquets and the large overarching chapels constructed above the endless catacombs where the remains of Laws, Curtz, Hanson, and Yori rested. They visited the tombs of Kilmer's men and shed a tear for the tragedy of them being driven to take their own lives.

Emerging from that darkness, they walked in the sun together, to the place where the Sanguine adventure started for Kilmer. They stepped out on the Green, the large, polished stone parade ground where King Leopold hosted his five-year celebration. Here they beheld the Star of Ehlona still burning in the sky, the overview of the historic Mauveguard Pass, and the wispy summits of the Blue Mountains.

Darla felt refreshed with the wind blowing crisp and cold through her hair. Her heart was satisfied in a feeling of warmth to be with Kilmer.

"My, my, Lord Kilmer, it's so beautiful," Darla told him. "I've never seen anything so beautiful."

"I have." Kilmer turned to look at her. "I want to remember you just how you are now." Despite the scenic splendor all around them, Kilmer only had eyes for Darla. Her thick black hair blew in strands across her face. Her bottom lip quivered with a slight chill.

"I want to give you something." Kilmer reached in his pocket and produced a little box. He opened it to reveal a golden band, one large diamond inset in its center, surrounded by an oval of smaller ones. The ring, set in multifaceted splendor, sparkled refracting the sunshine.

Darla turned toward Kilmer, and she suddenly could not breathe, her heart beating wildly, as Kilmer dropped to one knee.

"Darla, you have always been the one for me. Would you marry me?"

"Kilmer, are you asking me to be your wife?" Ring or not, Darla embraced him and kissed him. "I do want to be your wife. Kilmer! You take my breath away. Yes, oh yes."

The happy word spread, and soon the news, the talk of the kingdom, was that Lord Kilmer would soon be married.

Lord Whitney was the first to be told, and he discussed the matter with King Leopold. The news so pleased them after all they had been through that they decided the marriage of Lord Kilmer would be a public one. The king would hold another celebration. This one, the wedding of Lord Kilmer, would be planned to coincide with the dimming of the Star of Ehlona.

Preparations were made, invitations sent, and a feast organized. The Green would be decorated with flowers, white roses intertwined with red-and-blue ribbons and banners. Gifts were already starting to arrive from all the villages of the Mid-Run Valley.

The event would be a happy celebration, for the marriage of Lord Kilmer, and it also would be exciting to see the Star of Ehlona for the last time.

The kingdom worked together with the Star Prophets to calculate the precise time the diminishment of the Star of Ehlona would occur. They pored over the data and came up with a time to hold the marriage celebration that would culminate in an after-party to observe the star's disappearance. It had been the better part of a year now since the star first shone, and what a year it had been. People had gotten used to seeing the Star of Ehlona. They could not remember how dark the night was without it.

The date and time had been estimated by the Star Prophets and invitations had been sent throughout Odessa. As the date grew nearer to the one-year anniversary of the Star of Ehlona, the sense of excitement was palpable. Kilmer and Darla had never felt closer, and the entire kingdom was busy in preparations.

"Do you have any family you want to invite?" Lord Whitney asked Kilmer.

The question put Kilmer on the spot. "No family, I am an orphan. But I would like it if Sister Chavise and Sister Maldean could come."

"Oh sorry, I forgot," Lord Whitney said. "Of course we'll send an invitation to the orphanage at Plum."

Had he really forgotten?

On the night before the wedding people spent the night gazing one last time at the bright star knowing they would never see it again.

After much planning, finally, the day of Kilmer and Darla's wedding arrived. The atmosphere was full of electricity and many of the guests started to arrive. King Leopold had extended invitations to all the villages, and to their Head Councils.

Overhead, the Star of Ehlona continued to shine in its final hours, a fact that relieved the Star Prophets responsible for announcing the precise date and time. They worried that somehow their calculations were off, being not consistent with the Gods' calculations. What if they were wrong? They were concerned that it might go out the night before, but when it did not, that worry was replaced with whether the star would go out at all this night.

Gia and Glover, the Star Prophets primarily responsible for the discovery of Aberfell's blue comet, were in attendance. The two of them were spending more time together, and a wedding was a perfect distraction for them.

Visitors and guests from all over the Mid-Run Valley arrived and mingled. The atmosphere was light, joyous, and thrilling. A sense that they were witnessing history permeated the excitement.

Some more distinguished guests arrived: Barclay and Norwa with baby Aberfell attended by direct invitation of King Leopold, who paid all their expenses for first-class comfort in transit. Aberfell, the Supreme Historian, was a surprising distraction for the throng of people who wanted just the briefest chance to whisper some secret to the toddler. The baby with the vivid blue eyes had grown from an infant now and developed an intense alertness, an unusual awareness, at a rapid pace. When Norwa and Barclay finally took their seats, it signaled to the others that the ceremony would soon be beginning.

Chen-Li and his First Wives were in attendance, but not in their physical form. The dulled spirits of each of their Li's glowed in colors of white, gold, and blue. Their ghostly presence, a rare oddity, was something unique the guests had never seen before. They floated overhead as pale ghosts, and no one felt completely comfortable in their presence to attempt any small talk with them. Back at the Temple of Chen-Li, many hundreds of miles away, their physical bodies were guarded as they levitated in deep meditation.

Cordially invited, but unable to attend was Amtor and his wife, the healer Gilglad, due to his war wounds. Travel to Mauveguard Pass would be agonizing for him. But the former Minister of War sent wonderful gifts and extended the best wishes for happiness to the man who saved his life so many years ago at the Battle of Mauveguard Pass.

Sister Chavise, from St. Ehlona's Orphanage, likewise could not attend—she had been feeling under the weather, but sent her two former orphans the best well wishes from Sister Maldean and all the other orphans.

Darla thought all of this was more exciting than anything she could have possibly wished for. It was a dream come true. As she was being handled by a flurry of official servants, she stood behind a stage, looking through an opening in the curtain, watching the crowd fill in. The Green was filled with all sorts of people, none of them she knew, soldiers, priests, healers, and politicians. Seeing all these people, these strangers, made her nervous and her mouth dry. She tried to swallow hard and realized how nervous she really was. She felt a growing heat on her face, mildly dizzy, and at times just wanted to run away. Her maid of honor was Lara, Yori's widow. Her bridesmaids consisted of healers who had aided her soon-to-be husband in his hour of need. One thing that gave her strength was her background as an orphan—she was about as used to making new friends as a person could be.

"How are you feeling?" Lara asked her.

Darla closed the curtain and turned to Lara. "I am a little overwhelmed to be honest," she said with a laugh.

"Of course, you are. It's a big day for you. You are nervous now, but once you see Kilmer, it will all melt away."

Darla agreed with a nod, as Lara instinctively gave her a cup of cool water, which Darla was very thankful for.

On the other side of the stage, Lord Kilmer felt equally nervous but mostly excited. He was finally marrying the only girl he had loved. He wished his parents could see him now. How proud they would be. He thought about his sister, Mara; he wondered how her life would have developed by now, and what kind of woman she would have been. He wondered about all of them, where they would be, what they would be doing, had LaNew not murdered them. He could not help thinking about his old identity, Darius Plum, the person he used to be. He wondered how that boy would have turned out, had it not been for Hollow Face pushing him in the Plum River. So many fine threads of fate, intertwining in mysterious ways. There had to be a larger purpose for it all, he thought. There had to be.

Rhodes and Melvin were with him, each formally dressed in full military regalia with cords of yellow on their Red and Blue uniforms. Oaks was there too, now presenting himself as a young cavalryman in training; he was extremely excited, nothing unusual for him. Kilmer's best man was Lord Whitney, and he said he was feeling good, immensely enjoying the anticipation of both the celebrations, but mostly to see Lord Kilmer married.

Everything was going as planned and the people were happy, to the delight of Kilmer and Darla.

Horns blew announcing the beginning of the ceremony. After the horns, a choir of beautiful undulating voices created a lovely mood, and their heavenly tones echoed off the high mountain peaks from the Green of Castle Odessa. The chorus weaved harmonies together, felt not so much in the ears but within the cords of the heart, and somehow settled into the marrow of one's bones. The sound gave goosebumps to those who heard it.

After their voices faded, thick green velvet curtains opened, revealing the wedding party to the first public view. King Leopold walked in from behind them and headed out to the front of the stage. The wedding party of Lords Kilmer and Whitney, Darla and Lara, Rhodes, Melvin, and Oaks and the entire ceremony stood up in reverence to the king.

Leopold was dressed in a luxuriously thick red fur over broad shoulders, a double-breasted blue coat, and an elaborate golden crown of oak leaves. A wide leather belt adorned his torso, a dagger with rubies and sapphires tucked into it. He wore black pants with double stripes of scarlet neatly cropped into knee-high black boots polished to a mirrored shine.

The king motioned a greeting to the guests, allowing the applause to go on for a while. Then he gestured with his hand, and the guests began to quietly sit.

Then, the wedding began.

Darla looked at Kilmer, and he returned her look with a smile. King Leopold signaled, and the wedding party advanced toward him.

"Please join hands," King Leopold instructed Kilmer and Darla.

"I have something I would like to read," Leopold continued, opening a book to a prepared passage.

> *For all the times we have devoted, looking*
> *Over all the years we have went, searching.*
> *In our desire to grow wings,*
> *We flew high to find hidden things.*
> *Like the secrets in our minds,*
> *And in the center of the skies.*
> *But as we searched*
> *Our questions still cry.*
> *Then we find, to our surprise,*
> *That everything we were looking for*
> *Was here the entire time.*
> *Always right in front of us.*

"This is the meaning of love," the king said. He slowly closed his book and looked up at the couple. "Darla, do you take this man, Lord Kilmer, to be your husband in this life, until death gives him to you in the next?"

Darla looked at Kilmer, and replied, "Yes, I do."

"And do you..." King Leopold started, then stopped short. "Do you..."

Kilmer and Darla, and the rest of the wedding guests, looked at King Leopold. His pause was uncomfortably long.

But then, he continued, "And do you, Lord Plum-Kilmer, take this woman to be your wife in this life until death gives her to you in the next?"

The meaning of calling him Plum-Kilmer was lost on most of the guests—they did not realize the significance. But Kilmer did. In recognizing him as Plum-Kilmer, Leopold had just revealed out loud that he knew his real identity as a Plum. In front of hundreds of guests, and Darla herself, his deepest, darkest, greatest secret had just been revealed publicly; the king knew he was really Darius Plum!

Kilmer hesitated, not knowing what to do, or say, or what it meant. Was Leopold marrying him only to make Darla a widow on their wedding night?

"Lord Plum-Kilmer," King Leopold asked him again, "do you take this woman, Darla, as your wife until your death?"

Darla wrinkled her brow, and looked at King Leopold, having no idea what he meant by adding the name of Plum to Kilmer. She thought it may be some sort of title she did not know about. To her, it did not matter, but why was Kilmer hesitating? She now looked at him.

"As you have said it, I do, Your Majesty," Kilmer said with a slight bow to the king. Kilmer then turned to look at Darla. "My love for you has never been a deception."

"Very well then," King Leopold nodded. "By my authority as king of the Kingdom of Odessa, I grant you the titles of husband and wife, Lord Plum-Kilmer."

The crowd murmured in a joyous rumble.

But Kilmer felt paralyzed as the audience stood and applauded. None of them had any idea what had just happened. Darla leaned forward and kissed her husband. Kilmer kissed his new wife but had one eye on the presence of King Leopold, who stood motionless in front of him.

Finally, the king stepped closer to Kilmer. He congratulated him with a handshake, and softly spoke to him.

"I wish you both a lifetime of peace and prosperity. My wedding gift to you: the restoration of your family name, Darius Plum, son of Justus Plum."

Kilmer's heart was pounding in his chest, as the king reached under his red fur cloak, and pulled out an eight-inch dagger.

"I am sorry for the loss of your family, Plum. Please forgive me."

With an expert flourish, King Leopold spun the dagger around, extending the handle to Lord Plum-Kilmer, with the sharp edge pointing toward himself. Reaching down, he took Kilmer's hand and wrapped his fingers around the hilt of the blade.

Then, Leopold released Kilmer's hand and bowed his head.

The two of them stood facing each other, Kilmer holding the dagger, the king with his head lowered in front of him. There was nothing stopping him now from exacting his vengeance.

Knowing that it was harder to take a man's life looking him in the eye, King Leopold turned his head. And in so doing, exposed his neck to the point of the dagger.

They stood frozen in time. The audience could not fully see what was transpiring on the stage. While the others—Lord Whitney,

Rhodes, Melvin, Oaks—all flipped through the pages of the wedding schedule to find where they had missed this part of the ceremony.

Kilmer had been driven all his life to this moment. He fantasized about it from the time Hollow Face had pushed him in the river. From the time he saw his mother and sister run through with a sword, he desired revenge. When his father burst into flames in the middle of the town square—he blamed Leopold for it. He remembered every second, floating in the cold Plum River—every day he spent in poverty in the orphanage he desired this chance. Ever since losing his ancient family name, exchanging it for the lowly town hunchback, ever since, he had been dreaming of this moment for vengeance.

And now here it was. The moment was upon him.

He looked at the shiny blade in his right hand, and in his left Darla's small hand in his. Questions sent bewildered expressions across her face. He wondered what would happen to him if he did it? What would happen to Darla? Could his thirst for revenge be so complete that he would destroy the lives of all three of them? He held that fate in his hands.

Kilmer pulled the dagger back. He reached far back, ready to send it forward with maximum thrust, a determined expression upon his face, a redness of fire burst in his eyes. Exerting all the strength of all the former generations of Plums he thrust the dagger forward.

Leopold cringed for the killing blow.

The beautiful ruby-crusted dagger went sailing high overhead, across the stage, over the audience. End over end, it flipped in a long high arc. Across the Green it flew, over the stone railing, and dropped harmlessly down the heights of the Blue Mountains. The dagger tumbled down the rocky cliffs of Castle Odessa's three-thousand-foot drop.

"I choose life!" Kilmer shouted at Leopold.

Leopold exhaled slowly and stood straight. Kilmer could tell, the moment unnerved the man who had made a legend of his ability not to get unnerved. He now turned slowly to face Kilmer and looked him in the eyes.

King Leopold nodded at Lord Plum-Kilmer.

"Very well, Lord Plum-Kilmer. I will choose life as well."

The king turned, walked off the stage, and was not seen for the remainder of the ceremony. Privately, he retired to his chamber to decompress with his dog, Babbit the Magnificent, trying to keep his heart from racing. The aftershocks of making the biggest gamble in his life. But it paid off, and he would live to see another sunrise.

An eruption of applause rang out in waves from unknowing guests. The crowd descended upon them. Darla was beautiful, beaming in joy and well wishes. Kilmer's friends patted him on the back. But Kilmer, still in shock, his head swimming, felt light-headed over the events that just happened.

He started to wonder the unthinkable. For the first time in his life, was it over? Could he finally relax and be himself? The secret that had clung to him for so long was now revealed. Was it really over, or was he just being a fool thinking this was his moment?

"Ladies and gentlemen," Lord Whitney announced. "Allow me to introduce Lord Plum-Kilmer and his beautiful wife, Darla Plum-Kilmer."

Soft melodic strings began to play, and Darla and Kilmer faced each other.

"May I have this dance, Darla Plum-Kilmer?" he asked her.

"I would be honored, Lord Plum-Kilmer." And they started to dance alone as the audience watched them.

The chorus of beautiful voices rang out:

Our love is just beginning.
I can see it growing in your eyes.
And all the years we've been together.
Never as close as we are tonight.
Into your charms I suddenly surrender
I feel disarmed and longingly remember
That our love is just beginning.
Our love. It's our love.

"You are the best thing that has ever happened to me," Kilmer whispered in Darla's ear. He could smell the fragrance of perfume on her skin. "Thank you for being my wife."

"You came back to me," Darla said.

"But I didn't really. You came and found me."

She looked into his eyes. "No, you were lost in a very dark place, and you came back. You came back to me."

Sometimes at night when all the world is quiet,
I open my eyes and watch you sleep.
Somewhere in deep, familiar places
You're everything I want you to be.
If happiness is what you make it
Then you've made me complete in our love
It's our love. Our love.

As the song faded away, they kissed, holding each other tightly. The audience was enamored to watch them and applauded the celebration of their love. When the next song started, the audience joined and danced with them. The celebration had begun.

Thinking about King Leopold, Kilmer remembered the Battle of Mauveguard Pass and the words he shared with Amtor.

We are not enemies. We are safe now. We are safe.

Certainly, for the first time in a long time, Kilmer felt safe.

The celebration continued well into the night.

Then, just about two hours before midnight, the countdown to the disappearance of the Star of Ehlona began. Word spread quickly that the light from the star was a minute away from going out. These were the calculations from the best Star Prophets, on hand tonight and watching anxiously.

The countdown commenced and started from ten. The guests became even more excited, as their voices became louder: three, two, one.

The count reached zero, and the star still shone. The Star Prophets abruptly looked at their charts. *Where had they gone wrong?*

Then, without the fanfare, the Star of Ehlona went out, and the night got very dark.

Gia and Glover were four seconds off in their calculations. They were very close, but when the star did go out, they were looking down at their charts instead of at the star.

Gia stood expressionless with her mouth open. Glover said out loud what she was thinking privately to herself.

"A once-in-a-lifetime event, and we missed it."

"I really wanted to see it go out," Gia said, expressing her disappointment.

"Oh well," Glover said with a shrug. "Maybe next time."

Somewhere in the night

Lightning strikes the ocean

But it happens far from me

Much too far to ever see for certain

Excerpt from *The Witch's Songbook*

When you have nothing, you become more like the
water, leveling, and filling the empty spaces.
— Excerpt from *The Provenance* (Chapter Thirty-Two)

WHERE ONLY EYES
CAN REACH

Tʜᴇ Vɪʟʟᴀɢᴇ ᴏꜰ Hᴏᴍᴇsᴛᴇᴀᴅ ɪɴ ᴛʜᴇ Yᴇᴀʀ 843 HRT
(Tʜᴇ Lᴀsᴛ Nɪɢʜᴛ ᴏꜰ ᴛʜᴇ Sᴛᴀʀ ᴏꜰ Eʜʟᴏɴᴀ)

Amtor puffed at his pipe. A cloud of sweet-smelling smoke swelled around his head. He leaned against the corner of his house gazing up at the night sky, watching the Star of Ehlona dim from view. The night immediately got dark, darker than it had all the previous year. The surrounding woods plunged into inky, eerie shadows.

"The darkness is oppressive," he said. "I don't remember it being so black."

Gilglad, his wife, walked off the porch wrapping her arms around him.

"Come inside, my love, leave the darkness out here where it belongs."

Amtor touched his wife's hand.

"How is our little one?" he asked.

"Astar is asleep."

"They grow up so fast, don't they? He will be walking and talking soon. Did he enjoy his birthday?"

Gilglad laughed. "Yes, he enjoyed the taste of his first cake."

"Did you see his eyes?" Amtor laughed. "He made quite a mess of it."

"It all cleaned up nicely though."

A long piercing scream shattered the silence.

Instinctively, Amtor shielded Gilglad behind him from the direction where the screaming continued.

"Go inside and lock the door," he told her. She did as he asked.

Finally, the screaming stopped.

Amtor scanned the darkness. He saw nothing but shadows but could hear branches breaking in near proximity within the wood.

"Who's there?" Amtor shouted, reaching for his axe. An old habit: he never got more than an arm's reach away from having a weapon nearby. He pulled a torch from its sconce and waved it left, then right. Seeing nothing out of place, he walked deeper into the tree line, searching the area for what could have made the scream.

He felt unsettled. His instincts told him unseen eyes were watching him. Slowly, he proceeded into the woods with quiet, cautious steps, staying highly alert, his axe at the ready to kill anything foolish enough to spring at him. He could sense the unreal quiet of something trying hard not to be seen. Extending the torchlight in front of him, it cast shifting shadows among the trees.

Finally, the light fell upon a pair of silver eyes reflected ahead of him. His light illuminated the eyes to refracted neon in the darkened distance. Then, a quick rustle, a surprised movement, and the eyes scurried away. The noise of the thing going away faded from him rapidly. Whatever it was, Amtor and his big battle axe scared it away.

Now a more natural silence returned to the woods. The feeling of being watched was gone, and the feeling of being alone in the dark returned to him. He relaxed, knowing instinctively the danger had passed. Scanning the area, he found and tracked the crumpled grass, the broken branches. Investigating further he found a larger place more disturbed, close to the clearing, near the back of his home. From this vantage point, Amtor could turn back and see into the windows of his house easily. He could see the glow of the fire within, and Gilglad looking back out at him.

He waved at her, and she waved back.

This would be a perfect position to spy on him and his family.

Turning back now, he looked the area over further. He found blood—a trail of it led off into the distance. He knelt to find footprints, but then, he saw something else too—large snake trails. But these were much bigger than any snake he had ever seen. Massive, deeply channeled in the dirt and leaves, these snake trails slithered away from the place, after having stopped here for some time. Whatever made the scream was carried off by the snake that formed these trails. The other footprints were human, but they stopped here.

Amtor stood in the darkness, his eyes reflecting the torchlight. Just a rudimentary investigation told him all he needed to know to determine what had happened. The demons were back again. They had been standing in the cover of darkness by the tree line, spying on them. The serpent demon, and the spotted one, they had been here before; she had spied on him every month or so. This time, Amtor rationalized, someone came upon them and disturbed her. She could have stayed hidden in the shadows and continued spying. She could have let them pass. But the demon could not resist the temptation or ignore her ravenous hunger. She could not help taking an unwary victim. She could not control her lust for blood, and not able to resist the temptation, she attacked.

The demon had come to him in his dreams before. The horned demon with her blue skin, half-woman, half-viper, had spied on him in the middle of the night. Why she was here or why she spied on them, Amtor did not know. But he was ever watchful and protective of his family.

Amtor came out of the woods. Gilglad, relieved to see him, watched from the window and opened the door as he neared. He waved back without a look of concern, cleaving his axe one-handed into the cutting stump. Amtor tried to conceal his worry from his wife over something he himself did not understand. For now, he kept his knowledge of the demon to himself.

He walked around the back of the house and examined the spot he had covered with a large stone. He knew that under the stone was where he buried the golden dagger, the blade he found in the pit. He figured the demon was searching for it but could not locate it. If Langula knew where it was, she would have dug it up by now. The ground here was undisturbed, but spies seemed to be coming more frequently now, demonstrating their desperation, and how important the blade was.

Tonight, the blade was safe. But he had to remain vigilant for anything.

He returned to the corner of the house and picked up his pipe. It had gone out, which irritated him. A fine evening of pipe smoking ruined. He scanned the woods as he tapped the pipe against the corner of the house to empty its bowl. Then, he proceeded inside.

Gilglad unlocked the latch and let him in. He gently shut the door, securing it behind him and took a long last look into the night. Then, he pulled the shade.

"What was that scream?" Gilglad asked.

Amtor turned to face her with a grim expression. "Something sinister, I think."

Gilglad looked horrified.

"I saw signs of a struggle, but nothing else. Whatever it was, it ran away. I'm afraid it was an assault of some kind."

"The scream sounded like a person being attacked. Here? In Homestead? That sort of thing happens in Haverhill, not here," she said.

Amtor agreed. He took her into his arms. "Stay away from the tree line, and close to the house for a few days. Just in case."

Gilglad nodded. "But I was supposed to go to Hillsdale tomorrow."

"What's in Hillsdale?"

"The merchant with the rash. I promised I would stop by to heal him."

"Astar and I will come with you, if that's all right. For tonight though, let's make sure we pull the curtains. Without the light from the Star of Ehlona, it is darker out there, and anyone can easily see inside the house at night."

"Amtor, are we in danger?"

"No, of course not." Amtor had to smile; he held her tenderly. His body was so large, and hers was so small. "Who would dare threaten the Minister of War or his family?"

"Only a fool would challenge you," she smiled, and they embraced. But behind her back Amtor's face held a serious expression of concern. Gilglad watched him limp away, returning his pipe to its place on the fireplace mantel.

She alone went into Astar's room and checked that the baby was still asleep. She walked in and quietly shut the door. In a padded rocking chair, she sat in the dark. She listened to the rhythmic breathing of her young son asleep in his crib. Lifting her head and closing her eyes, she opened her senses. Using Astar's breathing as a metronome, she was able to expand her awareness beyond the room. She listened intently, not just with her ears but focusing on the center of her heart. Gilglad concentrated on every heartbeat. The echoes of time rhythmically pulsated like waves, fluctuating, emitting outwardly from her, then contracting back. She continued slowly, deliberately breathing in and out, her heartbeat in time, the waves ebbing and flowing around her. The baby's breathing assisted her to receive emotive signals. Like weaving a magic spell, Gilglad could sense, instead of see, the energy moving around her.

Her emotive waves produced a vision.

The spirit of the Goddess Ehlona materialized in front of her in a dim green light. Gilglad was neither afraid nor anxious, for this was the vision that she waited for. She felt only peace and a deep sense of overwhelming love. A curtain of sparkling emerald lights rained down all around her, and she became bathed in the love of the spirit of Saint Ehlona's powerful healing.

"Mother Ehlona, you are so kind," Gilglad said, the Goddess Ehlona floating in front of her. "You are beauty divine."

The Goddess spread her arms, emanating beams of soft green light illuminating the shadows behind her. Dressed in flowing emerald robes and jeweled in gold, her long blonde hair was blowing in an unseen wind.

My love, Sister Gilglad, the spirit of Ehlona spoke inside her mind. *You are my most favored. Let the emerald cloak of my love cover and bless you.*

"When, Mother?"

Soon. Stay faithful to the love in your heart, and my blessings will soon be upon you.

The vision dimmed. At the end of the vision, Astar stood in his crib and calmly looked at her in the darkened room.

While Amtor guarded the family against the blue-horned demon, she had been having visions of Ehlona, the Goddess, for over a year now. Both sensed a change was coming. There was static electricity in the air. A new reality drew near.

With these types of parents, what hope did little Astar have for a normal life?

That question would have to wait for the child to grow.

For now, little Astar merely stood and stared at his mother.

I can see the village lights from this height

Everything is so clear up here.

Excerpt from *The Witch's Songbook*

The screaming had stopped long ago.
— Excerpt from *The Provenance* (Chapter Thirty-Three)

CELEBRATION OF LIGHT AND LIFE

The Temple of Chen-Li in the Year 843 HRT
(The Last Night of the Star of Ehlona)

On the night the Star of Ehlona dimmed from view, another celebration occurred that most people missed. Once the wedding was over, the spirit of Chen-Li said his goodbyes, then he and his First Wives made a hasty exit. They sailed over the high castle walls and raced as white, blue, and gold phantoms, like shooting stars across the dark empty miles of the Mid-Run Valley. They streaked straight to their home at the temple. Chen-Li and the First Wives traveled the hundreds of miles almost instantaneously. Once back at the temple, where their physical bodies waited, a repetitive sound of three loud pops indicated their spirits had rejoined their bodies. Afterward, it took a moment for each of them to come out of their meditations.

By the time Chen-Li and the First Wives made their way outside the inner temple, a crowd of thousands of priests had gathered on the eastern ridge. They assembled to look up at the Gray Mountains to witness a once-in-a-lifetime event.

From the vantage point facing east, they could see Dragonbreath Mountain. In the dim light since the Star of Ehlona had faded, the resulting darkness would have made Dragonbreath undetectable in the shadowy distance. But this night, millions of golden orbs illuminated the high mountain summit, lighting the entirety of Dragonbreath and all the surrounding mountains. The dancing lights appeared in a celebration from millions of Timmutes in honor of their creator and the dimming of her star. Their microscopic society, created by the Witch of the Great Mapes Forest, worshipped their creator, and celebrated that they served her in life, served her needs in her weakness, and helped her escape the wiles of the world high atop the Dragonbreath Mountain.

Now the Timmutes on top of the mountain produced streams of spectacular golden lights on the summit spreading out like a bright web. In long winding chains, they illuminated the ridges leading up to the summit like crawling snakes formed from many individual lights. Upon every mountain ridge and valley, the Timmutes emanated from the pivotal point on top of the high summit.

> It looks like a burning wagon wheel.
> Like glowing spiderwebs.
> Like a bright glowing net cast over the mountains.

These were some of the comments from the White Eminence as the Timmutes' colorful orbs wrapped throughout the sharp, uplifted rocky Fangs. The steady stream of lights raced past the Temple of Chen-Li and continued westward, through the foothills, across the plain of the Mid-Run Valley, where they concentrated again in another central hub. This time they appeared in the Great Mapes Forest as their center moved to form more of the glowing spiderwebs. For the first time in history, the Timmutes made their presence known in lights, and it was a spectacular scene in the east.

Chen-Li walked out and viewed the western side. Here and there, the twinkling lights of the Timmutes could be seen in all directions, scattering out as far as the eye could see, right to the very horizon. The Timmutes were everywhere.

The mountains and the forests were alive, dancing in the lights throughout the Mid-Run Valley. The scene was a wonder to all who could see it. The Timmutes' commemoration of their creator would be the talk for several generations. It became known as the Grand Lighting.

The Star Prophets nervously flipped through their copies of the *Constellation Volume* to find any reference for this event. But none were found. There were no references to the Grand Lighting anywhere.

And so it was that the Grand Lighting filled a page all its own, in the back of the book, with no meanings or justifications provided. The Timmutes had spontaneously expressed themselves in the most unexpected event of all.

They danced in colors until sunrise. Then, as if by one accord, they dimmed in the new light of the next day. Most of them went dim simultaneously, but their dimming was an imperfect affair, which made it seem all the more heavenly in its elegance.

The priests of the Temple of Chen-Li stayed awake all night to watch.

As the lights of the Timmutes danced, another event was taking place elsewhere. In the Mid-Run Valley, when the light of the Star of

Ehlona went out, the light went out of Sister Chavise. She died peacefully and gracefully in her own bed at her orphanage in the village of Plum. She was attended by her only daughter, Sister Maldean, who cared for her beautiful mother, until she slipped out of this life with a smile on her face; a good life, well lived. She was the first of Saint Ehlona's blessings to finally dim in peace.

Sister Chavise was buried in a simple ceremony on the grounds of the orphanage, in a little plot with a smooth white rock marking her headstone. She was placed just behind the bean field, close to the place where she found Darius Plum, the boy who would later call himself Kilmer, hiding for his life in a slimy overturned tree.

In the years to follow, Sister Maldean would run the orphanage; since she was raised there by her mother, it was the only life she knew. She would make a bench by the tombstone and listen to the rushing waters of the Plum River, while thinking of her mother. She also reflected on the other sisters of the orphans, Kilmer, the soldiers of the Red Guard, and the Goddess Ehlona. In time, Sister Maldean would find a blessing and purpose in her life. To do so, would be the finest tribute she could pay this good woman, Sister Chavise, her mother, who taught her so much.

It's a volcano growing hotter

When your patience is being tried

And you just want to explode it

But you keep it all wrapped up inside

Excerpt from *The Witch's Songbook*

We should consider all possibilities, that is all.
— Excerpt from *The Provenance* (Chapter Thirty-Four)

HOSPITALITY OF THE ZORN

The Castle Odessa in the Year 843 HRT (One Month After the Star of Ehlona)

"He did what?" the Zorn screamed at the man. The prisoner hung in chains during the interrogation. The man was a minor council member of one of the villages. He was returning home from King Leopold's celebration at Castle Odessa when he heard a baby crying in the woods. Following the baby's cries, he discovered it was not a baby at all but a demon mimicking one. The next thing he remembered was waking up in Castle Orlo manacled to the wall.

"I can't believe it," the Zorn shouted. He extended a bony finger and lifted the man's chin to face him. The man's eyes widened looking at the Zorn's gaunt face, crooked teeth, overgrown chin, and deep hollow eye sockets surrounding his crazy yellow eyes. "Why are you tormenting me with your lies? Have I not been kind to you? You dare return my kindness with lies?"

"No, please, no," the man said. "It is the truth! I'm telling you everything I know. Leopold said it exactly the way I told you. Now, will you please free me? I want to go home."

"I want to hear it again!" The Zorn released the man and stood up straight. He put his arms behind his back and paced the dungeon cell.

"Let us reason together, you and I, and reach an understanding." The Zorn roamed to the far end of the dungeon. "You heard His Majesty, King Leopold, call him Lord *Plum*-Kilmer? Is that what you said? He said the word *Plum*?"

The man nodded. He licked his lips, and with a stutter, said, "Y-yes. That's the way I heard it. Does that mean anything?"

"And he said this in front of an audience of hundreds of people, at Kilmer's wedding?"

Once again, the man nodded his head yes.

The Zorn closed the distance between them as fast as lightning, coming to just an inch away from the man's face. "*You lie!* Only a fool would do that! And Leopold is a lot of things, but he is no fool! Are you calling Leopold a fool?"

"No," the man said, shaking his head. "No."

The Zorn turned his back. Then he shifted around slowly. The Zorn did not have enough skin to cover his hideously misshapen teeth, but in times of great distress, as this was, he could manage to curl his lip in a hateful snag of a crooked upside-down smile.

"What else did he say?" the Zorn asked through clenched teeth.

The man asked for a drink of water. The Zorn's expression changed to impart as much surprise and compassion as he could muster.

"Oh, of course, yes," the Zorn said. "Forgive my manners; you must be thirsty."

The Zorn daintily picked up a water pitcher with only his thumb and first finger, that sat on the stone floor of the prisoner's cell. He walked over and offered it to the prisoner.

"Here, let me show you that I can be kind." The Zorn tipped the pitcher into the prisoner's waiting mouth. The pitcher was full of stale urine as he poured it all over the prisoner's face and head. When he had emptied it, he threw the pitcher at the man.

"You think you're thirsty now? Wait until I pour hot coals down your throat. Now talk!"

"What do you want to know?" the man cried, spraying rotten piss out of his mouth and eyes.

"What else can you tell me about the king's celebration?" the Zorn said patiently with a tight sneer.

"Chen-Li was there. I overheard conversations with the master priest. Chen-Li helped heal some sick soldiers, Kilmer included."

"Ah! See there?" The Zorn looked over at Langula, who stood there with Monticello and two other demons.

One of the demons had blue skin, like Langula, and a full head of white hair. The other demon was shorter, stockier, and red-skinned with black curly hair. The Zorn noticed them but continued with his aggravation directed at Langula.

"That is why you lost contact, my dear. Leopold's search party dared come to the Sanguine Forest and you lost them," the Zorn said to her. "Chen-Li helped them. You know what that means, don't you?"

"He administered them his blood," Langula answered, looking bored.

"Exactly. Oh well, at least you got... how many of them did you get?"

"Four, five if you count the spotter."

The Zorn quietly repeated, "Four or five. You toyed with them too long. You could have—should have—had all eight of them! You and your constant need for fear to feed on."

Langula laughed.

"What's so funny?" The Zorn took notice.

She slithered through the room and circled the Zorn. "I played with them for too long? Is that what you said? Did I hear you right?

Did you say that Leopold publicly revealed Kilmer's true identity? What did you think would happen? Did you think you would unsettle Leopold by revealing to him that he could not trust the sole survivor of a family he was responsible for killing? What made you think that? Because that is what you would do? You would have killed the boy outright. You would never have given Darius Plum a chance to strike at you. You thought that you and Leopold were of one mind because you are of the same blood. But hasn't he taught you over and over again that he has a will of his own? He bested you, Zorn. He always bests you. Leopold is not your equal. He is stronger than you, he is your weakness. You have a blind spot for him, and he makes you look like a fool."

The Zorn narrowed his eyes at Langula. Then, he scrutinized the other three demons with her.

"Why is he blue?" the Zorn asked about the demon.

Langula quickly expressed her pleasure over her reproductive creations. "Oh, he is blue, what a marvelous blue, isn't he? I have named him Frost. Isn't he wonderful? Sometimes the traits come from the father, and sometimes the traits come from the mother. This one took after me, inheriting my blue skin."

"I thought I was assigning the names of the demons around here?" the Zorn said.

Langula shrugged.

The Zorn considered Frost. "Who was the father?"

"A little bit of the archer, Yori. Mixed in with that deliciously big one, the soldier with the split lips. The one I tormented until he hanged himself in a horse stable. He was marvelous."

Frost smirked with a crooked grin. "I would have liked to have gotten to know him better. We may have gained useful information from him."

Langula shrugged again. "He's just as dead anyway."

"What of the red one?" the Zorn asked.

Langula moved to the next demon. "This one's name is Grim."

"He looks Grim. He looks angry."

Grim stood breathing heavily, heaving his thick chest, looking at the Zorn from the top of his eyebrows.

"He's a little anxious, I confess. I do believe he is, without a doubt, the most vicious one so far."

"Is that from his father too?"

"It could very well be. The blood and reproductive material for this one came from Kilmer when he was your prisoner."

The Zorn shot her a quick angry look but then nodded approvingly. Then he walked over to the prisoner once more.

"I apologize," the Zorn said to him. "I got distracted, didn't I? But don't you worry, I did not forget about you. Now, what else can you tell me?"

"Aberfell was there," the man said.

"Ah yes, the boy who never forgets. The Supreme Historian. Quite a classy crowd." The Zorn looked over at Langula and the demonic. "Can you imagine what people are telling him? This so-called Supreme Historian? All their precious private information? All their dirty little secrets?"

"Why don't we capture him and force him to tell us what he knows?" Langula asked.

The Zorn shot Langula a surprised look.

"Because he is still a baby," the Zorn said with a laugh. "He cannot even speak words yet."

Even the demon Langula was not immune to embarrassment.

"Even as he grows, he will be problematic," Frost said. "He will never be alone. He would be a hard target with so many people constantly hanging on to him. His popularity makes him inaccessible."

The Zorn was impressed. "I like him," he said to Langula.

She could not help herself adding, "He has his mother's intelligence."

"Oh, there's more to him than that," the Zorn said.

The Zorn approached the demonic. Four demons: Langula, Monticello, Frost, and Grim. He looked them over carefully, then spoke, "We must leave Castle Orlo."

The demons looked at him, but none was so surprised as Langula.

"Leave the castle? Why?" she asked.

"It has served its purpose. The Sanguine Forest has served its purpose. Both are now forbidden, a blot on the map, a place off-limits to both man and beast. So, why stay? Chen-Li, King Leopold, and every hunter and archer and curious adventurer around, the word has spread; the Zorn and his demons inhabit the Sanguine Forest. As long as this place exists, we have won the battle here. But now we need to think of winning the war."

"I thought that was what we wanted?" Monticello said. "Didn't we want the realm of the humans to fear us?"

"They do fear us, Monticello," Frost said. "But they will fear us more if they don't know where to find us. The longer our position is known, it gives the mortals a target, a goal. Something worthy for them to gird up their courage and try to overcome their fear. They will fear us more if they don't know where we are. These humans, they fear the unknown most of all."

The Zorn smiled at him. "Your understanding is refreshing, Frost."

"Then what would you have us do?" Langula asked.

"Open the castle gates. Allow the vengeful spirits to haunt the Sanguine Forest as they will. They will keep it eerie and forbidden to the mortals. After all, we do have appearances to keep."

"Is that all?" Grim asked.

"No, that is not all," the Zorn replied, but this was the extent of his answer. "Not by a long shot."

The Zorn had a plan. He had thought the matter through. But at present, he did not feel inclined to share it with them. Especially when he knew that behind him a prisoner was still manacled to the wall.

The Zorn was getting paranoid of his nemesis Chen-Li and his trickery. The Zorn remembered all too well how Chen-Li snuck into his castle years ago in his spiritual form using the trickster, the Zornastic priest Nantz. He ended up stealing the magical dagger Soothsayer, a loss the Zorn had never fully recovered from. He turned and looked at the prisoner, and all he thought he saw was Nantz. But this prisoner was not inhabited by Chen-Li.

"What else can you tell me?" the Zorn asked the prisoner. "What other useful information can you give?"

The man stuttered and shook his head. He could not think of anything else to say.

"Are you afraid?" the Zorn asked, and the prisoner nodded affirmatively. "Why? What do you think I am going to do? Do you think I am going to kill you?"

The man looked at the Zorn with large eyes and trembled.

"You will be pleased to know that I am not going to kill you."

"You're not?" the prisoner asked.

"No," the Zorn reassured him and pointed to Grim. "I am going to let him do that."

Grim smiled through his razor-sharp demon fangs. The Zorn stood up and walked out past the demonic.

Behind him, the Zorn heard the screams of the man being ripped to pieces.

Look at me, here in the wilderness

Young and running free

The ungrateful child I turned out to be.

Now all the feeling is gone.

Excerpt from *The Witch's Songbook*

Be brave, lads. Fear will not defeat us here today.
— Excerpt from *The Provenance* (Chapter Thirty-Five)

THE HARD TRUTH

The Castle Odessa in the Year 843 HRT
(Six Months Since the Star of Ehlona)

King Leopold walked out of the large double doors of Castle Odessa and stepped onto the Green alone. A light rain drizzled down, and clouds obscured the high peaks. The wind had a cold, wet bite to it.

It had been three months since the Star of Ehlona burned out. The marriage of Lord Plum-Kilmer was just as long ago. Now the crowds had all gone away and the king was alone too, albeit with his ever-present aide. Also, it had been three months since he took the biggest gamble of his life, offering his throat to the man that had every reason to want to kill him. Leopold even provided the dagger and handed it to him to do it. Yet the gamble paid off, and both of them had buried their demons.

Leopold had seen so much death. He had been responsible for most of it. Some of them had it coming but some were innocent. Now the desire for life and peace overwhelmed him.

But could he ever be at peace? he wondered.

Contemplating these thoughts, the king crossed the Green, while his aide walked a reasonable distance behind him. The aide knew better than to disturb him, especially in moments of great reflection when the king was at his most melancholy. Leopold stopped in the center of the Green briefly, where he crossed his arms and looked down. Here in the geometric center of the space, a small round plaque of Blue and Red sat inlaid and flush into its surface, forever marking the center of the Green as a dedication to the sovereignty of the Kingdom of Odessa.

The king looked out into the mist. The red-and-blue flags were flapping in the strong, cold breeze. He put his hands behind his back and continued walking out to the balcony's edge, resting his boot upon the railing. The aide stopped behind him and momentarily had the fear that the king might launch himself over the edge. The recent trend of suicides had everybody worried.

Had the madness reached the king?

But Leopold had no intention of jumping. Leopold would never consider it while there were so many other people more deserving and since he had more dangerous tasks ahead of him.

King Leopold looked through the gloom, trying to catch a glimpse of the nearer peaks, but they remained obscured by clouds. He had better luck when he looked straight down over the railing. The cliffs dropped three thousand feet to the rocks below. His mind turned to Curtz, jumping from the highest tower of Castle Odessa. Had he even seen the view this clearly in his madness? In Curtz's mind, so separated from reality, he was unable to see any danger.

Leopold could not imagine it, even though he could imagine a great many things, as well as many possibilities, his greatest strength. But what he envisaged now, what he felt compelled to do, defied all logic.

"The signs are all there," he said to himself. "It must be done."

The aide approached him. "Excuse me, my king?"

Leopold hesitated, which is something he rarely did. But he wanted to be sure. At last, he turned confidently from the railing and once committed, commanded the aide directly.

"Summon my escort. Pack my fur cloak and seven days' rations."

The aide bowed in acknowledgment.

"Summon Lord Whitney to me here. Report back when the riders are ready. Go!"

The aide quickly obeyed. Two more aides appeared, armed with spears, waiting at a distance at the tall wooden double doors of the castle. They gave the king plenty of room to move. Leopold turned his back to them and continued to stare into the gloom, watching it move in gray wisps around the cold wind. He remained deep in thought until minutes later, when Lord Whitney arrived.

"Your Majesty?" Lord Whitney bowed. "You have summoned me?"

"Indeed." Leopold turned to face him. "I need to leave the castle. I am putting you in charge for the next week, maybe two, until I return."

"Yes, of course, Your Highness," he said. "May I ask where you are going?"

"On a fool's errand, perhaps. But something I must do for myself."

Moments later, King Leopold sat atop his warhorse that was adorned in red-and-blue armor, a white plumage of feathers attached, facing forward from the horse's head armor. The king had a band of ten riders: the best the kingdom had to offer. All of them veterans of Leopold's forces in the Battle of Mauveguard Pass. They wore their finest armor, colored in red and blue, thick and protective—this was the king's escort of elite forces, empowered to take the king of Odessa anywhere he needed to go, return him safely, or die trying.

The rain continued as the riders left the castle and rode through the Mauveguard Pass. The rain brought back memories of another time when the pass was flooded in rain and blood. The king's riders thought they heard the ghosts of the long dead and distant screams of the dying as they rode through. They traveled through the pass in silence, each one either reliving or trying to forget their memories. Leopold rode in the center of them but directed the way in silence to where they were heading. None of them knew where they were going, only King Leopold himself.

The end of the Mauveguard Pass gave way with Leopold turning the column south by southeast, and it confirmed the troops' deepest fears. They were heading into the Sanguine, the Suicide Forest.

After the rain stopped, they rode for hours, only stopping to rest the horses. None of the riders got any rest knowing where they were headed. Leopold could not sleep either. His mind was still deep in thought, and the men could tell something was wrong.

On the second day, the riders approached the boundaries of the Sanguine Forest. King Leopold gave the order to stop and dismounted his horse. On the outskirts of the forest ahead, a general anxiety rose in the battle-hardened men. Any one of them would give their life in defense of the king, but what lay ahead was something they could not fight with swords, spears, or arrows. Ahead of them, in the dark Sanguine Forest, only magic was might.

The sun had gone down, and an oppressive darkness lay ahead of them. The rain had returned, this time as a storm. Lightning struck and spiderwebbed through the dark clouds. The thunder boomed seconds later.

"Bring me my fur cloak," Leopold said in between flashes of lightning and rumbles of thunder. He unbuckled his decorative scabbard containing his favorite jeweled sword and handed it to one of his warriors. "Keep this safe."

"Your sword, Your Majesty?" the warrior questioned as he received it.

His fur cloak came to him, and he put it on. "Where I am going, it will not help."

The fur cloak warmed him. Leopold draped it across his broad shoulders.

"You men stay here. Wait for me until morning light. If I have not returned by morning, you are all to return to the castle and report to Lord Whitney of what you saw here this night. Keep a sharp lookout for anyone or anything."

"I will come with you, my lord," one of the warriors said. Then another, until they all were pledging to follow him.

"You have your orders. Stay here, until morning light," he repeated. "Do not go any farther into the Sanguine Forest. No matter what happens or what you see. Even if you see me or hear me calling for you. I can tell you now, it will not be me—it would be the work of dark magic alone. That could only mean the Zorn is preying on your minds. From here, I continue alone. Wait for me and go no further. That is an order. May the Gods be with you."

Leopold said no more nor waited for a response. He turned into the storm and walked alone into the Sanguine Forest. The men watched him fade away into the darkness. Each man had a bad feeling, a sense of inadequacy and restlessness, which turned into helplessness. This was the sacrifice of what they were ordered to do. They rested their horses and put up shelters against the storm. There, they watched diligently, waiting for the king's return.

Leopold had no trouble walking through the Sanguine. His boots would occasionally crush a skull, or some other bone of a long-dead

Zornastic priest. He walked farther into the depths of the dark forest, not really caring which direction he came from, or which way he was heading. A sense of direction did not matter here.

His first encounter came with the blue streams of the vengeful spirits, those distressed souls of priests unable to rest in the stillness of death, trapped between this world and the next. They let out howling screams and came to him in the form of shrieking heads longing for the warmth of his living flesh. They caused him no pain, only annoyance and some nauseating discomfort as they passed through him. He continued to walk in a brisk pace, making no effort to rebuke them other than wiping them from his eyes when they obscured his vision. Otherwise, he kept walking forward and deeper into the Suicide Forest.

He did not encounter bogs of quicksand, or swarms of locusts, scorpions, or hornets. Instead, the path was clear other than a few of the vengeful spirits. He did not break down from feeble-mindedness, confusion, or fear, and continued marching along in a straight line.

The Zorn had been expecting him and wanted to do nothing to discourage him to continue. Leopold himself was what the Zorn craved.

Leopold could sense he was getting closer now, and nothing slowed his progress in the slightest.

He walked into a clearing, and there in the distant lightning, Castle Orlo stood. The magnificent castle that evaded the sight of so many that had searched for it, yet Leopold had no problem finding it directly in his path.

Leopold took a moment. He had never seen the castle before. Its seven tall, spiraled towers and smaller domes were capped by a centralized one that covered the main forty-foot stronghold. The castle sat magnificently in blocks of stone. Then an angry look crossed the king's face. Despite his situation, he could not help being impressed by Castle Orlo.

As if by design, the main double doors loudly unlatched with a series of heavy *thunks* and moved slowly open. The golden glow on the inside spilled out, illuminating the dark woods. For a moment, Leopold thought the door looked like a pair of outstretched arms welcoming him in a deadly embrace.

Leopold had no reason to fear, for his confidence was supreme. He strode forward, never hesitating as he crossed over the threshold. Inside a glow of golden flame, from candles and torches hanging from sconces, lit the interior entryway.

Naturally by instinct, Leopold reached for his sword. Then, he remembered he had left it at the encampment. After securing a burning torch from the wall, he turned to watch as the doors slowly and deliberately closed behind him. Leopold watched them close and heard the latches clank in place. His only chance of escape just slowly closed behind him. The way out lay before him, not behind him.

The torches and candlelight cast shadows as the air became heavy and oppressive. The temperature dropped; his warm breath changed to vapor with every exhale. Adjusting his fur cloak tighter around his neck, he continued forward.

A double stairway wound up both sides of the walls, but they led to the same place, a balcony up above. The center aisle led to a double door under the balcony. Leopold knew where they led, information derived from Lord Plum-Kilmer's earlier adventure. That way was the way to some antechambers, and to the stairs down to the dungeons and torture cells. That was not the way he wanted to go.

He chose the stairway to the left, and with torch in hand, ascended toward the upper balcony. Along the way, he saw oil paintings framed on the walls. He held his torch to the first painting—a portrait of dark skeletal demons chasing wild animals over a high cliff, the animals tumbling to their doom. He continued up the stairs and another picture came into view. This one was of a large three-masted sailing ship that had been broken apart on sharp rocks in the middle of a storm and was sinking. The third painting along the way was of a small demon resting on a pale man's chest while lying in a bedchamber. All the paintings were of doom, destruction, and tragedy. Things that demons would hold in fascination.

Leopold reached the balcony and came to four doors; he opened the first one nearest him. All the doors opened to the same large room: a grand auditorium. Leopold now stood looking down inside an enormously round amphitheater, a place so large that sound reverberated from all directions. A terrace made of finely polished white marble wound its way around the wide circumference of the auditorium. The dome of the central keep towered high overhead, lit with a multitude of melting white candles casting shadows along its upper curved surface. Rows of smooth convex marble columns spiraled around framed balconies of private boxes obscured by curtains of moldy red velvet. The whole grand auditorium sloped downward and inward to a single point at the bottom, to a flat stage some hundred feet or more far below.

On the distant, dimly lit stage, a solitary figure stood. The Zorn stood with his back to the upper balcony. His body glimmered from the occasional sparkle of energy around him.

Leopold had come through the doors and stopped on the balcony. He saw the small lone figure below.

The Zorn stands alone to distract me?

After so many years of war, internal fighting with factions, and battling the Amalgamates, he was wise to tricks and this seemed like a trap. Leopold cautiously, slowly descended the stairs. Scanning the area, he noticed corpses of long-dead priests scattered throughout, grim reminders of the mass suicide that took place here.

As Leopold descended the steps farther, the Zorn turned slowly to face him over his shoulder. Leopold's footfalls came to a quick stop upon seeing the Zorn's face for the first time. This was no longer the man-sized crow he met in Hammerville, but the Zorn in his natural demonic state. He saw the Zorn for what he was: the Skeletal King.

The color of his complexion looked like stained ivory. The decay of his flesh had been so complete that his appearance alone generated fear, without the aid of any magical spell. Hideous for any who would look upon him, and King Leopold was no exception. But in Leopold's case, he felt less fear and more remorse for the condition the Zorn was in.

How did this wretched creature come to be in this condition?

The two watched each other in silence as the distance between them narrowed. The blue wisps of vengeful spirits streaked about the auditorium moaning in otherworldly agony. Leopold's heavy boots reverberated off the domed walls, bounced off the ceiling, and were the only sound other than the occasional scream from one of the blue hazy ghosts. Step by step Leopold closed the distance, until finally reaching the ground floor and the stage of the grand auditorium. There they came face to face. The entire way they maintained eye contact with each other.

Leopold expected to see the demon Langula, or some other minion. But none of them were in sight. Just because he could not see them, however, did not mean watchful eyes were not observing him.

The Zorn said nothing, as several blue ghosts darted between them. Then, at last, he broke the silence. "Welcome to Castle Orlo, Your Majesty."

Leopold looked at the Zorn. His visage was one of pure horror. His flesh was pale, torn and stretched across his bones. His eye sockets were deep with only tiny yellow eyes nestled in dark residual holes. A multipoint golden crown encrusted with precious gems sat crooked upon his head. Yet in his vanity, his clothes were fresh and new, always the double-breasted black uniform of his youth, buttoned up to his chin, with dainty red buttons holding his collar together.

"I am unarmed," Leopold said, spreading his arms.

"Almost," the Zorn told him, gliding away out of the light and into the shadow without contact to the floor.

Leopold slowly reached down and gently pulled the dagger from his boot. Holding it for a moment in his open palm, he let it fall to the ground with a sharp metallic echo. Throughout the chamber it resounded. He kicked it toward the Zorn.

The Zorn took no notice of the dagger as it skidded by his feet. "Now you are unarmed."

"Where is your demon?" Leopold asked.

"*She's* not here at present. I sent her on a special mission. Where's yours?"

"LaNew? I killed him."

"I can respect that. I killed twenty thousand of my Zornastic Order when I gave them my grand command."

"So we are alone then?"

"We are never alone," the Zorn said, motioning to the vengeful spirits. "Spirits of the dead. I can't get rid of them."

The Zorn considered Leopold. He stood in front of him with such confidence, commanding the space around him, in total control of himself. "You have grown into quite an impressive man. You remind me of myself at a younger age."

"I have come for a single purpose: the hard truth. We need to understand each other."

"I've been expecting it."

Leopold looked away. "When I was young, I felt powerless, because I was powerless. All I thirsted for was power. Ambition blinded me. Many people have died because of my ambition. I burned them at the stake, I burned entire villages."

"Umbrick? The village you grew up in."

"Yes, Umbrick. Locking the doors of the orphanage, I trapped them all inside. Then, I set it on fire. I killed them all. All the children, all the adults. I even murdered my own mother."

Now the Zorn's yellow eyes sparkled. "Finally, we utter the truth. Sister Luna was of no great loss to me or anyone else."

Leopold continued, "You have no idea what I suffered at the hands of that woman. All my suffering was my own mother's doing. Hiding under that ruthless disguise. Oh, the things she did to me. How I hated her! I enjoyed murdering her and watching her burn."

"I was once an orphan too, as you know well. My brother and I were raised in the orphanage of Sister Catosa. She was one of the original Sisters of the Orphans, endowed with the Beautiful Blessings of my mother, the Goddess Ehlona. But just a few months before Ehlona's blessing, and before I was born, another child was born. Sister Catosa had a daughter whose name was Luna. Only a few months older than my brother Marus and me, I had ten years to corrupt her. As we grew, we keep our liaisons a secret. I found her to be a… most willing subject, and she quickly aligned to my cause. Even after I escaped that place at the age of ten, even after I conjured my demon Langula, Luna kept coming back to me, and I bent her to my desires. When St. Ehlona's Orphanages expanded so rapidly after my mother's expansive plan, Sister Luna was groomed to run the one in Umbrick."

The Zorn paused briefly for a laugh. "How she deceived them all! Even that self-important brother of mine, Chen-Li, never had a clue that Luna was secretly a priestess of my Zornastic Order. She worshipped me. I found her to be very willing, very pleasant to be with, extremely receptive to the desires of the flesh. Before she even walked into the orphanage at Umbrick for the first time, she was with child. She hid it well. No one ever suspected. Until one night she walked out into the dark of the woods and had the baby there, in a misty cornfield. Langula assisted her. The baby, a male child, was put into a plain wicker basket and dropped on the steps of the Umbrick orphanage. Luna claimed to have found the child on the doorstep, left there by one of the villagers. No one suspected a thing. The orphanage took the baby in and raised the child as an orphan. But the child was Luna's all along."

Leopold's face steamed, but he controlled his temper.

"I just had a marvelous thought: the demon Langula was your midwife," the Zorn said with sarcastic wit.

"You abandoned me."

"So what? It is the way of the world. I was abandoned. We all go through this life alone."

"You handed me over to a life of abuse."

"It made you what you are."

"I killed my mother."

"She deserved it."

"You left me to die."

"No, I gave you power."

"Not anymore."

"Do you think you can change your nature, Leopold?"

"I am Leopold. I will forever be Leopold. Now I abandon you."

Leopold turned to go.

"Wait," the Zorn said. "Don't forget your dagger."

"Keep it," Leopold said over his shoulder, without turning back. "Since you can't locate Soothsayer, you need it more than I do."

The Zorn watched him climb the steps back up to the balcony that would lead him out. He called after him in a voice booming through the echoes of the large expanse.

"I may have abandoned you, but that was a long time ago! I am not giving up on you, Leopold! You are the king of the Kingdom of

Odessa! You will come around! You will come to my way of think-ing! You'll see! Once they all let you down. You'll see!"

Leopold reached the top of the auditorium. He kept walking through the doors while the Zorn's voice continued to reverberate in loud echoes.

"When they ridicule you, when they won't respect you anymore, you will come back to me! When you find all the people you trusted were just a lie, you will return to me! When you seek more power, your road will lead to me! When the end comes, only you and I will still be standing, you will beg to come back into my fold! Into my dream! Into my being! Your days are gone, never to return, they are gone and you will burn!"

The Zorn laughed manically.

Leopold fended off several more attacks of the annoying wispy spirits as he passed the old portraits of oil-painted bad luck and shuf-fled down the darkened stairway.

The last words he heard the Zorn say: "You have performed well for me as my puppet! Through you, you have delivered the entire Mid-Run Valley under my control!"

Leopold halted, as behind him in the darkness, he heard the Zorn's laughter. He turned so quickly that he dropped his expen-sive fur cloak in the corridor of the castle's entrance. He continued on, leaving it lying there.

As if by silent command, the heavy double doors groaned open loudly as he approached them. He stomped out of Castle Orlo and back into the Sanguine Forest. Of course, the Zorn would let him go—they had a kingdom to run together. As he stormed off, he heard the heavy castle doors closing behind him, but then the sound faded, and he never heard them close and latch completely. Turning back, Castle Orlo was gone.

The Zorn had given him enough to think about. Enough to torment him in his waking hours. He gave him no resistance in reaching the tree line out of the Sanguine Forest.

Soon the encampment of his men came into view.

When he appeared stomping out of the forest, the men leaped to their feet. The king's face was red and furrowed in what looked to be anger. But the king was safe and seemingly unharmed.

"Your Majesty," they said, each bowing in respect. But the king ignored them and strode past. He jumped on his horse, kicked it in the ribs, and rode off fast as lightning.

The storm had passed overnight, and daylight started to stream through the clouds in streaks of orange and red. The men hurried to collect their gear. One by one, a steady stream of disorganized riders rode off trying to keep up with their king.

Leopold was enraged. He tried to control himself as he knew rage was a spell the Zorn could have cast on him. But the Zorn did not have to use a magic spell; he merely had to tell Leopold the truth. The result was the same as if a magic spell had been used.

It all seemed like a bad dream.

Hush now, little baby, don't you cry

I'll hold you a little closer

And don't you ever forget, this loving embrace

In a world that's growing colder, colder, colder.

Excerpt from *The Witch's Songbook*

We are not enemies. We are safe now, they both said… We are safe.
— Excerpt from *The Provenance* (Chapter Thirty-Six)

SONGS OF EHLONA

IN THE VILLAGE OF HOMESTEAD IN THE YEAR 843 HRT

Chen-Li studied a long list of children born precisely when the Star of Ehlona first appeared. It was not an absolute science, as the precise second was a little inaccurate for the Star Prophets to calculate. But they did have some facts they were sure about. Like the date and a scale of time, down to roughly thirty minutes—that was fifteen minutes either way to the exact time they believed. The list of babies born during this period consisted of about thirty, with an additional twenty close to the same timetable.

Chen-Li's mission was to investigate all these children to locate which one would be the reincarnated soul of his mother, the Goddess Ehlona. He was not sure how to do this or what signs the child of Ehlona's renewed spirit would demonstrate. But that did not matter. He wanted to put his eyes on all of them in turn. Maybe he would recognize his mother in some sign of Ehlona once he saw it. Maybe not.

He and his First Wives searched those on the list. There were many peasant farmers and villagers, with some celebrities on the list. One of Chen-Li's own children from one of his many wives was on the list. There were also statesmen, soldiers, and healers. The easiest and fastest way for them to cover the most ground was in their Li forms.

Soon the Li forms separated from Chen-Li and his First Wives and were flashing in all directions through the Mid-Run Valley in dulled spirits. So as not to scare the general population, or start rumors of ghosts, they traveled as secretly as spirits could.

In their first attempts they saw nothing out of the ordinary. They went to the homes of new parents, not giving away any suspicions they were under observation.

One of celebrities on the list handled by Chen-Li himself was a little unassuming cottage in the village of Homestead. This was the home of Amtor and his wife, Gilglad.

His spirit soared over the Mid-Run Valley, turning west when reaching the Great Mapes Forest, and then descended from the clouds to float along the treetops where he could view them privately and unknowingly.

From a high vantage point, hovering at the tops of the trees, he scanned the home and surrounding area. Moving unimpeded through the branches, he was nearly invisible in his spirit form. He was like the gentle breeze.

He watched until, at length, he saw Amtor himself. This was the mighty warrior of the Battle of Mauveguard Pass. Chen-Li marveled at how stout the man looked. He was as large as a bear, tall and thick around the chest, his biceps like bands of thick muscle. Amtor had a thick mane of dark hair and a long lavish beard. Chen-Li knew Amtor had been handpicked by King Leopold, for his instincts and intelligence, as much as his physical presence and strength.

Chen-Li spied on him, watching him with curiosity. The large man, obviously still wounded, limped out of his house. He reached into his pocket and pulled out his pipe. After packing it with tobacco, he lit it with a flame from a stick he kept heated in the fire. He puffed and brought the pipe to life. Soon the surrounding area was full of a sweet bluish cloud of cherry pipe smoke. In his Li form, Chen-Li could not smell it, he could only imagine it.

He continued to watch as the giant warrior picked up a large axe as if it weighed as little as a small stick. Then he sat at the grindstone. The grinding wheel started to turn as one of his feet worked the pedal below. Soon sparks were cascading from the front of the rotating stone as Amtor honed the axe's metal. He continued to sharpen the blade and puff away at his pipe. Then, much to Chen-Li's surprise, Amtor started to sing in low baritone:

> *Now I see myself the way I used to be.*
> *Looks like somebody else gazing back at me.*
> *I remember fields so green, in the corners of my mind.*
> *I can remember stars so bright, every night I walked outside.*
> *But I,*
> *I can't recall it all, but I*
> *Aye, yah, aye, I seemed so different at the time,*
> *Aye, yah, aye*
> *I don't remember, I don't remember*
> *Anything at all.*

Gilglad came out of the door holding a child in her arms. She was a pleasant-looking woman with long brown hair combed back and straight. Chen-Li noticed a peculiar look about her; she nearly glowed. Chen-Li thought it odd but continued to watch and listen.

Gilglad picked up the tune Amtor was singing. Her voice struck a high note.

Hush now, little baby, don't you cry
I'll hold you a little closer
Don't you ever forget.
This loving embrace.
In a world that's growing colder,

Amtor joined in with her. They both chanted in perfect harmony.

Colder, colder, colder.

Then both sang beautifully with the other—Amtor singing in low bass tones and Gilglad singing in a high tenor. When the song ended, they laughed.

High in the trees up above, Chen-Li smiled. He knew this song. He remembered it from *The Witch's Songbook*. He knew it well and tried to stay quiet. It didn't mean much though, as many people sang songs from it. It was very popular.

This little home in Homestead was an idyllic place. Pleasant for Amtor, Gilglad, and their little child named Astar. Chen-Li could not explain it, but a feeling of love came over him. There was so much of it here, it permeated the air. He did not know if it was because they sang his mother's song, or something else, but something felt familiar here. Chen-Li had a hunch this all meant something in his search for the spirit of Ehlona.

As Chen-Li contemplated this from the high branches of the tree, he realized he was not alone. Far below, in the shadows of the brush, glimmered a movement that alerted him to the menace of another. Chen-Li was not the only spy with interest in Amtor's home, it seemed.

Chen-Li recognized it was the demon Langula herself, the Zorn's blue-horned demon, the entity primarily responsible for the possession of King Leopold's search party. But what was she doing here, so far north, slithering quietly among the underbrush? Chen-Li stared at her. She watched Amtor with equal interest as he did. But as with any snake, this serpent did not watch the skies for danger. Chen-Li held the high ground in her blind spot.

Langula's appearance piqued his interest in this family all the more.

Just then, the gravelly voice of Amtor spoke, "And how is our little Astar today?"

"Your son had pleasant dreams last night," Gilglad answered.

"Is that right? Well, you of all people would know."

Chen-Li looked down again. He could see the demon slithering, watching the family through the leaves of the bushes. He felt compelled to send her a little message.

As Langula silently stalked Amtor's family in the underbrush, she was violently propelled backward with such force it punched the air out of her and caused her to roll backward. Chen-Li had struck her using his new talent for materializing his spirit's fists. He struck the Zorn's demon for the first time ever, then floated above her in a perfect position to strike her repeatedly at will. Which is precisely what he planned to do. And she could not touch him in return.

"What is that?" Amtor stopped grinding his axe, hearing the rustle beyond the trees.

Langula's anger burned. She recovered quickly in time to see Chen-Li floating above her. His first blow caused her to coil like the snake she was. She hissed at the master priest, flashing sharp ivory fangs, which did not affect Chen-Li in the slightest. He focused his energy on materializing his fists for another quick strike against her. His hands began to glow red like fire.

But then, much to Chen-Li's surprise, Langula showed him a new trick she had learned too. She dissolved into a thin black plume of mist and vapor, and she was gone. On the Zorn's direction, and worried about her safety, she had been practicing a new skill and had successfully perfected it. Unknown to Chen-Li at the time, Langula had transported herself half a mile away from the danger of his fiery fists in the blink of an eye.

"Did you hear that?" Amtor asked Gilglad, standing up to face toward the tree line with his freshly sharpened axe.

"I heard something," Gilglad told him.

"Something is beyond the trees again."

Chen-Li looked over the area and could not find any sign of the demon Langula. He had attracted Amtor's attention and thought it best to make his departure. So, like a strong wind, Chen-Li streaked across the Mid-Run Valley on his way back to the Temple of Chen-Li.

Amtor waited and listened, sensing that some danger had presented itself, but now his instincts told him it had passed. He went back to the grindstone but kept a heightened sense of vigilance, maintaining one eye on the tree line.

A mist of sulfurous black vapors stirred about a hundred feet away from Amtor's home. The vapors swirled to materialize the demon Langula, just beyond the woods. She crawled low to the ground, obscured from overhead view by the tall trees. This time, the viper nervously looked upward. Not seeing any more sign of Chen-Li, she tenderly rubbed the sore spot on her chest, the place where he had struck her and knocked the wind out of her.

She knew that the direct approach for spying on Amtor would no longer do anymore. The Zorn would need to get creative with this problem. It presented too many dangers, for now it was all she could do to return to Castle Orlo and report what she saw, and what had happened. But first, while she was here, she would take her time along the way to feed. She slithered away in search of a tender young morsel.

Chen-Li crossed the vast plains, up into the mountains until he hovered over the roof of his wooden home. He dropped down like a phantom through the ceiling, entered his meditation room, and rejoined his body.

As usual, it took a moment of cooldown, then Chen-Li stood in his complete physical form.

He pondered what he had just seen. Perhaps it was wishful thinking, but he had the strong instinct he may have found what he was looking for. He resolved to keep an eye on Amtor's little house in Homestead. Chen-Li had to ensure no evil from his brother or any of his brother's demons would befall what he now had to seriously consider the best sign of the recycled soul of his mother.

It was too early to tell for sure. But somewhere the Goddess Ehlona had come back into this world. And this child, Astar, just went to the top of his list.

When the night is over,
and you feel so safe at home.
I want you to remember
You're not alone.

Excerpt from *The Witch's Songbook*

I find you guilty of crimes against humanity and
pronounce the sentence to all of you... of death.
— Excerpt from *The Provenance* (Chapter Thirty-Seven)

A BURDEN HEAVY

The House of Kilmer-Plum in the Year 844 HRT

Kilmer's ghost materialized in the dead of night roaming the darkened hallways of the House of Plum-Kilmer. Its flowing robe with a deep hood veiled its face from the realm of the living, as the ghost moved silently down the dark passageway. Moonlight streamed through the window, bathing the manor in tints of blue. All was quiet in the house except the ticking of the clock. It struck the time with a soft chiming of three bells. After which, the ticking of the pendulum resumed.

The hallway led to a bend where the stairs curved upward. The ghost silently wandered up the steps and past the round window that looked out upon the Blue Mountains' high peaks. The ghost reached the upper landing then turned to face the long hallway on the third floor. Without any contact to the floor, the specter moved, gliding across the hall until it came to a closed door.

It materialized through the chamber door without a sound, appearing on the other side and entering the bedchamber of Lord Plum-Kilmer and his new wife Darla.

The remaining flames in the fireplace warmly illuminated their cozy bed, where Kilmer and Darla slept soundly, his sword hung in a scabbard draped across the bedpost.

When the spirit moved in front of the fireplace, rather than cast a shadow, the ghost refracted the light like a kaleidoscope, in bright prismatic colors upon the opposite walls. As it past from in front of the fire, and moved to the window, the light changed back to a warm yellow glow.

Kilmer, sensing a presence, sat up.

"Hollow Face?" he said in a low whisper, squinting his sleepy eyes in the dark.

The ghost turned to face him. The glow from the window framed Hollow Face. Like in the old times, he still could not speak or whisper what he knew of the future, but propagated images in Kilmer's mind.

But appearing to Kilmer for the first time in a long time, the images Hollow Face projected were not prophetic ones of future dangers at all—those could wait. These were of happier times. Days of the past spent laughing and playing with his sister, Mara. Distant memories of yellow-and-white flowers, smiles, and laughter when they were children. It seemed so long ago. Hollow Face replayed scenes of Rosa attending to the clothesline, always making their clothes so clean and crisp, with the fresh smell of drying in the breeze. She was a good woman, a good mother, and took great care to make it so.

Justus walked along the village roads on his daily stroll for morning pastries. He wore his little floppy red hat and a luxurious blue-and-yellow coat. He approached the town square to chat on the courthouse steps with Kilmer: the real one, the well-traveled jovial panhandling Kilmer, with his toothless grin and friendly demeanor. Kilmer laughed with his father, holding his little dented tin cup. These were the memories, the way he remembered them, that he cherished.

Next Hollow Face showed him the people of the village of Plum, his friends from so long ago. Kilmer wondered what had become of them, where they were now, if they survived the massacre and were still living.

Images of Kory, Oaks, and Darla, Sister Chavise, Sister Maldean, and the orphanage of Plum, sent reminders of the time when Darla told him they were blessed. How right she was.

Lastly, Hollow Face showed Kilmer that ancient statue in the town square. The ridiculous bronze casting of the village founder and namesake of the river, Fortis Plum, with his broken mustache and heroic pose.

"Thank you, Fortis," Kilmer said. "Twice you have saved my life. You are a blessing to this family."

Past the statue, the vision ended at the cemetery. A single stone dedicated to the mortal remains of the physical body, which was once Fortis Plum the man, resting in his grave.

The ghost moved away from the window and back in front of the fireplace. Once again, as before, the ghostly refraction bent light into rainbows. Then Hollow Face showed him one more vision.

The vision was of a baby. The baby grew to a boy, and then later grew again to a man. Kilmer saw his face but did not recognize him. Once changed, the man held up a shining golden dagger in his hand. The dagger grew in size, the same way the boy did, from a small dagger to a moderate blade, then to a massively large sword. Then, in its largest size, the sword exploded, bursting forth in a powerful eruption, a massive fireball, one the likes of which the world had never seen. Then the vision ended with people screaming and dying.

"Your visions always have death in them," Kilmer said.

The vision faded away. The ghost turned and then he, too, slowly faded away from view.

"Kilmer?" Darla said rolling over to face him. "Did you have another nightmare?"

"No, not this time."

"Talk to me," Darla said, putting her hand on him. "What is it?'

"Just memories of my family."

Darla rubbed his shoulder.

"Darla? I need to tell you something. I need you to know about the Plums and the story about an old ghost named Hollow Face. I'm ready to tell you about everything."

Throughout the night Kilmer talked and Darla listened. She knew nothing about her birth parents, but Kilmer knew so much more than he had ever revealed to anyone before. After all those years in the orphanage, that night, the trust between them grew with the full knowledge of the truth. Finally.

In the days that followed, Lord Plum-Kilmer and King Leopold became closer as well. The king put Kilmer in charge of many operations of the kingdom. One of them was the training of new recruits. Lord Kilmer instructed new soldiers in the finer aspects of sword play, and in this capacity, both Oaks and Darla trained under his tutelage. Darla turned out to be a good wielder of swords. She dutifully learned the skill that would come in handy in the days to come.

But most of the time Lord Kilmer spent with King Leopold they sat predominately in silence. Neither one of them had the tendency to overshare anything. King Leopold enjoyed being in Lord Plum-Kilmer's company. The king and Kilmer kept their secrets safely locked away in their respective minds. Leopold never felt compelled to seek counsel in anyone other than himself. And as far as Lord Plum-Kilmer could tell, Leopold's governance of the kingdom was a kind and generous one. The king went out of the way to make life more bearable for the common people in the Mid-Run Valley.

Through the following years, King Leopold improved the legal system providing a fairer outcome, limited in authority, with processes and liberties of a more representative form of government. He donated gold for the well-being of orphans and the health of people everywhere. All in all, the king remained secretive and aloof, but the people learned to love him. Lord Plum-Kilmer and Lord Whitney remained close to the king, but even they did not share many of his confidences. There was always something dark and cold about him. But under the surface there was something warm too. This was most evident in the time he spent with his dog, the mongrel, Babbit the Magnificent.

"Do you think he will ever take a wife?" Darla asked Kilmer about Leopold one day.

"No," Kilmer said quickly. "He longs for companionship, but he fears the weakness of it. Not weakness for himself, but because he has a fear of having someone he loves used against him."

"He worries the Zorn would do that to him?"

"Among other enemies real or imagined. Instead, I feel like he endures his loneliness. He bears a heavy burden, as all people in power do. Maybe it is best if he just remains alone, married to the Kingdom of Odessa."

Darla gave him a shove, and Kilmer laughed.

"I'm never going to leave you alone though," Kilmer said.

"Between you and Kilmer's ghost," she spoke, "it may be a crowded house."

I want to be with you in the moonlight

For all my life

I want to see you dancing

With the stars shining from your eyes.

Excerpt from *The Witch's Songbook*

Zorn, my love, we need another plan.
Don't bother me, now. I am thinking.
— Excerpt from *The Provenance* (Chapter Thirty-Eight)

DISCOVERIES OF A LIFETIME

SOUTHERN STAR OBSERVATORY IN THE YEAR 845 HRT

It took more than two years for them to finally tie the knot. But eventually, the day came when Gia and Glover, the betrothed Star Prophets, were to be married. For certain, the two were made for each other. Anyone who knew them would say so. Like no other two people, they could comb over facts and figures and find entertainment, amusement, even find some degree of joy and relaxation from them. While others found vice in drinking, gambling, or carousing, Gia and Glover spent their free time in studious calculations. It was as if the Cosmic Creation made them from the same fabric. Who could argue? Maybe it did.

But there was the problem. The two were so overly logical and calculating, they could not solve the complex calculation of when to join in marriage.

After combing through their dynamic signs for themselves, they ultimately, and thankfully, agreed upon a common date calculation, rooted deep in the star movements, based on both of their ruling planets and the signs of the tides of the universe. To all other observations, it would seem tedious, but to them, just the right date was calculated with precision, great joy, and exuberance.

Finally, the day and hour came, when the universe was in perfect alignment to accept them and bless them, as man and wife.

As with the marriage of Kilmer and Darla, Glover and Gia had the same guest list. Chen-Li was invited, and as before, he attended in his Li form with his First Wives, Tyla and Myra. Lord Plum-Kilmer and Darla came. Aberfell, now nearly four years old, had grown into a child. He could walk on his own and could understand and speak most of the language. His parents Norwa and Barclay brought the child.

The marriage of the Star Prophets was held outside in the Mid-Run Valley under the pinnacle of the old stones of the South Watch Tower. Having favorable weather was part of their complicated calculation of the perfect wedding date.

And perfect weather it was.

The sun shone brilliantly that day as decorations and banners of purple and silver rippled in the breeze. It was a happy and long-awaited event. It had been over three years since their guests and friends were last together in one area, and it was good for the soul to see everyone doing well, healthy, and happy.

At precisely the right time, as the sun was setting, the far western sky mellowed to a bright red that seemed to be burning on the horizon, and Gia and Glover took their vows of acceptance to each other. No one could have planned a more beautiful ceremony on a more beautiful day. But then again, that was the point of being a competent Star Prophet.

After the vows were complete and darkness was creeping in, Gia and Glover embraced and shared a long kiss. The onlookers applauded. The fires ignited to give light to the party throughout the evening. The whole Mid-Run Valley seemed to glow in golden warmth.

The banquet table was loaded with delicious foods, pastries, roasted meats, fresh fruits, and vegetables. The wedding party mingled, talked, and laughed loudly. Fresh fish was consumed with elderberry wine, beer, ale, and sweet lemon water.

The music started, and Glover and Gia danced alone at first.

Sometimes the river overflows
Just like my aching heart
And I wonder where the water flows
Never to depart.
But I know, that it flows
Farther down the stream
That's where I dream
About the lover of my heart.
The lover of my heart.

The music stopped and they embraced again. When the music started, the happy newlyweds invited the whole assembly to dance with them, which everyone joyously did.

The party went on for longer than planned. The food and sweets lasted long through the evening; the strong wine and drink was plentiful.

All in all, the marriage of Gia and Glover was the perfect ending to a great five-year string of cosmic events. They had been through a historic phase that would undoubtedly go down in the record books as the only time where Star Prophets, of all people, could make discoveries worthy of celebrity. They were almost sad for the generations of Star Prophets who would follow, and those who preceded them. Those dutifully mundane Star Prophets who lived and died without seeing a single event. But not only did Gia and Glover discover just one static sign, but two. First the blue comet of Aberfell, then the Star of Ehlona. Two major static signs, discoveries of a lifetime.

By now, the darkness set in all around the Mid-Run Valley, and the party began to wind down. Chen-Li had long departed with his First Wives, not having bodies hindering their participation in these celebrations. Aberfell had long fallen asleep, and his parents had taken him home.

Gia and Glover were saying goodbye to Kilmer and Darla when something most unusual happened.

"What is that light over there?" Kilmer said, looking in the distance to the north.

"What is that?" Glover asked.

"There." Kilmer pointed northward. "Do you see that strange green light on the horizon?"

"Oh yes, now I see it," Darla said.

Glover and Gia walked in that direction. They squinted and scanned their eyes to the north. Eventually, they saw it too.

"Could it be?" Gia asked.

"Greenish lights?" Glover said to Gia. "It couldn't be."

Suddenly they startled at about the same time. Despite the remaining wedding guests, most of whom had traveled a long way to be with them, they ran away through the tables, upsetting and overturning them, heading toward the long set of stone steps to their observation platform.

"What is it?" Kilmer yelled after them. But they were gone.

"Do you want to leave?" Kilmer asked Darla.

"No, not now! I want to find out what has gotten into them."

"Me too," Kilmer said, and both ran after Gia and Glover.

They climbed the stone stairs up the platform.

At last, they entered breathlessly into the chambers of the South Watch Tower. Glover was standing with a raised looking glass to his eye, scanning the northern horizon. The greenish lights were still there, but then they faded away.

"Did you see it? Did you see it?" Gia questioned him over and over excitedly.

"Positive confirmation of event ending at 9:41," Glover said in his most rational and technically scientific voice. Gone were the newlyweds; now present were two professional Star Prophets.

"Ending at 9:40," Gia repeated. "No, wait. Ending at 9:39."

She opened the *Constellation Volume* and frantically flipped the pages open. She was searching for a specific page indicating a specific event.

"I still can't believe it!" Glover exclaimed.

"Shush, shush," Gia told him. "Where is it?"

She continued to flip the pages of the CV.

Kilmer and Darla were still breathing heavily from ascending so many stairs.

"Can someone tell me what is happening?" Kilmer asked, holding Darla from falling over in exhaustion.

"*Please!*" Gia said. "Quiet! Give me a chance to find it. The event ended at 9:39, and it started at 9:31."

"9:30 sharp," Glover corrected.

Suddenly, Gia stopped flipping pages of the CV.

"Here it is!" she said, mumbling what she read. "A green energy, radius twenty feet, duration 9.05 minutes. There it is!"

A silence filled the room.

Gia and Glover looked at each other quietly at first.

"*A third sign!*" they both shouted in unison.

"Another static sign?" Kilmer said. "What is it?"

"I can't believe it. A *third* static sign," Gia said. Seeing the confused look on Kilmer's and Darla's faces, she started catching her breath. It was evident that her new husband, Glover, fully understood, but Kilmer and Darla had no idea.

"Kilmer, the sign you saw—it's the Emerald Fire. The sign indicated in the *Constellation Volume*, the green energy field, the size, the duration, there can be no mistaking it. Kilmer! You discovered the third static sign!"

"I did?" Kilmer looked at them dumbfounded. "Whatever just happened, I'm sure I do not deserve credit for it. What is it, anyway?"

"The Emerald Fire is a sign of, well, it's kind of hard to explain," Gia said.

"Kilmer, Darla," Glover took a shot at it, "the Emerald Fire is a sign for occurrence of the Great Healer, Valen. Supposedly, Valen will come into the world, when the conditions are right, to cure the world's ills in a very precise way."

"What kind of way?" Darla asked.

"Through love," Gia said, smiling at Glover. She looked at her new husband, and he walked over and put his arm around her.

Glover spoke, "It is written that Valen will love the world and all humanity so much that her power can heal the world."

"Aberfell was a big one – the Supreme Historian," Gia said.

"And the Star of Ehlona was spectacular," Glover said.

"But the appearance of Valen in the world, well, that's just..." Gia lost the ability to speak. She started to cry. "That's number three! Three static signs in a lifetime!"

Gia and Glover embraced and cried tears of joy, jumping together.

Darla said to them, "To think it took all your efforts to calculate the perfect date and time to be married, and then as if the universe approved, a third static sign appeared."

Kilmer and Darla were in awe at what had just transpired. Looking out the window they watched as the beacon fires from the other three Star Towers illuminate their hilltops in the inky distance.

Gia took a torch off the wall and extended it to Kilmer.

"You found it," Gia and Glover said to Kilmer and Darla, "you light the beacon."

"Are you sure?" Kilmer asked Gia.

"You get the honor," she said with a nod. "I'm sure."

Kilmer took the torch and Darla's hand, and together they climbed the stairs to the upper level; there, the cone of treated wood waited for the tinder spark. Kilmer and Darla touched the torch to the bottom of the beacon, and for the third time in a generation, the beacon of the South Watch Tower ignited its flame, signaling a new static sign had come into the world.

The three beacons illuminated the sign to the whole world that a new God had entered their world and had come to heal them—with love.

There could be no better wedding gift.

THE END

EPILOGUE

The Fire Within

Memories of that night haunted him. Even though he was only four years old, Astar could never forget the night his mother died in the fire. Things were never the same after that. He was too young to understand completely what happened, but what he remembered vividly was the intensity of the emotions. Mostly, he remembered the panic in his father's face.

What Astar remembered the most, was his father carrying him out of the house and laying him at a safe distance away from the fire. The flames burst out of the windows of their little cottage in Homestead.

"Stay here!" Amtor told Astar and held up the palm of his hands to emphasize the importance of it. "Do not go back into the house! Understand?"

Astar nodded his head, then watched Amtor turn to go. He told his son not to go back into the house, but Amtor had to. Disappearing into the flames, Amtor went back to save his wife, Gilglad.

It seemed to take an eternity for Astar. He stood up and ran to the well. Dropping the bucket, he fastened the rope around the metal clip on the crossbar. Quickly he pulled the rope, up came a bucket of water. While doing this he watched the door of the cottage, hoping to see his mother or father again. The bucket came up and as it cleared the stone sides of the well, Astar reached out and grabbed it, loosening the rope from its handle, freeing it.

Astar, now holding a bucket full of water, did what he was told. He did not go back into the cottage. But he got close enough to the flames to feel the heat, although there was no heat. He approached the fire even closer until he could see inside the window of his room. Inside he saw two dim shapes, the shadows of his father and mother. They were struggling against each other.

Astar splashed water toward the flames, an exercise in futility. Running back to the well, he affixed the rope back to the bucket's handle, tossing it into the well again. Fetching another full bucket of water, once again, he loosened the rope and turned to take the water to the fire again. He resolved to keep doing this until the fire was out.

Ready to return with a fresh bucket of water, Astar saw that the fire had gone out, as suddenly as it started. The windows of the house were broken, and wispy streams of smoke lingered, but the flames were suddenly gone.

"Mother! Father!" he called out. He circled the cottage, still holding the bucket, ready to splash any sign of the remaining fire.

At length, his father, Amtor, stumbled to the door. He was alone.

"Are you hurt? Where is Mother?" Astar asked, his eyes wide. "Father? Where is she?"

Amtor did not say a word. He collected his breath, then rushed to embrace his boy.

"Where's Mother? Where is she?" the boy cried.

Amtor ran his hand up Astar's back, consoling him.

"She's gone," Amtor told him. Astar could feel the anguish in his father's voice. Amtor cried again, "She's gone."

The boy dropped the bucket. Water splashed out without notice. Astar hugged his father and sobbed. They knelt, embracing each other on the ground outside.

After several minutes, Amtor painfully rose, his old injuries newly re-aggravated. He helped Astar off the ground. Together they walked inside the cottage.

Inside the house was a mess, tables turned over, dishes broken on the floor. The fury of the flames scattered papers and clothes around the house as if a powerful force exploded within. A path led from the door to the back rooms. There, the bedchambers were located.

Walking back to the bedchambers, Astar saw his room. The flames seemed to have hit the hardest here. His bed was tipped sideways against the wall. The cabinet doors and drawers were open, its contents spread out across the room. But it seemed strange, nothing was burned or damaged by fire.

Amtor tipped Astar's bed from leaning against the wall, setting it back on its feet. The mattress, stuffed with straw and feathers, was placed back on the wooden bed frame. The sheets and blankets all returned to their place like it was before the fire.

"Here now, we are lucky the mattress did not burn. Thankfully, you can sleep here tonight. We have been truly blessed."

Astar nodded, looking around the room.

"Where's Mama?"

"She's not here."

Astar sniffed. "Where did she go?"

"Your mother is no more, my son." Amtor embraced Astar and cried again. "But it will be alright. You will be safe. We still have each other."

Astar merely stood there looking shocked.

"Come on, we've got a lot of cleaning up to do," Amtor told him. The two of them roamed around the house, making things right again. Before long, Amtor was feeding Astar, washing him, then put him to bed. It was hard, but Astar finally fell asleep, even with tears in his eyes.

The next day Amtor's friend Genson, Homestead's blacksmith, came to visit with his son, Micah, who was the same age as Astar.

Amtor received Genson most pleasantly. "Amtor, we wanted to check on you. We thought we saw a fire come from this way last night, but then it went away. Are you and Gilglad, and Astar, faring well?"

Amtor's eyes glazed over in tears. "Gilglad is gone, Genson. She is gone."

"Where did she go?"

"No, the fire took her. Gilglad is gone. She's dead."

"Gilglad? Dead?" Genson looked over Amtor's shoulder. There were no sights, no signs, no smells of fire. He was immediately worried. "Where's Astar?"

Amtor pointed to the cellar door. "He's down in the cellar."

"Can I see Astar?" Micah said softly, pulling his father down to him. Genson raised his eyebrows to Amtor.

"Astar could use a friend." Amtor said.

"We all could," Genson told him.

Genson and Amtor went inside the cottage, while Micah went around to the side of the house where the cellar door sat at an angle from the ground. The first knock went unanswered. But after another successive rapping on the cellar door from Micah, the door slowly cracked open, exposing the darkness beyond.

Micah lifted the heavy door. Briefly the sunlight flashed across Astar's face as he sat on the dirt floor. Backing away from the cellar door, Astar lodged himself between two sacks of potatoes. There was hardly room for both of them, but Micah managed to squeeze in front of Astar and shut the heavy cellar door behind him. The space in the cellar suddenly became quite dark.

The two sat in the gloomy silence, each comfortable to be sitting in the dark. At length, Micah could hear Astar sobbing, "My mother is dead."

"What happened to her?"

"She burned up in the fire." Astar sobbed more.

A long scratching sound produced a quick spark. Astar held a match on fire. It illuminated the small space within, throwing glowing yellow light on their faces. Astar lit a candle, and its wick continued to shed a warm haze. Astar put out the spark of tinder with a few shakes of his hand. Micah got his first clear view of Astar.

"I can't believe I will never see her again," Micah said after a while.

"Now you know how I feel, and I know how you felt when you lost your mother."

"We didn't even get a chance to say goodbye to her either, or tell her how much we loved her."

Astar sat with his knees up to his chin. He ran his hands through this thick unruly dark hair. His eyes filled with tears. Leaning closer to the flame, his cheeks rounded, as he blew out the candle. Darkness quickly filled the cramped space in the cellar again, as the two boys sat quietly together, both sobbing. They stayed in the cellar until the smell of onions and dirty potatoes in burlap bags became unpleasant.

Astar could never forget that night or the murky details that surrounded it. He didn't discuss it more than in a general nature with his father, as Amtor always dodged the subject.

"It hurts too much to talk about," Amtor would tell him.

But the more the boy grew and the more he learned, over the years he realized he had more questions than answers about that night. Something was not right about the way he remembered it. And the more he learned, the less he understood.

All he truly understood was that Gilglad, his mother, was dead.

AFTERWORD

The Third Scroll

Almon noticed Aberfell had fallen asleep. Aberfell, the Supreme Historian, at over 256 years old was the oldest living person in the world. He rested peacefully in his rocking chair, in the little cabin made up entirely of Timmutes at the top of the tallest mountain in the world, the Dragonbreath Mountain summit. Papers and scrolls lay scattered throughout the place. Almon looked curiously at them. One scroll, tied with a thick black ribbon, stood out. As Aberfell lightly snored with his mouth open, Almon pulled the scroll from the others. He carefully untied the black ribbon and quietly unrolled it. He opened it to the page of Yori's and Isse's disappearance in the Sanguine Forest.

Aberfell eventually opened an eye.

"Ah! Caught you," Aberfell said, looking at Almon through bushy eyebrows.

Almon did not seem embarrassed at all. "Am I not allowed to read your scrolls?"

Aberfell leaned back in his chair. "I call that one *Kilmer's Ghost.*"

"This is the legend of my ancestor, Kilmer?"

"Yes, even more than you understand of your ancestor. What's more, his ghost is connected to you as well."

"Where are all these stories leading, Aberfell?"

"To this." Aberfell produced a third scroll. This one was tied with a green ribbon. "The last scroll. The one with an emerald ribbon is my last story. That is where all of this is leading."

Almon looked at the green ribbon. "And what do you call that one?"

"This one is called the *Temple of Valor.*"

GLOSSARY

CHARACTER NAMES

Aberfell   *The baby who remembers everything, the Supreme Historian*

Amtor   *Wounded Minister of War of the Kingdom of Odessa*

Blaize Plum   *Head Council of Haverhill, General of Amalgamates*

Chavise, Sister   *One of the three sisters who left the Temple of Valor to find Ehlona in Husband. She was blessed with the Orphanage of the South*

Chastain, Sister   *Elder Star Prophet close to retiring*

Chen-Li / Marus   *Warrior, name of Marus, son of Heironomus and Ehlona, meaning Body and Spirit*

Curtz   *Member of search party, short, clever, and fast.*

Darla   *Orphaned friend of Kilmer*

Darius Plum   *Son of Justus and Rosa Plum*

Fortis Plum   *Trader, tracker, hunter, and adventurer of Clan Plum*

Frost   *Blue Vampiric Demon of Langula*

Gia   *Star Prophet*

Gilglad   *Healer and Amtor's wife*

Givens   *Member of search party, cavalry horseman*

Glover	Star Prophet
Grim	Red Vampiric Demon of Langula
Hanson	Member of search party, former Amalgamate
Hazor / the Zorn	Son of Gods: Ehlona and Hexor. The Skeletal King of Orlo, the Master of Evil
Heironomus	God of Light
Hexor	God of Darkness
Isse	First Archer's spotter
Justus Plum	Head Council of Plum, husband of Rosa, father to Mara and Darius Plum
Kilmer	Saves Amtor's life during the Battle of Mauveguard Pass
Kory	Orphaned friend of Kilmer
LaNew	Sadistic captain of the Red Guard
Langula	The half-woman, half-serpent demon
Laws	Scarred swordsman from search party
Leopold	An orphan of St. Ehlona's Orphanage, he becomes the first king of the Kingdom of Odessa.
Luna, Sister	Headmistress of St. Ehlona's Orphanage, Umbrick
Mara Plum	Daughter of Justus and Rosa Plum
Marus / Chen-Li	Son of Ehlona and Heironomus
Melvin	Member of search party, youngest, low-ranking, inexperienced
Monticello	Spotted Vampiric Demon of Langula
Myra	One of the First Wives
Oaks	Orphaned friend of Kilmer
Oskar Whitney / Lord Whitney	Cousin of Jakob Whitney, an engineer in Bowling
Rosa Plum	Wife of Justus, mother of Darius Plum
Tomar	Star Prophet
Tyla	One of the First Wives
Zorn /Hazor	The Skeletal King of Orlo, the Master of Evil, son of Ehlona and Hexor

COUNTRIES

Kingdom of Odessa   Leopold's growing Kingdom

CITIES, TOWNS AND VILLAGES

Blaize   *Village*
Bowling   *Village*
Chase   *Village*
Darby   *Village*
Estes   *Village*
Hammerville   *Village*
Haverhill   *Seat of the House of Erland, village.*
Homestead   *Village where Amtor and Gilglad make their home*
Jorleston   *Port and Lighthouse*
Olzen   *Village*
Plum   *Village*
Port Harbor   *Largest Port*
Umbrick   *Destroyed village*

PLACES OF NOTE

Blue Mountains   *Mountain range of the west*
Castle Odessa   *Leopold's castle in the Mauveguard Pass*
Castle Orlo   *Hazor's castle*
Dragonbreath Mountain   *The highest point on the map*
Gray Mountains   *Mountain range of the east*
Mid-Run Valley   *The central lowlands*
Sanguine Forest   *Haunted forest*
Spiron   *Nomadic tribes*

KILMER'S GHOST

Temple of Chen-Li   Marus's / Chen-Li's temple and home
Temple of Valor   Ehlona's Temple of Healing
Wilds, the   Untamed lands where the ground dips
dramatically to create enormous cliffs

CREATURES

The Timmutes – a society of microscopic humanoids
The Demonic – flesh-eating demons

ORGANIZATIONS AND GROUPS

Acolytes of the Temple of Valor
Amalgamates (Army of the Mid-Run Villages)
Nomadic Tribes of Spiron
Red Guard (defunct)
Red and Blue (Leopold's army)
Star Prophets
White Eminence
Zornastic Order (defunct)

TIMELINE

511 HRT   Heironomus blesses Fortis
Plum (aged 30)

741 HRT   Fortis Plum Dies Aged 260 years

786 HRT   Death of the Seventh Son
of Fortis Plum

832 HRT   Village of Plum Massacre

835 HRT   Kilmer and Kory join Amalgamates

837 HRT   *The Battle of Mauveguard Pass*

840 HRT   *Aberfell's Blue Comet observed*

841 HRT   *Birth of Monticello / Yori's*
                Disappearance

842 HRT   *Leopold's five-year*
                anniversary celebration

843 HRT   *Kilmer and Darla's wedding*

844 HRT   *Gia and Glover's wedding*

1041 HRT   *Almon and Aberfell – Epilogue*

I hope you have enjoyed *Kilmer's Ghost*,
and the time we have spent together.

Joe Lyon

Joe Lyon was born in Springfield, Ohio, on May 13, 1965. He grew up creating monsters and characters for his stories and homegrown comic books. In this, his first fictional epic fantasy series, *Astar's Blade*, Joe creates a world some have called "wonderfully epic with great texturing and grand scope worldbuilding." Joe has a master's degree in business administration, and is a former Military Intelligence School graduate and US Army veteran. As a musician and prolific songwriter, he has written over a hundred songs, a book of poetry entitled *Poetry is Cool,* and the first book of the *Astar's Blade* series: *The Provenance.* Joe currently lives in Aiken, SC, with his family.

JOE LYON

The House that Died

BASED ON A TRUE STORY.

By the time you read this, that old house will be gone. Mercifully torn down as a public safety hazard. That old house on Jefferson Street sat for years in bad disrepair, overgrown with weeds, with things falling off it. The porch had long collapsed, blocking the front door. The walkway was cracked and broken, and tall weeds grew through the cracks, reclaiming that ground in the name of the wild.

The last time I drove by the old place I could still see its past, as it was seared into my memory from dulled black-and-white photographs from the early Sixties. The house looked better then, solid and freshly painted, the yard exquisitely manicured and trimmed. I can still see the ghost of my father working outside. His favorite pastime was lifting bulky packages of shingles up a set of two heavy wooden ladders attached together, to pound nails in a new roof over our heads. That was almost sixty years ago. A great job when he did it, never knowing it would last as long as it did; it was never supposed to. Over sixty years later, a gaping hole as big as a Volkswagen Beetle had given way to the elements, providing an entryway into the moldy ruin of what was once our family home. A horrible disrespectful way for a house to die.

When I was a kid growing up, still to this very day, I can confidently say I had the strangest bedroom ever. It started with a standard door as its only entry, but two more curious little doors were located within—more about those in a minute. Looking outside the window from that room, I could see in the ground between our place and the neighbor's, a third more curious portal existed. Located in the ground, some twenty feet below, it consisted of a square concrete slab lying flat on top of a round cement mound. For years growing up, the thing disturbed me because I had no idea what it could be. But it covered something.

When I asked my father about it, he gave me the worst answer a father could tell his son: he told me to stay away from it. Well, being no kind of answer for a young inquiring mind, he should have just said, "Go check it out."

So, I did.

I gripped the corner of the cement slab and tried to move it, expecting it to be permanently sealed. Much to my surprise, and partially to my horror, the slab moved. It produced a grinding, gritty sound, like tombstones sliding together. I pulled it slightly open. A sliver of a dark opening appeared. I pressed my face to the opening. A deep darkness was all I could see. I dropped a small stone into the hole, listening to hear if it would land solid, or splash, but otherwise counting the seconds as it descended. In a couple of counts I heard the stone hit a rocky bottom in echoes. It was solid. No water. It had a floor, but it seemed a long way down.

With resolve, I pulled more of the slab away, gradually revealing the dark round hole in its entirety. The light of the day shone in, leaving a crescent shape upon its dry and dusty bottom. It was about seven feet down. Without thinking, I lowered myself over the edge of the rim, until I hung with my arms at full extension. Still unable to touch bottom, I let go. After a short drop, I landed in a little cloud of dust.

It felt old there, like a tomb, and smelled corrosive, the way it does underground.

I wondered if the floor could possibly break through and the Earth swallow me up. The thought occurred to me that I may have trapped myself in this round subterranean cavern, and if so, I had little hope of anyone hearing me.

Looking at the rim above, I hoped I had not misjudged. I jumped as high as I could, launching myself up and grasping the top of the rim. But only just barely. I held on momentarily, but then I let go. Now, knowing I could get out, the risk inspired me to stay longer, and I explored the large circular area.

It certainly was not my idea of a well, being too large; the diameter of the hole was about twelve feet, while a well seemed like it would be only a couple of feet at a maximum. Maybe it had been a sewer line, or old outhouse. I do not know, and I still have no idea what it was, or what it was doing there in the center of the city of Springfield.

I leaped up and grabbed the lip of the rim, pulled out one elbow first, then another, then used my stomach to leverage the rest of my body out. Inch by inch, finally I swung my foot free outside the hold. Soon, I was completely out again. I used my remaining strength to close the square lid back over the dark hole, removing any evidence I was ever there.

Years later, I confessed to my father what I had done. He seemed to be more curious than mad. I thought it strange that he would ask me what I had seen. His response deepened the mystery, as if he had never opened the lid himself. He never explained it to me because I do not think he knew either. In the end, I wish I could give a better explanation, but none exists. I chalked it up to one of those weird unexplained things.

There were two remaining mysterious doors back upstairs in my little bedroom. One of them was explainable—it was the eighteen-inch square wooden door to the attic. It could be lifted and slid over to reveal the only entrance to the rafters of the roof and the installation. Unfortunately, the little door was positioned right over my bed, right over my head, where I stared at it every night and tried to go to sleep. Every night I lay down, I looked at that little door, and just prayed that it would not open to expose some deformed slobbering face staring down at me. Every night I opened my eyes repeatedly and lived in fear of what might peek out.

The last door was my favorite. Also an eighteen-inch square wooden door but this one sat vertically flush against the lower wall. It had a latch on the outside, and from an early age I would unlatch it and crawl into the crawl space. Long, dark, and narrow, it had an unusually cool temperature. A string had been threaded through a series of round O hooks creating a long pulley system that turned on the lights that sat farther and deeper, about midway, in the long twenty-foot narrow space. Pulling the string and turning on the light revealed a long shelf about twenty feet long, about one foot wide. The shelf and the far wall were painted metallic gray. It had a unique smell in the crawl space. It was not unpleasant, just that it smelled like old fabrics. On and under the shelves a variety of odds and ends were stacked: an interesting collection of old photographs, books, clothes, baby stuff, musical instruments.

I had two fears of the crawl space. The first was that someone would slam the door and lock me in, either unwittingly or to be cruel. For that reason, I seldom crawled to the very end so far inside. Instead, I stayed closer to the door, listening for the sound of anyone approaching, or walking up the stairs beyond. If I heard either one of these sounds, I quickly scrambled out so as not to get trapped and locked inside.

The second fear came at night. I would lay in bed, staring at the little door. No matter how many times I had been in the crawl space during the day, I never denied the chance of it opening slowly, with a gradual creak, to reveal the same deformed slobbering face that I saw every night appearing from the little overhead attic door.

No matter how I situated myself in my bed, I always seemed to be facing one, or both, of the strange doors.

The house had many other weird things about it. The garage had an attic where my dad kept an old thrasher, like the one used by Death.

I write about these things as lingering aftershocks of watching late-night creature features with my three older sisters, even after we had all been told by our parents not to. God, I love those girls. The nightmares I had, and the many nights I woke up the whole house with my screaming, are the phantoms of my youth. A young boy can dream vividly in a weird room with weird doors.

I was the youngest of our family, not the baby of the family, a term I hated and still do, just the youngest. And not by just a little. My youngest sister is twelve years older than me. All of them Virgos, incidentally I married a Virgo, my son is a Virgo, I am surrounded by the sign of the Virgin. Two of my sisters had the *exact* same birthday: September 18, making them what is called Irish twins. And my remaining sister and my wife have the *exact* same birthday: September 13, making them Irish twins of different mothers. Weird facts.

Being the youngest I had the unfortunate experience of death at a young age. I think that had something to do with why I am so morbidly fascinated with death. Some people do not like talking about it. But to me, it is the ultimate subject. Death is something that is always there, hanging over our heads like a sword dangling from an unseen thread, but we like to convince ourselves that it's not there. Personally, I feel I live a better life more focused on death. It reminds me that time is short, life is fragile, life is tragic. We need to do everything we can before our time runs out.

I was in a band called Purple Toad. And one of my favorite things about being in it is knowing that we submitted some songs to Atlantic Records in a demo around 1985. One day, we got a letter on Atlantic Records letterhead that basically stated, "Thanks, but no thanks." But do you know what? I was not disappointed in that rejection letter at all. Instead, I was overjoyed, knowing we got further than most. At least we tried—we failed—but at least I can say we tried. I am oddly okay with that.

I am no psychologist, but I think it is the fear of death that makes most men get married. I know many will not agree, but I think it is true. There comes a point in a man's life when he wants to settle down. Most of us cannot live a riotous lifestyle for more than a couple of decades, no matter how we want to. We slow down, we sober up, we stop thinking of the right now, and start thinking about the future. And what does the future hold? Death. I am laughing as I write this. I am not sure how and why women get married, so I will only confine my perspective to myself and my limited view of mankind.

I never liked to take anything so seriously that I could not laugh at myself. I have never been very afraid of that, or of failure. But I can see why most people are.

That brings me back to my book, *Kilmer's Ghost*. I hope my stories entertain you. In the end, that is really all I am trying to do. A coworker told the woman who would be my wife that I was just a fool. I am a hopeless fool at heart, can't really help myself, so I write books, write songs, and put myself out there by being the fool, the man-child I know I am. I hope you like them, and I would appreciate hearing from you, either to tell me you like something, or just to tell me that I suck. I can take it. You can drop by my website and drop me a message, I would love to hear from you.

I wish you the best, until we meet again.
— Joe Lyon

CHECK OUT MORE STUFF BY JOE LYON:
WWW.ASTARSBLADE.COM

OTHER BOOKS BY JOE LYON

The Provenance (Book One of Astar's Blade)

All his life, Almon knew the Plum-Kilmer family had been haunted by spirits of the dead. For over two hundred and fifty years, the ghost had cursed his family, but not Almon. He thought the curse had finally run its course and may have skipped him. When the ghost finally does come, it strains his sanity. Unprepared, in growing madness, he is driven to the mountains. There, the ghost waits for him, either trying to save him or lead him to his doom.

This is the story of the Provenance, the Origin of Gods, Ghosts, and Demons who created an imperfect world. The story of forbidden knowledge, of unseen forces designed to stay hidden from mortals. If you continue, be warned—they know when they are being observed and are powerful enough to curse those foolhardy enough to be the observers.

So, open the pages carefully, dear reader, and prepare yourself for the Provenance.

Temple of Valor (Book Three of Astar's Blade)

It had been a year since the Star of Ehlona shone, leaving the world to wonder if the soul of the Goddess of Beauty had returned. But while a weary world looked to the heavens for answers, a new terror was being unleashed from below. Deep in the steamy darkness hatches a plot bent on vengeance. When powerful forces collide, there is no safe place. Will any survive in the final battle over Astar's Blade?

www.ingramcontent.com/pod-product-compliance
Lightning Source LLC
Chambersburg PA
CBHW070306040726
47501CB00018B/223